HERO

By E.A. STEWART

LEGENDS OF VALERÓS SERIES
Wheel and Serpent: 1
Traitor: 2
Hero: 3

ACCIDENTAL HERETICS SERIES
Book 1: *Bone-mend and Salt*
Book 2: *Trebuchets in the Garden*
Book 3: *Crux Lunata*
Book 4: *Song of Valerós*
The Mad Woman of La Catalane: A Novella
The Blue Door… and More Accidental Heretics Tales

RAIN CITY INCIDENTS SERIES
(writing as Annie Pearson)
The Grrrl of Limberlost
Artemis in the Desert
Nine Volt Heart
The Pirate King

HERO

LEGENDS OF VALEROS: *3*

E.A. STEWART

Jūgum Press

Published by Jūgum Press
505 Broadway East #237
Seattle, Washington U.S.A.
www.jugumpress.net

For Jacyn, always.

HERO

Canços de Montpelhièr

From the Secret History of the Flaming Cross
— Andonis de Zêna

AT THE NEW YEAR 1215, while I lived in Montpelhièr, a prelate convened a council of Roman priests and bishops to discuss what to do with the Languedoc counts and seigneurs who still protected the Cathar heretics. That same year, the Knights Templar were keeping the boy-king of Aragón in the city, waiting for the pope to designate the child's regent.

People gossiped about the prelate's council and the king in the hostels, on the docks, and in the streets, and condemned the flood of French, Catalan, and Aragón soldiers and mercenaries in town that cold winter. However, none of that was any of my business.

While I lived in Montpelhièr, I lectured in battlefield medicine at the School of Science and Medicine. Yet I feel that one science is not enough for any thinking man. Because I love music and the companionship you find among musicians and singers, I also spent time collecting songs of the troubadours. In the course of that pursuit—of music and friendship—I met a particularly intriguing and handsome jongleur, a singer of others' songs. I made a mistake at first, guessing him to be a wine-shop wastrel, dissipating his talents, singing for enough silver to gamble long past curfew, then paying for his drink and bread with the sous he won off less talented men who couldn't match his skill at dice, backgammon, or that perverse Egyptian card game he liked to teach.

Then I saw that fine-looking jongleur perform at Comte Nuño's villa, where lords of the south gathered to feast. On that occasion, he wore a glossy blue velvet jerkin in the Italian style, tight fitting over a delicate ivory-linen tunic. His long hair, usually bound in a braid and worn inside his shirt, was unbound so that white-blond locks flowed over his shoulders.

In the count's court, the jongleur played an oud, a far lovelier instrument than the lute he carried into any tavern where I'd seen him perform. That magnificent oud, with strings and exquisite tuning and tone, usually mark the player as an exotic, a man from Persia or Cairo or Andalusia or other foreign lands where people do things differently than these southern seigneurs of Montpelhièr and Toulouse and Narbonne.

After strumming a few strains of each new song, he'd toss his hair back and begin to sing. Whether he sang in a gorgeous baritone or an amazing falsetto, his voice captivated every woman and most all men in the court.

His voice struck my heart like an arrow, but the way he tossed his hair back, so fey, you could see he knew how beautiful he was. And flaunted it.

In that gesture, I found him irresistible. Under the guise of collecting troubadours' songs, I began haunting the taverns, hoping to hear him sing, longing to learn more about him, wishing he'd notice me.

When I saw him in a tavern at Twelfth Night, I approached, seeking to learn his story by singing a song myself, to show I cared about music like he did. Through perseverance, I won his story, though privately I wanted to win his heart.

Extraordinarily tall, long-limbed, and blond, he looked every bit a Celt, but I later learned he'd been born and abandoned in a crusader camp in the Outremer, rescued by a community of knights' mistresses and wives—or so he said. I collected several songs amid our adventures during the cold midwinter when we were friends. One song in particular remains in my heart.

‡

Cançons de Montpelhièr

I remain happy, summer and winter,
Through heat and cold.
I admire slush as much as apple blossoms,
And believe an entombed hero
Is greater than a living scoundrel.
And I find my fresh new love beautiful,
A delight beyond compare.
I see rockroses in the icy mud
And sunshine in greyest skies.

1

Pleasure So Sweet

Tuesday, Twelfth Night, 1215
Last of the old moon, Montpelhièr

A singer of troubadour songs and a knight of Aragón, Chrétien de St-Joachim celebrated his final night in Montpelhièr by contributing to the entertainments in the court of Comte Nuño. He sang of love and adventure in a joyous mood, choosing his father's favorite home-coming song while revelers clinked wine cups and called season's joy and saints' blessings to each other.

With most of his family far away in Toulouse and Valerós, Chrétien had few friends in the room, besides Orlando of Troyes, who drank to Chrétien's health three times. Chrétien didn't mind being a stranger here, because he was departing from Montpelhièr at dawn to go home to Toulouse.

"*Feliç nit dotze!*"

Men shouted Twelfth Night felicitations to each other, sloshing wine on their crimson, orange, or woad-dyed blue silk and velvet jerkins. Their empty sword-sheaths glimmered with elaborate silver and shell inlays, their boots gleamed in the candlelight.

"*I feliç any nou!*"

Women murmured happy new year, kissing each other's ears, hands up to protect their embroidered sashes and collars pinned to lustrous silks and linen dyed saffron and garnet and aquamarine. Jewels in their hair sparkled under candle branches. They embraced with a rattle of their necklaces, as if their hearts were always filled with love.

Amid a knot of priests enjoying the party from near the fire, an aged, red-headed cleric waved to catch Chrétien's eye, then steepled his fingers and blew a kiss in a gesture of gratitude for the music.

The cleric called, "Felicitations to the seigneur of St-Joachim. Your music makes my soul soar."

Chrétien called himself lord of St-Joachim, though it was only a money fief in Barcelona that he'd won from his brother in a dice game. In truth, Chrétien grew up far from there, the son of a crusader who'd retired to land won from the king of Cyprus as a reward for an adventure outside Jerusalem. A head taller than most in the room, when Chrétien performed he wore his flaxen hair unbound, so it streamed down his back, icy pale even in warm candlelight.

He sang the last song of the night the way his father used to sing it to his mother. Across the room, he saw Orlando de Troyes gazing into the dark eyes of his wife, both of them seeming to forget their wine, their food, the world around them. Soon, Chrétien would also gaze in peaceful repose, at home in Toulouse with his own true love.

> My love holds me in her power.
> Her pleasure tastes so sweet
> Her love goes into my heart.
> I desire nothing else in the world
> Than to be home by her hearth.

He'd been disappointed in September when, as a sworn *bonfraire* of the crusader brotherhood, the Confraria de la Crotz, he'd drawn the short straw and was compelled to serve as bodyguard for the child-king of Aragón. Now, at last, his replacement had arrived, Karles of Barcelona, formerly a personal guard to the old king of Aragón. Chrétien had finished his last day's duty and said adieu to the boy Jaume, leaving only this night to celebrate before he bid all of Montpelhièr adieu. *I'm off to see my true love, who's more beautiful than Adonis, more noble and true than any knight in songs or poems.*

He slipped thoughts of his lover Durán into the final chorus.

> My love holds me in his power.
> His pleasure tastes so sweet.

No one at this raucous party noticed the tribute. Chrétien began to wrap his oud, preparing to depart. Comte Nuño approached, offering a cup of wine.

"Chrétien, a word."

The lord of this villa—and of Roussillon and Montpelhièr—Nuño was about thirty, but his bright-white mane and height marked him as unusual, even without the gold-embroidered velvet jerkin and breeches. He'd be handsome if he hadn't broken his nose so many times, indicating he was more a man of action than a creature of court life. Nuño stood tall among men in the south, yet Chrétien bent his head to speak with him, as he did to most men.

"Monsenyor."

Chrétien accepted the coin Nuño slipped into his hand, though for this jubilant final night, he didn't require recompense for joyful singing. He also accepted the cup of wine, one more than he'd usually drink, and saluted the count.

"Xin-xin!" Chrétien toasted in Catalan, his father's favorite salute when two wine cups tapped. Over the winter, Chrétien learned that he and Nuño shared two things. First, immense regret about not being at Muret when King Pedro d'Aragón was killed in battle. Second, they shared a commitment to protect Pedro's son. "This is farewell, Monsenyor. Thank you for all your kindnesses. I shall be on my way to Toulouse at dawn."

Beyond Nuño's shoulder, Chrétien noticed a lurking figure who seemed out of place. It was the miniscule young monk who sat in school lessons with the child-king and who showed up in every court and tavern where Chrétien sang. His name was Feris, but Chrétien continually misspoke and called him *Furetto* because of the man's ferret-like face. The kind of untrustworthy man who'd never look you straight in the eye. It added to Chrétien's joy: to be rid of that ecclesiastical shadow when he quit this town.

"Departing tomorrow? You will just miss your good friend Ramón-roger, who's coming for the prelate's council. In his letter today, there's a missive for you." Nuño fished inside his jerkin and retrieved a sealed packet. "He believes I shall be elected regent..."

A letter! It had to be from Durán!

No, it was from Ramón-roger, the count of Foix. Chrétien lost Nuño's voice in the din of the great room while reading the missive, which turned his world upside down.

Hola, bonfraire.

I have no time for proper greetings. The prelate's council intends to destroy Raymond of Toulouse. And Nuño. And me. This is the greatest danger since we lost Pedro *el Rei.* Worse, I fear Nuño's worries have harmed his mind if not his soul. I'm calling on your oath of honor, to protect our world for the sake of your brothers, your father, and all you love. Stay in the city and help Nuño until I come. You'll find a way.

Your *bon amic* insists on coming with me, to help plead what he and other seigneurs are beseeching from the prelates and the council. As if your oath isn't enough to keep you in Montpelhièr.

— Comte de Foix, your sworn brother, et cetera

Sodalitas, fidelitas, virtus

Ramón-roger signed the missive with the motto of the *bonfraires:* fraternity, fidelity, virtue. He was a *bonfraire* who'd fought along-side Chrétien's father on crusade, and so was a sworn brother-in-arms to Chrétien and Durán. Now he called on Chrétien's oath, which meant that Chrétien must act or risk besmirching his father's honor. All the dancing angels in heaven would weep rivers of tears.

And Durán was coming to Montpelhièr! Durán, who hadn't sent letters since All Saints. If Ramón-roger's letter had come a day later, Chrétien might have missed them when he rode home to Toulouse. Surely, a few days waiting here was better than a lonely, cold ride home to find Durán gone.

But why would Ramón-roger bring Durán, the seigneur of the House Montcava and a heretic, to a city dangerously full of prelates and priests? *This council is the greatest danger since...*

His finger traced the answer at the end of the missive. *Your bon amic insists on coming...*

"It can't be enough." Nuño's voice came to Chrétien again over the din of the party. He was still recounting his worries. "Though I'm the boy's closest cousin, I don't have friends in Rome or among the prelates. What if the council gives Jaume back to Simon de Montfort, to be his puppet? Who can I trust as a friend at this dire time?"

"Peace, Monsenyor." He'd see Durán soon. In Montpelhièr. The decision settled on him like a winter cloak. No, there was nothing to decide. It was his duty to remain here. "The count of Foix asked me to stay and to make myself useful to you while we wait for him to join the prelate's council."

"A sweet gift from heaven!" Nuño seemed far too excited about such mild news. "Did Foix tell you how worried I am for this city? For all of us?"

"I am at your service, Monsenyor, since I no longer have duties to protect Jaume." Chrétien needed real work—*"You'll find a way"* — to fill every lonely moment until Durán arrived. (When Durán would press his well-formed, sturdy body against Chrétien's, sparking a frenzy of heated excitement.)

"I had no idea," Nuño turned thoughtful, "that God might answer my prayer by sending one of the best trained, most brilliant knights in Christendom to help me battle danger. A genius swordsman who can be more than a king's bodyguard. Who can guard the honor and safety of all of us."

"*Aiieee!* No. I can't offer that much. I'm only one man." Chrétien nervously fingered the count of Foix's letter. "*I fear Nuño's worries have harmed his mind.*"

"*Òc*, but people tell stories. And Ramón-roger wrote in his letter to me that Chrétien de St-Joachim had accomplished far more than other men, as if he were helped by magic."

"I protest, Monsenyor. Foix and others must be telling tales. I do only whatever I must when challenged. You know from my time here that I'm the laziest knight in Christendom."

"Everyone in the Pays d'Òc knows you helped the great crusader Hugues de Beaurain survive prison in Béziers."

"Um, it didn't require sword work until we were already free." In that prison tower, Chrétien won ten imaginary gold marks off Hugues, gambling to kill time while imprisoned. Durán and his brother had freed them; else, they'd all be a pile of bones clutching dice in a Béziers tower.

"And you helped prevent the assassination of Pedro d'Aragón in Andalusia."

"It's true that I rode across most of Iberia to stop it. But my genius sword work was against the caliph's bodyguards." And it was Chrétien's nephew Yusuf who had stopped the assassin. "You don't have battlefield challenges here, Monsenyor. No massive drums. No chained and enslaved giants to defeat."

"You rescued the boy-king of Aragón in Carcassona last spring."

"We used martial planning and endurance in the saddle, not genius sword work." And a woman, three small boys, and two dogs mattered more in that rescue than Chrétien's sword.

Nuño persisted, clearly agitated, while Chrétien grew concerned about the man's state of mind. "You've served well here as bodyguard to the new king of Aragón."

"Your city is full of Knights Templar, and that boy is guarded tighter than a winched-up trebuchet. I will do what I can for you and Ramón-roger, but I have no more to offer than any other knight."

Comte Nuño's effusive enthusiasm made Chrétien cautious. Once Durán arrived, he'd let Ramón-roger solve Nuño's problems. He and Durán had no business anywhere near a prelate's council. Where had Durán gotten such a reckless idea? The two of them should return immediately to Toulouse and enjoy the feast Chrétien's mother would prepare. A feast better than what the demi-angels served in the realm of the ancient gods.

Nuño leaned close, whispering. "The Church's agents have a plot to create havoc and then blame me and the other counts. We'll all be excommunicated and dispossessed, if not burned on a pyre or left to rot in a dungeon like the lost viscount of Carcassona."

Chrétien shook off daydreams of Durán's touch and Numa's cooking. He first had to find a way—as the count of Foix ordered—to determine whether Nuño was losing his mind or in grave danger. "How do you know, Monsenyor?"

"We have ears in every tavern and monks' choir. Even among renegade monks and wandering bishops. But I'm not sure which of my own men I can trust." Nuño drew back. He glanced around as if nervous.

"You believe you aren't safe in your own town." Chrétien said it quietly, so it sunk into his marrow, freezing him through with a special kind of fear. If Nuño was right, and not mad, then...

"Òc, you see? I need one superior knight I can trust. Foix says that's you." Nuño surveyed the merry party in his great room, musing. "Our crusader fathers and grandfathers are united in heaven,

which creates a special filial duty for you and me and others prepared to fight evil in the south. But this is a party, not a war council.
Meet me tomorrow morning to talk more."

Chrétien stood to leave, deeply disliking the sense of fear when
he didn't know what to fight, and also resenting his duty to an oath
when the only command was a handwave. *You'll find a way.*

"Oh, Senhór Chrétien. Yesterday I asked your nephew Yusuf
to work for me as a clerk. I invited him to live at my villa while the
prelate's council is here. See if you can convince him to accept my
invitation. We aren't any of us safe while all these zealous Churchmen are camped in the city."

2

O My Captain!

AFTER NUÑO'S URGENT WHISPERS in the feast hall, Chrétien's mood turned foul, mulling what he'd just learned.

Nuño, whether mad or perfectly sane, believed that the city and the entire countryside faced extreme peril.

Foix declared the council represented supreme danger—and Durán insisted on coming into the heart of it.

His nephew Yusuf attended school here, a foreign-looking scholar from Cairo in a city filled to overflowing with Churchmen seeking to condemn goodman heretics and schismatics.

Chrétien had to find a way—as the count of Foix ordered him— to ensure their safety, with only a few days in which to do it.

In order to still a cataract of disturbing thoughts flowing through his head, when he could take no action in the dead of night, Chrétien headed out to finish the night in a tavern. Throughout the early winter, bored and lonely when not on duty, Chrétien spent late nights in hostels and wine-shops, singing to build goodwill among all the doss-house soldiers and townsmen that he'd scalp at dice later in the night. Sadly, most men in this city remained comfortable only with dice and backgammon, loathe to enter into more sophisticated games of chance that Chrétien could teach them.

In the villa's foyer, he greeted Vincent, the young sergeant who led the *gardes du corps* that patrolled the streets in this district. And whom Chrétien regularly won coins off whenever they played back-gammon in Nuño's bachelor-barracks. He liked Vincent. The man had lost his family in the French carnage at Béziers and now put his passion into serving Nuño as the south's hope for future justice. However, in spite of his muscular build, Vincent had a fluting laugh that made it hard to take him as seriously as he took his role as Nuño's sergeant. Vincent turned back to banter with his second-in-command,

Guillaume, who was wildly imprudent at dice and had the same gorgeous auburn hair and god-like body as Durán, but had the face of a man who'd taken Greek fire in the conquest of Constantinople. Chrétien called to both men in the local tongue.

"*Feliç nit dotze!*"

Chrétien had left his best oud with Nuño's people and carried instead his second-best instrument, one he'd bought from a French mercenary in Narbonne, who called it a lute. That satchel under his winter cloak, his walking staff in hand, he stepped onto the frozen streets of Montpelhièr, humming to raise his spirits.

> I desire nothing else in the world
> Than to be home by my true love's hearth.

Frozen, lonely Montpelhièr would brighten at the arrival of the gentle and god-like Durán, whom Chrétien loved more than his own soul.

If we have souls. He could hear his father's cynical assertion. Or else Chrétien had said it aloud and it echoed on the cold streets. Everyone claimed that it's never this cold in Montpelhièr, but here he was, as cold as a naked leper, slipping and sliding along frozen mud and cobbles.

And wanting to relieve the fear that rose as soon as he'd understood the danger into which Durán might be riding. The words in Foix's letter still echoed.

This is the greatest danger since...

Chrétien first came to Toulouse the year after the French invaded at the request of the pope. The danger there was familiar, and he'd learned to dodge it. But beyond fear, Foix's words kindled a fury in Chrétien's heart.

Since we lost Pedro.

Pedro was a good man, and Chrétien estimated him to be about as good a king as people could expect. What most infuriated Chrétien was that Pedro had been his personal friend, with whom he'd endured battle and rough travel. Then his friend had been betrayed and destroyed by the morass of ambition and hatred that had seized the Pays d'Òc in a stranglehold.

A troubadour should write a song about what Pedro had attempted for the sake of freedom in the south. However, for the past year, Pedro's name was seldom mentioned. Stories of Pedro's magnificent campaign in Andalusia were spun into falsehoods; the king's efforts in the battle at Muret were twisted into slander. Pedro remained unheralded by the poets, so when Chrétien wanted to sing about heroic knights, he had to rely on Outremer crusader songs.

"Mercy. Please." A thin voice called overhead in the local tongue. *Misericòrdia, se vos plai.* "Forgive me. Like God forgives."

Chrétien passed too near where the *gardes du corps* had hung a man in a barrel pillory. The bishops' court condemned the fellow as a heretic, and Nuño's guards had to carry out the punishment, which was hideous for a murderer but seemed too cruel for what the Church called heresy.

"Mercy. I beg you."

Unable to do anything for the man, Chrétien glanced around for another route. He knew better than to enter the square where the pillory hung—near enough to the bishop's villa that the suffering could be watched, but the stench wouldn't carry to the noses of those who had passed judgment. The poor man. It'd been two freezing days. Surely the tragic fellow couldn't live through another frozen night.

This council is the greatest danger...

He detoured down an alley to escape the tragedy, a passage so narrow that two men could hardly pass each other. It led to the mews where the Knights Templars' horses were sheltered. The stable's closed shutters kept out the frigid weather, but the odor of a well-tended stable seeped into the street. The sweet smell of horse seemed like a balm after the grief raised by the torture of that poor man in the barrel pillory.

Tramping through the frozen mud of a city that was not his own, Chrétien wished for his cozy, safe home with Durán in Toulouse. Perhaps Chrétien would give up his knightly vows and convert, become a blindly peaceful heretic of the Cathar goodman persuasion like Durán, never touching swords again. He knew how to stay away from the Church or anyone would might betray him to the bishops' court.

He tripped on a loose cobble, steadying himself on a cold stone wall, twisting to keep from smashing his lute—and swearing a mild oath in Catalan. "*L'infern i el diable!*"

If he became a good heretic, he'd have to give up swearing. And meat. And wine, too. That wouldn't happen. His mood blackened amid the maze of streets—which should be dark, but because of the feast-day, people were out with torches, calling bright hellos and wishing everyone goddamn joy in the new year. Chrétien's inner spirit cast back ten years, when he'd stomp through the streets in a black mood until he found a fight to relieve the itch in his palms to do harm. *Òc*, pound a *baquelar* into the pavement. That would be a fine thing tonight, to ease the fury he still felt over Pedro's death, murdered by the same hatred that caused trouble to descend on this city where Durán intended to join him.

He shouldered his way through a dozen mummers dressed in a courtiers' idea of rags, half the men with faces painted to look like women, the others wearing painted leather masks. Dogs. Or maybe wolves. A ghost. A shiny pink thing—perhaps a pig? They sang a pitiful winter song about babies and mothers and burning logs on the fire, all while begging coppers for the poor. Although the song was in French, their singing wasn't bad enough that they deserved to be punched, however malevolent Chrétien felt at the moment. He hurried on, passing one group of celebrators who'd wrapped themselves in black wool scarves, making them invisible until they stumbled into the shadowy light cast by torches outside a pair of villas.

Every group he passed spoke another dialect or an unrecognizable foreign tongue. Every accented version of the local tongue, from Marseille to Toulouse and beyond. Catalan of every spice on either side of the Pyrenees and into Aragón. A host of tongues from the Holy Roman Empire, or so he assumed, having never traveled there. The rowdy collection of men gathering in Montpelhièr that winter might make a good moral tale, like that story priests like to tell. What was it called? The Turret of Babble? Something like that.

At the edge of the student quarter, Chrétien sought an alley to relieve himself, setting aside his staff and the satchel containing his lute. As he finished and sorted his tunic and jerkin, the sounds of a fight echoed from around a dark corner. Though his father always preached otherwise, it seemed that God answered prayer, at least on this Twelfth Night.

"*En tot mal guany!*"

Someone was damning a soul to hell in Catalan. Violently.

Chrétien left his satchel to the inspection of a skinny, shadow-dark cat and snatched his staff from where he'd propped it against a wall, the walking stick which also served as a quarterstaff to chastise anyone playing pickpocket or thief in the late hours.

Curses from the fight echoed in the street so loudly, you'd think other citizens might be ready to intervene.

"*Baquelar!*" A hideous rogue.

"Weasel!"

"Stupid ass!"

Weaker cries for mercy, in Catalan: "*Clemencia!*"

Three taller figures—alas, students, who never fight properly—kicked at a small form curled up in the frozen mud, hands over his head and knees drawn up for protection.

"Stop!" Chrétien shouted, imitating a Provençal accent. Then he tried French. Then his own Catalan. To his great pleasure, they failed to stop at his command. They did look his way, all three in painted mummers' masks. In the dark street, he guessed red dogs. No—foxes.

An opportunity to step ungently on some student toes.

"*A mal punt.*" An unpleasant situation, that's what his father would say, with a smile.

At the moment when the tallest of the attackers raised his boot to stomp again, one sweep of Chrétien's quarterstaff brought the man down onto his backside, breaking the ice-skin of a puddle and drenching him.

The other two turned from their victim to advance on Chrétien, but one was stopped by a noisy whack on his shin from Chrétien's staff, a knock that'd keep the lad wondering for a week whether his leg was broken.

The third student stepped back, treading on the first student's hand, who exclaimed, "Donkey's cock!"

Chrétien tended to agree.

"*Per l'amor de Déu!*" Chrétien pounded his quarterstaff on the cobbles. "Stop, if you want to keep your own cock."

That one ran, the thud of his boots echoing up the street. The other two stumbled to their feet and lurched away in the same direction, cursing Chrétien's father, mother, and cousins back through six generations.

"Thank you, gentlemen!" He called after them. "It has been my Twelfth Night pleasure."

However, that effort wasn't enough to relieve the itching of Chrétien's palms. Disappointed, he kicked at one of their discarded masks. Still, he owed thanks to someone else's angels of deliverance who had given him the gift of that brief tiff.

"*Merce Déu*. The Good God rains blessings wherever we go."

The small figure, still hunkering in the frozen mud, called thanks to God in Catalan. Then repeated it in the local tongue, while struggling to get up off the frozen street.

Chrétien grasped the fellow's forearm to haul him up. "Here, up you go, my friend. Out of the muck."

But he scraped his knuckles on the pavement, and then it felt as if he'd grabbed a stick instead of a human arm. Fearing he'd snap a bone, Chrétien instead embraced the small fellow's shoulders and hauled him to his feet. Unsteady, the beaten lad stumbled against Chrétien, who again embraced him to keep him upright. A mere boy.

The lad stood no higher than Chrétien's belt buckle and might be ten or twelve. Impossible to guess, because the urchin had a face that showed he'd starved, not so long ago, and he hadn't yet been fed right. He was as thin and tetchy as that cat in the alley, his mud-streaked shirt cold to the touch.

"Where's your coat, *fadrin*?" Chrétien used his father's pet word, spoken when his sons needed encouragement or comfort.

"I lost it when I ran away from the fishermen."

He'd have to guide this wretched lad to safety. There being no revelers with torches in this street, Chrétien tried to recall where in this passage there might be a bench or low wall.

"Wait here." Chrétien leaned the lad against the wall of a house, along with his walking stick, and jogged around the corner. The cat who'd guarded his lute scampered off with a yowl of protest for the surprise. Chrétien grabbed the leather satchel, turned—

And the boy was directly behind him, holding Chrétien's staff.

Even in the dark night, the stars offered enough light to show the lad's eyes didn't seem to focus, and he swayed. Those *baquelars* must have gotten in at least one good kick to the boy's head. Which meant Chrétien could not leave him on his own, coatless, on these frozen streets. The city's *gardes du corps* would be picking up those stick-like bones to carry off to whatever Montpelhièr used as a potters' field.

"Come along, *fadrin*. Let's get you a bite of bread." His satchel over one shoulder, stick in hand, he guided the unsteady boy up the street toward his favorite hostel, one owned by a Cyprian countryman who understood how to spice pottage properly.

At Aubèrja de Cyprus, Chrétien knew better than to ask for a place by fire for a ragged, bruised boy, but since it was Twelfth Night, a few local lads had a bonfire in the square where two streets crossed, hot enough that you could feel its heat even on the bench at the hostel's common-room door.

"What's your name?" Chrétien pointed to the bench. The boy sat, shoulders hunching meekly, the posture of a boy who'd long been made to obey. Chrétien hissed softly and bit back a curse to encompass all of mankind.

"Sanço." The boy said *S-aun-cho* in the peculiar way you heard on the other side of the Pyrenees.

"Where are your people, Sanço? On which street can we find your house?"

"I don't have a house. I'm not from here." Sanço's accent confirmed that he was from somewhere closer to Barcelona than the Pays d'Òc. "I'm traveling to find my lord, who's a crusader knight, to beg him to come home and save our village. May the Good God light my way."

Jhezu del tron! Chrétien had managed to pick up a goodman heretic refugee in a town crawling with Templars, French crusaders, and priests from every kind of monk-house, all sent by Rome to deliver judgment on the lords of the Pays d'Òc. No lord here was free to rescue a waif's village when their whole attention was on saving their own souls in the face of the Church's judgment against their kin. Thankfully, Durán knew better than to speak about his heretical beliefs to strangers. This child did not.

Yet in the flickering light of the bonfire, Chrétien noticed what he couldn't see in the dark streets: a whack on the boy's forehead, rimmed now with dried blood; painfully chapped lips; a snub nose so red and raw it hurt to look; hair dark as the night—or filthy as the street—falling into his eyes. The sullen boy peered out from under the fringe, as if perpetually guessing what bad might happen next. He had knotted cords on his arm, the kind men used on campaign to track the days, but that couldn't be what the boy did, for he had perhaps two dozen cords knotted, hanging from his skinny arm. Perhaps he'd gleaned them, hoping to trade for food.

"Wait here, *fadrin*—Sanço. Let me get you something to eat. I'll ask where a lad like you can doss in this city. I promise to find the proper help to keep you safe."

He left his cloak with the boy, stopping short of wrapping up the waif the way his mother would.

Pons, who owned this hostelry, greeted Chrétien as a friend, crying, "My beloved singer! You are better than my own son!" Pons amassed good silver for wine and ale on nights when Chrétien came to sing. A mid-sized man with powerful shoulders, Pons oiled the fringe of hair circling his bald pate, so that on the street he could be mistaken for a monk supervising a different kind of gathering place.

"A place for lost boys?" Pons puzzled over Chrétien's query, his eyebrows embracing each other like long-time shaggy friends. At Chrétien's request, he rustled forth a small, day-old *brioix* loaf and whacked a chunk off a wheel of cow's-milk cheese. "That would be with the nuns at St-Lazarus House, near the east gate. They take babies no one wants and children lost in the streets. If they're young enough."

Chrétien thanked Pons with copper pennies. Outside, the boy Sanço waited. He'd enshrouded his cold bones in Chrétien's cloak so only his eyes showed. He watched the other lads, who cavorted around their bonfire and paid no mind to the skeleton-boy on the bench. A thin, dirty hand darted out of the scratchy woolen folds of Chrétien's winter cloak to grab the bread and cheese.

"*Gràcies, el meu capità i senyor.*" Sanço saluted Chrétien as his lord and master, speaking in hurried Catalan. "May the Good God of Light bless you for your kindness, where none is expected or deserved."

Too much gratitude for a copper's worth of bread. Too much heresy spoken aloud in a town full of Churchmen.

"They say the nuns at St-Lazarus House will give you shelter." Chrétien hoped his voice contained certainty about the nuns, because he was uncertain about the boy. "But do you know how to confess that there is only one God? They're Roman nuns."

"Òc, lo mieu capitani." The lad switched to the local tongue. "I know how to make my way safely in rough waters."

"Can you find your way to the east gate? The nuns' house is right by the gate. Do you know the city to find your way?"

The boy's reply seemed positive, spoken through a mouth filled with bread and cheese, a few crumbs escaping.

"Why were those students beating you?"

"I found a sou under the ice in a puddle. They watched me free it, then one claimed it was his and that I stole it. But the sou was already mine. A gift to me from the Good God, who protects those who live a pure life and say the proper prayers."

Chrétien again hissed softly at the poor state of humankind and again doubted this boy's ability to speak correctly to nuns. He fetched three coppers from inside his jerkin and held them out to the boy. "Do you have a pocket, Sanço? To keep these pennies from thieves?"

"In my boot." Boots? Well-traveled leather, the soles and tops strapped with hempen rope wrapping. "Senhór, you make me see how I am blessed among God's good people. You rain down kindness equal to how our Savior blessed us and taught us to always do good unto others."

No, Chrétien wasn't in the business of raining kindness. And the effusion of gratitude embarrassed him. He returned to Pons's hostel calling adieussiatz to the lad. Go with God. After all, he expected the cloak and boy to be gone before he returned.

3

A Knight in Paradise

CHRÉTIEN BENT TO ENTER the low door of the hostel and was jostled when a man brushed past him on the way out. It was too petty a slight to provoke a fight, though Chrétien whispered, *"Baquelar,"* because it's roguish for a man to bump another man without at least a nodding apology.

At Chrétien's mild curse, the man paused, turned back to stare, eyes black as coals. The fellow had a round face and a moustache that Chrétien considered foreign, but he couldn't call up where in his travels he'd seen that kind of long and well-tended moustache, or black tresses that fell unbound around his shoulders. At first the man glared, but after studying Chrétien for a heartbeat, he offered a wry smile. With a hand bearing a dark mark or stain, he tapped his brow as if in salute, and then disappeared, like a ghost or a good old-fashioned djinn.

Chrétien intended to do a good deed by singing in Pons's common room, which would be filled with men who had nowhere else to be on Twelfth Night. But Chrétien's former day-work guarding the child-king seemed to follow him into his night haunts. Feris the monk lurked near the door, casting about as if seeking company; however, he had a wheedling manner that most men shunned, which left him alone near the door. Given that Feris's job was to ensure the child-king's schoolmasters adhered to Church teaching, it didn't take a suspicious mind to think Feris worked a second and third shift, making sure Chrétien's songs were free of heresy.

Since his father had raised no fools, Chrétien always stuck to *canços de guerra*—crusaders' trail songs and sad hymns about the loss of Jerusalem. The kind of soldier-songs dipped in date-sugar, mawkish odes praising the camaraderie with which God blessed true soldiers. Sentimental pap that left men in the room sniffling over their wine and, most nights, heedless when dicing later.

But didn't Nuño say that he had spies in every tavern? Chrétien inspected the room, wondering if any of the men here belonged to Nuño. He sat near two large men who huddled together in the corner, pale like Chrétien, but with hefty Northerners' beards. One had plaited the center of his beard, so it hung in a braid down to his collarbone. They didn't notice Chrétien, talking with each other nose to nose, but more like conspirators than lovers.

"He's gone. So, tell me, are you taking his silver?"

"I don't like his moustache," said the one with the braid in his beard. "But it's midwinter, so there's no other work on offer. You? Are you answering the recruiter's call?"

"I told him I had to ask my wife in the morning."

The other man scoffed. Drops of spit caught on his moustache. "You have no wife. Only your own good right hand."

"No matter. The fellow said I must speak to no one."

"That's bothering me. Why should a Christian care about who knows he's hiring good quality men at arms? What is he really hiring us to do?"

Chrétien sniffed at that notion, but everyone in the place was sniffing and spitting, so those two fellows didn't notice Chrétien's unvoiced scorn at these two declaring themselves "good quality." Other men in small convivial knots spoke in the local tongue or in Catalan, French, or a Lombardy tongue. Nothing lofty, for there were no haughty knights or squires here, no one else escaping court parties like Chrétien had.

Since it was a feast-night, there were no men in well-tended linsey-woolsey, clean boots, and oiled cuirasses—the married men who often hustled an escape from their wives on the excuse they had to look their best if a captain might come by to hire men. This night's small crowd was made up of men with nowhere else to celebrate, men who dossed in hovels or tight bachelors' quarters and so spent every night in a tavern or wine-shop before turning to their lonely doss-house cots. The crowd contained no students, because every decent ostler or tavern-keeper in this neighborhood forbade entry to students, to avoid quarrels, Church interference, and the students' typical inability to pay for the wine they drank and furniture they broke.

Chrétien drew his lute from its satchel, checking that it fared well in that brief adventure. Happily, the satchel Durán gave him had kept the lute from harm. Durán wasn't such a perfected heretic that he couldn't buy a leather satchel on market day to hold his lover's lute. Chrétien settled into the comfort of singing in an ordinary common room, more at ease than in a lord's great hall.

The iron kettle of pottage on the fire spread its perfume, along with the nose-tingling smell of cypress burning, masking the odor of too many men in winter's close quarters, their lanolin-rich cloaks hung near the fire, stinking of sheep and man-musk. The room was crowded with battered trestle tables that had spent the summer in the courtyard, pitted from years of gamblers' abuse. Rushes on the floor. The click of backgammon tiles.

He sank into a morass of loneliness, missing Durán, sipping on self-pity, because Durán was about to ride into danger with only Chrétien to protect him. He sang in a falsetto as if this were a woman's song, though every word described his *bon amic* Durán.

> My ship has come to a good port.
> My silver has turned to gold.
> The greatest knight in the world
> Granted me his kisses.
> A king should be so honored.
>
> I envy no man or woman
> If my beloved holds me for one night.
> I've never enjoyed more honor
> Than that kiss and one night
> To regard his dark, perfect body,
> Lithe and hard worn.
> I shall never speak of what it was
> To hold him in my arms.

Feris the ferret-man departed. With the monk-spy gone, and to cheer up, Chrétien sang the song his father once declared best represented his religious faith, the ditty about the independent-minded shepherdess. A provocative *canços d'amore*, a hare-minded idea that he'd send these men to their lonely beds with sweet thoughts.

One chorus into the song, another man arrived in the common room, whom Chrétien recognized first because of his long dark locks and the blood-red velvet hat he wore. Earlier that week Chrétien saw that he had another disciple who appeared at whatever tavern Chrétien chose. This man was hard to read: perhaps ten years older than Chrétien, seated furthest from the fire, and shrouded in his grey woolen cloak. A priest? If so, it had to be the secular kind, like Father Anselm at Valerós, not a member of any order. This disciple, like Feris, marked the words Chrétien sang, as if memorizing the songs.

> The shepherdess set her dog after the hedge-priest.
> 'I do nothing for anyone but my own,
> Unless you pay with gold.
> You can preach goodwill among men.
> But I have to make my way in the world.'

The man moved up to sit near Chrétien, where the rushlight burned brightest. "That song offers a dark view of God's creation."

He had a smooth, mellifluent voice and a smile like a fox waiting for mice in the vineyard. That was an unkind thought, since this excruciatingly handsome man had a warm and friendly smile; however, Chrétien couldn't rally a kind thought after his earlier fight with the worst scum of humanity.

"My father," Chrétien said, "taught me to never question God's view of His creation, because an answer will not be forthcoming."

"But if you wait long enough, perhaps you'll know."

"No," Chrétien said. "It never comes."

The man had more to say. "But the song describes a sad paucity of the heart, to reject the joy of new friendships. It might be a humor of the blood that a physician could cure."

"It isn't 'friendship' that the shepherdess refuses." Chrétien shrugged off any worry that a priest might judge him too cynical. If this man was indeed a priest.

"I'm called Antoni." The man held out his hand. "We shouldn't be strangers. May I take a turn?"

Chrétien withheld his lute, behaving as if this Antoni had reached for his instrument, not merely to shake hands like a bleeding Norman. He moved away from the bench, yielding to Antoni, who stood and sang *a capella.*

> The other day I woke in Paradise.
> God greeted me as a comrade,
> He who made the valleys, seas, and mountains.
> He said, 'Brave knight, why did you come?
> Why have you left your *bon amics?'*

Chrétien sat back, leaning against the plaster wall. Pons the hostler set food on his table, a bread trencher filled with a pottage from the hearth. The hot lentils and root vegetables smelled like a winter stew his mother might serve. He let it cool while he watched that fellow Antoni sing.

The man was the color of the Great Sea. Not the water, which changes with the weather and the time of day. But the people, the sun-ripened warmth you saw everywhere along the rim of the Sea, except of course in the Norman and French colonies on Sicily and Cyprus. Antoni wasn't as dark as Chrétien's father or brother, but he was the opposite of Chrétien's whey skin and flaxen hair. He had the mouth of an orator, not a singer, with full lips that matched a voice that seeks to convince you, not comfort you or remind you of what it is to feel deeply, to retell the stories of who you once were. Which is what you're supposed to do when you sing others' songs.

Antoni gazed with dark eyes, like forest pools beckoning in the deep woods, seeming to promise that only you, you alone matter in this world. Chrétien became convinced that he was being pursued for romantic or carnal purposes. Antoni's singing was a flirtation, a come-hither. In former days, Chrétien would have appreciated a pleasant diversion in a dull posting like Montpelhièr. However, he was true to Durán, and his loneliness was temporary. It had been years since Chrétien last fretted himself into a heat because of an empty bed.

Chrétien refused to hold the man's engaging stare. Instead, he studied other men in the room. Then Antoni's *cruzado* song beguiled his attention.

Darius, Alexander, David,
All the kings of old,
These cannot compare
To what I can do, whether or not
You choose to help me, dear God.
I have merit and what kings call chivalry.
I can accomplish what those kings failed.

An adage from my grandfather insists:
'A man who waits and does nothing
will lose all time and chance.'

This song was—

My enemies sought to harm me.
They betrayed me into slavery in Syria.
Yet I thank them now.
A beautiful woman loved me.
She cut my bonds and set me free.
I'm now delivered from torture,
No longer in poisonous peril.

The brazen fellow sang a *canço de guerra* about—

When I rose from my first night in Paradise,
A good lord sought my service.
My lord tells all the world:
'This knight is greater than every knight.'

This song was about the don of Morella's adventures in Syria, where
he escaped slavery and stole Numa away to be his wife. But that
bold, flirtatious Antoni added a false refrain at the end.

If a man does not follow God
And remains enslaved of pleasure,
How can he gain salvation?
Only the One God shows the true way.

Antoni held the last note longer than the strength of his voice
could support. A smattering of men in the common room beat on
the table to show their gratitude. And Antoni settled onto the bench
beside Chrétien. Too close.

"That song? You stole a man's soul and sold it to the devil in the final verse," Chrétien said.

"That song captures the true spirit of our crusader heroes. Not the kings, but the real fighters." Antoni smiled, as if offering his beautiful smile as a blessing. Which further raised Chrétien's ire. He was not in the mood to be played with by a pretty rascal in a tavern, whether he was a priest or not.

"But the last refrain is an utter lie." The last lines rekindled the rage Chrétien had carried through the streets earlier. How dare any troubadour—or singer in a tavern—ascribe a zealot's morality to the don of Morella? "If I know anything about that particular crusader, I know he never once said, 'Only the One God shows the true way.'"

"Indeed?" Antoni answered mildly. "I found that song in the library of the music school here in Montpelhièr."

He touched Chrétien's hand where it rested beside a wine cup on the table. Though Antoni stroked gently, rubbing his thumb over Chrétien's knuckles, it wasn't a gesture done in the hostels of Montpelhièr. A man in a grey wool robe, whether a lecturer from one of the schools or a monk who'd left his monastery, did not touch a bannered knight who served two counts of the Pays d'Òc. No matter how handsome and kindly the man appeared.

Chrétien glanced down at that impertinent touch, seeing the blood on his knuckles where he'd helped that filthy orphan up off the cobbles. He withdrew his hand. He had no reason to flirt with this rogue. "You presume too much with your song."

"Perhaps. The coda? I made it myself, to keep nosy Churchmen from censoring a great crusader's life story."

"It is false. A slander against his life."

"You know the songs about that crusader?"

"As much as any man."

Chrétien rose to depart, tossing coins on Pons's table for the uneaten stew and wine. He wasn't confessing anything about his father to a flirtatious stranger in a melancholy tavern.

4

Snick, Snick

OUTSIDE PONS'S HOSTEL, THAT bruised child was gone, of course. Chrétien called to the other boys on the street, who were busy feeding a broken milking stool into their bonfire.

"Where's the boy who was sitting here?"

"He puked and then ran away," one shouted back. He wore a mummer's mask too large for him. A red fox.

Glancing at the bench, Chrétien confirmed that someone had indeed been sick. A scattering of rocks lay nearby.

"And you threw stones to make sure he ran away?" Chrétien fumed. These boys were too small for him to vent fury like he had with the drunken students.

"That little sneak-thief? He has the plague!" one thin voice yelled in answer.

"A blight from the Evil One!"

"Cow pox!"

"Wolf pox! We had to protect ourselves."

Chrétien had done his best for that boy. Still, he walked home deeply unsatisfied. A lost urchin in the cold. A child-heretic, surviving on his wits, as Durán had once done, before his parentage was discovered. An orphan sent across the city alone to find shelter with nuns. Far worse than Chrétien's personal complaint, that he was stuck in Montpelhièr for more frigid, lonely days. Chrétien should have done more for the child. The wind had picked up since he'd entered Pons's hostel, and now a sodden wet snow fell, which made it highly likely that he'd freeze while searching the city for that lad, who at least had Chrétien's cloak for warmth.

A large crowd of drunken students wearing fox masks passed, indistinguishable from the ones Chrétien had kicked off that orphan. Five heartbeats later, a half-dozen *gardes du corps* came through the streets, led by Sergeant Vincent and obviously intent on returning to their barracks, out of the chill night.

"*Bon nuoit! Feliç nit dotze!*" Vincent called to Chrétien. His accent still had a trace of Béziers, his childhood home. "May God lead you down a good path."

"I shall do my best," Chrétien said, "but who knows how the dice might fall."

Vincent's fluty laughter echoed in the cold dark air.

Though Chrétien returned the guards' festive felicitations, the jolly exchange did not warm him on the walk home, because he couldn't quit thinking of that orphan, hoping he'd found his way to the nuns and was not lost and frozen on the streets. He vented his anger at the malicious ways of the universe by stomping the iced-over puddles, which cracked and popped in delicious ways, but also gained him wet boots in addition to his jerkin and tunic being soaked through from wet snow by the time he arrived at Nuño's compound, which included the smaller villa where Chrétien lived. A knight who'd grown used to his own cozy Toulousain villa in winter, Chrétien now slept in a cell where an ancient monk had numbered his days with scratches on the stone walls. The villa had once been a monastery, but those monks had built a new home for themselves outside the city gates, so the villa now lay within Comte Nuño's compound.

Home before dawn after the feast-day, Chrétien took down his weapons and fetched a whetstone from his kit to lull his resentment with the rhythmic *snick, snick* of stone on steel. A song he never tired of hearing.

In his recent duty, helping Orlando de Troyes protect the child-king and his schoolmates each day didn't call for sharp steel, but Chrétien may well need it ready at hand when they finally rode back to Toulouse, hopefully not before. So, he sharpened the entire armory he'd brought to Montpelhièr.

Two swords, though only one of Damascus steel.

Three cross-hilt knives, all Damascus steel, because at one time he'd finished a job as mercenary with enough silver to buy two, and the other he'd snatched as a memento from his father's armory.

Two smaller throwing knives, also inherited from his father.

An odd arming sword with a curved blade that his father had won in his journeys, or that had drifted around the Great Sea, traded again and again until it came into his father's possession.

Chrétien's mother brought that odd blade with her when she came to live at Chrétien's house in Toulouse. She gave it to him for protection on this duty-post, though Chrétien didn't know what use it might be. Perhaps on horseback, fighting other knights with curved swords. However, he didn't expect cavalry work, and his next duty would be to convince Durán to return home. Where they'd be safe from any trouble here that started before or after the lords of the Pays d'Òc gathered in Church council rooms.

Years before, he'd insisted that the disorder between the Church and the Pays d'Òc lords had nothing to do with him. However, his bond with his milk-brother Tomás dragged him into protecting Tomás's wife and her child. She'd barely been saved from being burned as a heretic after the siege at Minerve. He'd hunkered down to attend to family duties with Durán, who besides being more beautiful than an angel, was also half-brother to Tomás's stepson. That family obligation was as strong as any blood-ties could be. What he and Durán owed to their extended family required the same passionate protection that their father had given his sons, their mother, and all his loyal knights.

Durán said he was a Cathar goodman though he had the good sense to shut up about it around anyone who might report him to the bishops' court. Chrétien never argued with him about salvation and how to obtain it, or whether God intercedes for goodness's sake or leaves all men to struggle through on their own, which Chrétien's father asserted to be true. He couldn't adopt Durán's hopes for a better incarnation, but he would not let Durán be dragged into the dark chaos spawned when the Church condemned the mild, peaceful goodmen as heretics. On their way to Andalusia three years ago, Durán had tussled with the archbishop in Narbonne and managed to escape judgment. Like every goodman in the Pays d'Òc, Durán foreswore fighting and became even more adamant about walking weaponless in the world after their adventures in Andalusia. Therefore, although Chrétien no longer worked as a mercenary, he still needed to keep his sword sharp to protect Durán when needed.

For the seigneurs and counts of the Pays d'Òc, he didn't owe as much. Except as a *bonfraire* of the Confraria de la Crotz if they called on him.

Snick, snick. Sharpen enough steel in a stone cell, soon it's as if you can taste it. Too tired for more chores, he wrapped his blades in their soft calfskin covers and tucked them in the rafters, out of the reach of any schoolboy who might wander into this part of the villa.

Chrétien slipped the whetstone into its leather pouch, again noticing where he'd scraped his hand raw on the cobbles in the street. He'd forgotten it, foolishly, and now poured water from a goatskin bota and rubbed his fingers clean, hoping he hadn't rubbed black rot from the city mud into the wounds. Except, oddly, the flesh wasn't broken. Threads of dried blood traced the lines across his knuckles, but his skin was unbroken.

Lying on his cot, closing his eyes, he fell into his habit of composing letters to Durán, reporting on his day. Though the *punxor*, his own true love, hadn't written to Chrétien since All Saints.

> *Cor dolç.* My heart beats every moment with yours. I close my eyes every night, remembering your beauty. Your goodness. Your pure heart. The notch where your thigh meets your truly gorgeous hips. Why haven't you written, you blasted ass-bite? Your Good God has kept me here too long, to punish your indolent failure to succor my courage. But soon you'll come, and I'll enjoy your touch again.

He drifted toward sleep, and then was jarred awake.

"*Sona com un gat malalt.*" *You sound like a sick cat.* "You have worthy work. And good lords to serve. Stop moaning."

Catalan words from the voice Chrétien missed most in the world — beyond Durán or his mother Numa or his brother Tomás. He heard Don Miquel de Morella, the father he'd lost, as if hearing that song at the hostel resurrected his father's voice again.

Can't even say "the father whom God took too soon," since Miquel would say God had nothing to do with it. Rather, it was a poisoned blade plunged into Miquel's belly by his enemy a dozen years before. His mother Numa insisted it was a miracle Miquel had lived that many years after he'd been sliced open. But if angels or saints were handing out miracles, why couldn't they let Chrétien have his father alive and cursing for another dozen years?

Miquel telling stories.

Miquel explaining the thin boundary between courage and recklessness.

Miquel chiding him in the practice yard. *Do better. Strive to be a better man.*

Stop moaning. You have good lords to serve.

A knock at his cell door. Not Miquel's ghost, but a military hand. Chrétien pulled on his tunic and answered the knock.

"Comte Nuño has called for you, senhór."

Chrétien retied his hair, made sure it was tucked neatly down his tunic, then straightened his jerkin. As Durán often insisted, Chrétien was vain, but he cared only about what certain men thought of his appearance. He followed Nuño's aide-de-camp through the labyrinth of the villa's hallways in pursuit of answers to Chrétien's key question: was Nuño touched by the moon?

5

Count on Me

THE AIDE-DE-CAMP LED CHRÉTIEN to the count's stable. Dressed in stained riding leathers, Nuño had been out on horseback and was finishing up the chore of wiping down his horse. Both Comte Nuño and the horse breathed out white vapor in the cold dawn light. Chrétien breathed in the comforting odors of a clean stable.

"What do you fear most?" Nuño began the conversation as if they'd already been chatting.

What Chrétien almost said: being bored, boxed in, or left idle. But he was sober enough to offer a better reply. "An enemy I cannot see who means me harm."

"This is the worst it's been."

"The weather, Monsenyor?"

"The problems in the south. Though it's been bad for years. People in Béziers and Minerve and other towns suffered terribly."

"But now?" Chrétien prompted. While sharpening steel in his cell, he'd quelled his irritation at having been in Montpelhièr so long, but this line of conversation opened new fears.

Nuño said, "We've had a respite for the past year. It seemed then that the French king might stop Simon after we warned him about Simon's ambitions growing quite large."

Simon de Montfort had led the French forces to quell heresy in the Pays d'Òc, but last year rumors flew that Simon wanted to be king in the south.

"We all hung our hopes on Philippe Auguste after..." Chrétien wasn't going to say it. After Pedro was killed at Muret.

"Once the Church took the child-king of Aragón out of Simon's possession, Philippe no longer cares. He has other rebels to conquer." Nuño glanced around, taking in who else was in the stable with them. Two servants pitched hay to the animals. Two younger boys at the far end of the stable milked cows and made each other laugh, squirting milk at the cats. "But now Simon wants the Church to finally depose Raymond of Toulouse, to end heresy there."

Chrétien twitched, seized with trepidation. "There is nothing I can do to help with that." He'd do what he could for Nuño, but Church business was more than Chrétien cared to be involved in. Yet, Durán insisted on coming to the council, to plead for the other seigneurs.

"Certainly not." Nuño tapped his foot, irritated. "We spent all of December trying to uncover the plot Simon and the Church are hatching."

"We?"

"My men, who are my ears in the city. They say foreigners are recruiting mercenaries in the taverns. I believe it's for the Church's plot against me."

"So, they're looking for desperate men who want to be hired before they starve?" Chrétien recalled the two men in Pons's hostel the night before. "Who is recruiting? No one has approached me."

Although a warrior's warrior, Nuño fidgeted, like a man who can't get his words out. He glanced around again as if checking for listeners. "Let's finish this talk in my rooms."

Chrétien followed Comte Nuño down a short hall to the count's work room, which wasn't much larger than the ancient monk's cell where Chrétien slept. The work room was outfitted like a soldier's traveling camp instead of the silks and finery in the count's great hall. Three sturdy camp chairs with worn leather covers took up the corners, except the remaining corner held a camp-chest, apparently last used as a bench. A plain plank table served as a desk, as if Nuño lived perpetually in a war camp and wanted his city house to feel the same. Nuño must mend and oil his own tack, for it was scattered about the table top, so the room smelled of harness oil and horse.

Nuño pointed to one of the leather chairs, indicating where Chrétien should sit. In that small room, Chrétien couldn't stretch comfortably in any way without his boot encountering Nuño's. The count sat at his bare-board table, running his hands through his hair like a man who hadn't slept, so his white bush of hair stood on end, as if he were bewildered, looking every bit like a mad man.

"They haven't approached you either? Of all the men I sent to listen for rumors, only one claims to have been approached." Nuño shoved at torn piece of harness on his table, as if it were the object of his ire. "Yet I fear some of my men may have been recruited and now serve two masters. Is there anyone I dare trust?"

"Me, Monsenyor. Tell me about the man who seems to be recruiting mercenaries."

"My man thinks it's a fellow he encountered when sailing home from Constantinople years ago. In one port, men from a Genoese privateer called one of their crew *Il Priore Moresco*. They claim this Black Prior can heal wounds with his hands."

"A Moor who's a priest?"

"No, only dark from the sun."

"What does he look like?" Chrétien asked. "A man was hiring mercenaries in a hostel where I sang last night. He brushed past me, but all I noticed was a ridiculous moustache." And menacing confidence, though Chrétien didn't describe that to Nuño.

"If it's who my man thinks it is, the Black Prior is from a secret mystical brotherhood called the Order of the Wheel and Serpent. People say those knights can perform magic."

"There's no such thing as magic." Chrétien said it, feeling as if Miquel repeated it in chorus. His father didn't believe in mystical happenings any more than he believed in divine answers to prayers.

Nuño laughed. "Why did I think you'd say that?"

"What magic trick does this mystery man perform?"

"He cuts himself and then heals the wound. I hear it's shocking to witness."

Chrétien shivered—it wasn't a warm room—and rubbed where he'd hurt his hand the night before. Except he hadn't hurt it. "Perhaps I've met him. Does this magic man stand about this high?" He held up his hand to indicate how tall he remembered the flirtatious Antoni to be. "With long curls of dark hair and a nose like an old Roman statue?"

"No, slender and bald. Or he has long black hair like a Turcopole archer. Did the fellow you met have this tattoo on his hand?" Nuño grabbed a rag of parchment from the litter on his desk and sketched with a piece of charcoal. A circle, crossed with lines to form an eight-spoke wheel, and an asp rising from its base.

Chrétien had seen a similar tattoo, but not on the flirtatious upstart Antoni. "Orlando of Troyes, the house-master for the boy-king, carries that sign."

"I asked Captain Orlando." Nuño ran his hands through his hair yet again, looking more distracted and harried. "He says everyone else from the Wheel and Serpent confraternity has died. That they were only badly-behaved squires who met in Constantinople, not conspirators recruiting mercenaries in Montpelhièr."

"Do you think this fellow works for the Church? Or is he hiring mercenaries to defeat both the Templars and your own forces in the city?" Both options seemed wildly improbable, leaving Chrétien to wonder if he should ride out to meet Foix and Durán, and then take Durán home before they became involved with Nuño's mad fears and schemes.

"I have beliefs, but not proof." Nuño fiddled with a buckle on the harness sprawled on his table. "I believe, first, there will be a murder—likely a bishop or priest the Churchmen don't like. Then they'll use the recruited fighters to create an uprising in the city."

"They? You mean the Church?" Chrétien was still judging the count, who seemed lucid, logical, in pursuit of facts, not lost in dreams.

"Someone in the Church. Perhaps the pope doesn't know about this. Maybe the prelate isn't involved. But I'm sure agents of the Church are plotting here." Nuño wadded up the tattoo drawing, crushing it in his fist. "You likely think I'm mad, because I'm guessing on thin evidence. But a similar plot worked for the Church years ago in Toulouse. Why not use it again?"

Years earlier, a prelate was murdered outside Toulouse, by no one knew whom. Yet the Church blamed Raymond of Toulouse, leading the pope within a year to ask Philippe Auguste to send French armies to invade the Pays d'Òc.

"In the middle of all the chaos created," Nuño said, "the Church will blame the counts and lords for everything."

"You're saying the Church's goal in this plot is to ruin the counts and viscounts and seigneurs." Chrétien was beginning to see the depth of what Nuño envisioned.

"Òc. From Cahors to Narbonne, from the Pyrenees foothills to Montpelhièr. Every seigneur, every family." As if he hadn't been clear enough, Nuño added, "The bishops sent lists to the counts of those seigneurs they suspect. Your friend Durán of Montcava is on the list. As are your brother Tomás and his wife. Your family. Your households in Toulouse and Valerós. For all of us, everything will be lost if we allow this plot to succeed."

Chrétien sat upright in the camp chair. This wasn't a mad man. Nuño's mind was as sharp as Chrétien's steel. "Oh, why do I think the dancing angels just ceased singing?"

"Indeed. If murder and chaos disturb the prelate's council, the Church will force us to ensure every lord in the south rids their lands of heretics. Can your family and friends do that?" Nuño pushed aside the harness, as if to stop fiddling with it. "Senhór, you've been in Béziers. You know what a burned city is like. You were at Minerve, so you know how burning flesh smells. I cannot stop imagining the past years' terror coming to all the towns, to where my friends and family live. And, as you know, it's nothing like battle, because these people cannot fight back."

Nuño found a strip of linen on his table and wiped his face, hiding his eyes. But with those words, Nuño had caused Chrétien to imagine, too vividly, Simon's army coming to the villa where his own mother and lover lived. A house full of children and loyal house-knights. Friends he'd traveled and fought with.

Together with the animal smell of harness oil, an image burned like a branding in his mind: Durán and Numa facing a pyre.

Chrétien cleared his throat so he could speak again. "What can we do to stop this plot, Monsenyor? It seems impossible."

"Be a man I can trust on the street every day, in the taverns every night. Wear your steel everywhere. Hear what you can to help us discover the men behind the Church's plot."

Compelled to act, Chrétien knelt on the cold stone floor, holding his crossed forearms before him.

"By this cross, I swear to you, Monsenyor, to undertake all you need, risking the salvation of my own soul to serve you. I promise this faithfully, upon my own father's honor."

"*Aiieee.* Please get up." Nuño hung back, his arms folded, hands tucked in, where the sleeves of his jerkin had been lashed to the leather body. "You make me ashamed. I've never asked a man to risk his immortal soul."

"You didn't ask. I offered." Finding an assassin—or more likely, merely a rabble-rouser—didn't seem like a soul-risking endeavor when his family's safety was at stake. "You can count on me."

"Thank you. I hope that you are the man to help us. Foix insisted you are a great warrior."

"Ramón-roger must be jesting with you. He laughed himself sick when I declared I was the best swordsman anywhere near the Great Sea. Then he called on me to fight, and I spent half a year coughing up dust in Andalusia."

"This time..." Nuño hesitated again. Chrétien fought the impulse to pull words out of the man, eyeing the pliers resting on a half-mended harness. "They say the Black Prior studied with that djinn, the Old Man of the Mountain. Just like you and your brother. We need your own Nizari assassin magic to combat him."

6

Assassins

"No." CHRÉTIEN SAT BACK, defeated by Nuño's sudden foolishness. The honeyed animal smell of harness oil now irritated his nose.

"Yes. That's how the Black Prior heals himself. He studied with the Old Man who led the magical Nizari assassins."

"Stop. I was seven years old when I heard stories of those fighters, enough to make you wet your breeches." How had this intelligent conversation suddenly flown away with dark angels? He didn't consider Nuño to be mad, merely horribly misinformed. "That's all the Nizari assassins are, a tall tale to frighten crusaders into surrender."

"Yet everyone says you were trained by the Nizari. In Cairo." Nuño offered his open hands, indicating that he fully believed this ridiculous story.

"*Ai Dèu!* How long will that foolish lie persist?" Chrétien sighed. "My father's agent claimed to have found teachers who possessed the Assassins' secrets. He'd disappeared up the Nile with my father's gold in his pocket by the time my brother and I disembarked in Cairo and reported to our new fight-masters."

"Then it is as people say." Nuño sounded like a man clinging to a last hope. "You have secrets that can save us from a magic-wielding assassin."

"Magic is not an option, Monsenyor. Your fears are leading you down a wrong path. I regret saying your problems are impossible, if that's what led you to think of magic."

"But in Cairo you did in fact learn—"

"Our masters imparted skills that involve steel and staves, not magic. They also drank to excess and beat us with iron rods. There are no Nizari assassins." Chrétien spoke in a low but emphatic voice, beating his knee with one hand for emphasis. "Those men in Cairo were imposters. Anyone who possessed Nizari secrets would never share them with Christians. Anyone prowling in your city and claiming to have studied with the Nizari assassins is only another lying mercenary."

This time Nuño sat back, folding his hands, his arms hanging between his knees. "I was counting on—"

"Magic?" Chrétien posited one of the sadder questions he'd ever asked. He had to steer Nuño away from this worthless hope. "To my certain knowledge, there are no magical assassins. I am the most rational man you can find. I seek enemies and defeat them in battle, without magic. That's what I promise you—to search, not blinded by foolish notions of magic or ghosts."

"Or heresy? You are bonded to people the Church calls heretic."

Chrétien made an impertinent move, resting his hand on Nuño's knee. "Upon my father's honor, I do not expect to be reincarnated, either as a higher angel or a lowly newt. My prospects for heaven are as great as my father's, who was a crusader in the Outremer."

In fact, Chrétien expected his soul would end up in the same place as his father's, wherever that was. He held no sentiments about that and did not believe anything could make him care deeply about anyone's fate beyond Durán. And his own brother Tomás. And Tomás's son Yusuf. Tomás's stepson Sebastian. His mother. All of their families.

Nuño accepted Chrétien's claim, tragedy writ over his face. "Our situation here is hopeless."

"No, Monsenyor. This assassin has no more magic than I do. We shall find him. We shall defeat him, along with whoever is paying him to make trouble." Chrétien rose from the camp chair.

"We have only three days. I'm sure these plotters will act by Friday. What can you do in so little time?"

"Whatever I must, as I swore to you that I would. I'll search out recruited mercenaries until I find your assassin. You can rely on me."

"*Mercé.*" Nuño choked on his thank-you, gratitude which Chrétien had not yet earned in any way. "These Church fellows are united by an ideal, but each seigneur in the Pays d'Òc has only his personal oaths that bind or separate him from other lords. Pedro couldn't unite them, and certainly I have no hope of that. I can only rely on a few personal oaths from men of honor, like you."

"Monsenyor, I'm only a mercenary knight who—"

"No, you're a man I can trust." But Nuño did not ask an oath from Chrétien. He instead offered a scrap of parchment that he'd already signed. "Here's my license. My insignia will let you carry a sword in the city where most men are forbidden. And…"

Once more Nuno fell silent, yet it seemed he wanted to ask something more.

"What more do you want me to do, Monsenyor?"

"I'm still master in this town, as Count of Roussillon. As long as God grants me that place, I am the law here."

"No one debates that, Monsenyor. I'll do whatever you ask."

"If you meet a man bearing that tattoo," Nuño's hand rested on the crumpled drawing of the Wheel and Serpent icon, "you may kill him with impunity."

"No, Monsenyor. I won't kill him. It's more important to learn who his paymaster might be."

•

After offering Nuño a decent farewell, Chrétien went to fetch his steel out of the rafters in his cell. He whistled as he buckled on his sword and tucked two cross-hilt knives in his belt and a throwing knife in his boot. At least one good thing had come out of the morning. The city streets became more appealing now that he had Nuño's permission to bear a sword instead of a less useful staff.

A timid hand knocked on his cell door soon after Chrétien felt satisfied that he was as well armed as the best swordsman in Christendom needed to be when seeking a magical assassin.

"*Desencusatz*, senhór." Rafel, one of Nuño's servants, spoke the common tongue with a local accent. "There's a…a…I think it's a Twelfth Night mummer at the villa's door, begging to speak with you."

"Thank you, Rafel."

The visitor must be his nephew Yusuf, come for breakfast after the feast-day. Chrétien didn't know anyone else who'd sing as a mummer in the streets until dawn. He followed Rafel to the foyer, which was half again colder than the other rooms in the villa. In front of the great cypress wood doors that barred attackers and unwanted guests stood the waif who'd survived the street fight.

Swaddled in Chrétien's now mud-caked cloak, the boy fell to his knees, head bent. "O my captain! Please forgive me for failing you. Yet God is my guide and master, so I am here now."

"How did you find me?" *Aiieee! Why did you find me?*

"I saw that man who watched you from the door. So, I followed him to ask if he knew my captain. That way I'd know where to find you if you got lost. When I came back from the jakes, you were gone. But I knew to come here because that man who follows you told me."

"What man watched me?" Because of the conspiracy in the city, Chrétien did not need anyone watching him.

"The one who looks like a..." the boy's eyes darted "...a weasel. I asked him where to find you."

"I didn't tell you my name." Chrétien fought shivers, blaming the cold foyer. And yet, no man could feel comfortable being followed by a monk-spy, especially one who resembled a ferret, but at least it was man he knew, not a stranger who'd add more concern than Chrétien already had.

"He knew your hair when I described it. He says you're the *cavaller fada* who guards baby boys for Comte Nuño."

Chrétien scowled. *Fairy knight.* Sanço reported Feris's words, with no idea what the miniscule monk meant.

Sanço shrank back at his expression. That broke Chrétien's hardened, mercenary heart. No one wants children to cower in fear. The boy said, "I'm sorry I wasn't there when you looked for me. It was a call of nature. I swear you can count on my true and noble heart whenever you need me."

"Count on you?" Chrétien had counted only on mud crusting his winter cloak, if he ever saw again.

"It is as we are taught from the cradle." Sanço tipped his head as if listening for that teaching voice. "You are responsible for me now, since you saved my life. God has given you the blessing to be my spiritual father as well as my savior here on earth. For that, I owe you obedient service together with the love God placed my heart."

"I don't think so. That wasn't taught in my cradle." Chrétien folded his arms, returning from broken-hearted concern back to looking for the swindle the urchin was playing on him.

"But you promised to help find my lord, to make my village safe again. I have traveled the world in search of my lord. God and his merciful angels led me to you. He placed me in your care."

Chrétien wasn't given to making promises, so he couldn't think what he might have said that the boy mistook as such an enormous commitment. "Here's what we'll do." Chrétien, as a crafty soldier, sought the nearest escape. "Let's have breakfast. And then we'll find a coat that fits you."

"*Gràcies*, my captain."

"I'm not your captain. After breakfast, I'll take you to the nuns at St-Lazarus."

That look of dismayed hopelessness once more flitted over the boy's face. He seemed well-practiced at knifing his way into men's hearts. "That's not what the Good God intends for you and me."

"I was raised from the cradle not to guess what God intends." Chrétien deeply disliked putting on a hard face when speaking to this urchin. However, he'd already done more for this lost boy than anyone else in the city. He needed instead to find those who were threatening Nuño and the seigneurs and the city, preferably before Durán arrived. "We'll ask the nuns. It's their job to know what God intends."

The boy followed Chrétien to the villa's kitchen, still talking. "Can we seek my lord on the way to the nuns' house?"

Chrétien tossed up his hands. "Is he in Montpelhièr?"

"I'm not sure where he is. I hadn't heard of Montpelhièr till I came here, but we must ask. I couldn't find him in Narbonne or Marseille. Or on Sardinia or Sicily. And I haven't yet been to the other places we heard he might be, like Edessa or Jaffa or Cairo. Do you know where Jaffa is?"

Jhezu del tron! Chrétien hunched under the responsibility that followed him to the kitchen. The mistress of the villa, Mme Marguerite, Orlando's wife, would have his nuts off with her sewing shears if she discovered that Chrétien had dragged a filthy, lying beggar into her house.

In the kitchen, with all the meandering thoughts of Miquel from the night before, Chrétien saw his beautiful brother Tomás at the table, from years before. Then he blinked and his nephew Yusuf manifested, Tomás's son. Luis the cook was feeding a platter of boiled eggs with toasted bread and honey to Yusuf and his companion, Qasim. Luis claimed it was his duty as a Christian to take care of starving students when he could. And the cost came out of Chrétien's allowance from Nuño. Therefore, not an unusual morning encounter.

But to complicate this particular morning, Sanço fell to his knees, his hands folded in supplication, pleading with an astonished Qasim, who had himself once been a beggar on the wharves in Valencià.

"My most honorable lord, may the Good God rain blessings on you. You must save us all."

7

Honey and Fire

"BONJORN, MON ONCLE!" YUSUF glanced up from his feast, honey dripping on his lower lip. His tongue sneaked out to stop it. "We came to ask you the very same thing. You must save us."

One never encountered Yusuf without his close comrade Qasim, muscle-thick like a warrior and the incarnation of common sense, a foil to Yusuf, reed-slender with wit as sharp as a penknife. Yusuf handsome in black fustian, like his father Tomás used to wear, and Qasim powerful in brown leather breeches and double-thick jerkin, brass studs hammered across its front.

While staring at Sanço the supplicant, Qasim had frozen in place, a piece of toasted bread near his open mouth, honey drops falling onto the table.

"Sanço, get off the floor." Chrétien needed to assert his authority, before the boy's scam grew to be even more ridiculous. "Luis, can you please give my young friend breakfast by the fire? And then please send him with Rafel to find some clothes. Doesn't Mme Marguerite save the students' castoffs to give to the poor?"

"*Aiieee,* my captain! I must beseech my lord." Sanço's voice quivered, on the edge of tears. Or pretending to be. "It is what God has commanded me in this life."

"You," Chrétien pointed to the boy, "are commanded to be silent when I ask it of you."

Smoldering, Sanço followed Luis to the other end of the kitchen. Qasim and Sanço stared at each other across the length of the room. The cooks' noise allowed Chrétien and his nephew to talk, with only Qasim hearing them.

"I'm setting up a school for assassins." Chrétien pointed across the kitchen. "That's my first student."

"*Merce Dèu!*" Yusuf exclaimed. "I mistakenly surmised that you'd rescued an orphan off the frozen streets."

"I'd set out to...oh, never mind." Chrétien shook his head. He'd get no sympathy from these two for his rash act of charity. "What do you want me to save you from? If it's gambling debts, you have to ask your father. But only when I'm there, so I can watch the storm."

"No, I'm here in Montpelhièr as a scholar." Yusuf scorned the idea of gambling. He set aside his bread. "And to accrue debt when gambling, you must lose. You taught me to avoid losing."

"As my own father taught me. Tell me, young senhórs, what got you out of bed so early after a feast day? Besides breakfast at my expense. Are you finally joining me in the training yard more than a single day each week?"

"I'm willing," Qasim said, "but I haven't won the argument for both of us to be there."

"Quit asking, uncle. We're here for scholarship, not battle tactics." Yusuf took a bite and then was too nice to speak through food in his mouth; therefore, the story came slowly through eggs and toast. "Comte Nuño employed me as clerk for the prelate's council."

"Yes, he told me," Chrétien said. "And he suggested you leave school and live here for your own safety until the council is done."

Qasim answered, having no problem speaking with a mouthful of toast. "We're cozy where we are. We have the nicest landlady. She even manages our laundry."

"Yesterday," Yusuf continued, ignoring both Qasim's and Chrétien's interruptions, "I was working in the gallery of the council room. And—"

"Yesterday was a feast day," Chrétien said. "The council wasn't convened."

"That's what I said." Qasim let his trencher catch the crumbs as he spoke. "An entire day freezing in that hellacious gallery when we could be feasting."

Yusuf didn't defend his decision to work on a feast day. "There's a visiting priest, a disciple of that priest Dominic Guzman. Do you know of him?"

"He settled in Toulouse late last summer," Chrétien said. "He preaches that Roman priests should go barefoot like goodmen teachers if they want to convince heretics to change their ways."

"Yes, that one." Yusuf took an infernal long time to finish chewing his toast. "Yesterday, his follower, who's called Bernatz, convinced the prelate to allow him to inspect the libraries of all the schools in the city. To remove any traces of heresy and dissent."

Chrétien snatched the last two boiled eggs from the platter just as Qasim began to reached for them. If Yusuf's story was going to take forever to tell, Chrétien needed his own breakfast.

Yusuf said, "This monk fellow, Bernatz, promised to complete his examination by Friday."

Qasim smacked up the last of his honey. "Three days from today."

"So, we need your help," Yusuf said, "to hide any books the foolish monk Bernatz might want to destroy."

"I know nothing about books. Never even held one." Chrétien knocked one of the boiled eggs against the heel of his hand. Its shell shattered with a satisfying *crack*. "I learned to read from parchment scraps of love songs and chandlers' lists of supplies to move an army. Why do you two scholars need a swordsman?"

"About seventy years ago, a fellow called Raimon of Marseille adapted planetary tables from Al-Andalus for the Pays d'Òc," Yusuf said. The story now promised to take even longer to tell. Qasim folded his arms, which seemed to be how he bided time while Yusuf offered scholarly wisdom. "I corrected his work, so astrologers can work from accurate numbers."

"Of course, you did," Chrétien said.

Yusuf preened a bit, mistaking Chrétien's comment for a compliment. "And I placed it with two of my own original texts in the Astrology and Mathematics library. Scholars all share their work here, even if they aren't yet magisters."

Chrétien said, "You came here to study mathematics, didn't you? That doesn't sound like too much dissent, even for the Church. All you did was fix some numbers."

"Except the scholars I cite in my books include names that Bernatz will seek to remove."

"Then you'd best take your books home and hide them under your bed. Better yet, move here as Comte Nuño suggested. I'll let you hide your books in my rafters." Chrétien swallowed his first bite of egg, that nibble reminding him that he'd eaten too little the night before.

"Yes, but it's worse than that."

"Yusuf's been lecturing from his books." Qasim stuffed a chunk of toast in his mouth, gumming up his words. "They'll want him to answer for citing heretics and Saracens in his philosophy."

Chrétien harkened back to Nuño urging him to persuade Yusuf to leave school. "What kind of number heresy do you lecture about?"

"My notes on astrology and numerology cite teachers I studied with in Cairo, which included texts from the Jewish thinker, Maimonides." Yusuf lifted his head, proud of this. Chrétien also felt pride in his genius nephew—though he had only the vaguest notion of who the fellow Maimonides was—but didn't have spare moments that morning to endure Yusuf's tendency to deliver scholarly lectures in response to simple questions.

"You're asking my help," Chrétien said, "when you already know the solution. Stop lecturing and remove your books from the library. Today." He whacked his second egg. *Crack-k-k.* "If the Church claims an idea is heresy, there's no use nattering on about it. Unless you think you'd enjoy the trouble."

"But that requires I sacrifice everything it means to be a scholar. We search for truth." Yusuf spoke with such passion, Chrétien pondered what it'd be like to be eighteen again, to be capable of being so earnest. "About forty years ago, the old count in Montpelhièr declared complete freedom for all who come here to teach. The old count wasn't a scientific thinker, but he understood that good teachers and philosophers need freedom to think. To learn."

"I'm old and fit only to stay by the fire with a blanket and bowl of gruel." In fact, Chrétien was thirty. "But I can tell you what I learned when they burned the heretics at Minerve."

"The purpose of that," Yusuf said, "was to frighten the countryside into obedience, like beaten dogs. You and I—and Qasim—we aren't terrified animals."

Chrétien said, "When human flesh burns, it smells sickly sweet. It'd turn your stomach, except the screams keep you from smelling at first. Then it's a month or more before you quit smelling it in your hair, on your clothes. In your dreams."

"Woof." Qasim's eyes roamed until they rested on the hearth across the kitchen. "I am honestly scared as a dog of what they might do to anyone they declare a heretic."

Yusuf disregarded both Qasim's comment and Chrétien's caution. "My books in the library—that's only the beginning of the problem." He shoved his trencher aside, tapping the table to emphasize what he had to say. "If the Church removes books it doesn't agree with, generations of learning will be lost. Medicine, music, mathematics, astronomy."

"Astronomy? Is that the science for guessing where the stars will appear the next time the clouds are gone?" Chrétien asked.

Yusuf didn't respect that question enough to answer. Instead, he said, "When you teach us in the practice yard, you have a dozen rules to repeat, that we must live by. At the heart of my life, I believe in the texts that I study and lecture from. What do you believe?"

Chrétien readily knew the answer to that, because he and Durán had indulged in discussions of what it meant to believe anything at all. "I believe that you can only solve problems with rational action, which sometimes means drawing steel." As he spoke, both Yusuf and Qasim stared hard, and at that moment, he felt judged. Was he performing his usual role as the wise warrior uncle? Or failing? "However good you are with your sword, it's not magic, only practice. There is no magic."

"That's all?" Yusuf said.

"No. Most important, forget what the heretics claim. You only get one chance to live. Everything you need to fix, it ends at the grave. You won't come back to try again, either as a ghost or reincarnated as the most loyal dog."

"Right." Yusuf clapped his hands. "And so, uncle, instead of leaving today for Toulouse, please stay and help us with a bit of rational action that will save the library."

"I know nothing about libraries," Chrétien repeated. Unfairly, he refrained from revealing that he wasn't leaving Montpelhièr that day.

"Communities of scholars beyond Montpelhièr will help us hide them. Doubtless, the Church will change its mind. It did in Paris a few years ago. Made rules, then forgot them." Yusuf wrung his hands, as if ready to beg. "Come with us, uncle, to help plan how we might smuggle out those books that shouldn't be lost."

Qasim nodded vigorously, though to Chrétien's knowledge, Qasim should have all the scouting skills Yusuf required, since he'd been raised scavenging on the docks of Valencia.

"Why do you require help from one of the greatest swordsmen in Christendom to help steal books?" Chrétien didn't want to rescue books, which seemed like something you'd hire a sneak-thief to do.

"We aren't stealing them. We're moving them to a safer place. A temporary measure."

"If you say so." Chrétien did not think that explanation would protect his nephew if anyone involved was caught moving even one book to a safer place than its library.

"You think this isn't a worthy endeavor," Yusuf protested. "You think we're still children."

Chrétien put the last of the egg in his mouth. An indignant Yusuf was always a sight to behold. Chrétien suppressed the impulse to provoke him.

"Let me introduce you to a magister at the school. If I can't convince you to help, perhaps he can," Yusuf said. "I've paid to sit in his lectures since Christmas. All the other lecturers stopped over the feast days, but this magister teaches in mid-winter."

"And the week after Easter, when every other lecturer stays home," Qasim said. "The magister's Easter lectures must be fun after all that repenting and ashes." Like Yusuf, who'd been born in Cairo, Qasim had agreed to be baptized when he joined Tomás's house, but neither Qasim nor Yusuf sat easily with Roman Church philosophy or common practices in Christendom. Yusuf must have inherited his grandfather Miquel's cynicism and then shared it with Qasim.

"Instead of reading texts to students," Yusuf said, "the magister speaks what he knows. He brings in patients—paupers and beggars he treats for no fee—to demonstrate both diagnosis and treatment."

"Some days it's gruesome," Qasim said. "Blood and weird goo from inside people. And vomit. But the magister makes you laugh just at the moment when it seems insufferable."

"Some days," Yusuf said, "the magister takes students to watch surgery at *l'Espital de l'Esperit*. We're going to a lecture there today."

"It's always gruesome when he demonstrates at the Hospital of the Holy Spirit," Qasim said. "And it costs twice the fee of usual lectures. Unless you volunteer to clean up the vomit and gore."

Yusuf said, "The magister is quite persuasive. If you speak with him, you'll understand why it's urgent that we protect these books."

"If I help in any way, it's because my brothers and true comrades need help." Obstinate irritation crawled up Chrétien's spine, twinning itself with an unexpected resolution. "I swear it on the ghost of my father. I don't perform heroic deeds for utter strangers."

"Oh, good!" Qasim dusted toast crumbs from his hands. "Then you *will* help us!"

Yusuf clapped once in subdued glee. "So, meet us at the music library. At midday?"

"Music library? There's more than one?"

Qasim said, "Every school has its own library. The lecturers are all jealous of each other."

"Not all of them." Yusuf folded his arms, disputing.

Qasim waved that away without answering. "Not one of them would leave his books in another school."

"That is why this is…" Yusuf began, then paused.

Not a good idea. Chrétien could finish the thought but instead waited for Yusuf to continue.

"…not a university. Not like Paris. It's only a collection of little schools, where batches of men have banded together around mutual points of interest."

"And deep pits of jealousy for other lecturers," Qasim said.

"If that's true, and since you are such a snob," Chrétien wagged a finger at Yusuf, "why didn't you go to the university in Paris?"

Yusuf and Qasim glanced at each other, as if the Gemini twins agreed on an answer, though they often debated with each other merely for the sake of arguing.

"We like the food better here," Qasim said. "And the people aren't so…" He held up his hands, not finding the word.

"So very French," Yusuf said. "Not that I blame the people of Paris for everything their knights did in Béziers and Minerve. But, you know, in general."

"All right." Chrétien resumed the plan. "Each school has a library, with different kinds of books to be saved. And you want me to wander all around that part of the city inspecting libraries for the best mode of thieving."

"No, uncle!" Yusuf sounded eager. "We only need you to help us find a way to remove a few books from the Literature and Music library. We shall thank you throughout life, as it unfolds before us."

"I suppose that's better than being paid," Chrétien said.

"Also," Qasim said, "as my mother always said, many hands make quick soup. And therefore, we'll be less likely to get caught."

Chrétien glared at Qasim, willing him to understand what a bad idea this was, but Qasim just smiled. He knew, but he was going wherever Yusuf went, and he'd do whatever Yusuf wanted.

"Today is the day," Yusuf said. "Better not to wait. Like you said earlier, my good uncle."

The orphan had quietly eaten his breakfast at the far end of the kitchen. Rafel appeared to fetch him away to find better clothes. When Sanço passed Qasim, the boy turned to say, "The Good God will not let you abandon your people, my lord." Then he followed Rafel with his dirty head held as high and proud as any courtier in Nuño's great hall.

Yusuf and Qasim exchanged a long, determined, and serious look—apparently in that infuriating secret language sometimes shared by brothers, true comrades, and lovers.

"What in the name of all the dancing angels is going on?" Chrétien again snatched food from under Qasim's hand, this time the last piece of toast. He also took the bowl of honey, dragging it closer to him than Qasim could reach.

Yusuf shrugged.

Qasim shrugged.

Qasim watched Chrétien chew the last of the breakfast that Luis the cook had given them.

Chrétien enjoyed that toasted bread, having smothered it in butter and honey. For the sake of everyone's continued safety— Yusuf and Qasim as much as Durán and Comte Nuño—he needed to spend the day learning whatever he could in the city. A brief excursion to the scholars' district would be no distraction, though he wasn't sure what he could learn there. And, out of honor due to his father and brother, Chrétien had no choice but to do whatever it might take to protect Yusuf and Qasim from any harm that came from their heroics. And perhaps at the library Chrétien might have another chance to convince these two young men to leave school and stay here at Nuño's villa.

"I decided against training my orphan to be an assassin." Chrétien rose from the kitchen table. "I'm taking that boy to live with nuns in an orphanage. I shall meet you at your music library to discuss what you need from me. Or whatever your astrology says I'm supposed to do to keep the world in balance."

"Thank you," Yusuf said. "We'll meet after the sext bell."

Chrétien took a moment to remember when the sext bell rang. He wasn't raised where priests rang bells, didn't train where there even were priests, and didn't often work as a mercenary where priests had bells to ring. In the same way he had to remember each time how to cross himself, because he wasn't raised that way, Chrétien had to repeat the names of each bell and when they rang.

Matins, when monks got out of bed in the middle of the night to sing psalms.

Lauds, for more singing in the dark and for waking the bakers.

Prime, to mark sunrise, which must be a courtesy for blind men, because you can see the dawn without a bell.

Terce, when the guards change after first breakfast—at least that's how Chrétien understood it.

Sext, about the time farmers and mercenaries eat their second breakfast, and when street vendors begin selling food for midday.

Nones, about midafternoon—or did they ring a bell simply to bother your nap after dinner?

Vespers, at sunset, though again, you can see that it's sunset without a bell ringing.

Compline, another bell for priests to say prayers in the dark, about the time really good dicing begins each night.

While Chrétien figured the time for the sext bell, the two young men argued over directions to the library. Qasim seemed to have a better idea of the way through the maze of streets and which were the better landmarks to watch for.

Then Rafel reappeared with that wretched boy. Chrétien determined that it was time to examine the streets of Montpelhièr with new eyes, while finding a home for a lost boy.

There's only forty thousand people in Montpelhièr, they say. How hard could it be to find an assassin plotting chaos?

8
After a Feast Day

"LET'S GO!" CHRÉTIEN CALLED to the boy, his breath a heavy fog that seemed to freeze and fall to the icy streets. The snow had stopped, leaving only a film on the ground. Montpelhièr remained entombed in the unusually hard frost that seized the city a week earlier. Chrétien wrapped up in the scratchy wool cloak that Rafel had brushed clean, then inspected Sanço in his castoff clothes.

The homespun leggings must have once belonged to a taller servant, rolled up above less-ravaged boots and tied at the waist with a hempen cord. A beat-up leather jerkin hung over two woolen tunics, all with sleeves so long the boy's fingers disappeared inside. Mme Marguerite, the mistress of the boy-king's school that Chrétien came here to guard, had done well by the urchin. No longer in rags, but not so grand as to attract street thieves. A knit cap hid the boy's ragged dark hair, so the sharp-featured face that peered out seemed even more wan and starved. And stubborn.

"*Avant!*"

Chrétien called to the boy again. The best swordsman in Christendom should be able to at least coerce a beggar lad up the street.

The nuns' house, called St-Lazarus, was across the entire city, the opposite direction from where Yusuf wanted Chrétien to inspect his book problem. He trudged the icy streets, slipping on cobbles, humming a song to supplement the guilt he intended to heap upon his beloved Durán for not having written since All Saints.

> You made a thousand promises,
> Made me give up grievance and regret,
> To forget all my old distress.
> But you ensnared me,
> Like a gambler with false dice.
> Just as my heart opened,

You smothered it,
Heaped cruelty on my soul.

Too much? Chrétien thought not, since he'd been stuck in a cold, strange city, while at home Durán slept in a warm bed and couldn't be bothered to write one message. Chrétien's sword swung when he stepped over an ice puddle, reminding him that he'd be patrolling these streets when night came, seeking magic that didn't exist. It'd be a relief, though, after a morning filled with the needs of an obstinate orphan, an equally obstinate genius nephew, and Qasim, a stoic young man too in love to reveal any secrets of his *bon amic*.

Three turns down the winding streets toward the east gate, he passed a mustard-yellow door under the sign of a red rooster. Given the mix of men who frequented that hostel at night, it seemed as good as any place to ask about a Nizari assassin haunting the city. He could at least advance the work of making the city safe while he resolved his ill-considered decision to help a lost orphan.

Chrétien pushed the hostel door open, pausing to point to where Sanço should wait outside on a bench. He left his cloak with the lad in case the new jerkin wasn't enough on this cold morning.

"Rollo!" He called for the hostler, a *mestitz* Norman from Sicily who claimed the inn's standard fare was a faithful rendering of his mother's delights. Even though Rollo's mother's family had lived two hundred years on Sicily, a land where people know how to cook properly spiced food, every night Rollo served a mélange of meat parts and root vegetables stewed in a bland cream broth with bread dough baked on top. Just like Rollo's mother used to make.

Rollo appeared from the back, calling hello in Norman French and then the local tongue before he recognized Chrétien standing near the door. He had a long face and a long nose to go with it, narrow brows and thin lips buried in a heavy bush of a beard, plus weighty bags under his eyes, as if sleep perpetually escaped him. Yet Rollo had a warrior's body, not the soft flesh of many hostlers.

Chrétien greeted him in Arabic, a tongue they had been pleased to find that they both shared, having grown up on islands that had traded Saracen and Christian masters for five hundred years.

"I'm sorry, my friend. But we won't have food until the Nones bell rings in the middle of the afternoon." Rollo glanced over his shoulder toward the inner doorway that led to the kitchen, its carpet covering still swaying from Rollo's passage into the common room. "And we don't allow gambling here until after the compline bell. Nothing until when you usually come."

"I stopped by to ask you about..." Chrétien found Rollo's repeated glances backward distracting. Rollo didn't want him here, though whenever Chrétien came to gamble or sing at night, Rollo flirted with him, even more outrageously than that fellow Antoni did the night before. Chrétien had believed that, like him, Rollo preferred the sweet part of life to be with men.

The heavy rug over that door swung, and a veiled woman emerged who also spoke Arabic. She had a basket of fresh bread that she placed on the serving table, tucking a linen cloth over it. Without ever glancing in Chrétien's direction, she wagged a finger at Rollo, pointed to Chrétien, and then left them without a goodbye.

"There's no gambling during the day. Nora doesn't like it." Rollo spread his empty hands. "I can only allow it at night, after she's gone to bed."

Chrétien, knowing that must be embarrassing for Rollo to admit, changed the subject to explore what he wanted to learn. "I came to ask if anyone visited your hostel to recruit mercenaries." He spun a story about needing employment, though what he needed was to discover who was paying this phantom recruiter.

Rollo answered, as if eager to please—and then be rid of his visitor. "There's a fellow who's been in three times. You might suit. He only hires Catalan or Aragón men who lost their work when Pedro *le Roi* died at Muret. Or men from towns like Béziers that Simon's French army burned or destroyed." Rollo glanced over his shoulder again when the woman called in Arabic from deep in the hostel. "The men he talks with all nurse a grudge against Simon de Montfort and complain that southern seigneurs won't fight to protect innocent goodmen. Claim they want to be heretic protectors like Pedro was."

"What's his name?"

Rollo answered in Norman French, rather than the Arabic they usually spoke together. "He's called Zorzi de Gênes."

"Can you tell me what he looks like? Does he bear a mark like this?" Chrétien sketched the Wheel and Serpent in the crumbs on the tabletop.

"He's dark. Has a jolly round face, like the kind of happy man you want among your comrades." A torrent of words in Sicilian-accented Arabic flooded from the kitchen, about chores that must be done if they were to earn a single *sou* in this bedeviled city. Rollo's shoulders hunched up. "I didn't see that mark. If he comes here again, shall I tell him you're seeking work?"

"Yes, but can you tell me, does this man do magic? Or pretend to? Cut his hand and then heal it again?"

"I never saw it, but others claim he's a sorcerer with a sword. But you know," his hand grazed over Chrétien's, "many men seek magic to spice their lives. Will you come sing one night soon?"

Vowing to attempt it, Chrétien dropped three copper pennies on the table, reached under the linen that covered the bread to seize a small loaf, and then ducked back out to the cold street, where he found Sanço hunkered under the eaves to avoid the wind. The boy scrubbed at his nose with his sleeve to warm it, and then said thank-you too many times when Chrétien gave him the small loaf of unbuttered bread.

At the next inn where Chrétien stopped, the smell of mutton filled the room. The master of the house, a local called Jofré, wielded a flesh hook, pulling meat from one cauldron and dropping it into another pot atop an iron trivet. Jofré grew up in Montpelhièr and had been on crusade with Philippe Augustus. Chrétien instinctively spoke the local tongue with his best possible accent.

"I'm seeking a man who's been hiring mercenaries. His name is Zorzi. And perhaps he's from some part of the Holy Roman world."

When Chrétien pressed for details, Jofré claimed that the dark man recruiting at his inn wanted only mercenaries who resent here-tics for all the trouble they cause. "He seeks men who spend the most time complaining. Who curse heretics because they bring chaos wher-ever they go. Men who'll pick a fight with any heretic that might be trying to eat a peaceful supper."

"You allow heretics here?"

"I chase away any black-robed beggars preaching heresy. But I don't ask how a man prays if he can pay for his doss and supper."

While Chrétien was asking questions about magic healing and the shape of Zorzi's moustache and the Wheel and Cross sign, he passed over three more pennies, indicating that he wanted mutton wrapped in thin bread.

Jofré the hostler sliced off a piece of mutton while explaining that he hadn't seen the magic, but everyone talked about it. "A sorcerer with a sword, some say." But Jofré didn't believe in magic and insisted this Zorzi was only a man like any other. Average height. Perhaps dark. Jofré remembered the moustache, and then was eager to ask something of Chrétien before saying adieu. "Please stop by tonight. Perhaps you'll see him. We like when you come to sing. Men spend more freely."

"I shall try."

Outside, Chrétien found that Sanço had made friends with a muddy, long-haired yellow dog and couldn't be moved from where he perched until he'd shared two pennies' worth of his mutton with the dog.

"He kept me warm while I waited for you," Sanço explained. "Therefore, as the Good God would wish, I owed him a favor, the same way I owe you my life."

Chrétien wondered if the trek across the city was so long that Sanço might forget to say his creed at the convent. Would they make it past the door before Sanço spoke heresy again?

They made more stops along the way to the east gate. He learned in one hostel that a dark man who might be called Zorzi sought to hire local men who are good Roman Christians.

"Lots of able-bodied men resent the trash that's come to this city," one hostler claimed, a chubby Frankish man named Louis who'd come to Montpelhièr after being on crusade with Philippe Augustus. Though an outsider himself, Louis nursed a grudge against the displaced Aragónese and Catalan men in the city.

Chrétien replied without committing to anything, answering in the local tongue and doing his best to cover his own Catalan accent.

Louis spoke freely, though, because Chrétien's questions opened a well of feelings.

"It's all because Pedro let his men down when he got himself killed at Muret. Now we have riff-raff drifting in to take our women. Why should this town be loyal to Aragón? They are all half Moor or worse. What did those *mestitz* counts and kings ever give us?"

"More freedom than most places," Chrétien murmured, but Louis didn't rise to the bait, because he'd gone on a tirade about a mummer's trick the man had performed, pretending to cut his hand and then heal it with magic.

"You saw this?"

"Of course not," Louis said, taking a penny from Chrétien for a slice of cheese. "But I had to serve wine and ale to all the fellows begging to hear the story from those that did see the magic."

At the door, Sanço again huddled with the yellow dog. He wouldn't listen to reason when Chrétien sent the dog on its way.

"We don't know where it lives, *fadrin*. It needs to go back before we lead it too far from its home."

"Didn't your father teach you that it is unkind and immoral not to care for God's creatures?" Tears ran down Sanço's sunken cheeks, streaking his face. "You have hardened the warm heart that the Good God gave you."

Chrétien did not, in fact, have a hard heart, and he regarded the tears as this child's way of wielding Chrétien's feelings as a weapon. "I have the common sense that the One True God gave me. And if I want a sermon on morality, I'll go to church." He spoke of God in the Roman way, hoping to remind Sanço to tone down all the heresy about a Good God and an Evil one. He poked the boy to get him off the bench. "Here, I have a piece of good cheese for you."

"My heart is too full." Sanço had his nose in the air again. "I cannot accept that you will not open your heart to the kindest and gentlest of God's creatures."

"Do your feet work when your heart is full? Because you'll freeze if you don't follow me. Right now."

"I shall pray for you, my lord."

"Silently, *fadrin*. Silently." A silence that had to last through an investigation of hostels and hopefully might last through any questioning the nuns might make.

By the time Chrétien listened to a fourth hostler, he was more confused than when he started. The last man, as squat as the ragged white dog that sprawled over his foot, spoke. "That fellow only hires Lombards and Genoa and Pisa men." The hostler's common room smelled of baking bread and garlic and burned beans, causing Chrétien to long for a second breakfast. "The kind who refuse to work for local seigneurs. Me, I can't afford to refuse any man's coin. I don't understand why anyone from the Holy Roman Empire ever came to this city if they hate us so much."

The squat hostler claimed the recruiter was as Roman as the pope. With long hair and a moustache. "Yes, he's called Zorzi de Genèva. And everyone talks about his magic." The hostler, however, had always been too busy to see any magic with his own eyes.

At each inn, Chrétien had drawn the crossed circle and snake in the crumbs or flour on a tabletop, asking the hostlers if the recruiter had that sign on his hand. Each hostler studied it, no spark in any eye, shaking his head in denial.

For all of us, everything will be lost if we allow this plot to succeed.

Chrétien needed a different tack, because he hadn't learned news that Nuño didn't already possess, except a name. Zorzi. Who might be jolly or cruel. Who might have magic or swordsman's secrets. Who recruited Aragón loyalists to protect heretics. Or men who hated heretics. Or men who simply hated foreigners. Or did Zorzi only seek foreigners? None of it fit together.

And what he needed to know most of all was who Zorzi's own paymaster might be.

9

St-Lazarus House

CHRÉTIEN FOUND SANÇO DANCING outside the door of the last inn, begging to find the jakes before they went any further, refusing to pee in an alleyway.

"We aren't barbarians," the boy sniffed. The burden of dignity that the lad bore seemed excessively heavy.

Back on their way, Chrétien made a couple of mistakes in choosing the passages among curving streets, errors he discovered only when they'd once more passed the same smoldering bonfires left from the feast-night revelries. The unpleasant dying-fire odor of wet charcoal bothered Chrétien. He finally found the memory that disturbed him: being imprisoned for a month in Béziers, where even after a year, the odor of the crusaders' torching of the city hung in the air, like the miasma in a plague city.

In that desultory mood, Chrétien paid scant attention to Sanço's chattering stories. The lad seemed to prefer his own voice to silence, as if to know he wasn't lost again.

"When *francimand* mercenaries burned our houses. There was nowhere safe on the Aragón frontier except—"

Thinking that the boy's fantastic stories could not be healthy, Chrétien stopped him. "There aren't French soldiers in Aragón."

"O my captain! What do you know of Aragón?"

"A great deal. I was with Aragón's army at the battle of Las Navas de Tolosa three years ago."

"Perhaps you know Andalusia, but not Aragón." Chrétien decided not to argue with a lost street urchin, letting Sanço chatter on. "Our part of the country is still ruled by a *taifa* general. We who are Christian called Pedro our king but pay taxes to a man who pretends to serve the caliph. The faithless *francimands* who attacked us worked for the caliph in Andalusia. When the great king Pedro defeated the caliph, these sinful men turned bandit. Then they came to our town when our *taifa* was off serving the caliph, so we could do nothing. All men of Islam had been called by the caliph to fight and then never came home, and all our Christian men had followed Pedro on crusade."

"It wasn't a crusade." Chrétien spoke automatically. "Only an expedition of peace, defending Christendom against the caliphate."

"And yet, alas, Pedro *el Rei* did not choose to reclaim or defend my home, which is why you must help me find our lord, to take back our village from these evil men."

Near the east gate, Chrétien led the urchin down an alley in the direction pointed out by a baker's boy three streets over. The alley emptied into a tiny square, another cross-street polluted by the odor of firebrands from the previous night's festival. The largest house had a carved stone cross over its heavy wooden door. The house itself was backed up against the city wall not far from the east gate, though a maze of narrow streets led from the pitted and scarred door of the house to the actual gate.

"This has to be the place," Chrétien muttered, taken aback at how despondent the scene appeared. The other buildings had their backs turned against St-Lazarus House, with their windows looking out only from the highest stories. Grass left from summer had been trodden to straw in the frozen muck accumulated at the base of each building. A few scrawny rosemary plants straggled and drooped from stone urns. But it was winter, and an unusually cold one. Ice destroys any memory of summer and joy.

"This isn't a good place," Sanço whispered. He clutched Chrétien's cloak as if to hide in it.

Chrétien, removing his bare hand from the warmth of his cloak, raised his fist to knock, but the door swept open before he touched it. He stood nose-to-nose with the loveliest woman he'd seen in this town, her pale face flushed from the cold air, her breath bursting in a cold cloud before she saw Chrétien there. She stepped away from Chrétien and finished speaking to someone behind her.

"*Merce a Dèu*, Magister. Thank you for coming so early on this cold morning. We all appreciate what you do for our prioress. No other physician or surgeon seems to help her."

"It's nothing." A man's voice echoed inside, a beautiful mid-range voice speaking the local tongue in an unusual accent. "I'll send the proper coriander over this morning. You understand how to prepare the concoction? If not, I will send a preparation to you."

"I shall prepare it myself." The beautiful nun then smiled at Chrétien, ready at last to greet him. "May we help you, senhór?"

Chrétien cleared his throat, since it had been seared raw by cold air. "I am told that the House of St-Lazarus will take lost orphans."

Her eyes scanned him, judging. "You seem sufficiently wealthy to provide for your own orphans. Or bastards."

So pretty, yet so harsh. "He's not mine. I found him lost on the street last night. And I'm merely a bachelor-knight visiting this town. I have no ability to care for others' orphans."

"I am Sòr Maria. Our prioress will examine the boy to determine whether we can provide shelter." She opened the door wider. Chrétien pushed Sanço ahead, but when he stepped up to follow, Sòr Maria put up her hand to stop him. "We'll send you a message. We don't allow men in our house."

At the same moment that she claimed this, a man in a blood-red velvet hat stepped out the door, as surprised as Chrétien that they were seeing each other here.

"No men allowed?" Chrétien repeated the nun's claim, seeing the man called Antoni at her door.

"Only this physician." Her voice seemed to scoff at Chrétien.

"*Bonjorn,* my friend." Antoni greeted Chrétien, then spoke to the nun. "My friend is the glorious jongleur of Cyprus."

"You know this man, Magister Antoni?" the nun asked. That possibility thawed her reserve, so her demeanor became no colder than the frozen streets.

"He's a knight living at Comte Nuño's compound. Seigneur Chrétien de St-Joachim." Antoni smiled at Chrétien as if he intended to melt all of Montpelhièr with his warmth. Chrétien, however, remained impervious to the man's overt seductions. "But what brings you here, my friend?"

A woman's voice called from within, and Sòr Maria answered, then bid Antoni farewell and closed the door, leaving the two men on the steps of St-Lazarus House.

"You are a physician?" Chrétien asked, still surprised. The nun had called him "magister," Master Teacher. That would never have occurred to Chrétien, especially after the previous evening's seductive encounter, after the man had followed him through half a dozen hostels and taverns over the past weeks of feast-days. "You sing well for a doctor and a teacher."

Antoni beamed, as if Chrétien meant the highest compliment. "And what are you doing here?"

"I pulled a lost orphan out of a fight last night. They say this is the best place for such creatures."

For no apparent reason, Antoni broke into song.

> He is dearer to me than my own heart.
> The great knight Miquel binds me to him,
> Promising the joy of friendly alliance.
> Neither sword nor ship can part us.

"Stop, *se vos plai!*" Chrétien begged. "Your choice of song comes too close to my heart."

Antoni tipped his head, curious. Or puzzled. "Truly? You did know that crusader, Miquel of Morella?"

"He was my father." Chrétien hadn't intended to reveal any details of his life. He gazed past Antoni, a movement at the street corner catching his eye. A man shooed away a black cat. That ferret-monk Feris watched, more like a guilty man than a holy man. Chrétien restrained his impulse to snatch up the little man and demand to know what sin he'd committed that sent a spying monk on his tail.

But Antoni was speaking to him, standing so close that Chrétien smelled basil and garlic on his breath, which he usually smelled only when nuzzling with Durán after a happy supper. The unexpected intimacy startled him, so that he stepped back, seeking distance.

"A father such as the famous crusader Miquel would be proud to see his son rescuing orphans." Kind words, spoken in the same seductive tone as the night before in Pons's common room.

"It's nothing." Chrétien echoed the words he'd heard Magister Antoni repeat from inside St-Lazarus House. "But how did you know my name and where I live?"

Antoni offered the kind of smile usually used to melt men's hearts. As if God enjoys a good jest or seeks to make fools of men, the door opened behind the two men, and the house spit out the waif Sanço.

"*Brut peccador!* Heretic!"

The beautiful nun stood at the threshold of her house, shouting invectives that weren't known to be prayers of St-Maria. Then she turned on Chrétien. "How dare you bring this—this creature, this filthy demon to our house!"

She shut the heavy door with as loud a thud as a small woman might muster. Chrétien should have done more to remind Sanço of his creed and how to speak to nuns, but he'd been too distracted, trying to fit together pieces of Comte Nuño's puzzle.

"*Fadrin?*" Chrétien spoke as mildly as he was capable, it not seeming that the child needed more scolding after a nun had called him a dirty sinner. Chrétien averted his eyes from Magister Antoni, to keep from laughing.

Sanço folded his arms, the long sleeves of his jerkin slapping his chest. He spread his legs in defiance, his dark face scrunched with a scowl that pressed his eyebrows toward his chin.

"The big old lady in her chair insisted I didn't say my creed loud enough for God to hear. Then her witch-women tried to pull off my shirt, like Saracens do before they sell you to pirates."

"I suspect those women wanted to rid you of fleas. I'm certain that they weren't going to sell you to pirates." Chrétien closed his eyes. One glance over to where Antoni stood would cause him to burst with the hilarity of this wild-child stomping furiously on frozen cobbles.

"No? They touched me all over, like pirates do. That's why I—I—I..." Sanço gnawed at his lip. "I bit her."

"Oh, *fadrin*." Chrétien sighed. "A gentleman of honor never bites a woman."

"You are a gentleman of honor, my lord." Sanço seemed to be near tears. "Why did you want to sell me to those witches?"

"I wasn't selling you. I was going to give them money to care for you. People don't sell children here."

"No, they go to Marseille, where they can earn better gold selling children to pirates and Saracens."

"I don't think so." Chrétien did not feel heroic about saving this particular orphan. "These are good women who care for poor children. Not witches."

"You are a noble and kind lord," Sanço said, serious as the devil, "but you know nothing of the world. You live like a blind man in a world of pampered lords."

While wishing to reply with a dozen denials, Chrétien changed the discussion. "We shall have to find another place for you."

Magister Antoni held out his hands, as if in a prayer of supplication. "Perhaps I can help. The lad would be welcome in the house my countrymen keep in Montpelhièr. Is he willing to work, perhaps in the kitchens? We don't beat children or force them to say unnatural prayers."

"*Merce*, Magister Antoni..." Worried about what obligation this offer might incur, Chrétien stuttered half an answer.

"No, *merce*, magister." Sanço answered, though the invitation had been directed at Chrétien.

"It's a great opportunity for you, *fadrin*." Inside, Chrétien screamed: *Will I never be free?*

Sanço bent backwards to look up to Chrétien, his voice shifting into a formal appeal. "Senhór, it is only to you, Our Savior's anointed knight, that God has assigned me service in this life. I cannot be parted from the duty that God has blessed me to fulfill."

Antoni seemed gracious about the refusal. "Will you let me treat that cut on your forehead, my dear child?"

"No, *merce*. I'm fine."

Antoni seemed about to ask a second time, but at that moment, the heavy door of St-Lazarus House opened, and the beautiful nun called, "Magister Antoni, the prioress calls you back."

Antoni disappeared inside. In a moment, the door opened again and a thundering herd of children pounded out to the little plaza, shouting and shoving.

As the screaming mob brushed past them, Sanço stepped close to Chrétien, clinging to his cloak. Chrétien endeavored to speak in his kindest voice. *"Fadrin,* I cannot keep a child here. Life in Magister Antoni's house would mean—"

"He smells like a pirate," Sanço said. "I will not go with pirates again. Their hearts know no mercy. They cut children into pieces and feed them to the fishes."

A few heartbeats later—moments filled with the shrieks of St-Lazarus children in a game that involved shoving each other into mud and cobbles—Sanço added, "I know in my heart that you, noble lord, shall unite me with the great lord who rules my village. And you shall help to rescue all of my people."

A childish voice shouted from across the small, decrepit square. "It's the heretic boy!"

Chrétien, not thinking it through, adopted Sanço's wide-legged stance, folding his arms, a stance that intimidated any challenger in arm-to-arm combat, since he stood a head taller than most men.

However, instead of accepting Chrétien's protection, Sanço ran full-bore into the mob, shouting his own invectives. The indigent urchin drew calamity wherever he went, as if by magic.

"Pirate spawn! Slave bait!" Sanço shrieked. "Did you stand naked when your mothers sold you?"

That's when the chunks of stinging charcoal and bruising stones began to fall.

Chrétien bounded across the shabby square, thrusting Sanço behind him, then slipping on ice. The stones fell on him. He heard only one shrieking child.

"O my captain!"

A Physician Found

From the Secret History of the Flaming Cross
—Andonis de Zêna

I was born on Sardinia forty years ago, the same year that Saladin seized the caliphate upon his uncle's death and upended the careful balance of power in the Outremer. That was also the year the Byzantine emperor restored trading rights to Venice, which was not the happiest news in Genoa.

My family lived on Sardinia in a Genoese outpost where my father's many brothers and cousins were merchants, growing rich off the sea trade between our world and the Outremer.

Please don't think the worst of me for being the son of a mercantile family; it's not as if we were farmers or operated a gold-thread factory. When I was ten, my parents perished in a plague. My uncle took me to join our family in Genoa, and that's when my quest to become a healer and physician began.

While we sailed to Genoa, my uncle Zorzi became ill, and by the grace of God, when all others had given him up to the angels, I laid my boyish hand on his brow and prayed to St-Jude, the apostle who knew Jesus and who intercedes in hopeless causes. My uncle was healed. After giving his thanks to God for that miracle, my uncle recognized that I might have a vocation to serve God here on earth. He took me to a monastery a few leagues outside Genoa, a house of scholarship that has schooled our family for generations.

Rodolfo Rossellini, the abbot at the monastery, took me on as if I were his own son, becoming the first of the many mentors God has provided to guide me in this life. He identified and encouraged my talents for languages and healing, teaching me Latin and Greek, and asking another of the monks to improve my Arabic, which tongue I'd previously picked up playing with the half-Saracen boys who lived on Sardinia.

The wonder and joy of writing these languages, as well as learning to write in my native tongue, which the Roman Church calls the vernacular, filled my days until I was fifteen and fully grown to the size of a man.

‡

Cançons de Montpelhièr

The plain brown rossynols,
The bird the French call nightingale,
Sings in the blossoming hedgerow,
Seeking and taking and giving love,
Fluting its song of joy, nodding to its mate.
The swift-flowing rivulets are delightful,
And the pastures are enchanting,
Because of the new joy that rules my heart.

10
Hospital of the Holy Spirit

"THAT'S WHAT PIRATES DO. Cut you open, just like that." Sanço's querulous voice whistled in Chrétien's dreams. "Then—whoosh—they feed you to the fish. But you're dead, so the great fish won't toss you up on the shore like Jonah."

"There's no fish here." Qasim's voice. "And no pirates."

"We have to stop him."

"Hush, child. The magister is about to teach again."

A chair scraped on stone near Chrétien's ear, the screech crawling up his spine. Then a man's voice sang softly. A hand stroked Chrétien's head.

> The world is only wind and dreams.
> But I can perform the fabulous.
> I can regain Damascus and Syria
> That idle lords lost from Christendom.

"You shouldn't feel this good," Miquel whispered in Chrétien's ear. "Not after getting your *cabeza* whacked open with a stone."

"I can do anything if there's enough wine." Chrétien believed he said it aloud. His throat burned, drier than the desert at the Horns of Hattin.

"Please lend me your attention, my good students."

What tongue was that? What man speaking?

Antoni, the man in the tavern who kept trying to seduce him.

"Let's begin the second half of today's lecture, which is a diversion from how we usually come here to treat the poor of the earth. This is a unique opportunity for you to observe the use of battlefield medicine on an actual soldier." Antoni's voice paused, changed pitch. "Though from my experience, a warrior-patient will whimper as much as any child you save from the gutter."

A rash of laughter broke out. The shuffling of leather shoes on a stone floor.

Antoni spoke again. "What do you notice at this moment? You, *jove mèstre*. Please tell the others."

"He's waking, which is good." Yusuf, his nephew, whom Antoni called young master. Chrétien would know that sweet voice anywhere. Like Tomás's voice, though his brother couldn't sing a note.

Antoni spoke, while Chrétien tried to swim out of dreams. "And why is it good for this injured patient to wake now?"

"Too long asleep after a head bash can signify a deeper injury." Yusuf's voice again.

"*Bien.* Other thoughts?"

"Because we don't want the patient to be lost in poppy dreams for too long." A deep but froggy voice that Chrétien didn't know.

"Excellent, young master. Are there exceptions?"

A chorus of voices. "When it's a hopeless case." "When all you can do is relieve pain." "When the patient is on his way to God."

"Here you are, *fadrin*," Miquel whispered. "You aren't dead like me. Not yet. That's what the magister says."

Chrétien opened his eyes. Dark cross beams overhead. Smoke-colored plaster. A thousand candles burning, brighter than a hundred suns. The heat burned like a summer's midday in Cairo. Then he smelled the smoke of a charcoal brazier. And the tallow candles, smoking the room with the funk of dead animal.

He lay—no, sat—blanketed in sheepskin, the wool against his bare skin.

"Senhór Chrétien." Antoni's voice, coddling him, beguiling him. "You had an accident. We cleaned and bandaged cuts on your forehead and behind your ear. And leeched the worst bruises."

"No leeches!" Miquel cried. "No leeches! The devil can take all the leeches home to his hell-hole."

"Stay still, my friend." Antoni's voice calmed all the disquiet that Miquel's voice roused. "With your permission, we still need to stitch the deep cut on your hand."

"Magister." A voice further away. "Does the patient need relief from pain when you stitch such a large hand wound?"

Hand? Chrétien struggled to sit up, wanting to wipe the cobwebs from his eyes.

"Careful, *fadrin*," Miquel whispered. "Take a breath. Get the lay of the land."

Chrétien blinked away the crusted rime around his eyes. At the edge of the warm yellow glow of blazing candles, a semicircle of men stood, most with arms akimbo, watching Chrétien as if he'd come before a panel of judges, their faces all grim, as if determining how many punishing lashes the crime deserved.

"Let's ask the patient," Antoni said. "Senhór Chrétien, do you need relief while I stitch your hand? Poppy syrup? Wine?"

"Save the wine to clean the wound." His voice sounded like scraped gravel in his own ears.

"Observe, students." Antoni's voice rose. "This is a moment when the patient's wisdom exceeds the physician's."

The crowd shuffled, most chuckling.

"*Bien.* We begin." Antoni gently rolled back the sheepskin, exposing Chrétien's left hand where it rested on the chair's arm. He began to unwrap the linen that swathed it, quickly revealing blood-soaked layers, which he peeled with even greater delicacy.

Until he revealed Chrétien's hand, lifting it so others in the room could see how it—

"*Jhezu del tron!*" Miquel swore. "It's burst open clear to the bone. That's going to hurt."

Chrétien stared. Then turned his head so he couldn't see it, only smell the hot, wet, copper scent of too much blood escaping his body. At the end of the semicircle nearest to him, Yusuf and Qasim stood, Qasim's arm wrapped around the ashen-faced, squirming orphan.

"Hush, *fadrin*." Qasim tightened his embrace of the child. "You can only stay if you are silent."

"It's my fault!" the child whispered. "I am the Judas goat."

Yusuf stroked the boy's head. "No, he makes his own choices."

Behind Yusuf, that little priest stood, the one assigned to ferret out heretics and rebels, who'd sat in the boy-king's classroom all autumn and into the winter. He now watched Chrétien receiving the care of a sweet-natured physician, who hummed as he worked, as if conjuring the peace and beauty of a summer's day. How had Chrétien managed to call a priest-spy to follow him everywhere? He always took care, to protect Durán. *What did I do?*

"Threw yourself in front of very naughty children." Antoni answered a question Chrétien hadn't meant to ask aloud. "They'll be repeating prayers every hour and supping whey and plain bread for a week as punishment. Meanwhile, I shall prescribe you good meat and wine. Now, again, do you want spirits before I begin?"

"Just do it," Miquel said. "It's nowhere near the first time."

"I'm ready," Chrétien said.

"It is most important," Antoni pitched his voice to his students, "to clean the wound thoroughly. Some philosophers prefer water, but I prefer the strongest spirits at hand." A metal flask in his hand, he poured hot wine over Chrétien's hand.

"Stings like the devil," Miquel whispered. "Worse than getting the cut is the stitching up."

"At this point," Antoni turned toward the circle of students, "most patients scream for God's mercy, to stop the pain. What does the thoughtful physician do next?"

"Stop his gob," Miquel said.

A student called out, "Put his belt between his teeth."

"Ah, the wisdom of the common man," Antoni said. Chuckles echoed in the room again. "Do you need to bite on your belt, senhór?"

"Just do it." Chrétien repeated Miquel's comment. Not like in a dream—he never dreamed about pain—but more like he floated above the chair, swathed in a shearling blanket.

Antoni hummed that tune again. Once more Chrétien smelled the green, herb-filled smell of summer. Not gore. When Antoni touched his hand, forcing it to bleed again, Chrétien felt Durán's hands from the first time they touched, when Durán offered to splint Chrétien's broken shin bone. That touch set his blood on fire, burning up and down his limbs as his heart pumped fire through his veins, so he knew right then that it was impossible to live without his heart beating and it would forever be impossible to love, to breathe, to find any peace if Durán ceased touching him. And yet now here he was, his life's blood soaking the linen wrapping, trickling over the back of the magister's hand as he touched Chrétien while humming a song that made the room sound like a sun-buzzing summer's day, with crickets and chirping birds.

In the same way the world tipped sideways when Durán touched him, it tilted at that moment, because Miquel whispered in his ear and the magister, still humming, stroked Chrétien's fingers in a way that meant he wanted to claim Chrétien's touch, which wasn't available for love or money, because there was only Durán filling his heart, Durán running in his veins instead of blood. But then, at the hiss of Miquel's whisper, Chrétien turned from Antoni's ardent touch while again catching sight of Yusuf standing so formally, though you could see, like lightning in a summer sky, how tied that young man was to Qasim, while each of them rested a hand on Sanço's head, stroking his hair when the boy wiggled in agitation, as if between them they could calm that child's torments.

> Now that it is summer,
> I shall sing!
> Orchards bloom white.
> No more frost.
> Every pasture is green.
> My love holds me.
> Now I have hope.
> No one else brings solace.

"Next, my good students?" Antoni stopped singing. He lifted his head for a moment, drawing all the attention in the room. "It's crucial that any grit or slivers be removed. Whatever the cause of an open wound, you must diligently search for the smallest trace of foreign matter. Now, I ask you, dear students, if you have water with which to wash a wound, what must you do?"

"Boil it!" A chorus answered in unison.

"Excellent," Antoni said. "It is not merely my own philosophy. We've learned from the best of the ancients. Tiny bits of evil, invisible to the eye like demon spirits, lay in wait for the opportunity to invade a man. You must be diligent in washing away evil."

The cleaning of the wound was the worst of it, but not because of the throbbing or the prick of the tweezers Antoni used to explore the wound, but because it took so much time that Chrétien pondered the worst. Could he finger the neck of his lute ever again? His sword hand hadn't been harmed. He could hold a shield with even a mangled left hand. But music?

Antoni softly sang again while he worked, humming whenever he frowned while concentrating even harder on exploring the open wound, which required frequent dousing of water and wine to wash away the blood.

> The world is only wind and dreams.
> But I can perform the fabulous.

"It's a song about Miquel the crusader." Antoni spoke too low for his students to hear. "Did he teach you how to endure pain?"

"Teach?" Miquel growled. "My boys sucked courage with their mother's milk."

Magister Antoni began stitching, the familiar (to Chrétien) sense of the smooth slip of needle and thread binding the wound closed. Antoni begged the students to take turns coming close to observe, while he advised on the kind of thread to use. "Make sure you always have the best silk from the best traders. Trust Genoa for that, not Venice." And more comments on how to obtain the best needles. "Spend the money for the best steel, and guard it close to your heart. Use an ivory needle only if you must. Burn the point in a candle."

The magister knotted his stitching closed and then snipped the thread with tiny gold-handled shears. He doused the hand with wine again, washing away the last of the blood. He gently wrapped the hand in a long length of linen gauze.

"And now, good students, our patient is ready to return to the world." Antoni tugged away the sheepskin blanket at the same time that Chrétien moved to stand up.

The warmth of the room whispered against his bare skin while Chrétien stared at the white linen paw that had replaced his hand.

"O my captain!" Sanço called from between Yusuf and Qasim.

Another voice in the herd of students exclaimed, "He has more stitched scars than bare skin. Was that truly a demonstration of pain relief for ordinary men?"

"I'm not about to question the magister," another voice said.

"A warrior," Miquel growled, "isn't like other men."

"Come, my friend. Here's your tunic. Now I recommend," Magister Antoni's hand brushed Chrétien's chest and rested, too familiar, on Chrétien's elbow, "a good lunch and all the wine you can drink."

"I recommend," Miquel said, "that you protect your own and find the magic assassin. And quiet that filthy brat. I cannot endure any more talk of pirates."

When Chrétien turned to answer, Miquel wasn't there. Of course not. He was buried on Cyprus. Yusuf stood nearby though, with Qasim a hand's breadth away, both of them restraining Sanço from running to Chrétien's side.

Though Magister Antoni still had one hand on Chrétien's shoulder, two men from the gaggle of students crowded close to the magister, eager to greet him, their attention only for Antoni. As if Chrétien weren't there. As if he'd disappeared like Miquel.

"We are blessed to have you in our school, magister." The man spoke the local tongue with a heavy French accent. He wore a brown gown like so many physicians did, but of a fine-gauge wool, the sleeves showing a silk lining. His downy goatee did not hide his receding chin. "I read your treatise on amputating and cauterizing battle wounds. Your insights surely come from God."

"You are kind to say so, Magister Jacobus." Antoni's voice was warm and kindly, like it had been while he treated Chrétien's wounds. If Jacobus was called magister, then he was another lecturer from the school.

The second man, also in a physician's brown gown, though less costly, had trampled Chrétien's foot in his eagerness to be close to the magister. He said, "I beg you, Magister Antoni. Let me assist you next week. As you promised at All Saints." This man's voice scratched, as if he had an ague. He coughed, his spit flying over Chrétien's bare arm. If Chrétien weren't taller than most every man in Montpelhièr, it would have been his face.

"If you'll let me examine you tomorrow, Magister Lucas. It seems you've had that cough since All Saints. I'm worried about your well-being."

"It's only a rheum, like everyone in Montpelhièr has had since this bad winter began."

"Ah, I've had extra success with the common rheum here. Will you come to me tomorrow if I promise to share the secret of my rheum-defeating potion?"

"Lungwort?" Magister Lucas said. "I've used such a potion since the first day of Advent."

Magister Antoni smiled broadly. "You need my secret, for yourself and for your practice as a doctor."

The two eventually finished praising Antoni, who then turned his attention back to Chrétien. First, he insisted that Chrétien needed food, and Yusuf begged to come along. Qasim would follow, of course, if food was involved.

After they all set out in search of a meal, Yusuf asked Antoni where he was from, and where he'd learned to be a physician. But while Chrétien tried to hear Antoni's story, Sanço's sharp voice stung his ears. The boy told yet another series of lies, prompted by Qasim, who should know better than to bait a child's fantasies. When Chrétien glanced around, Miquel walked beside him, while Yusuf listened to Antoni tell a story from his heart.

Chrétien stopped in the street, shaking off Antoni's guiding hand, blinking as if waking from a dream.

"Where's my steel?"

11
Weak Soup

"I HAVE YOUR SWORD, uncle. Yusuf holds your cross-hilt blades."

Besides calling Chrétien "uncle," Qasim's perpetual calm affected Chrétien deeply. He resisted embracing Qasim with relief, grateful that the young man had taken care of the important things.

However, Qasim said, "You must thank your pupil Sanço. He gathered and carried your weapons to the hospital. Wouldn't let anyone else touch them until Yusuf and I appeared."

Antoni seemed curious. "How do you come to carry a sword in the street? Comte Nuño forbade carrying arms when the prelate came to town."

"My uncle is the count's own man," Yusuf said. That relieved Chrétien from having to reveal more. He pulled at his jerkin, feeling the special license from Nuño in the inside pocket.

Their little crowd crossed the city, seeking a blood-fortifying luncheon. Qasim fell back to walk beside Sanço, who still trailed after Chrétien, chattering. Qasim kept saying "What happened next?" prompting the prattling to continue.

"After we crossed the mountains," Sanço said, "we guessed we'd do better to join the crusade, because they were going to the Outremer. We knew our lord was in the Holy Land."

In an intoxicated state, Chrétien traveled the streets with Sanço's high-pitched voice piercing his dreams. He glanced back at Sanço, but in doing so, caught sight of his own swathed left hand. Such a hindrance for a swordsman who had to find a magical assassin.

"It seemed the best way to travel there," Sanço said after Qasim once more asked *But Why?* "Sadly, we had more work in the crusaders' camp than ever, taking care of the little ones. And we were always hungry. The crusade had grown too big and guzzled up all the food in the countryside. Did you know that crusaders are hungry all the time? Have you been on crusade?"

"In Andalusia with Pedro d'Aragón," Qasim said. "Yes, we were often hungry on the way home."

"With Pedro? That's the crusade that took all the men away from our village. Christians went with Pedro. Others were mercenaries for the caliph." Sanço sniffed. "Besides being hungry, I lost my dog when we journeyed with that crusade. People said a wolf got her, so then we didn't dare leave that crowd to travel on our own. Who wants to be eaten by a wolf?"

"Not me," Qasim said.

Antoni kept hold of Chrétien's elbow, guiding him through the streets. Miguel again hounded him, walking alongside Chrétien's other elbow. "Your orphan reminds me of your brother at that age. More prepared for adventure than other boys."

"I was always as ready as Tomás." Chrétien defended against the idea that Tomás was better than him. "We strove to be equals."

"Still and all…" Miquel stopped in the street, then stepped back to walk alongside Qasim. "*Jhezu cristo* and all the singing angels. What are you doing here?"

Qasim brushed a hand on his ear, as if bitten. He glanced about, but then turned his attention back to the orphan, while Miquel stood still in the street, hands on his hips, that expression he had when he was fuming mad, beyond all endurance. Antoni led Chrétien around a turn in the street. Miquel was lost to sight.

Sanço sniffed once again, wiping his nose on the long sleeve of that new-to-him jerkin. "I miss my dog. She was called Lluna. Maybe it was the wolf in the moon that got her."

Antoni led them to the common room of Pons's hostel, assuring Yusuf that he knew for a fact the food there appealed to their patient.

"What luck, uncle, that you've already met the magister. That saves us time." Yusuf turned to Antoni. "My uncle Chrétien has pledged to help rescue our texts."

The stone that led to stitches didn't seem lucky. And Chrétien took two heartbeats to remember what he'd promised. And why. Ah, yes. "We're rescuing your astrology texts. So that the Church doesn't destroy them. And burn you as a Saracen-loving heretic."

"All my texts have been moved. So, this afternoon," Yusuf ignored the part about heresy, "we will rescue important texts from the Literature and Music library."

"Ah." Antoni studied Chrétien, the same way he had when administering medicine. "What good fortune. You'll help us save the troubadour songs about Miquel. Your father would be proud."

Miquel folded his arms. "You don't have to do a damnable thing to make me proud."

Shivering, Chrétien moved to a bench near the fire, as if his bones had chilled that morning and couldn't be thawed. The others gathered around him, Antoni at his side, Yusuf and Qasim once more across the table. Chrétien watched the warm repartee between the magister and Yusuf, feeling left out of their discussion of science. He glanced at Qasim, to see if Qasim also perceived that the physician intruded upon their family intimacy, but Qasim jumped up to intercede when Pons the hostler tried to toss Sanço back out on the street. Chrétien couldn't hear Qasim's entreaties, but Pons shrugged his well-padded shoulders the way many men did on Cyprus. He pointed toward the kitchen.

"Don't tell me that creature is a servant to any one of you gentlemen. I can see what he is. Your imp can eat in the kitchen. If he knows how to mind his betters."

Qasim walked to the kitchen with Sanço, murmuring what must have been encouragement, because Sanço straightened his shoulders and marched ahead with resolution, his nose once more pointed high, suffering the lowly indignities that inundated him.

"What ancient philosopher dreamed the remedy of leeches?" Yusuf's voice rose, asking a question about the lecture. "And you surely don't believe in the superstition of letting blood."

Pons interrupted, delivering wine and bread, promising a lentil pottage soon, which Chrétien scarcely heard because, ugh! Leeches! The word made the wine turn bitter on Chrétien's tongue. Worms had sucked his blood.

That disgust, and the throbbing in his head pulsing through to his swathed hand, made it hard to hear the debate between Yusuf and Antoni. Chrétien still felt as if he were far away, watching everyone at a great distance.

"My personal experience is that a heliotrope potion is more useful for blood disorders than bleeding. But I believe..." Antoni's eyes darted about the room, seeking who might overhear, "that the great Persian teacher Rhazes has more to teach us than any credulous philosophy of bleeding."

"The morbific principle?" Yusuf asked. Chrétien recognized the pupil wanting to be praised by the teacher. He wasn't so old that he'd forgotten what that was like.

Antoni tapped his temple, a twitch of a smile at the corners of his mouth, rewarding Yusuf with a gesture that acknowledged the student's correct insight. "Then you know the great Rhazes argues that fermentation happens in the body, like it does in our food and drink, and that's what generates disease."

Qasim folded his arms, the way he did whenever Yusuf wandered into scholarship and forgot his friend. Chrétien didn't trust that his head was clear, since it seemed that Antoni practiced on Yusuf the same subtle seductions he'd tried on Chrétien the night before. Perhaps Qasim perceived it too. Chrétien worried too much about his throbbing hand to volunteer the abundantly evident truth: the sharpest Damascus steel could not cleave Yusuf and Qasim apart. Antoni merely wasted his effort if he intended to beguile where two young men were as tied to each other as the twin stars in the constellation called Gemini.

"We know," Antoni was saying, "when Pope Innocent sent Simon de Montfort to make trouble in Toulouse, he asked the bishops in Paris to stop the lecturers from teaching Aristotle and Avicenna in the schools there."

"Yes," Yusuf said. "I've been to Paris. However, some lecturers there ignored the pope."

"Indeed, they must," Antoni said, "because the modern advances in healing and health from Salerno and Toledo rely on Avicenna and Aristotle. All good science is now based on what we are learning from those great philosophers, and from Rhazes in Persia."

"While I resent the overly cautious thinking among lecturers here, I'm not blind." Yusuf, as usual, picked at his food, distracted by his own thoughts. "They are so deeply conservative because they saw what happened in Béziers and Carcassona and Minerve. As intended, those tragedies served as a warning, so the lecturers remain in harmony with the priests and the pope. What will such caution mean for teaching medicine and science in Montpelhièr?"

"What does it mean?" Antoni touched the back of Yusuf's hand; Qasim came to attention as if poked. "It means that new discovery and new philosophy will belong to other men in other cities. The physicians here will only write glosses of already translated work."

Chrétien watched, with no ideas of his own to contribute, while he ate the food that Antoni insisted would fortify the blood and restore his life's spirit. But it tasted of ashes. That swaddled hand lay in his lap, useless. Trying to remember what he should be doing felt like chasing gnats. Find answers to help save the city, help Nuño, provide safety for Durán while he attended the prelate's council. The most important things.

A whisper. "And protect Yusuf. Family before other promises."

Magister Antoni remained intent on keeping Yusuf's attention. "My own magister, who trained in Salerno, often said, '*Come le cure come*.' Or as all teachers in Toulouse and Avignon say, '*Coma suenhs cossí*.' Now, what does it mean to claim 'Like cures Like.'"

"It's the physician's key question, isn't it?" Yusuf couldn't help being the perfect student. Qasim seemed that he'd prefer to eat his own boots. "What can we discover that is similar to this diseased thing that can therefore cure or prevent the disease?"

"Indeed." Antoni again signaled his respect for Yusuf's intelligence. Qasim stole Yusuf's bowl of soup and proceeded to eat it, as if not hearing the magister at all. "Our science must give the structure and philosophy for our experiments and practices, to know what has been provided in nature. Pursuing this knowledge is my life's work. Recording what we prove and practice is the legacy we promise for the future."

Yusuf said, "Will you tell me, magister, how you induce a trance and preserve it during surgery? Or must I do more than pay for lectures to learn your secrets?"

Qasim stood. "I'm going to see how Sanço is faring in the kitchen." He headed for the inner door, leaving Chrétien to ponder whether Qasim ever strayed that far from Yusuf's side.

Magister and student chatted more while Chrétien listened for a memory of what he was supposed to do. An image burned in his mind. Something he had to see but didn't want to.

Durán. Your brother Tomás. Your family. Your households in Toulouse and Valerós. Everything will be lost if we allow this plot to succeed.

"*Òc,* that's the thing, *fadrin.*" Miquel reclined beside Chrétien, as if he too needed the fire to warm his bones. But his bones were buried on Cyprus. "We're looking for a stranger. Spies spying on spies. Like I did in Syria."

Chrétien stood, swaying with the rush of blood to his head, knowing what he needed to do next.

Antoni was on his feet in the same moment. "Senhór, you'll disorder yourself. Sit." He coaxed Chrétien back to the bench. "Let me see." He adjusted the bandages on Chrétien's head, then removed them. "You don't need these now. Air has amazing curative powers for cuts."

As soon as Antoni removed the bandages and stepped away, Chrétien went in search of the hostler.

·

Pons was busy tapping a wine keg at the long table from which he also served bread and stew and ale.

"*Eh, el meu amic.*" Chrétien collected every bit of his accent from early life on Cyprus, intending that Pons see him as a comrade from their homeland. "Two men were here last night. Huge beards. One of them braided in the middle like a Northman."

Pons blinked, his eyes casting about as if trying to remember. Slowly, he nodded. "Mercenaries from Marseille. Last fought for Philip Augustus up north somewhere. Or so they say."

Chrétien persisted. "Another man spoke with them. I think he's recruiting mercenaries. A man named Zorzi. I'd like to find him."

Pons's eyes emptied, as if he possessed no thought at all. Then shook his head, turning his attention back to the wine keg, not letting Chrétien catch his eye. "The sole captain who's been here lately seeks only men from Marseille, the kind who cry in ale cups because the pope won't mount another crusade, keeping them from practicing holy murder. Men who want work but don't want to bow to a

French lord, or the Duke of Burgundy, or—God forbid—go to work for the Holy Roman Empire."

"Freelance work is hard to find in winter." Chrétien wanted to tease out more information. "Can you please let any captain who comes in here know that I need work?"

Pons denied any greater knowledge, shaking his head so hard it dislodged half the fringe of hair he'd oiled in place. "Now, my friend, are you going to get that urchin out of my kitchen?"

"In a moment. Do you have more ideas about what house might take in a lost orphan?"

"You tried Lazarus House?"

"They didn't suit."

Pons fingered his thin beard, as if scratching for an idea. "There's St-Niccolò hotel by the north gate. They take boys who can work."

"Is that another Church orphanage? Our luck wasn't so good with the nuns."

"Church?" Pons found that funny. "No, as secular as you and me. More like a hostel than an orphan's house. Run by a bunch of Pisans. They say it's clean, though. Even priests and monks go there."

Pons gave directions that would again cause Chrétien to cross half of Montpelhièr. Why had he made such a complicated commitment to a street urchin? His sense of honor should be tied up only with his promises to keep his family safe. But he couldn't leave the child back out on the street.

Chrétien pushed open the door to Pons's kitchen to fetch his orphan. Heat from the fires poured over him like a balm. The boy had Qasim and the cook listening spellbound to more of the lad's incessant chatter.

"Then we were crusaders journeying to the Holy Land, marching to Marseille. They say we were ten thousand strong. We scoured the bushes all day to find every possible rabbit, rat, and stoat, which we boiled on turd-fed fires at night. When sermons were shouted every morning and night, they said we'd be greeted as crusaders in Marseille, because we were on our way to free Jerusalem with the love of God in our pure hearts."

"How did they greet you in Marseille?" Qasim prompted. "I've never been there, but they say it's a grand city."

"The householders in Marseille nailed their shutters closed and barred the doors. No one on the streets, no priests in the churches."

"No one?" Qasim prompted him again. Chrétien didn't like feeling annoyed by Sanço's fantastic tales—it's what boys do—yet he wasn't sure why Qasim encouraged the lad, but Qasim's curiosity encouraged Chrétien's patience.

"Indeed." Sanço sniffed, wiping at his nose. "At the docks along the Great Sea, captains and sailors cheered and shouted for us to come aboard their ships. It seemed to take forever, but it was only three days until a captain begged me to come aboard his ship. That's when I was separated from my cousins who'd traveled from my village. We went aboard two boats, anchored right by each other."

"That's bad," Qasim said. "I'd hate to be parted from my friends."

"But we were happy, because the sailors all shouted, 'Hurray for the little crusaders!' in a hundred different tongues."

"A hundred?" Qasim said.

Sanço considered this seriously. "Maybe a thousand."

Why not ten thousand, Chrétien wondered. It'd make an even more enticing and fantastical story.

"'Hurray for the little crusaders'? Did that make you proud?" Qasim spoke respectfully, but Sanço shot him one of those hooded hateful looks, like a poisoned arrow, then pointed his nose in the air and continued his fantasy.

Sanço said, "I walked up their boarding plank, sat where I was told, wrapped in my blanket, which was all I had left from home. I got sick as soon as the ship broached the shore break. That's what the sailors say it's called, that roll of waves between the harbor and the Great Sea."

"I got sick when I sailed, too," Qasim said. "I swear on the black saints of Valencia that I'll never go to sea again."

"Did you puke?" Sanço seemed to return Qasim's respect.

"For two days."

"Did they shout at you for puking on the ship? Call you the most evil names?"

"I leaned over the side," Qasim said. "My master held me, kept me from falling in."

"You were lucky. I got sick on my clothes." Sanço returned to his lies. "At nightfall, the rowers lifted their oars. The ship ceased moving forward. Any soul who spoke was slapped to shush him, so the only sound was water lapping against wood, right behind where I sat braced against the side of the boat. I was thinking how there was only a plank of wood, which used to be a tree, between me and the bottom of the Great Sea."

"*Aiieee!*" Qasim said. "I felt the same way when the storm tossed our boat."

"It would have been better for all of us," Sanço said, "if we had indeed gone to the bottom of the Great Sea. At that moment an enormous hook grabbed the side of the boat, right by my head. The boat rocked and rocked, and I puked again."

"That's when it's bad," Qasim said. "When you've tossed up everything in your belly, but you're still heaving. Was that the worst?"

"No. Another boat lay beside us. Two men crawled into ours and stood talking with the captain in a tongue I didn't know. It was coming on night, but I could see these men were darker than most of our crew. I guessed they spoke the Saracen tongue."

"That's likely," Qasim said. "People say Saracens are good sailors."

"Good? I haven't met good sailors." Sanço curled a lip in disdain. "The men on our boat began handing us over the side. I was one of the last passed from hands on our boat to hands on the other. Because they spoke that strange tongue, it was the next morning until even one of us understood that the captains in Marseille had sold us to Saracen slavers."

"Christians sold you to Saracens?" Qasim voiced dismay. But it was the dismay of one who believed the story. The story that Chrétien found as improbable as the assassin he was trying to find.

"*Òc.*" Sanço offered a heartbreaking expression, eyes brimming, ready to release tears. "And I never did see my comrades from my village. We lost each other that night. It was as sad as losing Lluna to wolves." Sanço glanced at the door, then cried in dismay. "*Aiieee! El pirata Moresco!*"

A man stood in the doorway of the kitchen. Dark beard, hooded black wool cloak. A ridiculous moustache.

Chrétien bounded out of the hostel in pursuit of the man who might be called Zorzi, pausing only to tuck his knives in his belt and then snatch his sword.

12

In Search of St-Niccolò

IT HAD TO BE THE same man he'd bumped into the night before.

"Stop!" Chrétien called to the man in the local tongue. "I want to talk with you, my friend."

The cuts stung on his forehead and behind his ear. The street spun. He was dizzy as a drunken man. Had the physician done something else to him? He had no time to watch for hazards in the street while he tracked where the man ran. Chrétien hit a puddle whose ice layer was too thin to bear his weight. Icy water lapped over the sides of his boot, wetting his stocking.

Though his head pounded as if held in a vice while a blacksmith hammered, Chrétien was fast, even when carrying weapons, so he kept the slower man in sight as they passed aged stone houses that had been manors in earlier days, but now were buttressed with three-story merchants' houses, where workers and householders busy at the day's tasks scarcely glanced at the running men.

Sturdy girls hauling water from a city well stepped close to the houses to avoid brushing against Chrétien.

Adolescent boys scrubbed pots with sand in an alleyway.

A *thunk* down one street drew his attention for a single heartbeat. Workers turned the crank on a windlass, raising a heavy stone block for the upper story of a new church. The screech of stone matched the ringing in Chrétien's ears.

He caught sight of the moustached man rounding a corner and pelted after him, picking up speed as he entered a street of tailors, then shoemakers, all with their doors shuttered so they could work inside where it was warm.

One more street over, he dodged a pair of youths rolling a barrel along the bumpy, slick roadway. When the street pitched upward, the barrel rolled back on the boys, but Chrétien was gone before they got on their way again.

A hostler's wife sold pottage from a booth outside an inn. Her booth's awning swayed in the wind; strings of mushrooms, onions, and garlic danced where they hung over the woman's head.

"Lookout, water!" Another woman cried in the local tongue from an upper story.

Lookout, water! Miquel cried in the Catalan cant they spoke in their household on Cyprus.

Chrétien bobbed, not knowing which direction to duck, and slipped on ice. The promised brown water cascaded to the street beside him. He leapt like an old-style bull-dancer to get away, slipping again, smashing his spine on the pavement.

Then he had a boot on his chest and a nicked dinner knife at his throat.

"You're that long, tall boy from Toulouse." The man who held Chrétien down with his boot drawled in the local accent. He wore a polished leather cuirass, studded front and back with brass nails. A dark wool scarf wrapped his neck, trapping long brown hair in its folds. "That fey singer who wants a mercenary master."

"Took four *sous* off me at dice last week," a second man said. "Another Catalan man come to steal from us."

A dozen or more men appeared behind the attacker, each swathed in black wool, all of them muttering, their words escaping the wool wrappings in white clouds of fury.

Stranger, go home. Over and over, in the local tongue.

They weren't wrapped to block the cold. Rather, these men hid their faces so only their eyes appeared. Yet even with a headache, Chrétien saw that they were all young. Fifteen, perhaps. And in spite of Comte Nuño's proclamation about carrying weapons, each held a barrel stave, a broom handle, a broken wheel spoke, most with a nail or two protruding from one end.

Miquel drawled, "*A mal punt.*" An unpleasant situation.

Chrétien sought leverage, with one hand swathed in gauze, where spots of red had already leaked through.

"Stop! Stop!"

Howling, a furious creature flew like an enraged hound at the man who held Chrétien down, clawing at the man's clothes, shouting an impressive string of imprecations and insults.

"No biting, *fadrin!*" Chrétien commanded, interrupting Sanço from using his teeth on yet another foe.

The man in the cuirass tried to brush the boy aside but couldn't get his hands on the squirming child. Chrétien took advantage of the distraction to leap to his feet, resting his hand on his sword's pommel. "Let's speak peacefully. We are all men of Christendom."

Miquel held the child by the shoulders. Sanço looked around wildly, as if trying to find what held him back, before sighing mightily and accepting the restraint. "Master, I cannot care for you properly if you run after *baquelars* and pirates. It's my fault you were injured this morning. You must let me…"

"Hush!" Chrétien needed to focus on the man who'd pulled a knife on him, who stood with arms folded, backed by the friend who held a grudge over four *sous* Chrétien won off him at dice.

"My friends," Chrétien began as amiably as he ever did, "I hold a license from Comte Nuño that permits me to carry a sword on the streets of his city. What lord protects you when you pull a knife on a man who's done you no harm?"

"My four *sous*." The complaining gambler spit the words.

"We don't need Catalan and Aragón riff-raff in this city." Cuirassman set his jaw. "Demand that your food is cooked just so. Can't speak a proper tongue."

"Always bragging about beating the caliph in Andalusia," the losing gambler groused, "as if the *francès* and *espanyols* didn't have bigger armies."

"Sniffing at our women." The first man spat his disgust. "We don't need you in our militia. Or on our streets. *Mestitz* Moors, the lot of you."

"I have never sniffed a single woman in your town." Chrétien jerked Sanço to his side to make it clear the boy was under his protection. Miquel let go of the boy's shoulders. "And I must be the most pallid Moor ever. Whiter than the ghost of a Moor."

Both men wanted to be done with Chrétien, likely because of Comte Nuño's license for the sword on which Chrétien rested his good hand. His attacker, still holding his dinner knife as if it were a useful weapon, pointed the blade to Chrétien's swathed hand.

"Don't expect you got that in a fair fight," he growled. "But we won't attack a crippled and broken man. We're telling you now, men like you don't belong in this town."

He and his friend pivoted on worn boot heels, as if they'd gotten the best of the argument, and stalked up the street and around the corner.

Chrétien called after them. "Tell me the name of your captain. Comte Nuño would like to speak with him."

He expected no answer, which left him with his orphan to be inspected covertly by others who belonged on this street, while he quarreled with his headache and ringing ears and his ghost-father, pondering how he got from falling in the cobbled square outside St-Lazarus to here, threatened on a street he didn't recognize.

"Your kind friends said to meet them at their library." Sanço tipped his head far back to gaze up at Chrétien. "Are we going there now?"

"After I've found a place for you at St-Niccolò hotel."

Wagging a finger to silence Sanço's protests, Chrétien walked back up the street to greet the woman who sold food from a booth. She smiled, brightly expectant, until it turned out that Chrétien wanted directions to the north gate, not to buy food. He gave her his last two copper pennies while asking for details.

"It's St-Niccolò hotel that I'm looking for."

She spat at his boot. "You rogue. Take your boy and leave our street." She pointed at a taller church to what must have been the north. "Stop there and beg forgiveness. They'll give directions if you can't find the hotel."

Chrétien wanted to argue, like he had with the pretty nun, that the urchin wasn't his, that he'd committed no sin and planned no sin. But things had already gone as badly on that street as could be, and Miquel was tapping his foot while Sanço wiggled at his side, as if seeking to climb out of his own skin. So, Chrétien struck out for the north side of the city with a ringing headache and a throbbing hand, and a singing ghost at his side.

My son shows valor
Before ten thousand aggressors.
He holds our castles against charlatans.
A liar makes no advance in his noble land,
For he has merit and wisdom to guide him.
His words and songs taste like honey.

At his other side, Chrétien had a pointy-nosed orphan who could not hide his bitter resentment while telling a story that seemed intended to admonish Chrétien to behave better.

"When the pirates captured the slave ship, they cut off the Saracen captain's head and threw it into the sea. We had to work, they said, or they'd cut us up too. The bigger boys had to row, but I was too little, so I carried water to the rowers. One of the big boys got sick. He was burned black from the sun and also burning up inside. The pirates carried him away, and then they cut him open to put out the fire in his guts."

"I've never heard of that," Chrétien said.

"Indeed, nor I," Sanço said. "But they failed to put out the fire, so my friend died. They rolled that boy over the side of the boat for the fishes. And when the fishes came, the pirates speared dozens to roast for dinner. For days and days, we had no food morning or night except the fishes that ate the burning boy."

"Does this tale have a moral purpose?" Chrétien asked. The pitch of Miquel's pestiferous singing matched the shrill ringing in his ears. Having one's head cut off sounded like pure relief.

Sanço kicked a cobble. Miquel ceased singing.

"It is the kind of blessing the Good God delivers. Some friends will stay with you, even after they've been fed to the fishes."

"May ten thousand angels dance their way into the flames." Miquel stopped in the street, shook his head at what he didn't want to hear, then walked off, headed west, clutching his head in the same way that Chrétien wanted to seize his own skull.

Only then did Chrétien notice Miquel was younger than he'd ever known him. Not much older than Yusuf, who resembled Miquel enough to be his brother. Why hadn't he noticed that...

"I didn't know the burning boy, but whenever I brought him water, he smiled and said, 'Merci beaucoup.' That means gràcies in the *francès* tongue, doesn't it? Every *gràcies* is like a small gift from the Good God. Like the way I said *gràcies* when you saved me, because your kindness came from the Good God."

"Sanço, silence please!"

Lightheaded, Chrétien wanted to repeat Miquel's imprecation but it wouldn't be enough to make Sanço stop speaking heresy where anyone could hear. He blinked to clear his vision. They'd come to where he expected to find the St-Niccolò hotel. But from the outside, the aged villa looked far too fine to be a hostel, starting with the metalwork embedded on plank-wood doors: a pair of brightly polished men, kneeling and each holding out a hand to the other.

A Physician Trained

From the Secret History of the Flaming Cross
— Andonis de Zêna

The year I went to study in Toulouse, 1190 by the Roman calendar, was the same year that Riccardo Cuor di Leone and Philippe di Francia set sail from Marseille for the Outremer. That was a grand year for my mercantile family, because my uncles and cousins in Genoa provided many of the ships that sailed to and traded with the Outremer. Genoa had been turning its forests into ships for many years, doing a better job of it than most other shipbuilders in Christendom.

I was judged as not ready to go on crusade, but I did not experience despair, because Abbot Rodolfo instead sent me to Toulouse to train with a physician who had also studied at the Flaming Cross monastery as a child. Excited about journeying out into the wider world, I didn't think of what it could mean to say farewell to long-time friends. A few years after I left, Abbot Rodolfo died of pleurisy, one of the diseases which I learned to treat as a physician in Toulouse. I still think of Rodolfo with fondness for all he did as a teacher—and with regret that I couldn't be there to heal him.

In Toulouse, I studied under the physician Francisco di Salerno. As his name indicates, he studied medicine under the great teachers at Salerno. That means that Francisco emphasized theory and philosophy, as much as medicine. Francisco also put great store in the magnificent scholar Avicenna, which he pronounced in the Arabs' way, Ibn Sina, since he had spent much time with such scholars at school in Salerno.

Also under Francisco, I first learned that translation is more than a punishment any tutor might assign a boy. In addition to what he earned from fees as a physician, Francisco was part of a coterie of scholars, sponsored by local seigneurs and counts, who were translating medical knowledge found inside Greek and Arabic books that few could read. Beyond learning everything I could by observing Francisco's practices and listening to his lectures, I studied his glosses on texts he translated, which led me to the activity that caused my heart to soar in Toulouse.

I became a major contributor to the translation efforts of physicians and scholars who struggled with sublime texts on science and medicine, knowledge trapped in unfamiliar tongues. But these were tongues I already read and wrote fluently.

I had one other mentor in Toulouse, whom I met through Francisco's scholar-friends involved in translation work. Ezra ibn Isaac had been a translator in the famous libraries of Toledo, where more Arabic and Hebrew texts on science and medicine are preserved than you can imagine. I heard from other translators that Magister Ezra was famous for the speed and accuracy of his translations. Though he wasn't a physician, he invited his friends who were doctors to comment and explain while he worked through translations of texts that most of Christendom has never seen.

Ezra taught me to read and write in his own native tongue, which of course I'd never learn in any monastery or among any Christian scholars. And—this is a source of wonder and gratitude in my life—he introduced me to Averroes and more of Aristotle than I'd ever seen previously.

Magister Francisco alluded to the scholar Averroes but had no texts to show me. I was friends with Ezra for two years before he allowed me a glimpse of that forbidden text. And I spent another year as his apprentice before he allowed me to copy from the texts that he had preserved.

It was easier to learn how Ezra ibn Isaac ended up in Toulouse than to learn anything from Francisco—who as a fellow brother in the Order of the Flaming Cross should have been much more forthright with me.

Francisco stayed in Toulouse instead of going home to Genoa because he had a wife and children. Ezra, however, left Toledo and came to Toulouse because of his wife and child. Now, the story I've heard from other travelers in Andalusia is that what they call the People of the Book are allowed to live side-by-side in harmony. Those who aren't of the Saracens' faith pay a tax, the way Genoa taxes Venetian ships who seek harbor. But Toledo returned to Christendom in 1085, after three hundred years of Muslim rule. If Francisco's wife and children were happy in Toulouse, Ezra's wife and mother became increasingly uncomfortable in Toledo, feeling harassed in the streets. He found a sponsor through cousins who had moved to Narbonne two generations earlier. And then he packed everyone up, sewed his books safely into goatskin wrappers and wax, and moved to Toulouse.

We still converse through the message-circuit of physicians and translators. Not long before my monastic brother Francisco died, Ezra left Toulouse for Narbonne—the incursion of French Christian zealots in that part of the world left his wife uncomfortable again, so they've moved into a neighborhood with his Narbonnese cousins. He left texts for me with Francisco, so you can imagine how eager I was to return there to learn what I had inherited from my monastic brother. I shall repeat no more about my time in Toulouse, except to say I spent the most joyous years of my life there.

‡

Cançons de Montpelhièr

A man who finds no pleasure in song
Lives the life of a sad jester.
I long to live in joy.
I'm neither a fool nor fickle.
Anyone who forgets delight

And forbids pleasure,
And censures other people's joy,
Is a complete fool.

13
Possessed!

"TOO FANCY." SANÇO JUDGED St-Niccolò quickly.

Chrétien agreed. Too fancy for a hostel that might hire street-boys in the kitchen. Lattice windows on the first floor were each covered in linen soaked in tallow and resin. Given the unexpected cold of the Montpelhièr holidays, these must all now be hung over with tapestries inside to defeat the draft. Windows on the upper stories had panes made of sheep's horn. If the owners employed orphans for anything in this house, it would be for extravagances like peeling sheep's horn to fill windows.

Though not convinced that this hostel would welcome an uncouth boy like Sanço, Chrétien knocked, his hand barely fitting between the two polished metal men on the door. It opened so fast, the aged man who appeared must have waited only one footstep from the archway.

"*Bonjorn, senhór.*"

The man rubbed his bare hands against the cold. Bald. Indeed, seemingly hairless. His narrow jaw jutted as if persistently asking questions. Behind him, sweet scents rolled from the door to the street, where Chrétien and Sanço exhaled white clouds on the cold street. Ginger, cloves, cumin. As if they'd wandered near a kitchen kept by Chrétien's mother.

"*Bonjorn.* My countryman Pons, of Aubèrja de Cyprus, suggested that your house might find a place for a good boy who has nowhere else to go."

"Home," Sanço whispered beside him. "I want to go home."

The old gentleman glanced down his narrow nose, inspecting Sanço. "He's quite young. Are you sure you don't want to keep him until you're tired of him?"

"I can't keep a boy. He needs a warm place that will feed him and keep him safe. I appeal to your heart."

The old man tossed his head back, laughing, his skin stretched tight over bones, as if he had no flesh. He reached his skeletal hand out, grasping Sanço's arm above the elbow. Sanço squirmed away, but the old fellow must have felt how thin the lad was. "If he doesn't give us any trouble, the house can share…" He glanced past Chrétien, distracted. He called out, "Brother Guido, come give us your opinion. As our long-time customer, you can render judgment for me. Is this boy worthy of our house? Can he be saved?"

The chubby monk he'd hailed huffed across the street, a middle-aged cleric in a drab, well-worn brown robe, from no order that Chrétien recognized. A long-time customer. While Chrétien puzzled this, the old man at the door finished what he had to say to Chrétien. "The house can share half a virgin's fee with you. That's the best offer we can make."

"*Jhezu del tron!* No!" Chrétien meant to grab the boy and flee, but the monk inserted his bulk between Chrétien and Sanço and pulled back the boy's heavy wool hood and stared into his eyes. Then he yanked up the sleeve of Sanço's too-big secondhand jerkin, his pudgy hand grazing over the raised welts on Sanço's forearm.

"A hedge-witch's child? Not for your house." The monk ran his finger along those welts. "I believe he's possessed."

Chrétien reached to grab the boy, but Sanço wrenched his arm free of the monk's grasp, squirmed out of reach, spit in the monk's face, then kicked. Just as Chrétien finally grabbed him, Sanço raked the monk's cheeks, drawing thin dots of blood.

"Possessed!" Guido cried. "His demon curses the Holy Spirit."

"No, Brother Guido. You are mistaken." Chrétien wanted to restore peace and get Sanço back under control.

Meanwhile, the old man struggled to close St-Niccolò's heavy, iron-straked door. He paused, only to offer a one-handed rude gesture to Chrétien, who shouted his father's favorite invectives. "Jove's pissing monkey, I'd let the devil's own adulterous sister have the boy before you, you goat-legged spit-licker."

The monk grabbed Sanço's arm again. "I'm taking this demon child to the bishops' court for judgment."

"You shall not!" Chrétien shoved at the monk, who stumbled and fell on his backside in the ice. Before the monk could cry out one more condemnation, Chrétien hoisted Sanço over his shoulder and stepped around the floundering monk.

However, the monk's continuing cries of "Possessed!" drew people from their doors and caused workmen to stop their labor, all slowly moving toward St-Niccolò hotel.

Then a clutch of seven men shoved their way through while tying white linen kerchiefs over their faces. They began chanting, "Our land, our Church, our ways."

An old woman yelled, "He attacked Brother Guido!"

"Guido's a drunk and a fool!" A voice cried from an upper window, but was shouted over by others.

"We protect the Church and true Christians!" another deeper male voice called. "What are you doing here?"

Chrétien struggled to shelter Sanço behind him, wedging the boy against the hotel door, hoping the lad might have enough sense to shut up and stand still. What was he doing here? Seeking a safe place for an orphan that wandered into his path. What he was supposed to be doing? That branded image burned in his mind. Durán and his mother Numa standing before the flames.

He was supposed to be stopping the plot that threatened Nuño and the lords and seigneurs of the south.

However, near the corner of an alleyway, steps away from the seven-man wedge that challenged Chrétien, that moustached round-faced man appeared, grinning like a thistle-eating he-goat, snow speckling the woolen hood he wore.

"*Hola, lo mieu amic!*" Chrétien called out in a mix of the local tongue and Catalan. "I want to speak with you. Are you the man called Zorzi who's hiring mercenaries?"

The man stepped forward, still grinning. The two men regarded each other, nodding in respect. This might be Chrétien's best chance to learn who was paying to recruit mercenaries to create chaos.

Snow began to fall again, and the encounter would have proceeded toward peace, but once more that blasted orphan shrieked, as if he were truly attacked by demons.

"*El pirata Moresco!*"

The shrill pitch sent Chrétien's hand to his sword, because his heart begged him to protect Sanço. Chrétien might have had a life like this orphan if Miquel hadn't rescued him as an infant. Durán could have fallen as badly if he hadn't been lucky enough to be made a Montcava footman, and then been recognized for who he really was. Chrétien had more to protect than just Durán and Yusuf: his other hand reached for the long knife in his boot.

Except that hand was swaddled and useless.

The seven-man wedge took another step toward Chrétien with their staves and banned long knives. Chrétien drew his sword, confident that he could handle three, maybe four of the white-masked wedge-men, perhaps enough to frighten them away.

Yet it was only the moustached man who came for him, brandishing only a pole that might have once been a staff, but now had a long iron nail protruding from its end. His hand, wrapped too tightly on the pole, bore a swirling back mark, a tattoo. Chrétien tried to see it more clearly, but the man swung the pole at him in the clumsy sort of way you'd see in an infantry melee. Chrétien parried with the flat blade of his sword, knowing the power of his blow sent a painful shock down the pole to the man's hands. Before the man rallied to strike again, Chrétien stomped on the man's instep and brought the pummel of his sword up under the man's chin.

If he'd been serious, the blow would have broken the man's neck. But Chrétien hadn't intended that. While the man tried to rally, Chrétien kicked away that nail-headed staff and shoved the pommel of his sword against the man's sternum. If this was Nuño's assassin, the magic was that the man had lived so long with such poor skills.

The wind knocked out of him, the moustached man fell backward, caught by the seven men. Though Chrétien could see only their eyes, they seemed uncertain whether to pursue this fight. So, Chrétien tried what had worked to conjure peace a few streets over.

"Let's speak peacefully. We are all men of Christendom. I seek only to protect this orphan."

"If you're peaceful, why draw steel on us?" One man called out, while the seven men with linen kerchiefs hiding their faces stepped into blade formation again, which seemed a bit much for confronting a solitary man.

"I'm sworn to support Comte Nuño. If you truly care about what you say—your land, your ways—you too would support the count."

Maybe those words chilled the heat building in the crowd. Maybe it was the snow that fell (though everyone swears it never snows in Montpelhièr). Whatever it was, people became distracted.

A woman helped the decrepit monk onto his feet, adding distance between the monk and Sanço while she murmured words of comfort that settled on the irritable monk along with the falling flakes of snow. The masked challengers glanced at each other, uncertain. A man's voice from up the street called, "Can we get back to work? These bricks need hauling before our bums turn to ice."

The shifting wedge-men formed a curtain, so there was no sign of the moustached man. Then all seven had retreated up the alley from which they'd first appeared. The monk also vanished.

Which left only Chrétien standing on the portico of a brothel, with his sword drawn while across the street three old women and a small boy clutching a puppy regarded Chrétien as if he were a leftover Twelfth Night mummer. He returned his sword to its sheath, his swathed paw steadying the scabbard.

Amid all the residual tension, Sanço called across the square.

"My name is Sanço. May I pet your dog, my friends? I will be ever so gentle. I promise."

Chrétien hoped he was gentle with those stick-like bones when he pushed Sanço behind him with a swathed hand. He hoped the gesture commanded silence, because a throng of male voices echoed from up the street.

"Halt! Halt!"

A half dozen of the city's *gardes du corps* hustled into the mostly empty square. If there was a Good God who could defeat evil, their sergeant proved to be Chrétien's backgammon companion, Vincent. He was the same size as Qasim, though perhaps more muscular from regular training with his guards.

"*Mercé Dèu*, Sergeant Vincent! You have rescued me!"

Chrétien decided praise was the better greeting, though he wished they'd come several heartbeats earlier. Then he described for Vincent the recent confusion, skipping any mention of the brothel keeper and the irregular monk, instead describing the men shrouded in white kerchiefs, accompanied by a stranger that Sanço called a black pirate but whom Chrétien described only as a foreigner who'd been recruiting mercenaries for an unknown purpose.

"You carry steel, seigneur?" Vincent interrupted the story, pointing to Chrétien's sword and knives. "The count proclaimed that men cannot go armed while the Church prelate is in residence."

Chrétien produced the license from Comte Nuño that allowed him to carry steel arms in the city, unsure whether Vincent could read to decipher more than Nuño's mark. While repeatedly hushing Sanço ("peace, *fadrin,* please"), Chrétien jollied the guards, while his headache pounded, his ears rang like the sext bell, and the boy wiggled as if he wanted to crawl right up under Chrétien's cloak.

"Colder than a sword master's heart out here, isn't it?" The men agreed, adding that the snow was a plague, worse than any disease, all laughing bitterly until their sergeant hushed them.

Vincent returned Nuño's license to Chrétien. "So, you want us to beware of men in white kerchiefs?"

"Comte Nuño believes that men with ill intentions seek to disturb the city. Some wear black scarves, others wear white kerchiefs. I think all these men intend chaos."

"We shall beware." Vincent spoke in that heartfelt way that young leaders of soldiers do to make promises they likely cannot fulfill. He dropped his voice. "And we can only hope Comte Nuño has enough men to calm those that the Church has harmed."

When Vincent led his *gardes du corps* away, Chrétien pondered the problem that Vincent presented: how many men serving Nuño were like Vincent, with soul-deep wounds inflicted by Simon de Montfort and the Roman Church?

Sanço interrupted his contemplation with a litany of apologies. "You don't believe that monk, do you, my lord? I'm not possessed of a demon."

"No, you are not. I didn't like him either."

Sanço fell silent, staring past Chrétien at the small boy with the puppy who stood at the far side of the square.

"Stay by me," Chrétien cautioned. "No more fuss."

"My dog Lluna was just like that puppy." Sanço sounded wistful. "I wish I could pet that little dog."

"No, *fadrin.*"

But Sanço called out again, "Can I pet your dog?"

The boy across the street, squirming as much as his puppy, shook his head. He mumbled something.

"What did you say?" Sanço shouted, starting to move toward the boy and dog. Chrétien grabbed the back of his jerkin.

"Heretic!" The puppy's owner shouted. "You'll put a demon in my dog."

"I'm not a heretic!" Sanço shouted, bursting into tears. "I'm not possessed. I'm not!"

Chrétien clamped his hand over Sanço's mouth, tossing him over his shoulder in one swift motion. Disliking the undeserved sense of humiliation, Chrétien charged up the street, elbowing people out of his way, the boy's weight like nothing. At the corner, Miquel stood still as a ghost, grinning.

"Ah, my own blessed orphan." Miquel laughed. "Remember how no one in the world wanted you? Except me, *fadrin.* Oh, of course you don't remember. You were a wee babe."

Then Miquel stirred his bones and followed Chrétien and Sanço up the street, whistling.

"*Aiieee, fadrin.* Watch out for any more mercenaries looking for a long, tall boy who's sniffing around in business that's not his."

14
Wisdom in Translation

WHEN SEEKING THE SCHOOL for Literature and Music, Chrétien asked directions from old women, girls hauling water—anyone who seemed unlikely to be associated with overwrought mercenaries. They'd crossed half the city before Chrétien set Sanço down to walk on his own.

"You'll keep me with you, my captain? And help me find the lord of my village?" Sanço bounced ahead, walking backwards.

"I must help protect this city first. Then we'll decide what's next." Chrétien kept glancing at the boy, trying to see what infernal magic led people to throw stones and denounce a ragged child, who was more bones than flesh and who importuned only Chrétien. He decided to hold his temper about the boy's pestering, since the rest of the city's populace seemed to have lost their minds.

"He stinks of magic." Miquel's ghost offered a comment. He'd walked beside Chrétien since that blow to his head. A specter, singing in the same key as the ringing in his ears.

"There's no magic," Chrétien muttered. "As you always said."

"The boy stinks of something more than no bath. Maybe if you washed him, we could figure out what plague he carries." Miquel folded his hands in judgment again. "I hate to see a child suffer."

"You can't believe that I like to see it!" Chrétien cried.

"Pardon, please forgive me." Sanço answered Chrétien's cry in that peculiar backcountry accent. "If you'd let me serve you, as God intended, then we could avoid all the sad souls who do not let the light of the Good God into their hearts."

Chrétien couldn't speak to that, since his thoughts dwelled on why Pons, from damned-by-the-dark-angels Cyprus, sent him out to sell a child at a bordello.

"That old lady said we'd find the school you want right here at…" Sanço drew his breath. "*Aiieee,* is that man a pirate? Is he one of them?"

Ahead, a man at the edge of a stone building's portico shook an admonishing finger at someone who stood deeper in the shadows. It was Antoni, his long locks escaping his blood-red velvet hat.

"It's only the magister who healed me," Chrétien said.

Sanço sniffed.

A thin voice drifted into the street from the portico. "I am compelled to warn you. The monk Bernatz has your name from other magisters. He intends to examine you tomorrow. He knows where you live. You are watched."

"And I assure you, dear friend, that my work and my soul are protected by God." Antoni drew the figure from inside the portico, bracing him by the shoulders. Feris, the rodent-like monk who turned up everywhere.

Here was news: both men who'd followed Chrétien through the taverns of Montpelhièr knew each other. Further, Feris, whose job was to spy on the boy-king's schoolmasters, was warning the magister of dangers from the Church he served. So many questions bubbled inside him that Chrétien had to hold back from jumping in to interrogate the two of them.

"Magister, it's most likely that all lecturers will be examined by the bishop of Maguelone. Protect yourself," Feris said.

"Go back to your post, my friend. You'll find tomorrow that God protects His own. You have no call to worry for me."

"You are always so carefree." Feris sounded bitter. "This will be more than *gardes du corps* beating heretics. More than the pope excommunicating Comte Raymond and perhaps putting Toulouse under siege. They will come for you."

Magister Antoni watched Feris depart, waving each time the little monk looked over his shoulder. Then the magister turned into the portico and opened a door. Chrétien followed, since this was the school he'd been seeking, to meet with Yusuf and Qasim.

"Master," Sanço whispered behind him, "guard your soul."

Hearing them at his heels, Antoni glanced back, his face beaming when he recognized Chrétien.

"Lo mieu amic! Bona serada!" He called good afternoon in the local tongue. "I'm happy to find you again. Are you well?"

"I am." Chrétien believed he was fine…except Miguel appeared once again, peering at him over Antoni's shoulder. "But I overheard Frere Feris just now. Are you in danger?"

"No. My friend is given to histrionics. His order does not cherish him as well as he deserves."

They wound their way up the narrow stairs to the library, which was empty save for Yusuf and Qasim, and not much warmer than the icy streets below. The north wall had a window, its shutters open to allow the afternoon light into the room.

"Uncle, you've come!" Yusuf embraced him.

"I said I would."

"He has never failed us." Qasim then caught sight of Sanço and motioned him to his side, ruffling the boy's filthy hair. Sanço stuck to Qasim's thigh, looking up with smiling eyes, like a dog seeking comfort from his master.

"Don't compare boys to dogs." Miquel growled his criticism when he appeared yet again by Chrétien's shoulder. "You're jealous."

Chrétien shook his head, denying it, not wanting to speak to a ghost. It was only a headache that came from protecting his orphan against stoning.

Miquel snorted. "That young man gives the lost lad more comfort than you do. The boy is clinging to his leg the way you used to do when I dragged you into strange places."

Yusuf had turned his attention to Magister Antoni. "Brother Feris was here, seeking you. He says all the lecturers are to be examined and—"

"I met him on the street." Antoni glanced about the room. "You mustn't let it worry you. We have a plan. And these books are too precious for us to sacrifice them out of fear for our personal safety. Don't you agree?"

Yusuf adopted his best sage expression, nodding in agreement. Chrétien, however, wanted to assert that perhaps Yusuf's father would not agree to his son laying down his life for a pile of parchment. Before Chrétien could determine how to voice that idea, Antoni turned to him, his eyes warm and smiling.

"Your father would be proud to see you rescuing our books. It's the same self-sacrifice he showed when he smuggled Comte Raymond's family to safety when Saladin threatened Tiberius."

"Not the same." Miquel spoke in Cyprian-accented Catalan. "Plus, the family ended up in Acre, which Saladin captured later. But it is the same kind of smooth-talking heroics that Ricart el Lleó de Cor used to take possession of Cyprus."

"We have to move the books tonight, don't we?" Yusuf was agitated, his usual laconic movements exchanged for wringing his hands, lifting his shoulder.

"Yes, tonight." Antoni answered Yusuf, oblivious to Chrétien's struggle with a ghost. "But we needn't despair. I expected this. There's a merchant train in town. My countrymen. They'll help us if we deliver the books to them. Two of my students are helping at the Science and Medicine schools. How have you fared?"

"We removed the texts that need protection from the Astrology and Mathematics library," Yusuf said. "We hid them in our landlady's cellar."

"Good work," Antoni said. "But the safest way is to let my countrymen take them out of the city. Have you identified what needs protection here?"

"There's a thread tied to the chains for the ones I've identified," Yusuf said. "Do you want to look? Perhaps find more?"

Antoni examined the shelves of books, each attached to its shelf with a long chain. "That shelf matters to you." He pointed to an upper shelf, glancing at Chrétien. "That's where I found the troubadours' songs about your father's adventures."

"Truly?" Yusuf answered, excited. "Songs about Miquel?"

"Some rogue wrote down those lies?" Miquel stood near Qasim, who had folded his arms as if he were less comfortable here in the realm where Yusuf the scholar reigned.

"Yes," Antoni said. "Once you get these books out of the library, my countrymen will help bear them away."

"Magister, you are in danger, too," Yusuf said. "Are you leaving with the texts tomorrow?"

"I shall be safe." Antoni had his hand on Yusuf's arm, offering reassurance, but in a way that seemed to annoy Qasim, who moved toward them as if to interfere. But then, it bothered Chrétien too, because, as the uncle, he was responsible for protecting Yusuf and Qasim. Magister Antoni pulled his cloak closed. "I have to say adieu while I attend to my own texts. I'll find you later."

After Antoni left, his steps echoing down the stairs and the outer door closing behind him, Sanço once more fell on his knees, clinging to Qasim. "O good lord! We must go home to save our people! You cannot trust pirates."

"Never worry, *fadrin*—"

Before Qasim could finish his reassurance, Chrétien lifted the boy by the back of his jerkin, letting him dangle for a moment.

"You will sit quietly here, unless Qasim has an errand for you. No more tales. No more begging."

Chrétien pointed to a bench, and Sanço complied, his head bent, though it was still possible that Sanço mouthed silent complaints. Miquel sat on a stool beside him, his chin in hand as if pondering a problem, occasionally rubbing the boy's head as if to comfort him, like Qasim did. That sight tugged at Chrétien, because he believed he himself was especially good at calming children. However, he didn't know what to do with such a wild, imaginative boy. It was good that Miquel could offer comfort.

Except Miquel was a ghost, some bad dream that followed Chrétien since that blow to his head.

"With so much animal skin," Chrétien said, "you'd think this place would smell like an abattoir."

"It's all scraped and cured," Yusuf said. "All you smell in a library is dust."

"Where do they write?"

Yusuf pointed to the floor below them. "In another room. This is only for storage and study."

That lone window of sheep's horn allowed daylight, but it seemed that a reader who studied here hung a lantern on one of the wooden poles that ran that length of the room between shelves. The cramped room held three rows of wooden shelves where, apparently, scholars read standing up, pulling books down from the shelves to be read from a slanted table. Each book was affixed in place by a chain that looped through a hole bored in the shelf. Three rows of perhaps twenty books to a shelf, all made up of parchment bound between wooden boards and clamped in leather straps. At a cupboard, its doors thrown open, Yusuf examined stacks of scrolls wound on wooden spindles.

Qasim said, "So, you'll help us?"

"I will help." Chrétien wanted to be hunting Zorzi, to see what connection he might have to Nuño's mysterious assassin—especially to learn who paid him. "But only because your father will be irked if you're burned as a heretic while I'm living in the same city."

"I'm not a heretic." Yusuf said.

"He is, though," Qasim said. "I sit in the lectures with him. Yusuf doesn't believe what those priests teach."

"Heretics think their souls go into dogs or beasts when they die." Yusuf was indignant. "Science cannot even prove to us that we have souls, much less that there is a devil, or one God versus two. Or a full dozen. Hundreds."

"See? Heretic. And also, there is evil," Qasim said, "and devils. Creatures that science hasn't described."

Yusuf didn't answer for a while. Then he muttered, "Not a heretic."

"They like to burn people here," Qasim said. "Didn't you listen in that debate over—"

"No one likes to burn people," Yusuf insisted. "Those priests were putting on a bold front."

"You have a kind soul," Qasim said.

"Science hasn't proved that men have souls and so—"

"*Aiieee*, a pigeon! They carry the souls of good people. The ones we've lost." Sanço drew attention with a shouty whisper, then was down on his knees, crawling under the rows of shelves. Chrétien heard the cooing but didn't see any bird. "It's dragging a bad wing. Poor thing."

Preferring action to discussion, Chrétien said to Yusuf, "Do you want me to break the chains?"

"I found a way to do that in the Mathematics library." Qasim pointed to a pair of thick leather gloves folded over his belt. "It just takes time."

"Our problem here," Yusuf said, "is that we can't remove books from the library without being seen."

Qasim said, "The bound ones are too large to hide under our cloaks. And we have to carry away the scrolled parchments in batches. Which will take all night."

Chrétien checked the room, then peered out the open window. "I think we take the books out this way, along the roof, and then into the alley up the street past the school."

Yusuf came to look out the window, shaking his head with more than doubt. Which meant Chrétien had to prove his idea, because he wasn't about to send either Yusuf or Qasim out the window.

He folded almost in two to climb out when a clang and slap of metal startled him, but it was only Qasim doing his job, breaking a book's chain.

Wishing he had a cat's ability to wiggle through small spaces, he crawled out and then stood cautiously on the ledge that had long ago supported the stoneworkers who built this place. He crept along the ledge, with his one unwrapped hand to steady himself. Any fool on the street below could see him. Too tall, too awkward in boots. And too unsafe for either young man to attempt, since anyone carrying a book would have to leverage his body to swing up onto the roof, while praying the tiles remained in place.

Back inside, Chrétien thudded to the floor.

"Not a solution," he said.

"Too high?" Yusuf was disappointed.

"Too narrow to maneuver. Too steep to balance."

"Too high," Qasim said, "if you don't like breaking your head on the cobbles below."

Yusuf said, "Perhaps, then, a basket and a rope, lowered from the window."

"Where everyone in Montpelhièr can see?" Qasim argued against the idea. "And take the whole night to finish?"

"Then we smuggle out one book at a time," Yusuf said. "Through the front door. The back door opens onto the kitchen of a villa. A dozen people are there day and night."

"Wearing what?" Chrétien challenged. "A giant's smock?"

"You, *gai sauvatge?*" Qasim called Yusuf a wild jay, which seemed to be a nickname. "With a book in your shirt, you'd look like a quarterstaff about to birth twins."

"You, *ma belette muet.*" Yusuf responded with a sobriquet for Qasim: mute weasel. Which left Chrétien unsure whether they traded pet names or insults. "You could assume the disguise of a cooper's barrel. With thighs and boots."

"Magnificent thighs," Qasim said. "You have to admit that."

While Chrétien pondered the most sensible action, he glanced about, sensing something missing.

"Where's Sanço?"

"Right here." Qasim glanced over his shoulder, seeming to have gotten used to being the orphan's anchor.

"He chased that pigeon under the shelves," Yusuf said. "Did it fly out the window, or is it still hopping among the shelves?"

"Forget the pigeon." Chrétien felt his heart beat faster. Miquel was missing too. "Do you suppose he ran away?"

Yusuf and Qasim stared at each other, that Gemini twins' silent exchange. Yusuf spoke first. "No, he won't run away, now that he's found us."

Qasim said, "That boy carries magic we haven't seen before."

15

A Lost Inheritance

"MAGIC?" CHRÉTIEN LAUGHED, SINCE their bantering continued into the absurd. "The magic of how to be smeared with that much dirt and still stand up?"

"No, magic from old times."

"But what is it?" Yusuf was asking Qasim, who remained busy breaking book chains with his gloved hands.

"Perhaps from Persia?" Qasim puzzled, as though he were listening to a voice far down the street.

"Oh," Yusuf said. "Oh no."

The tone and tenor of Yusuf's *Oh no* echoed the pounding of Chrétien's headache, and spawned a greater sense of trepidation in his belly than when he'd seen Feris on the street with the magister.

"Yes. Appears to be true." Easygoing Qasim became more serious than Chrétien had ever seen.

"What does it say?" Yusuf asked.

"It doesn't know. Merely guesses," Qasim said. "Vibrations. A smell. Like old ivory and rotted silk."

"I shan't call on the dancing angels in heaven." Chrétien tapped his foot, impatient, wanting answers about the trepidation and hesitation that seemed to embrace all three of them. "I will call on the ghost of my father to remove you to the outer districts of hell. What are you talking about?"

Again, Qasim spread his empty hands, which must indicate that he didn't know. No, it proved to be something different. "Yusuf, you know I can't say. If you want Chrétien to know, it's up to you."

"I haven't even told my father," Yusuf said. "Numa believes it might hurt his feelings."

God's own judgment might conceivably hurt his brother Tomás's feelings, but Chrétien couldn't name anything else on this green earth that might. "Should I promise not to tell your father? I didn't tell him about the time—"

"That was Numa's worry," Yusuf said. "I only worry that it might cause my father to see ghosts again."

"I'm losing patience." Chrétien only then remembered Tomás's claim to have seen Miquel's ghost in Andalusia. "Did you inherit your father's predilection for entering into danger without warning your friends?"

As if preparing for an examination, Yusuf began pacing. Chrétien again marveled how much Yusuf resembled his father, so handsome, like Tomás before he was attacked and battered. "We all know that my great-great-grandfather came to Iberia from Morocco as a mercenary and then settled in Morella."

"Yes," Chrétien said. "We know from my father's tales." He glanced around, to see if his ghost remained close by, but there wasn't even a flicker.

Yusuf said, "Miquel inherited a—an—a guardian spirit. Like the ones that old women keep to guard their chickens from foxes."

"Ow!" Qasim startled, as if he'd been bit by something nasty. "Be kind, Yusuf."

Yusuf nodded with a seriousness that sent a jolt of foreboding through Chrétien's veins. "His guardian spirit went to Numa when Miguel died, because she was the only one there with him."

"You mean, when Tomás and I missed…" Chrétien couldn't make his throat and tongue form words. Yusuf might as well have taken his dinner knife and plunged it into Chrétien's heart. When Miquel died, the same night Tomás was attacked by his enemy, Chrétien lay in the arms of a one-night encounter. He missed his father's passing, missed his last words, and almost failed to rescue his brother. If he properly grasped what Yusuf was saying, both Tomás and Chrétien had missed receiving Miquel's guardian spirit.

His heart beat as poorly as that day when Numa claimed God had taken Miquel, but his heart knew that the old man was just plain lost to him.

"Not lost." Miquel murmured from behind Chrétien. "Other business called me."

"Yes, uncle," Yusuf said. "You had the good fortune not to be pecked mercilessly by an ancient creature who claims it has free will, but then plagues us against our own will. Who thinks it knows more than the prophets, but never has one useful thing to say."

"*Aiieee!*" Qasim stepped back from the bench where he was working, like a man who'd been struck across the face. "Stop insulting your qareen!"

Yusuf folded his arms. "You see, uncle, I received the guardian from *Aviá* Numa. I didn't get along well with it, so Qasim coaxed it into living on his shoulder. But that means the two of us cannot be parted. The qareen keeps Qasim at my side, to guard me."

"Not that I object," Qasim said. "I was already Yusuf's sworn comrade. So, it's just…a slight inconvenience." He winced, apparently once more punished by—what?

"Let me understand," Chrétien said. "You two—one more educated than most men on this earth, the other with more common sense than God usually gives men—are possessed of an invisible magical creature?"

"Yes," Qasim nodded vigorously. "That's it. Thank you for believing us."

Chrétien didn't know what to believe. "Why?"

Yusuf said, "It isn't magic. It's the enslaved servant of an ancient fire lord, consigned to protect me, as Miquel's heir."

"Ow!" Qasim cried again. "Stop it, Yusuf. Our protector insists it has free will. Please lend a little respect."

Yusuf opened his palms, as if helpless to comply.

"*Qui s'ho creu?*" Chrétien muttered it three times. *Who'd believe it?* But then again, his father had been muttering in his ear all day. Why not believe it? "Why don't you use your creature's magic to save your books?"

"The creature can't do magic," Yusuf said. "It only offers unreliable advice."

"And that's why we asked your help," Qasim said. "Our qareen says we need you."

"We're not sure why," Yusuf said. "But we've learned to listen, because the little bastard beast's cautions are sometimes useful."

"*Yeow!*" Qasim leaped from the bench again, waving his arm as if bitten by a dog or pecked by crows.

"It seems," Yusuf said calmly, "that the qareen has free will, but the rest of us aren't free to abandon or ignore it."

Chrétien could see both boys believed they were being controlled by an invisible— "What's it called?"

"A qareen," Yusuf said. "From ancient Persia. It has a name, but I'm sorry, we can't tell you its name."

"You could only know if you'd inherited Miquel's guardian," Qasim said.

"If you ever pray, uncle," Yusuf said, "you should thank God you aren't plagued with an ignorant and elderly guardian creature."

"Ow!" Qasim jigged in pain, then slapped Yusuf's shoulder in a less than friendly way. "Stop with the insults."

The door slammed open, startling all three of them, then slammed closed.

"I found a way out!" Sanço cried. "But it's skinny as a chimney."

"Where does it go?" Yusuf asked, abandoning the discussion of magical creatures to give full attention to Sanço.

"To a deserted stable, two houses over. It's as old as any casa you ever saw, falling to ruin." Sanço led Qasim over to inspect what he'd found behind the last shelf, which seemed to be a board serving as a flimsy door that creaked open to reveal the space between this building and its neighbor, with ladder pegs leading down. No one thicker than Sanço could move through that chimney.

Sanço tugged at Qasim's sleeve. "I shall help you, my lord! Then you will all be free to rescue my village."

Qasim had his hand on Sanço's head, praising him in Catalan for what he'd found. He asked, "Where is your village, young friend?"

"Morella," Sanço said. "Beyond the Aragón frontier, on the road to Valencia."

·

"So, we have to go to Morella," Miquel said. "And bring an army."

Chrétien had the job of receiving and stashing books after Sanço brought them down into the decrepit stable. It allowed plenty of time to ponder magical creatures and ghosts, and to ponder how he'd accidentally found an orphan and then a ghost who called on his filial duty. If only his brother Tomás were here to consult, Chrétien might know what to decide, instead of pondering unanswerable questions. Tomás was the current lord of Morella, and Yusuf was his heir, but none of them had ever visited the place.

He forced his thoughts to Nuño's challenge, to make the city safe, especially since down the alley to the street, bands of five or six or seven men passed every few heartbeats. Like clouds gathering for a storm.

"I'm here to protect Yusuf. And to serve Comte Nuño. I can't leave until the city is safe." Chrétien needed to finish helping Yusuf, so he could go patrol the streets in search of the so-called magical assassin, to learn who was plotting chaos for Montpelhièr. To protect the seigneurs who were coming to the prelate's council. Seigneurs like Durán, who should have known better and stayed home. Yet all Chrétien had done so far was rile several neighborhoods against him. "It's my duty as a *bonfraire*."

"But this is for family," Miquel said, "which is a greater duty."

"I'm stealing these books for family." Chrétien stashed another book behind what had been a cow's stanchion decades earlier. "I'm protecting Yusuf and saving troubadour songs about the great crusader Miquel de Cyprus y Morella."

"See?" Miquel prompted. "Our family has a duty to Morella. It's my father's and grandfathers' home."

"Yet you didn't choose to stay and protect it. Right now, I must protect Yusuf and Qasim, and help stop the plot against Nuño and the seigneurs. Then we can think about Morella." All of what he was doing for Nuño was about protecting family. (He resisted once more seeing that branded image of Durán and Numa before the flames.)

"That fierce lad must be a cousin of mine. Perhaps second or third degree." Miquel ticked ideas on his fingers as if calculating. "Family comes first."

"Why don't you help Yusuf and Qasim, then? They have your— what is it, a careening?"

"Qareen," Miquel said. "Yusuf is right. It's a nasty pest. He and his *bon amic* are both braver than me. Took dying for me to finally be rid of that nuisance."

"You could have waited."

"For what?"

"For me to be there that day when you left us!" Chrétien said it aloud, too loud, voice raspy with long pent up anger at the loss of his father.

"Senhór Chrétien?" A voice called from the alley. It was Magister Antoni.

Who appeared at the falling-down archway and stepped over the broken stones and timbers. Two men followed him, bearing a large box carried on a pole between them.

"I've brought my countrymen to bear away these books."

It took only a few words before the two men began loading their box with the books stacked behind the manger. The box proved to be a child-size coffin.

"No one will question them carrying a burden through the streets," Antoni said.

"Remind me again why we are doing this," Chrétien said. "I hear Yusuf's passion. And yours. But then I think, what are grown men doing, hiding books?"

"Because," Antoni shared his warm, sweet smile, "what will we have if physicians are forced to teach only what is already known, and only from a narrow philosophy?"

"I'm sure you will tell me."

"We will continue to have people who die young or who endure lives of hideous pain." Antoni spoke with as much passion as Chrétien had ever heard from the magister. "We shall continue unnecessary catastrophes. Babies born wrong who cannot be set right. Mothers who die giving life. Children who die no matter what incantation their mothers attempt."

"You are even more passionate and articulate than Yusuf," Chrétien said. "Which I hadn't believed possible."

"Thank you for your help, my friend. Now, what I see is a patient who has exerted himself far more than his physician cautioned. When you finish here, I must beg you to come home with me. It's only two streets over. You need a restorative. You look like you've been deliberating with ghosts."

Ignoring Antoni, Miquel breathed down Chrétien's neck, a resentful huff. "I needed to be with your brother that day. He'd have died too if I wasn't there to hold up his courage. Took you forever to show up."

"I have other chores, magister." Chrétien shifted to another foot, deciding how much he trusted Antoni, judging whether this was another flirtation.

"I understand," Antoni said. "But you want this hand to heal faster than nature can do. Let me help you."

Antoni offered the impossible, and Chrétien did want it. He needed that hand to fight the growing unrest in the city. To find the assassin and his paymaster. To play his lute, should he ever have a peaceful evening again.

A voice called, "This is the last one, my captain!"

Sanço jumped down from that narrow chute into the stable. He skittered at the sight of Antoni and his two companions. Chrétien tugged the boy close, unbuckling the belt that trapped the last board-bound book close to Sanço's thin chest.

"Fine work, *fadrin*. I want you to go with Yusuf and Qasim to my room in Nuño's villa. Now, quickly, before it's dark. Take the alleys. Stay out of the squares and thoroughfares. Can you repeat that to them?"

"Oh, yes, my captain. But where will you be?"

"Magister Antoni asked me to come to his house for a physic. I'll join you soon."

Sanço shuddered under Chrétien's hand. He pulled Chrétien down to whisper in his ear. "Be careful, my captain! Don't let him poison you." Sanço straightened and said aloud, "When do we eat?"

"Yusuf knows how to beg the cook at the villa for dinner. I want all three of you to remain there until I come."

When Sanço was gone, and after Antoni instructed the men where to carry the book-coffin, he joined Chrétien, holding Chrétien's elbow to lead him through alleys to his household. It wasn't as if Chrétien needed to be guided, more that Antoni liked the close contact.

"What did your orphan whisper?" Antoni asked.

"That I shouldn't trust you."

"Do you? Or do you not?" Antoni sounded amused, rather than offended.

"You had my life in your hand at the hospital, magister. If you meant me harm, you could have succeeded easily before now."

"Then you do trust me?" Antoni now sounded gleeful. "It's been my desire that we be friends since I first saw you sing in a tavern." He changed topics. "Weren't you taking that passionate, untrusting child to work at a hostel?"

"We had bad directions." Chrétien wanted his curiosity satisfied. "A priest in the street called the lad possessed. Even my friend Qasim says the boy carries some kind of magic. Do you sense it?"

"Most emphatically, no." Antoni tightened his grip on Chrétien's arm for a heartbeat. "At one time in my training, we studied possession. There isn't a whiff of the Evil One about that boy. Scabies and fleas, most certainly. I prescribe a bath. And a special calendula balm that I can give you."

"Why did you say that I look like I'd been talking to ghosts, magister?"

"It was only a manner of speaking. You have the pale look of a man who's lost blood and needs a hearty broth to restore him." Antoni stopped on the street to study Chrétien in the afternoon's fading light. "You don't believe in ghosts, do you? Are you hearing voices after that knock on the head?"

"Only a ringing in my ears."

"Ah, my friend. What you need most is a long night's sleep."

"Don't have time for that," Chrétien said. "Do you have a restorative you can pour into my blood? The opposite of bleeding?"

Antoni laughed. "Our science hasn't taken us that far. Perhaps one day our children's children will learn that secret."

"Men like you and me won't have children. We're lucky to have had fathers." The words tumbled out, leaving Chrétien confused about what he'd said and why. That perpetual headache.

He glanced around to make sure where he was. A square not far from the school of Literature and Music, where two streets crossed and four alleys opened onto the cobbles and the local well.

"Men like you and me." Antoni was laughing at Chrétien's words. "Other men's curious sons will take up our work when you and I quit the world." He paused before a low cypress door that opened out to the street, rapping on it with his staff. "I was about to say that 'a son's duty to his father' isn't a command from heaven. But I don't have that experience. There must be a special kind of filial duty that comes to a man who has a hero like Miquel of Morella for his father."

Far too tall, Chrétien had to duck to enter behind Antoni when the door was opened from inside. He stepped down one stone step into another world.

Order of the Flaming Cross

From the Secret History of the Flaming Cross
— Andonis de Zêna

You should know better what transpired in my family. On Sardinia, my father declared me, his oldest child, to be a genius. My uncle Zorzi declared I could contribute best to the family if I had a proper education and the kind of manners learned in Genoa. Some people say that our class of merchant-rulers have manners they call patrician. However, it's merely the way I was taught—how worthy people behave once they leave the wild state of childhood. Zorzi disapproved of my mother and her family, natives of Sardinia, whom he claimed were more than half Saracen. If I remained under her family's influence, Uncle Zorzi insisted, their dark Saracen blood would pollute my mind and my soul.

When I left Sardinia, my uncle Zorzi the Elder first took me to his villa, believing I was yet too young for the monastery, and also intrigued by the strange events of our voyage, when I healed him with my touch. However, after I'd spent two months at his villa in Genoa, his wife, mother, and grandmother all complained that I stared, I pried, I asked too many curious questions. What finally dispatched me to the monastery was Zorzi's female relatives' complaint that my weird eyes unnerved them. I'm still hurt when I remember that condemnation. As a doctor, I've many times experienced that patients are made brave and enter into healing with me if I can look into their eyes and capture their gaze. And anyway, I must forgive those women, for they are now all in God's hands and no longer walk this earth.

The Flaming Cross monastery was always my destiny. Our family has sponsored that house for two hundred years. There's seldom more than twenty-five devotional monks, but a hundred lay brothers farm the land and tend the holding. In my extended family, the older sons, middle sons, younger sons—all have gone there for a few years' schooling and polish before joining the family business.

It shouldn't matter to you, but the Order of the Flaming Cross is as independent as Genoa itself is from Roman-dictated policy and politics. Our order is as old as any Christian order, whether in Byzantium, Liguria, or Septimània. The legend, written seven hundred years ago, is that our order represents the first monastic impulse of Christian Visigoths who passed our lands on the way to conquer Iberia.

As Abbot Rodolfo taught, we are free men, free to follow our hearts wherever our experiences of the wonder of God's creation leads us. In addition to training lords' sons, the order has provided a free-footed bishop for every adventure that Genoa's ships and privateers have undertaken.

‡

Cançons de Montpelhièr

'My dearest troubadour,
I do not like you hiding in the cloister,
Or quarreling with your neighbors.
Rather, sing songs of love and mirth.
All the world is the better for that.'

'Lord, may I sing of my love for you?
Is it a sin if my song admires you and your love?
If so, I shall give up all song
And seek a monk's life.
What is the value of love
If I cannot confess it?'

16
Harmonics

CHRÉTIEN HAD SPENT A NIGHT once in the king of Cyprus's bed-
room (a tale best forgotten). He slept for a week in the Count of Foix's
villa in Urgell, and also in the viscount of Narbonne's city compound.
He'd dined in the royal *domus* of the kings of Aragón in Lleida and
in the villas of the richest merchants in Toulouse.

None of that compared to the warmth and exquisite beauty of
the room where Antoni led him. Jewel-tone tapestries covered every
wall. Thicker carpets hung over the shuttered lattice windows,
blocking the cold. A fire burned in a stone fireplace, but this wasn't
a kitchen. It burned solely for the comfort of anyone in this room,
the shadows of the flickering flames dancing in the ceiling, where
the thick beams supporting the upper floor hung a mere two hands'
breadths above Chrétien's head. A cozy cave, with tapestry-covered
chairs around a few tables, as if a small host often gathered in the
room. The room was redolent of spices. Cinnamon and saffron
clung to the folds of tapestries and carpets.

Instead of choosing a table, Antoni gestured to an arrangement
of cushions and thickly upholstered pallets scattered over piles of
carpets that blocked the cold from the brightly tiled floor. When
Chrétien sat as instructed, the pallets proved to be stuffed with
wool, not straw.

"Rest a moment, my friend, while we prepare the appropriate
restorative for you."

Antoni went to an archway to give instructions to a young man
in a tongue that seemed as if it should be familiar, but Chrétien
couldn't place it. He leaned back into the cushions, wrestling with
an animal desire to sink into comfort versus intense curiosity about
how a physician came to live in such grandeur.

When Antoni settled amid the cushions, Chrétien said, "You live well for a teaching physician who heals paupers without a fee."

"None of this belongs to me."

The young man appeared, and Antoni greeted him with a warm smile and repeatedly thanked him. A tray was settled in beside Chrétien, with a pot of hot water, a mug, a small bread trencher stacked with slices of chicken and mutton.

"Thank you, Elias. Can you please also bring a basin of hot water, and then after a bit, some heated wine? It's kind of you to aid my patient."

When Elias left them, Antoni said, "This villa belongs to my countrymen. They're traders from Genoa, where I spent my youth. In my order, we are not allowed to own worldly things, so I rely on the graciousness of my countrymen."

"Physicians have mendicant orders? I thought only priests undertook vows of poverty—and not many of them."

"I'm also a priest. A wandering bishop in my order."

"But priests in orders can't be physicians. Or do I not understand those rules?" A wandering bishop? Was Antoni a heretic as well? How did Chrétien keep stumbling into such associations?

Antoni said, "Only clerics in orders recognized by the Roman Church are prohibited. My brotherhood isn't restricted in that way. My order has preserved traditions older than the last few generations of power-mad popes." He paused. "While I treat paupers found on the street, Cistercians in Provençal monasteries have adopted blood-letting to treat carnal notions."

"Do I hear a note of censure in your voice, magister?"

"Some of us have differing opinions about the most important ways to help people."

"Why call yourself a wandering bishop? Isn't that an insult priests hurl at heretics?"

"Eat. You need the blessings of good food." While Chrétien followed Antoni's instruction, devouring the meat slices and bread, Antoni said, "I'm not a heretic, if that's what you're asking. I believe there is only one God. However, my order respects a line of bishops that extends back over hundreds of years. I was consecrated by my bishop, and wherever I travel, I find men like those in this house, who commune together because they were born into the same tradition as me."

"But Christian?" The answer to that question didn't matter so much to Chrétien, except he always liked to know which faction of heresy he might be involved with. If anything, he preferred the starkness of Durán's heresy: live simply, pray to God without priests, be kind to each other. "And choosing to live in poverty." He indicated the magnificent room with his injured hand.

"Like you," Antoni said, "I accept whatever housing the people I serve provide for me. Will you allow me to ask you an impertinent question?"

"You've been gracious to answer so many of mine."

"How can Miquel of Cyprus possibly be your real father? Or Yusuf your nephew? I don't want to offend you, but you are as pale as your linen bandages. Where do they breed men like you along the Great Sea?"

Chrétien wasn't offended. "A man isn't a father just because he planted a child in a woman's belly. That's a fool's notion. It isn't shared blood that makes a family."

"What binds a family then?"

"Promises and oaths," Chrétien said. "I never knew what man sired me or what woman birthed me. I don't know if they created brothers and sisters after they abandoned me. I have no children, no uncles, no aunts."

"How sad. No cousins? Mine are as close to me as brothers."

"I have all my sworn brothers-in-arms, including my milk-brother Tomás. I'd never desert my brothers, even if it meant my life. And they'd never desert me. We've sworn bonds that can't be cut by steel."

"How can you keep such promises?"

Chrétien considered that. "I'm competent and quick-witted. Which I learned from my father."

Antoni pursed his lips as he poured a concoction into a mug, but he did not pursue his question further. He said, "Let's return you to being the healthy warrior you were when you rose this morning. I found this tisane in a book of battlefield medicine, written by Greeks from a much earlier age. Your strength lies in your muscles and blood. Your muscles suffered only a bruising, so it's your blood we need to fortify."

He examined the cuts on Chrétien's forehead, seeming satisfied with what he found there. The cuts did not sting as Antoni dabbed at it with a warm, wet cloth. Antoni's dabbing at the one behind his ear felt too intimate.

"I need battlefield medicine?" Chrétien hoped he could still laugh at himself. He sipped the tea, which tasted like iron filings and bitter weeds. "The famous battle of St-Lazarus Square, where the crusaders took enormous casualties and gave up all territory to miniature warriors with stones?"

"But, to your father's glory, you retained the noble mission of saving orphans. I'm happy to see that these cuts on your head no longer need bandages."

Antoni motioned for Chrétien to offer his injured hand, and then carefully unwrapped the layers of linen, which had grown grey and muddy through the afternoon's adventures. At last Antoni revealed Chrétien's palm, with the raw, red wheal running down, crossed by fine silk stitches. Antoni smiled, seeming satisfied.

"It's doing quite well."

Chrétien looked away, changed the subject. "My orphan boy claims you smell like a pirate. Why is that, do you think?"

Antoni remained absorbed in examining Chrétien's hand. "If he thinks he's met pirates, it's more likely privateers, like the lords of Malta and Sicily employ. So, it's the spices he smells. Don't you smell it here? If there's a heaven, it surely smells as wonderful as a Genoese merchant's villa."

Elias appeared, carrying a basin of hot water and a tray with an urn and linen bandages. "And the heated wine, Magister? Is now a good time?"

"Yes, you came at the right moment."

After Elias returned with another urn, Antoni washed Chrétien's hand and dowsed it with wine that was almost too hot to bear. Instead of wrapping the wounded hand again, Antoni held it in his hands and began to sing the way he had when demonstrating field medicine to students at the Hospital of the Holy Spirit. Once again, the song dragged Chrétien toward the world of dreams, but this time he fought the descent of the veil that clouded his thoughts.

"Which is this trick, Magister? I can sing any man into tears or bursting with laughter. But you sing to move me to another world. Is it magic?"

"Not magic. Only a healing technique I learned when traveling among the Bogomils in Dalmatia. The unity of your soul, your mind, your body—that's God's miracle. I sing your body into harmony so it can heal itself. We're merely borrowing a few notes from the harmony of the spheres."

While Magister Antoni massaged Chrétien's hand, he hummed. Chrétien fought the desire to sink into the soft cushions, pull one of the colorful carpets over him, and sleep.

The fellow had a way of touching that in days long past had led Chrétien into the kind of dubious decisions that brought ridicule from his brother Tomás. He withdrew his hand from the magister's beguiling touch, since he was no longer enticed by other men's captivating ways.

"I love someone," Chrétien said, "and I am loved in return."

"That's obvious," Antoni said. "Any man can see it in how you move through the world. How you examine each man you meet. You wear another man's love like armor."

He retrieved Chrétien's hand and resumed massaging it. "All my work, all my studies have been to understand the power of natural things. From the purely mechanical, such as the best filament to use in surgery. Or the proper charms to restore health." Antoni walked three fingers up and down Chrétien's palm, which tickled. "The principles for collecting and compounding effective medicines are all about nature, not magic. I've learned when to gather herbs, which requires knowledge of the time of the moon and other astro-logical conditions, not hedge-witch magic."

"Magister, there's a man in the taverns whom they say cuts his hand. And then heals it, like magic. Is that magic?"

"I don't think so. Perhaps the man learned what I did from the Bogomils of Dalmatia."

This tickled something at the back of Chrétien's mind about Zorzi the recruiter. He almost asked Antoni: *Is that you healing in the taverns?* But Chrétien knew there was no magic. Yusuf had explained that the ancient creature Qasim carried was incapable of magic. And Antoni's answer satisfied Chrétien's curiosity—his healing came from science, not magic. And the man described by every hostler he talked with matched Zorzi, not the well-mannered magister.

Antoni again hummed while he stroked Chrétien's hand.

"Magister, is your music part of the power of natural things that you describe?"

"Yes. What besides music more strongly ties the body, the soul, and the mind together?"

"Casting a spell?"

"What superstitious people call spells are medical use of invocations, calling the mind and the soul to help the body." He released Chrétien's hand.

Chrétien studied the mess that was his left palm. Yet after the washing and Antoni's massage, it seemed not so angry, not so raw. Still, he wanted only to curl up and sleep. He shivered to keep awake.

"Are you chilled?" Antoni swept his hands over Chrétien's forehead, cheeks, and neck in the way that physicians check for a fever.

"No, I—"

The magister kissed him. First, lightly. Then deeply, like a lover feeling passion and seeking to spur it with his tongue. The potion seemed to course through Chrétien's veins at the same moment. His head no longer ached. He felt as if he'd inhaled a glorious spring day. His ears still hummed with Antoni's song. And he enjoyed that kiss far too much.

Chrétien pulled away, as if he were again a naïve young thing getting in over his head. "I have a love. I want nothing more."

"Of course. But do you have room for another brother, who'd swear to protect you with his life?"

When Chrétien didn't answer, Antoni released him and then urged him to his feet. "Come along, my friend. I have another duty. Come watch. Learn a few notes from the harmony of the spheres."

•

Chrétien and Antoni descended further into the house, down into what must have been a stable when Montpelhièr first came to be, but now was whitewashed and brightly lit by branched candle-holders hanging from the wall, burning what Chrétien guessed must be costly beeswax candles, from the scent in the room. Beeswax and frankincense.

A collection of men also descended into the room, mostly in silence, with a few who murmured brief greetings to each other.

Antoni said, "These are the drovers and guards of a merchant train leaving at dawn for Marseille."

"The escort for your saved books?"

"They have promised that kindness amid their other work. It's a custom in every villa like this to bless our countrymen before a journey. Are you well enough to stand for some moments?"

"I'm not ill at all."

"Of course you aren't."

Antoni continued to the end of the barrel-vaulted room and stood beside what must pass for an altar, though it appeared to be only a carved wood chest. Candlelight sparkled off what might be ivory or pearlescent shells. Or polished bone. The room had no crosses on the wall or carved statues or any other sign that it was used for worship, as if the chest could be lifted on poles and borne away, with nothing left behind.

The vaulted ceiling did serve as an excellent space for sound. First, the shuffling of leather boots on swept stone. Then silence when Antoni raised his hand in blessing, prolonged for so long that the silence seemed to have a pulse of its own. Then the silence broke, like the surface of a pool when a pebble is tossed. Antoni began to chant the common mass in Latin. The men chanted in response, as if they'd been trained to harmonize, like monks in a choir. Chrétien murmured the responses quietly as he always did, only to demonstrate that he belonged among Christians. Yet he was an outsider here. The mass concluded quickly enough (though never fast enough to suit Chrétien's impatience with ritual). He stirred to leave. But everyone remained in place.

A voice in the back sang a line of song. Chrétien couldn't see who sang. It was an adolescent boy or a eunuch with a clear, piercing pitch that sent chills down Chrétien's spine. Before Chrétien finished shivering, Antoni echoed the same line of song in his melodic tenor voice, in a tongue that Chrétien couldn't immediately identify, but guessed might be Greek.

The men in the room answered by repeating the words—or sounds—in harmony. Some sang close to the adolescent register that began the chant. Others repeated a single note in harmony with each other. A few deep voices set a kind of drone, like a bagpipe turned human.

When Antoni sang a line of song, each man took a half step to the right and put a hand on the shoulder of the man next to him. Chrétien was pulled into the moving mass. At each new line of the song, the men moved a half step, pulling Chrétien deeper into the huddle of singing men.

Antoni sang another line, warmer than the original soprano, but as chilling. The men in the room repeated the line in harmony. And then again. The notes rippled through Chrétien. He joined in, not knowing what words they sang, though he perfectly replicated the notes.

When he closed his eyes, it seemed as if the candlelight flickered blue. If he concentrated on the sound rising inside him, it grew from his chest, blooming from heart and lungs, more than just his throat.

How long they chanted, Chrétien could no longer say, but while the deeper voices continued to drone, the singers in harmony shifted to an interlaced repetition of alleluia and amen.

Then the pulsating silence again, until the men moved out of the communal embrace, said farewells, and shuffled up the steps.

Chrétien approached Antoni, wanting to express his appreciation for having been invited into that choir. But another man got there first, pulling Antoni into a whispered exchange. Antoni appeared to be arguing at first, then nodding his agreement. Watching the conversation, Chrétien reflected on this visit to Antoni's house, and found that he admired the man. In fact, after two sessions being the recipient of Antoni's expertise, the past day's adventures had led to brotherly feelings that Chrétien didn't expect. At last Antoni and that man finished their conversation, shaking hands.

Once alone, Antoni scanned the room, smiling when he saw Chrétien waiting for him.

"He's a charming fellow," Miquel said. "Handsome. And he's so in love with you."

"We're both too old for that. He's no mooncalf."

Antoni came to Chrétien, again grasping his elbow while he led him up the stone steps and into that cozy great room. "The merchant train carrying those books to safety is leaving tomorrow, a day earlier than planned. My countrymen's usual guards will meet them on the road tomorrow morning." Antoni let go of Chrétien's elbow, his hand running down to caress Chrétien's hand. "The merchants' drovers are armed, but they aren't trained men of steel. They don't know knights in the city and haven't been able to find mercenaries to hire. They need help out the gate and down the road."

"Are you asking me to help?"

"You may be the only person who can make sure our books depart on their path to safety. Can I beg you to ride with the drovers out the city gates until they meet their usual guards? They leave at dawn, so you'll be back in the city before the sext bell."

"I have other chores." Chrétien didn't want to appear to hesitate but didn't feel that his time was his own to commit. "I helped Yusuf with his concerns, but I have no reason to…"

"Dear, brilliant Yusuf," Antoni dipped his head, shaking it, "put his own name as the author of his books on astrology. Then added all the names of scholars among the Moors and Arabs. If the wagons are stopped at the gate, and Yusuf's books are found…"

Chrétien hesitated. The frankincense and candle odors filled his chest like a solid substance. "If Comte Nuño agrees to my absence in the morning, then yes, I shall help you."

Yes, he'd help get the wagons through the gate. It wasn't only honor or oaths to his brotherhood. Yusuf was Tomás's son. Of course, Chrétien would do whatever it took to protect him.

17
Snow

WHEN CHRÉTIEN EMERGED FROM Antoni's villa with the magister's potions in a bag tied to his belt, the sun had dipped below the western horizon and a light snow fell, illuminated by the lantern beside the villa door. His nose burned from the cold, but his headache was gone (and so was Miquel). His hand no longer throbbed. Better still, whether from the singing or Antoni's potion, a sense of well-being heated his belly, like after a night of good company, the best luck at dice, hot spiced wine, and the certainty that Durán had already warmed the bed.

> My love holds me in his power.
> His pleasure tastes so sweet.

Torches and lanterns burned near the heavy doors of the other villas around the square, casting twisted shadows onto the cobbles and the neighborhood well across the square. While Chrétien set his mind onto the next thing he needed to do (return to help foil the plot against Nuño and the southern seigneurs), the distinctive sound of men marching carried up from the school of Science and Medicine. A woman's cries echoed up the street over the sound of boots on cobbles.

"Mercy! I beg you."

A passel of soldiers entered the square, French in the style of the army that supported Simon de Montfort, with half a dozen men in chainmail and helmets at the fore and another half dozen behind. In the midst of the French soldiers, two men in physicians' robes walked, their hands bound in front of them.

It was Magister Lucas and Magister Jacobus, Antoni's friends from the Science and Medicine school. Magister Lucas raised his hands, coughing so hard that he stumbled amid the soldiers. A priest walking behind him poked the stumbling physician.

When they entered the square, two soldiers in the rear stepped back to bar the way, keeping the crying woman from following the soldiers and their prisoners. After the men had passed, heading toward the prelate's villa, Chrétien crossed to the weeping woman.

"Senhóra, what has happened? What can I do for you?"

"Do? There's nothing to do." She was small and pale, and spoke with a French accent, like Magister Jacobus had. Snow was sticking to her black veil. Her voice rose, then fell into tears again. "The Church has them."

"But they are magisters at the school. It must be a mistake."

"No. A priest came to inspect the library, and my husband, the fool, chained the door. He and Magister Lucas refused to allow the priest to enter. A matter of principle, they said, because the old count had promised the schools complete freedom."

"Oh no, ma dòmna." His mind flew to Yusuf and Qasim. Did they go to Nuño's villa as he instructed, or were they still in the Literature and Music library? Had this danger touched them?

Her voice breaking, Senhóra Jacobus said, "The priest warned that he'd bring men tomorrow to break the chains and open door. When the magisters cried out in protest, they were taken. What shall be done?"

"Perhaps Comte Nuño can help." Chrétien wrestled with the sense of dismay and powerlessness welling in his belly. Hearing again what Nuño had said—"These people cannot fight back"—Chrétien felt compelled to help this woman, because the Church was dragging scholars before the bishop. Not only did he have to save his willful nephew and the kindly Antoni, but this was certainly part of the chaos that Nuño insisted was coming. "Please let me seek the count's help for your husband and the other magister."

"But why would you help us? I don't know you."

"I met your husband today. I know his interests as a magister and a physician." He wasn't making a new promise to this stranger, only another piece to helping Nuño return Montpelhièr to peace.

The woman was in the middle of an embarrassing profusion of gratitude, given that Chrétien had yet to act for her, when cries rose from the other streets that led into the square.

Hurriedly, he said, "Go home, senhóra. Bar your door and remember that Comte Nuño wants everyone in the city to be safe."

Clashing sounds and shouts reached the neighborhood square before people appeared. Chrétien pointed the woman back up the street from which she'd come, waving her away. His hand fell to the pommel of his sword. But the cold steel was not reassuring. Without chainmail or a helmet or a shield, he might as well be walking naked into conflict.

Out of four of the streets, masses of men appeared.

"*Aiieee!*" Senhóra Jacobus choked on her cry of surprise. She turned and fled, back up the street toward the school.

From the north, the men emerged into the square, white linen hiding their faces, like the men who'd threatened him on the street earlier over that foul monk. The linen shrouds did not muffle their chants. "Our land, our ways." Repeated, in the local tongue. The men at the front carried cudgels and pitchforks. But no sign of the round-faced, moustached man who'd attempted to fight Chrétien outside that infernal brothel.

Another strand of men appeared from a side alley, kerchiefs tied over their faces that must have been torn from an Aragón field banner. Yellow and red stripes, the colors of the king of Aragón. These men chanted, "Our neighbors, our friends, our duty." Catalan mercenaries guarding their heretic cousins from the Church. What had that hostel master called them? The heretic protectors.

Out of another street, more men emerged, their faces painted black, black wool scarves around their necks—the same black wool scarves as the men who'd challenged him when he fell while pursuing the moustached man. They carried staves and hand knives, chanting, "Go home! Go home. Hide in the mountains." More cries went up. It seemed that they hated more than vagrant Catalan and Aragón mercenaries, because they also chanted, "Jew and Saracens, God will deny you heaven," all in the local tongue.

The moustached man appeared amid these men chanting that they wanted foreigners gone from the city. The fellow had a black wool wrapper hiding half his face now instead of standing with the white-kerchiefed, priest-protecting faction as he had earlier when he made a sad attempt to fight Chrétien. The fellow waved an all-black banner tied to a barrel stave. And this time Chrétien saw his hand clearly. It bore a tattoo of a snake rising in front of a circle crossed like a wheel.

"*Bon vèspre!*" Chrétien hailed his moustached nemesis. Then shivered. "Are you the captain they call Zorzi? I'd like to talk."

It wasn't the man's mischievous smile nor rapidly falling snow that chilled Chrétien, but rather the appearance from another street of figures dressed like mummers, all wearing red fox masks. Students chanting in Latin. Chrétien recognized the language, but it wasn't from the mass, so he didn't know what the words meant. But any man alive could identify the scorn and bile they spewed. They carried poles that might serve as fighting staffs and, worse, flesh hooks from kitchen fires.

For a city where men weren't allowed to carry swords in the street, torchlight flashed off a good deal of steel as these bands of men entered the square, facing each other. It portended disaster, but before Chrétien could return to Antoni's door in search of a safer exit, a young voice pierced the cold air. It wasn't the soul-shivering, mesmerizing adolescent voice that sang in Antoni's barrel-vaulted chapel. It was Sanço.

"Barbarians! Are you men or demons?"

The different threads of the mob, intent on harming each other, turned to the shouting child who stood at the far edge of the portico outside Antoni's villa.

"You let the Dark God into your heart. You curse the Light. Dark angels will rain ice on your perfidy. My lord will slice your gullet."

Chrétien lost all his curiosity about Zorzi and the gathering crowds. Instead, fear for Sanço's safety flooded his muscles and veins. When the stones began to fall, Chrétien swept Sanço into his arms, threw him over his shoulder, and kicked open the door of Antoni's villa. He set Sanço down for the three heartbeats it took to throw iron bars across the door. Stones struck the outside. Since all villas in the city seemed to be laid in a similar pattern, he followed instinct and ran for the kitchen, admonishing Sanço to shut up when the lad shrieked again.

"Stinks of pirates!"

The place smelled of cinnamon and spices, which had seemed so comforting only moments earlier. From the kitchen, Chrétien found an escape into an empty alley. He began the awkward chore of crossing the city through the snow with a boy over his shoulder and one hand on his sword's pommel. He dashed into alleys to avoid rioters while still trying to get a good look at whoever might be leading the mobs.

He was all the way to Comte Nuño's compound before he recognized that the trip had been made easier because he once more had two good hands.

18
Two Guardians

AT NUÑO'S VILLA, TORCHES burned all along the roofline. Archers on the roof had arrows notched in their bows, aimed at anyone who approached. Chrétien paused before he reached the door, waving until someone waved back and called his name. Nuño's armed men on the ground were closing up access to the villa, so Chrétien barely gained entrance before the bars and shutters were in place.

After brushing snow off Sanço and shaking his own cloak, and then remembering Antoni's kind instructions to be sure to eat, he carried Sanço to the kitchen, intending to beg rations from Luis the cook. To his great relief, Yusuf and Qasim were there, picking apart the remains of a chicken. Qasim had gathered a small store of discarded bread crusts from others' trenchers and was spreading one with butter. And stuffing his face.

Chrétien sent Sanço to the other end of the kitchen, where in a few moments the boy was telling another of his outlandish stories, surrounded again by the lads who served under Luis the cook. Mme Marguerite entered, the wife of Captain Orlando and mistress of this portion of the villa, seeking Chrétien after the commotion at the front door. He greeted her warmly, asking if she could take charge of Sanço.

Mme Marguerite agreed with a nod, but she had something else on her mind. "The Templars came at the nones bell and removed Jaume from the house." She meant the boy-king of Aragón. "They took him to the prelate's villa. I believe they expected trouble tonight. Nuño, Orlando, and Karles went along with Jaume."

"Then our king and his friends are safe, since no one is about to attack Templars." Chrétien sought to relieve the worry-knot in her brow, while also feeling jealous that the Catalan knight, Karles, in his first night replacing Chrétien as the king's guard was seeing more action than Chrétien had experienced over the past three months. "Nuño left enough men here to keep you all safe."

"If I can keep you all inside." She seemed stern when she crossed her arms that way. "You sent these boys to me, and they ran off before I could blink. And only two came back. Then you return with a mob screaming behind you."

"I promise they'll stay here this time." Chrétien almost choked on the latest of the promises he'd made that day, this one being a promise he had little power to keep. "However, I have to go out again. To assist Nuño. Please don't worry on my account."

"Except I'm supposed to give you a message from Nuño. If you can make your way to the prelate's villa, he wants to speak with you. So, will we see you again tonight?"

"Likely not. I appreciate your help. Yusuf and Qasim can sleep in my cell. If they agree, you can lodge my young charge with them."

"It's funny," she said. "Men call you cynical and arrogant—oh, don't wiggle your nose. You act that way on purpose. But here you take great care over a poor orphan."

"Nonsense. It's only a peculiar circumstance. There are too many orphans in the world for me to be worrying about all of them."

"If you say so." Something in her expression made Chrétien think she was laughing at him. Mme Marguerite then led Sanço to the fire, offering a custard in exchange for a promise to come away for a bath after it was eaten.

Flexing his hands for warmth, Chrétien was flooded with relief. The day had been so busy and strange, full of too large cares that he only now felt the worry of what it might have meant to lose use of his hand. But his fist was tight, easy to release, fingers limber. He'd play a lute again, and fight without concern or pain. Weeping with joy might be the only correct response, but there were still too many cares preventing that kind of indulgence.

Chrétien joined Yusuf and Qasim where they were eating. He began with his most significant news.

"Magister Jacobus and Magister Lucas have been seized by the Church. They chained the door to the Science and Medicine library and wouldn't allow the priest to inspect it. They are to be questioned by the bishop tomorrow."

Yusuf's eyes flashed. "And Magister Antoni?"

"The French soldiers who escorted the two magisters didn't seem to be looking for Antoni. They passed right by where Antoni lives with his Genoese countryman."

Yusuf sat more erect on the bench. "The magisters are protecting only the idea of the library. We have already removed every text that needs protection from that nosy priest."

"Magister Jacobus's wife is overwrought with fear," Chrétien said. "As I would be if it were you that French soldiers marched away in bonds."

"I…"

For once the scholar Yusuf had no lecture to deliver. Qasim reached over to touch his friend's hand, a gesture that others might never have noticed.

"Since I cannot command you," Chrétien said, "I'll only comment that men of wisdom would stay indoors where it's safe. Which is here, inside Comte Nuño's villa. The count advised you to withdraw from school for the winter, live here, and only go out to serve as his scribe at council sessions. Given the riots in the streets tonight and the seizing of those magisters, I agree with Nuño."

"I too agree." Qasim kept looking at Yusuf, waiting for his response. "Can we also fight every day in the practice yard?"

After several moments, Yusuf finally agreed.

Chrétien pointed their attention across the room to where Sanço was telling stories by the fire. The other lads seemed to complain when Mme Marguerite came to cart Sanço off to a bath.

"More pirate stories, do you think?" Chrétien asked Qasim. "I asked him to stop telling tall tales."

"No. Now it's monster fishermen." After Qasim swallowed what was in his mouth, it was possible to hear what he said. "At the last part of the story we heard, the pirates were shipwrecked and Sanço was rescued from the stormy seas by Christian fishermen. But they turned out to be as bad as the Saracen slavers."

Yusuf said, "Sanço was about to describe a great escape, when Luis the cook asked me to remind you that you owe four *sous* for your guests." He gnawed his chicken bones daintily, arranging them on the wooden trencher from which the bird had been served.

"That's when you let Sanço run off? I asked you all to stay here."

"We ran after him," Qasim said.

"He was quicker than Qasim, wiggling through the crowds." Yusuf elbowed his friend. "Time to admit it. Those thick thighs aren't made for speed."

"I'm as fast as you," Qasim said. "Uncle, the boy cried that you were in danger, that out of duty to God he must help."

"Let me guess. Pirates?"

"*Si.*" Qasim lapsed into his Valencià dialect, which sounded a good deal like Sanço's odd Catalan. "Demons of the Dark God."

Chrétien's jaw tightened. He rubbed his hands to warm them, refusing to cry *Why me?*

Qasim noticed the gesture, and then noticed that Chrétien's injured hand was no longer swathed in gauze. He pointed to Chrétien's left hand, asking a question with his eyes.

"Magister Antoni shared more of his healing methods," Chrétien said. "I'm as good as new. Though, look, you can still see traces of the stitches." He offered his hand for Qasim to see. Yusuf didn't examine it.

"Don't you admire the magister? As the best man of science?" Yusuf said. "Antoni is one of the few men lecturing here who truly deserves the title of magister."

"His healing is rather like magic," Chrétien said.

"Except it's merely science." Yusuf rubbed his hands like Chrétien had done, as if imitating. But then, it was cold at this corner since half the kitchen fires had been banked for the night.

Qasim seemed to want to say more. "Uncle, forgive me if you think it's not my place to say anything. But the boy calls me lord, because he carries magic."

"It's not magic," Yusuf said. "He carries an artifact, the way a lodestone and needle find true north."

"We think it's in those welts on his arm," Qasim said.

"Whatever it is, Sanço can sense the damnable qareen the Fire Lord sent to plague us," Yusuf said. "Thanks to the querulous qareen, we have a good idea of the hell that dark angels govern, without our having to go there."

"Ow!" Qasim clutched his ear, but then finished what he wanted to tell Chrétien, who had a thousand questions but remained silent while these two explained their thoughts. "Sanço calls me lord, but he considers you his master. He thinks you have inherited the duties of his village's lord. Who must have been Miquel, your father."

"Although we have never met your father," Yusuf said, "we have inherited the living spirit that must have plagued his soul. Like leprosy or scrofula."

Qasim batted at his ear. "Stop it, Yusuf. For my sake, please cease insulting it. It's only doing its job."

"Does this qareen thing breathe?" Chrétien asked. "It's alive? Not a ghost? Or a demon?"

"As Magister Antoni teaches," Yusuf fell serious, assuming his teaching-scholar posture, "there are more living beings in the world the Creator has made than we can see with our eyes."

"And that live longer than the great cedars in the ancient forests." Qasim sounded like he was quoting an authority. "And so, I am to tell you, such noble creatures deserve the respect due elders throughout Creation."

"You lost Sanço." Chrétien didn't care to sound like his own father censuring misdeeds.

"Yes," Yusuf said. "And then the Templars arrived and herded us back to Nuño's villa, away from the rioters."

Qasim scooted closer to Chrétien on the bench, perching like an attentive swordsman. "Uncle, we think Sanço's stories are true."

"As outrageous as they are?"

"Yes," Yusuf said. "Antoni says that three years ago—while we were returning from Andalusia with Pedro—a horde of children calling themselves crusaders descended on Marseille."

"Where they all boarded ships and then disappeared." Qasim's face settled into grim judgment.

"Antoni says people in Marseille believe the children were taken by sea-going slavers and pirates," Yusuf said. "Like Sanço claims."

"His story is too fantastic." Chrétien said it without believing it any longer. Deep inside, his affection for (and frustration with) his scrappy orphan had been growing all day. If the terrible and grievous stories the boy told might be true…

"Fantastic things have happened to me," Qasim said.

"And me," Yusuf echoed.

"Our own stories would sound as incredible as Sanço's tales," Qasim said. "And if those things didn't happen to him...well, he's suffering whether or not the tales are true."

"I believe him," Yusuf said. "Though I don't have much science to prove the truth."

"I'm not a science man," Qasim said, "so I can say it. Sanço's truths speak to our hearts. I believe him."

The two of them were so damnably convincing. And yet...

"Do you believe it when he calls Magister Antoni a pirate?"

"He's in shock from his adventures," Yusuf said. "Something about the magister reminds him of what he endured with the pirates. Memory is so unreliable. A smell or a sound can cause a memory to return, as strong as when you first felt it."

"Like when a stew is spiced in just the right way," Qasim said. "I close my eyes and think I'm in my mother's house."

"Sanço truly is seeking the lord of Morella," Yusuf said. "He was captured by slavers and Saracen pirates. It's not childish fantasy."

"Is that what your guardian spirit says?" Chrétien still sounded skeptical, but Yusuf and Qasim had wakened what had bothered him about his orphan. As fantastic as these stories seemed, the child believed it had all happened to him.

"What does Miquel say about the child?" Qasim asked.

·

Chrétien prevented all expression from crossing his face, the way he'd learned from his father.

Yusuf said, "The qareen can see Miquel's ghost. And speaks with him."

"Can you see him?" Chrétien pointed at both young men.

"No," Qasim said, "but I've been hearing one side of their conversation every time you appear today."

"That's lunacy." Chrétien wasn't convinced of his own words. A knot of pain and trepidation unfolded in Chrétien's belly. They seemed to believe Miquel was truly there, that it wasn't a specter arising from the knock on his head. "No ghosts, no magic."

"Yet our spirit guardian," Yusuf said, "says we must go to Morella. And it claims your ghost tells you the same thing."

Chrétien glanced around, seeking Miquel, who'd been absent since the chanting in the chapel and had not yet returned. He boldly redirected the conversation.

"I promised Antoni to escort the merchant train through the city gates to carry away your books tomorrow morning. And Durán is on his way to Montpelhièr with the count of Foix, so I promised Nuño to help protect the city until Foix arrives. I can't begin another adventure now."

"How will you help Nuño?" Yusuf waved away the plate of warm bread that Qasim pushed his way.

Since it wasn't a secret, Chrétien said, "Prevent riots. Keep an assassin from murdering a priest and blaming it on the counts."

"Not working out so well, thus far?" Yusuf sounded sympathetic, even though the words stung.

"It's not Chrétien's fault." Qasim bit into a piece of bread that had been heaped with roasted fowl, so he next spoke through a mouthful. "We distracted him with our library crisis."

"But now we're going to Morella?" Yusuf said. "Maybe I should get my books back from Antoni. Then we can leave before—"

"We aren't going to Morella right now," Chrétien said. "Everyone in this city has turned lunatic, so you need to forget about school for a season. As soon as the snow is gone, you will take Sanço to Valerós. Your father will make a plan to go to Morella."

Yusuf stared at Qasim, waiting for an answer.

Qasim, chewing his lip in concentration, listened to what was either the real or imaginary voice of their guardian spirit. Then he said, "That's the best idea. But it doesn't like saying goodbye to Miquel again."

"It likes a ghost better than us? After we've done everything it asked? Except the foolish parts?" Yusuf spoke with disgust, then shook his head. "Everything has been chaos from the moment I finally found my family. Why should life calm down now when I want to study? Why do we all have to pay for the sins of our fathers in past generations?"

"Not me. I don't," Qasim said. "I never met my father. Anyway, school is boring. I'm glad to go on a crusade to rescue Morella."

"It's Tomás who must decide," Chrétien said. "As the current lord of Morella."

"Then you can count on it," Yusuf said. "We're going to Morella. Likely the only question is when. Before Easter, don't you think? My father won't wait for the regular fighting season."

Before Chrétien could answer, Mme Marguerite returned with Sanço, who headed for the fire to resume his storytelling. Except now he was shining clean, dressed in better clothes than had been found for him that morning. Mme Marguerite sat on the bench by the fire, holding the boy in her lap. She ran her hand up and down the boy's backbone, a gesture of comfort similar to Qasim rubbing the orphan's head. Two large dogs—they were everywhere in Orlando's part of the villa—laid their heads across Marguerite's and Sanço's laps, soon half asleep from Sanço scratching between their ears.

After a few moments, Mme Marguerite gracefully removed herself from the pile of dogs and orphan to join Chrétien.

"Thank you for supervising the bath," Chrétien said. "No dire wounds found, I hope."

"Only those odd forearm welts. And scabies and fleas," Mme Marguerite said. "I insisted on a good ointment for that. A shaved head wasn't possible. When your orphan refuses, it's hard to insist otherwise."

"As I have learned," Chrétien said. "Is there a place for Sanço in the kitchen or among the servants? I hope that—"

"I cannot keep your orphan, senhór."

"It's only for a few days, until—"

"No, senhór. Only tonight, while we are locked in."

Mme Marguerite held her elbow in one hand; the other hand tapped her cheek in the stern way Chrétien had seen when she dealt with a particularly troublesome young boy living in the household as a schoolmate of the child-king.

"Senhór Chrétien, you know I'm the only woman in this house, together with my service woman. And we're both old as the hills."

"Hardly." Was she hunting for a compliment? Chrétien knew that her husband Orlando considered Marguerite to be beautiful.

"That's solely because Comte Nuño doesn't like women in his house in general. I'm here with my maid under his personal dispensation. But Nuño also cautions that we are living in an armed camp, not a peaceful home."

"Òc, I know you are more than busy, senhóra. But Sanço doesn't appear to need mothering. Perhaps a master in the stable can—"

"That's the worst idea, Chrétien, amid many bad ideas. I had believed you possessed at least the sense of a discerning donkey."

"Then what am I to do with the lad?"

"'A man who waits and does nothing will lose all time and chance,'" Miquel whispered, raising the small hairs on Chrétien's neck. "It's a good thing Tomás will see that we need to go to Morella as soon as we can."

"*Aiieee, mon ami!*" Mme Marguerite slipped into her native French...and seemed to be laughing at him.

"*Madame, quoi?*" He spoke wretched French.

"Chrétien, my dear brilliant and blind friend, Sança can sleep in my rooms tonight, but then, to adhere to Nuno's rules, we must find another place. Your orphan is a girl."

19

Strategy

A GIRL.

How could Chrétien possibly be expected to see that, since he knew a total of nothing about girl children? Why didn't the ghost and that careening thing see it? Or Qasim and Yusuf, who claimed to have detected Sanço's truths?

Except she was Sança.

If he'd listened closely, he might have heard that every time the child spoke its…her name. However, Chrétien had also mistaken Tomás's wife for a young man the first time they met. In his defense she was dressed in hunting leathers and looked more like a donzel than the dòmna of a castle. Still the fault was surely with Chrétien.

Oh God, what did I lead that girl through today?

But then, the previous horrors the child had passed through were enormous for either a girl-child or a boy-child. What kind of people lived in her home village that they'd send a young girl out to find the lord of Morella? To find Miquel the crusader, who had been dead for six years? The poor thing had crossed the Pyrenees and walked right past Valerós, not finding Tomás, who was closer to Morella than Marseille.

After saying farewell to Mme Marguerite and repeating instructions for Yusuf, Qasim, and Sança to remain at the villa, Chrétien set off. He'd discarded any plan to visit more taverns in hopes of finding the assassin who was sowing evil in the city, because he must meet with the count at the prelate's villa. As he set out for that villa, he tried to compose a report for Nuño of what he'd discovered that day while searching for a man recruiting mercenaries. But how observant could Chrétien have been, given that he believed he dragged a boy-child with him all day?

Thanks to Antoni's healing and the euphoric sense of strength he'd enjoyed since drinking that remedy, Chrétien managed a safe passage to the prelate's villa. He first climbed to a roof at the edge of Nuño's compound, greeting soldiers who had arrows nocked in their bows, prepared to stop attacks on the villa. He stuffed his cloak inside his jerkin and then scrambled across roof tiles, leaped over narrow passageways, and clambered over balconies to shimmy up to higher stories.

All the while, he pondered all the things to be done next, since Miquel didn't choose to come along and harangue him.

While scrambling across ice-rimmed tiles, Chrétien took to heart what Yusuf claimed. Of course, Tomás would go to Morella as soon as he heard the story. Without a pause. Chrétien could count on it, as much as spring would come and then turn to summer.

Disappointment settled in Chrétien's gut. Chrétien and Durán couldn't simply go home to Toulouse. Instead, he'd have to explain that they needed to follow a ghost and a small girl back to the Aragón frontier, to fight *francimand* bandits who served a *taifa* general who made people pay taxes to the Moors' caliph. Chrétien had little success thus far in making Montpelhièr safer for Durán and other seigneurs attending the prelate's council. Next, he'd drag his pacifist lover across the mountains to an unknown battle.

Did heretics like Durán believe in ghosts and invisible creatures and magic-laden girls? Could he persuade Durán to leave the Council without waiting for final decrees? The Montcava house-knights could assure safe travel for Durán, Sança, Yusuf, and Qasim to Valerós. Miquel's ghost could take care of himself. How to explain to Durán why they had to undertake the next adventure without sounding as if he'd swallowed a lunacy potion? At least, when they made their way to Castell-de-Valerós, Tomás would believe the whole tale, since his brother claimed to have spoken with Miquel's ghost.

The villa where the prelate had taken up residence was four streets over, but it took Chrétien until the compline bell to reach it, since the tiles were cold and slippery with new snow, and every handhold or leap to another roof had to be planned. In the square below, the chanting crowd was kept at bay by a phalanx of French and Lombardy guards with pikes, shields, and short swords. Across the square, four *gardes du corps* lowered the barrel pillory, which meant the poor fellow had died. Nuño didn't hold with keeping a barrel hung after the lawbreaker died, believing that by then, everyone had understood the judgment and reasons for punishment.

Chrétien swung down from a neighboring balcony to the prelate's portico, startling two guards there.

"*Bon vèspre.* I am Chrétien de Valerós, Comte Nuño's man. I came in answer to his summons."

That wasn't how Chrétien usually introduced himself. Why did he claim Valerós? Too much thinking about what he had to do next for that orphan, instead of what he had to do immediately.

Before they'd lead him to the count, Chrétien had plenty of time to think about what to report while he endured a long series of tasks:

Agree to surrender all his steel.

Agree to be manhandled by the guards responsible for ensuring that he'd surrendered all his steel. (They missed the blade tucked into his boot.)

Agree to further delay while a man brushed all the snow from his jerkin and boots.

Repeat his full name to a clerk, who recorded it in the prelate's list of visitors. "Chrétien de St-Joachim y Valerós, son of Numa of Cyprus, sworn knight to Jaume, king by Grace of God of Aragón."

Agree to "make his mark" beside where a clerk had written his name (as if Chrétien couldn't write his own name).

Repeat his creed. ("A precaution. They say everywhere in the city that heretics intend to murder the prelate and the bishop.")

After he'd finally passed all the queries, Chrétien was led to a small room that seemed to be an ascetic library or study room. A shelf along one side held a few books and scrolls. A small table and chair stood in the middle. Nuño was reading a roll of parchment by candlelight. He put the roll aside when Chrétien was announced.

"Have you learned anything today, my friend?"

"Close to nothing, Monsenyor." Chrétien leaned against the door post, since Nuño sat in the only one chair. He discovered that his body was weary, even though Antoni's potion warmed his heart and kept him thoroughly awake. "An agent is indeed stirring up factions in the city. But I haven't learned if Churchmen or others are paying him. I don't know if they intend to attack counts or priests, but they enjoy attacking each other. Hence, tonight's riots."

Nuño said, "Half the men picked up in tonight's melees claimed they were recruited to act for the Church. The other half say they were hired to work for me, and that their friends will come to my door tomorrow to be paid. Will the men you've met attack the prelate and the bishops?"

"No, Monsenyor. No one I met is prepared to go against the Templars or the army that Simon de Montfort brought with him."

"Yet tonight's riots are part of the chaos we expected."

"Yes. I…" Chrétien paused, because he had so little to report. "I found the man who's been recruiting mercenaries."

"Truly?" Nuño sat up, wide-eyed, too excited for the dull story that Chrétien was about to tell.

"It's not a tale worth repeating over a winter fire." Chrétien glanced around the ascetic room. "Like the kind of fire you'd have if you had a better host."

"The prelate's austerity doesn't signify. Tell me your tale."

"A dissolute monk stumbled on the street. People in the neighborhood thought I'd attacked him. Black-masked men came to protect the monk, and then the man I'd seen in the taverns joined them. He charged at me with a nail-studded staff."

"Did he bleed when you cut him? Did he heal himself?" Nuño remained too eager to find magic.

"The moment I disarmed him, he disappeared into the crowd." Chrétien pressed his point. "He's no mage. And he's no assassin. His moves were those of battlefield brute, not a trained warrior. They say he's called Zorzi, either from Gènova or Genèva."

"Zorzi de Zêna." Nuño sighed, sagged in his chair. "Who was a consul for Genoa. But I heard that he died last year. If he's still alive, he's ancient. Too old to be scheming for riots and assassinations. And why would Genoa care about our prelate's council?"

Alarm raced up Chrétien's spine. "Genoa? Could he have a son or other kin in the city?"

"I believe his son would also be quite old, but I don't know much about his family." Nuño sank further back in his chair, having lost all the initial thrill of Chrétien's revelations. "What do your inn-keepers say? Does this Zorzi perform magical cutting and healing?"

"None of them saw it. The so-called magic is only a rumor." Chrétien rubbed at his hand, deciding not to discuss his personal experience with wounds, since that story would only encourage Nuño further down the mistaken path of magical thinking. Though the connection to Genoa of Magister Antoni and the name Zorzi was too much to ignore. "I'm sorry, Monsenyor. I learned so little."

But Chrétien's nerves buzzed, alert to a question he couldn't yet answer about Genoa. How to learn more?

"Yet with the riots tonight, chaos is coming faster than we thought." Nuño had his head in his hands, sinking into despair.

"Let me tell you more." Chrétien knew at least enough to tell where the conflict seemed to come from. "This Zorzi fellow is recruit-ing men among several factions. In one hostel, he's seeking Catalans who call themselves heretic protectors and who hate Simon. In another, he wants men who hate heretics for causing chaos in the Pays d'Òc. Elsewhere he seeks locals who resent the Aragón and Catalan fighters that came here after the battle at Muret. Another bunch hate Lombards. And in another inn, he's been recruiting Lom-bards and men from Marseille who hate the French."

Nuño's handsome mouth settled into a thin, grim line. "Men set out tonight only to battle those they hate."

"Not all. The bands of students wearing painted fox masks from Twelfth Night want to fight only for sheer pleasure. And..." Chrétien paused, contemplating how to explain what else he knew, since he still wasn't sure how it factored in. "There are many Genoese coun-trymen in the city right now. Merchants, I'm told. But if this Zorzi is also from Genoa, perhaps there is a connection we haven't yet discovered."

"I know no reason for Genoa to send an assassin. Magic or not. If this were Marseille or Pisa or Venice, sure. But we aren't an enemy or competition for Genoa."

Chrétien should have asked Antoni more carefully whether he was healing people in taverns. Until he had answers, Chrétien couldn't help Nuño, except to change the subject and distract him.

"Monsenyor, what can you do for the magisters that the Church took into custody today? At least two teachers from the schools were taken away for refusing to allow inspection of the libraries. The bishop is going to examine them tomorrow."

Nuño dropped his hands to his lap, palms open to heaven, as if crying out that he'd done everything God called him to do.

Whatever possessed Chrétien to believe that the magisters' predicament might distract Nuño from despair?

"I cannot help anyone." Nuño once more ran his hands through his hair, ravaging the white locks until his hair stood on end. "If we survive the coming days, if we can convince the prelate and the bishops that we will obey the Church, then maybe we can take care of people. And restore order."

"Monsenyor, you are exhausted." Chrétien knew what exhaustion looked like. In truth, he too should feel it, after a sleepless night, an accident with the St-Lazarus children's stones, and several wearying walks across the city. But traces of Antoni's healing potion still coursed through his veins. If he had more of that remedy, he'd offer it to Nuño; however, he'd left it back in his cell. "Have you slept? That's the best restorative for wits and courage."

"It's as if sleeping might rob people of their salvation. I'm planning for what action to take next."

"Perhaps I can assist with your plan." Chrétien strove to sound encouraging.

"Instead of worrying about the assassin," Nuño steepled his fingers, then one hand tapped the knuckles of the other while he spun threads of his plan, "what if we confront the neighborhood toughs he has riled up? After tonight's disorder, we know where they are banding together."

Chrétien tried to guess what Nuño was considering. "Do you want to send *gardes du corps* to stop them before they can coalesce into mobs like they did this night?"

"What if instead of fighting," the pace of Nuño's knuckle tapping increased, "my guards herd people into the squares by the churches? I shall read a proclamation, begging for peace in the city in the name of our Savior."

"A proclamation?" Chrétien was unable to keep from voicing his doubt. "You will quell riots with sermons?"

"And also surround the neighborhood ruffians with *gardes du corps* and our visiting seigneurs' armies. And with the Templars' help, if I can talk their master into the idea." Nuño now rubbed his hands, relishing the idea he'd conceived. "I shall deliver my proclamation outside the prelate's villa."

"It will take a good sermon to convince—"

Chrétien still leaned against the doorpost, one knee bent. Nuño put his hand on that bent knee, startling Chrétien. "*Aiieee,* my friend. It's not the ruffians we need to convince. It's the prelate and the bishop and their whole cadre of judgmental priests. They need to see that I'm commanding peace among the people."

"So, a sermon to save the ruffians from the Church?"

"No, to save our land, our families, our way of life." He tapped Chrétien's kneecap, then returned to tapping a rhythm on his knuckles. "To keep soul stitched to body for seigneurs like you and me. For everyone that the Church suspects of perfidy."

"Your sermon will deny all the wild rumors and defend the precepts of the Church."

"*Òc,* Senhór Chrétien. You get my intent."

Chrétien pondered the wisdom of that, since it wasn't the kind of action he'd choose. While Nuño spoke, the connection to Genoa nagged at Chrétien's thoughts. "There isn't much I can do to assist you with a proclamation. But I may be useful elsewhere if this Zorzi is from Genoa."

Nuño looked expectant, his despair not yet rising to hope, but he appeared eager for options. "Yes, senhór?"

"I have on opportunity to escort a Genoese merchant train out of the city. A chance to ask questions. Who knows maybe we will discover this Zorzi and his motives among his countrymen."

Nuño closed his eyes for a second. "Are you certain of a connection to this Zorzi and our trouble in the city?"

"Yes, but I met another man from Genoa." Chrétien had come to respect Antoni and didn't want to believe his friend was tied to this plot. Antoni and Zorzi might be countrymen, but Antoni was only trying to preserve books the Church might destroy. "I'm unsure whether this other man knows Zorzi, but perhaps he or the merchants can help me understand why a man from Genoa is recruiting factions in the city to fight each other."

"Very well, senhór," Nuño said. "Use the license I gave you to escort these merchants. Find out what you can. When you return, I'd like you with me tomorrow when the proclamation is read."

"I will return by the sext bell." Chrétien again recited his private understanding of the bells, to ensure he'd remember.

"You and I were bred to protect people who cannot protect themselves. So tomorrow we take action." Nuño smacked his hand on his leather leggings. "I missed the battle at Muret. I will not miss yet another action to protect Roussillon and the south from Simon de Montfort and a crew of troublesome churchmen."

Given the trouble Chrétien encountered simply because one dissolute monk stumbled in the streets, he had to agree. "Fine. Deliver your proclamation tomorrow, near sunset. I'll stay with you, like your shadow, as your personal bodyguard." Unconvinced a proclamation could do much to quell the danger, Chrétien also wanted to be near the action, lest he need to protect Nuño, in the way he had not been able to do for Pedro at Muret. "Now, if you don't mind my impertinence, Monsenyor, I believe you need rest. And I need to go home and sleep. It's been a day."

"Safer if you sleep here, in this villa." Nuño rose, straightening his vest, running a hand through his hair again, failing to quell its outrageous ways. "You can have the room they gave to me."

"Please don't sacrifice your bed for me, Monsenyor."

"I won't be sleeping there. When the prelate heard about the riots, he declared that he'd sleep in the king's quarters. I shall sleep across the king's doorway, like knights of old did for their lords. So, I shall bid you good night."

Nuño was at the door, calling for someone to show the way, and Chrétien could not refuse the kindness of this city's lord.

Among the Bogomils

From the Secret History of the Flaming Cross
—Andonis de Zêna

In 1202, Innocent III was rallying Philippe and other rulers to return to the Holy Land and reclaim Jerusalem. My family called me home from Toulouse. With Abbot Rodolfo gone to God, I was made a bishop of my order, and then was asked by our family's elders to accompany crusaders to the Holy Land.

Our family businesses had long included transporting crusaders sailing from Genoa to the Holy Land. Therefore, it was our elders' wish that I learn more Arabic medicine and learn the practice of battlefield medicine in service to my family.

The crusaders in 1202, however, relied heavily on Venice for their transport. When negotiations over finances proved difficult, the entire crusading force was stalled at Zara. Rather than wait where the only healing required was camp sickness and knife wounds from drunken quarrels, I left Zara with one of my cousins and went on a scientific expedition to meet healers rumored to live in the hills of Dalmatia.

However intrepid I've been, as a curious and bold man of science, this expedition became an adventure that exceed my experience and challenged my wisdom and spirit.

First, the guide we hired proved worthless and disappeared. We were taken up by a band of men that we assumed were brigands. My cousin and I carried weapons—what physician goes out for any purpose without sharp steel on his person? However, I presented open hands and open arms, to indicate I was a man of peace. I believed that they might still have murdered me for the contents of my pack and pouches. But as if God chose to deliver me to greater knowledge at that moment, a branch fell from a tree, spooking the horses. One man was thrown into the rocks beside where I stood.

Without thought for my own well-being, I came to this stranger's aid. He'd hit his head but hadn't broken bones. The others of his company saw that I acted as a physician and stood aside to let me work. I didn't then have the skill I've gained since, but I had certain knowledge of head wounds and the natural healing ability with which I'd once saved my uncle.

One problem with a head wound is that you simply must allow time and the healing. While we waited for their comrade to be ready to travel again, I did my best to explain that I was a physician and why I'd come to this wild country. Though I'd read and translated Greek for many years, I'd seldom heard it spoken. Yet through friendly effort, we came to understand each other. When their comrade was well enough to ride again, they took me, along with my cousin, to the place I wanted to find.

The village where they left us was not what had been described to me by people I'd met in Zara, who knew only rumors. It was not a magnificent palace atop a mountain on an island, like we hear in fantastical tales about the wildest north lands. It was not guarded by magical creatures or three-headed dogs.

Instead, it was a simple village of mud-and-wattle huts, surrounded by a palisade made of sharpened logs, built only to keep out the wolves that roamed the forest. The people didn't need the palisade to protect animals, because they kept no animals except dogs and cats. They did not dine on flesh or the fruits of flesh.

You are surmising that we had fallen among the famous Bogomil heretics of Dalmatia. I said as much after I'd been there a week and learned enough language that I could ask more complex questions. But my new friends denied knowing that word, or even knowing about the Manicheans. They called themselves only "the Children of God" and believed that the world of the spirit and the mind was created by the Good Son of God, and the material world was created by an evil, dark son. I never heard them invoke the Archangel Uriel, which is the way of Bogomils (or so I've heard). They prayed the Lord's Prayer but considered the Cross a sign of evil. If they held to any rituals, such as marriage or communion, I never saw it.

Yet, however often I tried to ask if they were Bogomils or Manicheans or Cathars, they each and collectively turned my questions aside. It was as if I were a child asking why the sky is blue and where does the sun go at night and how can the moon shine one night and then appear again in the day.

Therefore, to describe what I learned in that village, I can only explain that they had made a study over generations of the power of the mind and spirit as being greater and more powerful than the body.

Winter came not long after we arrived in this village, and it was that hard winter, the year so many in the higher regions suffered from frigid nights, poor hunting, and illness. But in this village, it was as if my cousin and I had come to a magical place that did not know weather or illness or famine. We were cozy with only cooking fires and woven blankets and dogs to keep us warm. And there were as many dogs as people in that village. How they were all fed I don't know. They bounded out of the open gate each morning and then returned before night fell.

I couldn't have made my way back to Zara if I'd wanted to be-cause of the weather and poor roads in the forest. But I didn't want to leave. There was so much to learn.

I learned to use voice and touch to save patients from the initial suffering of their wounds or illness.

I learned to harness a focused mind with song and potions to achieve healing such as I'd never seen described in any texts.

I learned to compound potions and elixirs that most men would consider magical, but I have described these in my medical texts, so any other man can choose to create these concoctions. None call for any charms or invocations greater than the Lord's Prayer.

If you've heard of such healing and consider it to be miracles or the work of saints or magic or alchemy, I assure you it is not. These Children of God did not even consider their wisdom to be held secret. Their teachers insisted that it was each person's duty to go out into the world to heal, sharing a gift from God.

Now, can I tell you where to find this mystical place? I cannot. By the time spring came, I too felt the teachers' encouragement, to go into the world and heal. I am not a hunter or a woodsman, and my cousin was no more a woodsman than I am. By the time we were led to a trail that took us to a trade route and to cities, I could not retrace the way back, to find my dear friends the Children of God again.

‡

Cançons de Montpelhièr

Lord, I lived in your cloister for years.
My order will soon forget me,
Because I love you and serve you.
My cousin has never deceived me.
We shall, I believe, unite our desires.

20
Nuño's Bed

CHRÉTIEN WAS SHOWN TO a tiny room, more like a monk's cell than a guest room, that held only a cot, a small desk, and a chair. When the door closed, Chrétien sat in the chair, his mind not ready for sleep, even if his body had been pushed hard that entire day. He was wide awake, and his mind roamed widely.

Given Nuño's revelation about the original aged Zorzi of Genoa, riding out with the merchant train seemed the best action. Antoni had been correct that it'd be a catastrophe if the merchant train were caught with the texts. But what if Antoni had other motives for getting the train safely out of the city? Chrétien did not want to doubt his friend, but everything related to Genoa seemed too coincidental, even if Chrétien could not think of how the books might have anything to do with the unrest in the city.

However, accepting Nuño's invitation to use his license to exit the city might lead to further disaster. If any catastrophe caused to a search of the merchants' wagons, Nuño would then be connected with the rescued texts. Which included the same texts that had caused the two protective magisters to be taken into Church custody.

The better solution to ensure the merchants' passage was for Chrétien to risk only his own honor. The guards at the east gate had a barracks beside a tavern called *Sèt Estelas*—the Seven Stars—and he'd gambled with those men often, letting them win half the time as an investment, so that he had a friendly point of exit from the city. His father hadn't raised a fool.

His father.

Who harangued Chrétien to go on crusade to Morella, and then remained with Yusuf and Qasim and the orphaned Sança.

"Lord love all the dancing angels!" He repeated Miquel's favorite curse, gripped with frustration over the day's confounding events.

But he spoke the words too harshly, blowing out the candle with his exasperated exhalation.

Which plunged the small, cold room into complete darkness.

In the blackened room, he continued to vent his frustration by reciting an entire litany of the creative curses that Miquel had inadvertently taught his sons.

He hadn't seen where the tinder box might be in the tiny room, and he didn't find what he needed by feeling around the desk. Failing to locate flint, he was not about to open the door and ask for help from servants or guards, since he'd likely be subjected to another round of more questions than a heretic in the bishops' court. It'd likely mean rousing Nuño to explain why a knight with a Cyprus accent was sleeping in the count's room.

So, Chrétien tucked the throwing knife from his boot into the space between the cot and the wall, and went to bed, that being the only action possible in a pitch-black room.

The thin, hard bed was of course too small, and it was too cold to let his feet fall over the end. He turned on his side, doubling his knees, which then threatened to hang over the side of the narrow cot. He pulled the fleece covering tighter. The one luxury in the room. Too bad Nuño didn't feel free to command a better bed when he visited other men's villas. The tall count wouldn't fit this miniscule cot any better than Chrétien.

He therefore lay in the dark, curled sideways, the way he did at home with Durán, nestled against his lover's god-like body, where there's more comfort and joy to be had than anywhere else on earth. But the cold wall behind him had none of Durán's yielding warmth.

Dismayed by the pending sense of loneliness, he tossed about, lying on his back again, then finally getting out of bed to drag that chair to the end of the cot to accommodate his feet.

What it took, too often, to live in a land where people only grew to the height of his breastbone.

He lay as utterly still as possible and counted his heartbeats. Finished wrestling with the bed, Chrétien then wrestled with the remains of the day's thoughts, since Antoni's potion still kept his mind too awake.

"Miquel?" He whispered his father's name, trying to determine whether the ghost was with him, though Miquel never seemed to be silent when he was present.

No answer. This time, Chrétien was unable to block that pang of loneliness.

Why miss Miquel when the night was more peaceful without his father nagging him? Especially since he'd already agreed that he and Tomás would go to Morella come spring. He'd learned when he was still too small to get on a horse without a mounting block that nothing could be gained by rejecting his father's advice. Miquel had always been there to…

That was the problem with Miquel's absence now. As infuriating as the man could be, the ghost's absence led Chrétien to recall all the turmoil endured when his father died. The grief. The anger. The void that remained, even this many years later. Was there any magic that careening thing could command which would keep the shade of his father nearby?

Except Chrétien didn't believe in ghosts or magical spirits.

He considered Yusuf's expression as he'd explained all this strangeness. Yusuf, the most rational man on God's green and luscious earth. Yet what Chrétien remembered instead were the glances that Yusuf and Qasim exchanged when confirming what they believed. He recognized that silent language, when one heart so deeply understands its twin.

Which plunged him back into missing Durán. When Nuño had asked what Chrétien feared early that morning, Chrétien claimed he feared hidden enemies. Alone, honest, he knew what he feared most was loss—like when Miquel died—and loneliness. The kind he felt in this city after so many months without Durán. Durán and Foix couldn't be more than a day's ride away. And Chrétien had no success in making the city safe for Durán and the counts and the seigneurs.

May one of the lesser dancing angels please let me sleep.

He called on his best reserve action when his lover wasn't available for peace and comfort. He summoned sleep with a song.

With all my heart,
I love wholly and solely and absolutely
A man who cannot see or hear me.
What can I do?
My heart cannot leave him.
I am like an importuning pilgrim
Begging heaven for compassion.

Chrétien had not prayed in earnest and did not expect deliverance, but the blessing of sleep fell over him, like another blanket. His body refused the first touch of comfort, his muscles jerking him awake. But then he was at last in the land of dreams.

Warm.

At peace.

Flying weightless, with Miquel pointing to the sights on the earth beneath them, showing his son how a ghost sees the world he'd once loved. Then in that sweet dream, he was wrapped in the sweet space that felt like heaven, how he thought heaven must be.

In their shared herb-scented bed, in the divine heat of early Toulousain summer, only a yard of linen thrown over them, a thin layer of sweat separating their bodies as they recovered from their exertions, whispering to each other how it would be.

He explained to Durán how he'd touch him next, knowing how his hands would roam until Durán panted, begging for mercy.

"I have a better idea."

Durán plunged his tongue into Chrétien's mouth, nearly choking him, then wrestling Chrétien to a position that was meant to render him helpless.

Durán's weight on his body. Like the burden of carrying an angel.

He held Chrétien down, exerting his greatest strength like he did when they wrestled. Or when they played that Durán was the conquering hero, though Chrétien would never reveal that, in fact, Durán had no idea how to make evil use of his innate strength. That playful move, kneeling on Chrétien's arms, pressing on his knees so he couldn't move, until that divine weight threatened to crush him.

Surrender. He'd had enough. Yet Chrétien could barely twitch a finger to tap three times. Their signal to stop.

He tapped again, as much as he could move, paralyzed with the pressure.

Stop!

No sound came out. He couldn't shout in his dream.

Worse, he couldn't breathe. But he'd learned when he was a child how to wake from a nightmare.

Take a breath.

Something trickled in his throat. A gag.

A man's weight trapped his arms and legs, something pressed on his face. He couldn't breathe, and he couldn't wiggle free to shake off whatever smothered him. He'd passed the point where no air makes you desperate. He coiled the last of his strength and heaved aside the body that trapped him.

At his first gasp, that noise you hear on the battlefield, he twisted again, to snatch the blade he'd nestled by the wall.

A man's weight fell on him again, but this time that blade and his hand absorbed much of the weight.

That other sound from the battlefield. The last of a man's spirit, escaping to heaven with a cry of pain.

Chrétien thrust the body away again. Stumbling, stubbing a toe, he fumbled for the door and pulled it open. He shouted in the local tongue.

"Danger! Guards! Help!"

Two guards appeared, one bearing a torch. The sudden burst of light burned a flame in his eyes, but not before Chrétien noticed the guards' surprise at seeing a bloody Celt in the count's chamber.

Holding a dripping steel blade.

While one guard prodded Chrétien up against the cold stone wall, the other came in with the torch, which cast enough light to show the body on the floor by the cot.

Not any kind of Nizari assassin. Only Sergeant Vincent of the *gardes du corps*. Who'd served Nuño in hopes of justice for his family lost at Béziers.

May the angels weep in heaven. Poor Vincent.

How did that good man turn out to be a traitor to Nuño?

·

A too-long day of mayhem came to be followed by a longer night of pandemonium.

The candle on the desk was lit again. Three more candles were brought in, and quickly more people wanted entry than the room could hold. No one seemed in a hurry, while Chrétien again answered all the same questions as when he came into the prelate's villa, with new questions about how he came to be sleeping in this room.

The wait seemed tediously long while Nuño was fetched. At last, Comte Nuño appeared with two Templars and two priests. Chrétien knew the two Templars, a slight friendship, from boring days guarding the classroom of the king of Aragón. They were a matched pair with northern French accents. Dark heads and beards, they were extremely handsome. It seemed sad that such beauty would be wasted over an entire life in a celibate order.

Everyone had dressed hastily and therefore rank was difficult to discern among the priests. Nuño was more rumpled and creased than when Chrétien last saw him. A sleep mark across one cheek indicated that the count had indeed been dossing on the floor outside the king's room.

"What's happened?" Nuño spoke calmly, yet ran his hand through his hair repeatedly, so that it again stood upright.

"Unfortunately," Chrétien said, "one of your guards attacked me and is now dead."

He'd already told the story three times. At each telling, the rush of energy and panic from the fight had ebbed a bit. By the time Nuño and his coterie heard the story, Chrétien no longer retained any of the warmth and well-being from the healing experience with Antoni. He was cold. Hungry. Exhausted in every bone.

And dismayed that a man he knew, whom he'd considered a friend, had tried to murder him. And died for it.

A voice from the huddle of priests and Templars asked, "How did you come by a steel blade here? Did you take it from that man?"

"It's mine," Chrétien said. "I forgot to surrender the blade in my boot when I came to the villa."

"Monsenyor." A guard in the hallway spoke. "We take great care to examine visitors. But Seigneur Chrétien carries a license from Comte Nuño."

"Are you too free with your licenses, Nuño?" The smallest of the two priests sounded amused while chiding Nuño.

"It's because I had a knife that I'm alive." Chrétien resented how Nuño was addressed. "An assassin is dead."

The way that Nuño stiffened beside him caused Chrétien to recognize that his interrogator was Pietro di Benevento, the prelate.

"Monsenyor, I believe," Nuño said, "that it was a good decision. Seigneur Chrétien is trustworthy. He's helping me to search out threats to the safety of people who've come to Montpelhièr to attend your council. We believed an assassin had been paid to attack…one or more of us. Seigneur Chrétien has been seeking who that assassin might be."

"Assassin?" It was Fabien, one of the matching Templars. "That's a grand claim for a common guard fighting a Catalan swordsman."

"May all the dancing angels sing in heaven!" Chrétien cried, losing patience with the way the fight was being questioned over and over again. "The man who attacked me was seeking Comte Nuño. No one knew I was sleeping in his bed, alone in a dark room."

"But you said," Pietro the prelate spoke slowly, still seeming amused, "that this was Nuño's man, from his *gardes du corps*."

Chrétien felt Nuño's eyes on him. He nodded, indicating to Nuño what the count had said at dawn after Twelfth Night: *Is there anyone I dare trust?*

"Someone is recruiting dissatisfied men, for an unknown purpose." Chrétien sounded assured while masking what he and Nuño feared—that hidden Churchmen were behind a plot to generate chaos through riot and murder. "We worry that some of Nuño's men might have been beguiled into serving two masters."

"This fellow you've killed was Nuño's man." Pietro spoke slowly, as if explaining to children. "And everyone in the villa believed that I'd be sleeping here. No one knows I loaned my room to Count Nuño, or that he'd chose instead to sleep outside the king's room. Therefore, the man you call an assassin—Nuño's man—was seeking me."

A burning sense of danger flared in Chrétien's limbs. He told the truth, but accidentally implicated Nuño in this attack. It would have been better for Nuño if Vincent had escaped. A mystery would serve better than Nuño's sergeant dying in the prelate's austere cell.

"We need to understand this better," Pietro was saying. For a small man, his voice commanded respect. The two Templars drew to attention, which reminded Chrétien that he was without steel anywhere on his person. He couldn't defend himself if conflict rose with these people.

"I agree, Monsenyor." Nuño sounded confident, though Chrétien could not conceive how the count remained so calm.

"And we need to be at our best," Pietro said. "Shall we meet at sext bell in Guillaume's rooms?"

"Guillaume?" Chrétien repeated. That was Vincent's second in command. Did the prelate want to examine all of the guards? Interrogate them? "Do you want to visit Vincent's quarters? He slept with his guards in the bachelors' doss quarters at Comte Nuño's villa." Chrétien couldn't make sense of this suggestion. "Instead of going there, isn't it better to send men to look for what Vincent might have left behind?"

Nuño spoke quietly, his breath rousing the small hairs on Chrétien's neck. "Monsenyor means Guillaume D'Autignac, Bishop of Maguelone."

Chrétien's heart beat like it had while he fought Vincent, because of the threat of being called before a bishop for judgment. Before Chrétien could protest that he'd already related everything he knew, Nuño answered the prelate.

"I am eager to examine with you all the dangers you perceive in the city, Monsenyor."

The prelate wanted to examine Nuño, which increased Chrétien's alarm. Nuño would be pulled into tribulations with the Church before Chrétien found whoever was plotting murders and riots in the city. How fast could he find answers?

"You will come too?" The prelate addressed Chrétien. "At the sext bell. I think your contributions will be important to us."

It was impossible to solve the mystery by the sext bell of how Vincent came to be an assassin—or what that might have to do with the city's uprising. Yet he could only answer as he must. "Of course, Monsenyor. Upon my father's honor, yes, I will come."

Pietro called to the guards in the hallway. "Can you please clean this room? The rest of you may return to your posts. I'd like to speak to the count about his man." He reached up, placing his hand on Nuño's shoulder.

Chrétien could not determine whether that was the touch of comradery or of one lord dominating another. He said, "I'm at your service, Monsenyor."

"I referred to his dead guard," Pietro said. "You may go."

When Chrétien bent down to pull on his boots, still purposefully in the way of the men who'd been instructed to clean the room, he noticed the dead guard's outstretched hand. He tugged up the blood-soaked sleeve, gesturing for Nuño to look.

The Wheel and Serpent mark.

"Comte Nuño, shall I explain this to Monsenyor the prelate? Or do you want to?"

"What is it?" Pietro asked, not waiting for Nuño's reply.

"The sign of a cult that formed in Constantinople." Chrétien related a portion of what he and Nuño believed. "Men who pretend to practice dark magic. We believe they seek to assassinate the counts and bishops in Montpelhièr. To create chaos and confound the Church's mission."

The prelate and Nuño both offered blank looks at Chrétien's revelation, because great men know how to keep their thoughts private. That explanation was the best Chrétien could do to help Nuño at the moment. He finished pulling on his boots and grabbed his cloak, then fetched his throwing knife from the table, since it had belonged to his father and he wasn't about to lose it.

Fabien and Olivier, the pair of Templars, walked beside Chrétien and waited with him in the foyer while he begged for his sword and the rest of his steel from the guards. The two Templars were brothers. After Chrétien did his best to remind them that they were friends from child-king guarding days, he said, "Comte Nuño is doing everything he can to protect the prelate and the council."

No answer, but the brothers did blink in harmony.

So, Chrétien persisted. "There's a man from Genoa called Zorzi who's been recruiting men as mercenaries. His aim seems to be chaos, and we believe he's behind this night's riots."

Still no response. The brothers might as well have been statues that stepped off their plinth as celibate Templars. What a waste.

"He has a moustache like you see on Roman mercenaries and other *outré* mercenaries from that part of the world." Chrétien wiped his lip to demonstrate. "If you help find him, you'll help restore peace in the city. And protect the prelate's council."

After retrieving his steel from the guards in the villa's foyer, he offered weak farewells to his Templar friends. "I hope we meet again at the sext bell." Then he hiked back to Nuño's villa in the dead of night, anxiety burning in his chest. The snow had stopped. The stars shone in the thin cold air. And dawn was coming far too soon.

What a goat-licker's mess. A man Chrétien liked was dead at his hand. And, after two nights' and a day's exertion, he'd done nothing that would, in the end, protect his family from a renewed incursion by the French army as champions of the Church. And instead of helping Nuño, he'd inadvertently placed the count under suspicion for being in league with Vincent the assassin.

The streets had been cleared of the evening's havoc. The guards had returned to their posts. Chrétien strode across the square outside the bishop's villa, passing the now empty pillory barrel. He slipped into the narrow alley that was the short way back to Nuño's villa, through the bishop's mews and the barracks where many of the Knights Templars were dossing. When he came to the end of that narrow passageway, he paused, hearing voices where he'd thought the streets were deserted. Under the torchlight of a villa, he recognized Feris, his stalking monk, passing a bag to another man.

A cat yowled near the stables. The other man glanced around at the sound. Zorzi. Unmistakable.

Chrétien darted out of the alley, sprinting for the two figures, but less swift because he carried steel. And not silent.

The two figures disappeared into opposite alleyways, gone before Chrétien could lay his hands on either man.

At Nuño's villa, he shivered in the stable, because he'd given his room to Yusuf and Qasim. To console himself Chrétien cleaned his blades and prepared to ride at dawn.

But he had one answer now. He'd witnessed the link that proved the Church was involved in the chaos being roused by Zorzi's recruits. He knew the house where men from Feris's order lived, so he could produce Feris at the meeting the prelate called with Nuño and the bishop. His morning ride with the Genoa merchants should produce answers to how he might find Zorzi of the ridiculous moustache. If not, he'd beg more time at the meeting with the bishop, with Feris as his first proof of the plot in the city.

21

The East Gate

WHEN PRODDING TOMÁS FROM bed to the training yard after a long night of dice and wine, Chrétien always told his brother, *"We'll sleep later, when there's nothing left in the world to do."*

Here he was, dragging his boney rear end through the streets, exhausted after only one hard day and a couple of nights of damnably poor sleep. He was getting old. Instead of going to Morella, he should retire to sit by the fire under a heavy rug, like every old man who'd live beyond his best years.

However, the sun was about to rise. A day's work needed doing, and Chrétien was the only one now who could do what Nuño and the seigneurs of the south needed—to uncover the conspiracy behind the assassination attempt. He had no leads except the Wheel and Serpent tattooed on Vincent's hand. Chrétien had also seen that mark on Zorzi, so the thin connection to Genoa remained, leaving Chrétien with no other place to begin except to ride out as planned and inquire among the Genoese merchants.

More than a dozen merchants' wagons had lined up for departure, waiting for the guards to open the east gate. Chrétien asked the first drover he encountered and found that the Genoese train began three wagons back from the gate.

As wagons moved forward, Chrétien greeted every guard he recognized, asking how they'd fared over Twelfth Night, begging to join them for a night of gaming when he returned to the city.

"When will that be?" Sergeant Raoul asked. Raoul had won two *sous* from Chrétien the last time they diced together, and now clearly wanted the chance to press his luck. Chrétien congratulated himself for the foresight to let the sergeant win.

"Tonight." Chrétien explained that his merchant-friends would meet their own guards on the road to Marseille. "I'll be back here before the sext bell. With new silver in my pockets."

"We reserved the Seven Stars for our private use tonight." Raoul always invited Chrétien to their private games in the tavern. Private games made particular sense now, given the tensions that seemed to spark a quarrel everywhere.

"Let me contribute to the rent." Chrétien rummaged inside his jerkin, then produced a coin, the one Nuño had given him at Twelfth Night. "I'd enjoy another night in your company." He appeared as jolly as he was able, given that his insides churned with fear that a snooping guard would discover books in the wagons. Books that carried Yusuf's name alongside the names of Saracens from Cairo and Mozarabs and Hebrews from Toledo.

Chrétien idly gossiped with Raoul, who often had the most lascivious rumors. Raoul said, "Did you hear about Sergeant Vincent's *gardes du corps*? A dozen Templars marched them to the bishops' court this morning. What do you suppose that's about?"

"I wonder." Chrétien's insides knotted. If he didn't find answers on this short journey, there was little he could do for Nuño when he returned.

Raoul dropped his voice. "I think it's about Vincent. How many times have I warned him not to spend time with the discontents still complaining about Béziers? Some priest or *francimand* traitor was bound to take it wrong."

At the moment when Raoul's guards surrounded the first wagon in the Genoa train and lifted the cover to peer inside, ragged shouts echoed, repeating chants from the previous night.

"*Strangers, go home!*"

"*No heretics in Montpelhièr!*"

Chrétien disliked how much those chants added to the turmoil in his belly. However, the guards stepped away from the wagon, looking to Raoul, who muttered common invectives as he drew his weapon and motioned for the gates to be opened. He waved Chrétien and the drovers through the gate. "*Adèu, el meu amic!* Let's hope we recapture peace in the city before you return."

The exit from Montpelhièr cost Chretien only that coin from Nuño. Luck had come to Chrétien for the first time since Twelfth Night. Would it carry through the brief jaunt in the countryside? Yet his spirits remained low, worried for Nuño, as the sky brightened on the rosy eastern horizon.

After days of a wooly, snow-burdened cloud cover, a crystalline clear day dawned. Once they passed through the suburbs and came to the open countryside, scant snow remained, since the fields weren't shaded all day like the city streets. However, few horses and wagons had passed this way since the freeze first descended. That proved to be another lucky break. The heavy wagons churned up mud, but if others had passed ahead of them, the wheels would have sunk on mushy roads.

Chrétien's plan was what always worked for him: win friends through gambling or song, then press friendly questions once good-will was earned. He had little time, but he couldn't risk the Genoese seeing him as an enemy or becoming suspicious of him before he could ask what he needed.

He rode alongside the driver of the foremost wagon, eyes open for any challenges to the merchants' train, but he saw only milkmaids returning from their morning chores, boys herding goats and cows to frozen pastures. An eagle flew overhead, but otherwise, the smaller birds seemed to have remained in the cover they found when the ice and snow invaded this part of the country.

The country was wide open here so that, like the eagle, Chrétien could see any challengers from a distance. That ride through the countryside left him free to chat with each driver as he moved up and down the train, free to sing, though he couldn't recreate the mystical experience of chanting in Antoni's vaulted cellar. Singing, sunshine, a ride in the country, while smiling at his new friends. He chose a song of praise from Miquel's comrades.

> We choose to serve an honorable lord.
> He serves beside us like David the common man,
> A small man who dares face the great giant.
> But he knew how to put on the strongest armor.
> Only God could defeat him when he took to the field.

Song was as good as sleep for preparing Chrétien to return to the work of battling chaos in Montpelhièr. He suppressed his fears, that the meeting with the bishop and the prelate would cast doubt on Nuño's innocence. He'd be able to produce Feris, to prove the Zorzi rascal was being paid. Perhaps he'd learn more on this trail, as he and Nuño hoped, about what the Genoa men knew about Zorzi. Then Chrétien would be free to meet Durán and go to Morella as his father commanded.

The road, which Chrétien had never ridden before, curved to the south and up a long hill edged by large rocky outcroppings, with no pass through the rough hills except this road. Chrétien did his best with songs and stories to make friends with the wagon's drivers. They answered Chrétien's friendly questions about other journeys they'd made, the weather, how glad they were to be leaving the cold city, and their joy at seeing the first signs of spring in the hills.

When he felt he'd made a good footing with these men, he tried his first real question.

"I've been looking for new mercenary work. There's a fellow they say is recruiting and he's from Genoa? Do you know him."

A brushed away answer and a request to sing "*We choose to serve an honorable lord.*"

There was no way to not sing the song. As he did, he rode farther along the wagon train, asking the same question three wagons further on. When that failed, he rode further down the line, asking if he should look for more employment at the merchants' house, since Magister Antoni was his friend. Those drovers had no idea how the merchants recruited drovers. Or the mercenary guards that were to meet them on the road.

He got one honest answer for all his efforts. "Signore, there's not a merchant from Genoa I know that will hire anyone but another man bred in Genoa."

So, nothing for his morning's effort. He'd have to hunt Zorzi when he returned to the city. And take Frere Feris straight to the meeting with the bishop and the prelate.

At the pinnacle, the trail unfolded onto a broad flat space free of bushes and trees. It had often served as a campsite, given the stone-lined fire circles. From the angle of the sun, it was about time to turn back to Montpelhièr. In the mid-morning sunlight, he could see a great deal of the countryside, though he didn't know how to identify landmarks since he hadn't explored after he came to the city in the autumn. He could make out in the distance what he believed was the road from Béziers where it broke through the hills. Now was the last available time to ask these men of Genoa about their business and how they knew Antoni.

Then a wagon became stuck. Chrétien watched, increasingly anxious about finding any information, as the oxen had to be un-hitched from another wagon, then hitched with the stuck wagon's team for extra strength.

Soon the sext bell would ring. Chrétien paced the broad empty space at the pinnacle, worrying about the meeting with the bishop and the prelate. Chrétien had his own course to find answers that might help Nuño at that meeting. Otherwise, they'd be stuck with only the truth in the interview with the bishop, and only the thinnest proof of the plot to create chaos in Montpelhièr.

If Chrétien couldn't produce Zorzi, Nuño had no facts to pre-sent the prelate. If the Churchmen were indeed behind the chaos, even if the prelate weren't himself involved, then the truth would be altered and the prelate would be shown no reason to be fair with Nuño. In either case, the outcome was...

Chrétien again forced his mind away from that branded image. Durán and Numa before the flames.

A wind rose when the merchant train finally reached the pin-nacle, making the day colder than it had been, ruffling his horse's mane and the grass it browsed. At the edges of the trail, the boughs of holm oaks and pine trees danced in the wind. Chrétien asked the lead drover to confirm what he'd guessed that he saw in the land-scape. He proved to be right about the road to Béziers.

The drover pointed to the other side of the city. "That's the road to Marseille."

Surprised, Chrétien said, "But you are traveling to Marseille." Wasn't that where Antoni had said his countrymen were headed?

"No." A man spoke behind him. Antoni's warm voice. He'd emerged from one of the wagons. "The merchants are meeting a ship from Genoa at Maguelone. Sailing close to the shore will be safer than the roads."

He dismounted and greeted Antoni, grasping the magister's hands, which were warm. Chrétien's felt like ice. "I expected you to remain in the city, magister."

"I want to confirm the success of today's passage." Antoni then spoke to the lead drover in what must be his Genoa tongue. The drover disappeared to do whatever the magister had asked.

Asking the drovers about Zorzi was impossible now. Chrétien reassessed his plan, preparing to ask questions of Antoni by first teasing his friend. "You don't trust us to save those books?"

"I long to trust all of you." Antoni offered his sweet, seductive smile, but he was serious. And he hadn't released Chrétien's hands from embrace. "However, I need my own peace of mind."

"Will you ride back to Montpelhièr with me?" Chrétien gently pulled his hands free. "I'm done with what you needed from me. Comte Nuño expects me this morning." As did the bishop of Maguelone and the pope's prelate. On the ride, he could ask Antoni questions about Zorzi and about yesterday's healing. Chrétien hoped for anything that could lead to uncovering this conspiracy.

Instead of accepting Chrétien's offer, Antoni drew him close, his arms folding around Chrétien's shoulders. He stood on tiptoes to kiss Chrétien, who tried to turn away. Antoni held him so close that his breath fluttered across Chrétien's lips.

"I pray to God, asking for so much more between us."

"Yet you know I love another man, body and soul." Chrétien grasped Antoni's shoulder, freeing himself forcefully, wishing his repeated rejections might be taken seriously. "I'm not capable of other desires."

By saying that, Chrétien's current plan was undone by his devotion to Durán. The ride to the city together would be uncomfortable.

A motion drew Chrétien's attention to where the Genoa merchants' train was preparing to continue its journey. A party of riders appeared from up the other side of the hill.

"Are those your merchant-friends' regular guards?"

Antoni scarcely glanced where Chrétien pointed, his eyes still locked on Chrétien. "Indeed, I believe so."

"Then is this farewell? Or will you ride back with me?" Chrétien couldn't give up this one chance. If he was wrong about the Genoa connection, he hoped Antoni's intelligence in conversation might bring new ideas to pursue. "It's past time for me to return to my chores for Comte Nuño. We should ride now."

Chrétien stepped to his horse, preparing to gallop to the city. Below, from the direction of the city, a rider came into view, climbing the hill. Chrétien hadn't mounted his horse before the rider reached the pinnacle. It was Feris, atop a horse that had been forced to work harder than an animal should. Chrétien caught the horse's harness, doing what one did to calm it while trying to calm his own rising confusion. He understood the connection between Feris and Zorzi, because he'd seen it himself. What was Feris doing here? A greater connection with other men from Genoa.

The monk slipped from his horse, seeming frantic, and ran to Antoni, greeting him effusively, his high voice adding to the whistle of the wind.

"*O mio fratello!*" Magister Antoni answered in the same dialect he'd used with the drover. He smiled, shaking a finger at Feris, admonishing him with seeming kindness. Then he switched to the local tongue. "I explained last night. This journey is not the best course for you. You must return to your order. Please don't beg me again with your claims about love."

"*Aiieee*, my friend. I've come to warn you. Templars are pursuing this wagon train." Feris pointed back down the roadway he'd just covered. If it were summer, dust clouds would follow riders. But in this frozen weather, other travelers could be seen only as an irregular dark blot moving across the countryside. "I'm here because I love you. I'll do anything to protect you."

Embarrassed to be caught in an unexpected quarrel between would-be lovers, Chrétien listened to Feris and Antoni argue, hoping to hear from Feris whether his arrangement with Zorzi involved Antoni too, though that seemed improbable. Of course, the monk-spy in love with the kindly magister would have seemed improbably to Chrétien only yesterday.

Casting about to look anywhere but at the two arguing men beside him, other movement in the greater distance caught Chré-tien's eye. A large party traveled to Montpelhièr along the road from Béziers. Banners flew at the fore and along the line of what must be armed men. The yellow-and-red striped banner of the Comte de Foix. It must be the count who rode at the front of this expedition, and by his side, another banner flew. The crimson banner of the House of Montcava.

His heart bounced behind his breastbone. Durán was arriving a day sooner than Chrétien dared hope.

And riding directly into danger if the bishop accused Nuño of plotting against the Church.

Chrétien scanned that distant line of knights, looking for the banner of Durán's brother, Sebastián of Valerós. He didn't spy it but remained elated by the appearance of Durán's banner. He'd see Durán at the sext bell. Relief and worry mixed acidly in Chrétien's stomach making him aware he'd hardly eaten since the previous night.

"I feared this." Antoni's voice interrupted Chrétien's joy. "We shall have to negotiate."

Feris's thin, high voice became more pronounced, still arguing with Antoni.

"It's not you they want, magister. It's him." Feris pointed to Chrétien. "The prelate wants to question Seigneur Chrétien about last night's riots. Monsenyor Pietro is an even-tempered fellow, but when he learned that Chrétien de St-Joachim left the city, he sent those four Templars out to bring him back."

"Then this is farewell, magister." Chrétien touched his horse's nose, whispered to it. "I'll ride back to the city with the Templars, since my work for you is done now."

And in Montpelhièr, he'd only be able to tell the truth while offering no solid proof to save Nuño, unless right here he could persuade Feris to return to the city with him. But at least he'd finally see Durán. He turned again to prepare his horse to ride.

"I'm sorry about that, my friend." Antoni sounded mournful. Feris looked like an anxious beggar. "You should stay with us."

Feris whimpered. "Why keep him and not me?"

Chrétien, weary of Antoni's seductive ways, was embarrassed for Feris, who proclaimed his unrequited passion for the magister. Meanwhile, his own true love was riding into chaos.

"Magister! You must send Seigneur Chrétien down to the Templars!" The words tore from Feris's throat. "If they meet your wagons, they'll discover you've taken all the science books."

22

The Pinnacle

"ALL THE SCIENCE BOOKS?" Chrétien turned to face Antoni. "We removed only books the Church might destroy."

"No." Feris remained overwrought. "Antoni took the school's entire collection of medical and science texts."

Antoni spoke mildly, in spite of Feris's wild words and Chrétien's probing glare. "That's not true, dear heart. You exaggerate. I took only the original Arabic, Greek, and Hebrew texts. I left all the vernacular and Latin translations. For my purposes, the translations aren't worth wasting parchment."

Chrétien tried to understand the depth of this betrayal. He'd been convinced that the removal of the text was temporary, for Yusuf's safety, not that he was participating in outright theft. And Antoni had deceived Yusuf more cruelly than what he'd done to convince Chrétien.

The merchants' hired guards arrived at the pinnacle, their horses clattering on the rocky ground. They shouted greetings and were embraced by the drovers. Antoni raised his hand, beckoning the man who appeared to be captain of the guards. That man, the same build as Antoni but darker by several shades from sun, embraced the magister. After they kissed, the captain whispered in the magister's ear at length.

Feris shifted, his face flushing red as he stared at the ground.

Antoni turned from the guards' leader. "Seigneur Chrétien. This is my cousin Bonaventura."

"*Bonjorn.*" Chrétien remained too distracted by Feris's news. "Magister Antoni, you can't steal an entire library. The Templars, the Church, they will—"

"We rescued these texts for a higher purpose." Antoni spoke in that mild, comforting voice, the one he used when healing. "We can't let the Church put a stop to science, to keep us from what we yearn to know about God's creation."

"Yes, but…" As if he'd caught Feris's frenzy, Chrétien couldn't voice his dismay.

"It's a sin against the Holy Spirit." Antoni chose the words that Chrétien had heard when Churchmen challenged heretics.

"Let's give the books back. We can tell the Templars we found the texts, that we were tricked and didn't know who put them in the wagons." Chrétien, standing there alone, remained uncertain how to act. "You are no thief."

"I cannot steal what belongs to me." Antoni's voice dropped back to the soothing tones he used while healing, with the hum that promised a summer's day. "Because God has given me the strength and insight to uncover and practice the wisdom in these texts. I shall be the Word made flesh, made by God to heal and to teach, to make men more than well, but also wise."

"Antoni, your notion is too large to comprehend. I beg you to consider another way." Feris folded his hands, genuinely pleading.

"Through me," Antoni's voice rose over the sound of the wind sweeping the pinnacle, as clear and musical as when he chanted in that chapel, "men will be made free of the bonds of ignorance. We shall build a new university in Genoa, to teach battlefield healing and scientific methods. I shall lecture on plagues and the diseases that pass like invisible spirits among people."

"The schools will ask the lords and the Church to find these stolen texts. Your theft will lead to relentless pursuit." Chrétien turned to the frantic monk, as if Feris might assist in persuading Antoni to reason. "Tell him how wrong this is."

"Antoni, I know you won't take my advice." Feris was calmer than he had been. "But you do know I love you."

Chrétien said, "Come away with me, Brother Feris. This will besmirch us both."

Feris shook his head. "Magister Antoni possesses special wisdom from God. I'd sacrifice my life to remain at his side."

Antoni sounded weary. "Since you've come this far, you shall come along, Brother Feris. It seems there's no other humane choice. But you know I cannot love you."

That would ring in Chrétien's heart as a deeply embarrassing moment, hearing the rejection of another man's impassioned plea to be allowed to love. But the Templars now were close enough that Chrétien could hear the thud of hooves on the ground. He had to act.

"I'm going to meet the Templars," Chrétien said. "They came looking only for me. I shall ride away with them, because it would be folly to invite them among the wagons."

His desire to protect Yusuf from the Church's investigation prompted him to persuade Antoni to give this up and leave with him. He asked Antoni again, was refused again. He had the reins in his hands, prepared to mount. "Do what you will, Antoni, but this is farewell. Feris, ride back to the city with me."

Feris stood like a man in battle shock, staring at Antoni, wringing his hands as if in prayer, an overwrought lover who didn't recognize there was no hope for the object of his passion.

If Chrétien couldn't persuade Feris, he wouldn't have proof for Nuño about the connection between Churchmen and the man who was recruiting rioters. Antoni had refused Feris's affection, which should have left the wretched monk with no option except Chrétien's protection to return to the city.

"Feris, let's go." Chrétien felt he needed to be harsh. "Zorzi was a poor choice, but it's worse if you throw away your work for the Church to beg a man who's refusing you."

"I never chose Zorzi," Feris said, his voice quivering. "Only Antoni, who owns my heart."

"Frere Feris, no!" Chrétien pleaded.

"See? He made a choice." Antoni spoke with his usual mild calm. He grasped Chrétien's hands. "You should make the same choice."

While Antoni spoke, Chrétien's hands firmly in his, a trio of the Genoa guards surrounded and disarmed Chrétien, one battering his solar plexus, another kicking his legs out from under him. He squirmed to his side when a third man tried to kick his head.

Feeling hideously alone among the drovers while these guards bound him, Chrétien cried, "Antoni, what have you done?"

"My cousin Bonaventura insists you cannot go now, Chrétien. Not if you want to keep Yusuf safe."

Then two guards did the same to Feris. And the two bound men were loaded into one of the wagons. One of the drovers paused at the wagon's edge to smile at them. Zorzi.

"*Bonjorn,* my friends." Zorzi stuffed a gag in Chrétien's mouth, tying it too tightly. He left Feris without a gag, which was just as well, because the poor monk was weeping and would have choked if they'd gagged him.

So, no Nizari assassin. Only a drover from Genoa.

Likely, not an agent of unknown Churchmen. Only a foil for a plot by a greedy, obsessed physician.

Chrétien had never known the right questions to ask. Though none of these drovers would have ever answered truthfully. He'd failed as soon as he left the city. Worse, he hadn't even had a notion to suspect and then find out whether the two men of Genoa that he knew about in the city might have a connection with each other.

Zorzi shoved Chrétien to the floor of the wagon. Once the man was gone. Chrétien wiggled to sit up so he could see the clearing.

The guards and the drovers, eighteen men in all, formed a wedge. The Templars didn't seem to recognize what was arrayed against them when they arrived at the pinnacle, though it was exactly the formation that Chrétien would have chosen if he commanded eighteen men to attack four. Likely the Templars had no expectations, having been hailed and made welcome a few horses' length before they reached the top. Within a few heartbeats, the men of Genoa had closed on the Templars, pulled them from their saddles, and murdered them.

A scene to make cast-out devils weep.

But Antoni's people were the devils.

While the other drovers stripped the Templars' bodies and rolled them into the trees, Zorzi returned to the last wagon and searched through Chrétien's jerkin. He removed the leather pouch with Chrétien's coins and the license from Nuño.

The guards distributed the Templars' armor and weapons among the other wagons. Chrétien couldn't see, only hear the directions they called to each other. Four of the guards removed and stashed the horses' saddles and gear. When the guards mounted to ride, they tethered the Templars' horses to walk behind them, along with Chrétien's and Feris's horses.

During the preparations to get the merchants' train back on its way, Antoni sat by a dead fire ring with two of the wagons, taking medicine from a box at his feet and wrapping each of the men's hands. Through the sound of the wind in the trees, Chrétien heard the enticing tones of the magister's healing song.

Captain Bonaventura called for the wagons to move. Zorzi, the last man standing in the clearing at the pinnacle, crossed to where the Templars' bodies had been rolled. He tossed a packet in with them.

Nuño's license, which had allowed Chrétien to carry steel. Steel now stashed somewhere in these wagons.

Although he ultimately needed steel to fight his way out of this, Chrétien began the monotonous task of getting free from the too-tight bindings. A chore so monotonous that he considered if perhaps he should just sleep for a while.

Sleep, to escape the sense of shame at being beguiled into this dark and dangerous disaster.

A Plan for Genoa

From the Secret History of the Flaming Cross
—Andonis de Zêna

By trading my healing skills for food and shelter, we soon joined a group of priests traveling from Constantinople who carried us with them from the forests of Dalmatia to a seaport, one where my family keeps a trading house.

Not long after the auspicious fire festival on the first day of May, a ship came to port. The shipmaster was our cousin Bonaventura, who was of course pleased to give us passage back to Genoa, along with a quartet of young knights returning from Constantinople. After Bonaventura gave them enough bitter resinous wine from his cargo, they were full of tales about a secret order they had joined. Young Zorzi, my other cousin, made such good friends with those knights that they initiated him into their confraternity. He brags of it still, because it's the closest to knighthood that my cousin is likely to come. We are a merchant family, not warriors.

The first ill tidings that Bonaventura shared: our uncle Zorzi the Elder had died. A family council at the end of the summer would decide who was best suited to take my uncle's places as a consul in Genoa. Bonaventura's excitement about this was palpable, and I agreed that he was most suited to that new role.

Two days at sea, the next ill turn occurred. Bonaventura took a sickness in his belly, likely from something evil he ate when ashore. He fell so ill that when the sun set, he begged to die. Yet by the time the sun rose again, I'd restored him to his hearty self.

We talked then, Bonaventura and I, of how we could better serve our family. My cousin was astounded to hear what I'd spent the winter learning. His spirits soared further, with grander ideas than I'd ever dreamed.

"Genoa needs a university," Bonaventura said. "We shall be renowned for scientific and spiritual medicine. And our family shall lead the way."

His idea fit well with the teaching I'd carried away from that village high in the mountains above Dalmatia. But Bonaventura wanted us to do more than share spiritual gifts with the afflicted.

"We shall offer crusaders and traders more than Venice can dream of. Genoa shall become the center of teaching and the source of great physicians practicing battlefield medicine."

I became convinced that, indeed, that was how I might best serve God, my family, and my order. It was more than Bonaventura's infectious joy, or the pleasure of a sunny day afloat on the Great Sea, or his flattering praise for my ability to heal. His vision for a great school was like a balm poured over my soul, which I hadn't felt since leaving the village of the Children of God.

"We begin as soon as we are home," Bonaventura said. "Our uncles and cousins will be our investors and will help advance our mission in every way."

"Not this summer." I was forced to slow his ambitions, because I needed to recover my mentor Francisco's library in Toulouse. Then I needed a year at a university to learn what I had not yet gained from my peace-seeking friends in the woods. I needed more of the philosophy and teachings of the ancients and from Rhazes, the great physician of Persia.

Therefore, Toulouse and Montpelhièr became part of Bonaventura's plan to make Genoa indispensable among crusaders.

"And I shall help," our cousin Young Zorzi said, rubbing the tattoo on his arm that he'd picked out with a needle. He'd learned in the past winter how to heal himself, but he'd asked my help when his tattoo became inflamed after he'd tapped in the red ink. He'd made the ink from mercury and sulfur stolen from my apothecary box, so while I helped with his healing, Young Zorzi had to endure lectures from me about the moral hazard of theft.

"And yet, we heard stories in the mountains," Young Zorzi said, "about the Greek who stole fire from the old gods. And about how Jacob stole his brother's birthright and was blessed by God."

He repeated that argument through the summer and into the autumn. I contended with his stories only in my heart. And although he was my cousin, when we stopped to trade at Sardinia, I purchased a new apothecary box, one with a lock.

‡

Cançons de Montpelhièr

He frightens false knights more than a gryphon,
While his own men pledge their hearts to us.
He captivated me and stole my heart.
We are more faithful and true than David and Jonathan.

23
Unrequited Love

THE WAGON JOLTED ALONG with two bound men bouncing under the canvas cover with only a well-used horse blanket separating them from the wagon's plank floor. Chrétien longed to sleep, both to escape from the hell he'd ended up in and to regain strength. But when he closed his eyes, he remembered Durán's banner headed for Montpelhièr. Nuño facing the prelate and bishop without a friend to prove the truth.

Could Durán and Ramón-roger, the Comte de Foix, protect Nuño? Or were they all doomed by Vincent's assassination attempt?

Chrétien's mood worsened. Feris could not shut up, first despairing and reliving that massacre, because apparently the little monk had no battle-wits. Then Feris despaired over everything God hadn't given him that led to the stomach-churning ride in the back of a frozen wagon. Because he was gagged, Chrétien couldn't beg that their captors might put a cork in the monk.

"They didn't need to tie me up." Feris spoke through his sobs. "Why won't Antoni trust me? Why not take me seriously? I'm condemned by my stature, my face, my voice. I look and sound like an adolescent. I stand no taller than ordinary women of Montpelhièr, and therefore I'm lost in a crowded street, or among all the monks and priests at mass. My mud-colored robe should mark me as a member of a respectable order, but if I'm out without my monk-brothers, I'm propositioned by men. In the streets, in the hostels."

Chrétien formed a sense of how the bonds at his elbows and wrists were configured, determining how to get free. If he didn't guide his mind to only that chore, his cheating thoughts would pick up the wail of Feris's complaints, and he'd again be asking how he'd been beguiled to this end.

And where was Miquel now, when Chrétien needed him?

He'd listened to Yusuf's request for help, but he should have removed Yusuf and Qasim from the city. Immediately.

He'd listened to the enthralling magister, who praised Miquel's courage and then put his tongue down Chrétien's throat.

He'd listened to the magister charm Yusuf, playing on Yusuf's passion to be respected as a scholar.

He hadn't listened to his orphan, hadn't even seen that she was a girl. *Smells like pirates!*

He'd stayed in the city to wait for Durán, and now he wouldn't be there when his beloved arrived.

Listening to that self-pitying monk, Chrétien was increasingly tempted to roll over and smother the fellow, to relieve him of his suffering. For both their sakes.

"Since childhood," Feris's complaints spun off in another direction, "my heart had been taken by love for Our Savior and service to the Holy Church. Then a large portion of my heart was consumed when my brother-monks and I rescued Antoni after he left the Bogomil heretics in Dalmatia."

Duelist heretics. The mind and the body ruled by different gods. Chrétien didn't buy a bit of it; his father had inoculated his sons from the cradle, so they couldn't be cheated by charlatans. Yet here he was, having been captured by enemies while thinking he was on a jaunt in the countryside.

At each moment that he paid too close attention to the monk, Chrétien smelled fear emanating from the fellow. All the while, Chrétien continued to feel along his bonds, seeking ways to part them from his flesh.

"Those brothers are now swept up by the teachings of that indigent teacher, Dominic Guzman. I agree that men of God must adopt poverty to prove that we are true disciples of Our Savior. I agree that's the way, if we hope to have any persuasive effect on those heretics who reject both meat and gold in hopes of a better life after death. It is our duty to teach that there is no life after death except in Our Savior."

If Feris's whine could sever cords, Chrétien would gladly put it to use. His efforts to wiggle out of bondage had so far rubbed his wrists raw and threatened to dislocate his shoulder.

"But on earth," Feris's voice shifted to wistful tones, "what signifies heaven to me is when my dearest friend—my only friend—Antonello sings. Or when he lectures, sharing the wisdom and talent that God has given him to heal the sick and to comfort those who cannot be healed."

Chrétien rested his efforts, fearing that he'd make his flesh swell instead of shrinking away from his bonds. He worked instead to be free of that gag, using tricks he'd practiced in far different circumstances. Wiggling his nose, he smelled his own sweat, refusing to think it smelled like fear.

"Here, the magister is called Antoni delle Manigentili, my Antonello of the Gentle Hands. When we met, I was sunk in illness from battle and camp life. Life with my monk-brothers became torturous. But my Antonello warmed me by our campfire and then laid his gentle hands upon me. I was healed when I woke at dawn the next day. Many moments each day, I still long for that warm fire and those gentle hands. But in this world, he is Magister Antoni of the medical school." Feris's voice shifted back to the high register of complaint. "And I am the lowliest of mendicant monks, because that is what my order chose for me. Poverty and loneliness."

Chrétien found modest success. His own wicked tongue and narrow jaw did their work, and he was free of the gag at last.

One thing had to be said first.

"Peace, Brother Feris." He coughed, his throat dry as a desert in Egypt. "You're old enough—what are you? Twenty?"

"Twenty-five."

"Then you're old enough to know that a man like that will never return your love. Never in all eternity. He charms men so he can use them. Then tosses them aside."

Feris didn't answer.

Chrétien persisted. "You gave an oath to your order, like I gave an oath to my brotherhood. Perhaps you believed you were still serving the Church when you paid Zorzi."

"Paid Zorzi?" Feris whispered the words.

"I saw you near the Templars' mews. You gave him money to recruit men for the riots."

"No, nothing like that. Antoni's destitute cousin was always begging for money. Antoni asked me to give it to him, to say it was the last time, that he needed to go home to Genoa."

"It wasn't from any of the Churchmen?"

"No. Just a favor for Antoni. He knows I'll do anything he asks. Like you. He asked your help, and you couldn't do otherwise."

"No. He beguiled me. He played on my sense of honor and my need to protect my nephew Yusuf. But he used me to steal books and escape." Chrétien sensed that wasn't all Feris had to tell. "What else did Antoni talk you into doing for him?"

"I told him about events in Nuño's compound every day. And what I knew about life in the prelate's villa."

So, Chrétien's shadow had been reporting on him. Just not to the Church. Chrétien wasn't relieved; however, if Feris was reporting, perhaps he'd seen or heard things that Genoa shouldn't know.

"What did Antoni ask—and what did you reveal—about the boy-king?" Chrétien had to know how much danger these Genoa men had created for the king of Aragón.

"Nothing. I told him from the beginning that the boy's guards are layers and layers deep. Impenetrable."

"Thank all the dancing angels for that."

"Except that's when Antoni began asking about you, Seigneur Chrétien. That's when he began following you in the taverns."

"What did he want from me?"

"His cousin Zorzi—they didn't know I overhead—insisted that you could help."

"With the books?"

"No, with all the chaos Bonaventura wanted Zorzi to create. The riots were to serve as a distraction while they removed the texts. He recruited mercenaries for no other purpose than...Oh, why did Antoni need so many people to help him, but had no time for me?"

Chrétien bit back a frustrated shout. When he'd pieced it together in the dark last night, it seemed too impossible to connect the books to the chaos, even as he saw the threads of Genoa between the players. When he'd seen Feris, he believed he had the answer about a plot by Churchmen. But here it was laid out, insipid danger, simply for Antoni's gain. And Chrétien had been pulled into that danger, unable to see the many deceptions at work.

Now he was a bound prisoner incapable of keeping his oath to either Nuño or Durán to protect them with his life. Still, in his heart, Chrétien wanted what Miquel had in the last part of his life, to grow old, away from the world of chaos, the person he loved most at his side. A chance he'd miss if he couldn't free himself from these bonds and find his sword.

This morning he'd worried that failure meant begging mercy from Churchmen who served the pope seeing that people needed hope, not judgment. Now he was without his chainmail or sword, humiliated through his own vain-glorious choices. His kidnappers likely weren't bringing him along for Antoni to seduce. Yet, if they meant to kill him, they'd have left his body with the Templars on that blasted hill. He needed to concentrate on escape, not moan on about failure. He needed to do the opposite of what Feris did.

They jolted along the roadway, like animal carcasses going to market. Mercifully, Feris lapsed into silence. When it was possible to smell the sea, the destination for the wagons, Chrétien nudged Feris with the toes of his boot. That was as much movement as he could manage while bound so tightly.

"Brother Feris, a man like that will never return your love. But it has nothing to do with you. You have to find a good man, who sees your soul and loves you for it. I have a lover. That's why Antoni didn't beguile me the way he did you."

"Didn't beguile you? Then why did you do everything he asked you to do?"

"I...why, I..."

Chrétien made choices the only way he knew how, for honor and loyalty. He quivered at the humiliating thought of that being used against him, shaking like a beaten dog.

And felt his bonds loosen.

Which seemed to free his mind to form a plan as the wagon lurched along. He couldn't, however, act without involving his fellow prisoner, who stirred beside him.

"Things can't get worse, can they?" Feris asked. "Antoni's cousins won't hurt us, right? They just don't want us to tell anyone that Antoni stole the science library."

"It won't get worse." Chrétien did not understand why Feris sought reassurance from him. "I promise to protect you, in any way that I can, if it seems that harm might come to you."

"It must be nice to be a warrior." Feris became wistful again. "Who can make promises to protect others."

"Listen. I am going to escape. The next time the drovers stop to rest the oxen, I'll steal away with my horse." Chrétien planned as he spoke, willing the words to be true.

"How?"

"No matter. Do you want me to help free you, too?"

"No, I want to stay with my Antonello. He shall soon perceive that I am always loyal."

Working to keep his distaste for Feris's desperation from his voice, Chrétien said, "I have to ask you, by all that you consider holy, to keep quiet while I escape."

"I...I..."

"Brother Feris, make me one promise."

"If I can."

"Do not let yourself think that you might win Antoni's love by betraying me."

Feris breathed so deeply, Chrétien could feel the rise and fall of the man's chest.

"Feris, let me be free to go home to the man who loves me. If you want, I'll take you away, so you can find—"

The wagons stopped. Voices called out in their Genoa tongue. Chrétien turned their words over. Where were they corralling the horses? Was everyone around the wagons? The closer he listened, the clearer it was that the guards had ridden on, leaving only the drovers with the wagons.

Chrétien sat up, brushing off his bonds. He reached down to untied the lashings around his boots. Now, to find at least one steel blade. Then a horse. And he'd be gone. Though the thought of losing his own sword and Miquel's knife left Chrétien sick with regret. Better to have his own life though, and also to get away fast enough to send Nuño's men after Zorzi, with the truth about the city's chaos revealed.

"Farewell, Feris. I wish the best for you."

"Adieu. I shall pray for you."

Chrétien accepted any help offered to make his way out of the mire he'd waded into. But the offering of a prayer was not a promise that Feris would not betray him. He had to gamble that things couldn't get worse.

Voices shouted from farther down the merchants' train.

"Hey, my good friends. Untie us. We have to piss. We shall be forever grateful."

Qasim's voice.

"The Good God will grind your bones. You shall next live a pig's life, snuffling in darkness."

Sança, of course.

Yusuf must be there, too, since the Gemini twins were never more than an arm's reach from each other.

Aiieee, things could get worse. Now he had to get his own people away from a herd of trained fighters.

He needed more steel. Several horses. Better luck.

Or magic.

24
Harborside

CHRÉTIEN EDGED SILENTLY FROM the wagon and slipped into the shrub oak and cistus brush at the trail's edge. He saw no one. No one saw him. Once he moved several steps from the horse blanket where he'd bumped along through midday, the air smelled even stronger of the sea. It was marshy here. His boots were quickly soaked through. But then, even if the sodden trailside weren't seeping into his boots, the persistent drizzle would soon soak every other part of him.

He sidled along in the cover of winter shrubs and small trees, inspecting each of the wagons for weapons to steal while the oxen stood in harness, their hot breath sending blasts of steam in the dripping mist. The drovers and the guards had gathered at the head of the wagon train. Beyond them, occasional gusts of wind ruffled the waters of a small harbor. The Genoese merchants seemed to be the day's only visitors. They'd begun to load a ship, smaller than any transport Chrétien had sailed on. The other dozen vessels were fishermen's skiffs, the fishermen seeming to be home out of the rain and the rising wind.

At least, that's what Chrétien guessed at first. After he'd spied all the details of the men of Genoa loading their ship, his eyes caught forms in the mist. The locals watched the visitors from open sheds near the wharves, from the doorway of the single tumble-down inn near the water's edge. While Bonaventura completed business with a trio of villagers near the wharf—they seemed to be arguing vehemently—a man near a stone shed seemed to stare at Chrétien. Which deepened Chrétien's uneasiness, though it couldn't be possible that anyone saw through the mist to spy Chrétien amid the oaks and cistus. The mist turned to rain, dimpling the harbor water.

Should he shout to those lurking villagers for aid? No, the Genoa gang would overwhelm the villagers, and the guards and drovers had already proved their murderous capabilities.

At the front wagon, guards surrounded Qasim, Yusuf, and Sança, whose hands were bound in front of them. The guards debated who should escort each captive into the bushes in answer to Qasim's demand for relief.

Chrétien slipped back along the deserted wagon train, at last finding a Templar's sword in one wagon. The thin rain dripped from his hair, trickling inside his linen undershirt as he crept back under the tree line. He decided it was all well and good that Antoni had forced him into this adventure. Otherwise, Yusuf and Qasim and Sança would be standing at the edge of this little harbor without him. If he were still in the city, it'd be like the long living nightmare when he'd failed to be there while Miquel died and Tomas was tortured. This time, Chrétien was there to act for his friends.

All the Genoa men were all excessively deferential to Bonaventura and Antoni. If Chrétien could take either man as hostage, he'd control the scene. However, he had only a thin slice of moments—while Yusuf and Qasim were still unbound and could assist—to capture Bonaventura.

Waiting for the moment to act, which would be when Qasim returned from the bushes, Chrétien coiled every muscle, ready to lunge like a wolf.

Bonaventura left his argument with the villagers, tossing a dismissive wave over this shoulder as he crossed to the wagon train, again calling command to his men.

Slinking beyond where the drovers and guards huddled, Chrétien prepared to leave the cover of the trees. In four paces, he'd reach Bonaventura, who didn't sense the swordsman in the rain-drenched cistus brush behind him.

Chrétien took a silent step forward, ready to seize the man. They would all be free.

Miquel suddenly appeared, right beside him. "You can do it, my boy!"

Sança jerked upright, pulling away from the drover's hand on her shoulder, staring where Chrétien emerged. She yipped like a hound that caught a scent. Bonaventura turned, spoke one word of invective in his infernal tongue.

Two guards, noticing where Sança stared, came for him, swords drawn. That ended Chrétien's moment of action.

"*By all the angels dancing in the rain!* I just stepped out to piss." Chrétien resisted shrugging them off when they grabbed his arms and removed his recently acquired sword. "We're all Christians here, aren't we?"

"That's not clear," Qasim called. "My helper seems more bar-barian than Christian. Wanted to hold my hand back there. The whole entire time."

"Mine did that too!" Yusuf called. His face was calm, clear, hope-ful, like when Chrétien first met the child Yusuf. It made you want to rescue him even more whenever Yusuf put on the face that asserted he knew how to rescue himself. "His hands were warm and soft."

"My man was warm, but not soft," Qasim answered.

Provoked, those guards argued heatedly, egged on by responses from Qasim and Yusuf, until Bonaventura shouted for his men to finish loading the ship.

While guards were binding Chrétien's hands again—and also binding Qasim and Yusuf—Sança shook free of her inattentive guards and ran to Chrétien, grasping his thigh ferociously.

"O my captain!" She tipped her head back in the rain to see him. "You don't know pirates." She wrinkled her nose. "'Cooper-ate,' they'll say. And you must. See how I do it. You must learn to be agreeable, my lord."

What Sança did not say: *I told you they were pirates.*

"Sanço, lad!" Qasim called. He must know Sanço was Sança, and therefore they'd agreed to keep secrets. And Qasim echoed what Sança told Chrétien. "Do just as you're told."

They were told to huddle together under an oiled canvas sheet, where they stood freezing in the wind and rain, trying to keep Sança warm for what seemed like a full day.

"Why did you all leave Nuño's house?" Chrétien didn't want to be the censorious uncle, yet here he was, wishing that this once the Gemini twins had done as he'd asked.

Yusuf said, "Antoni sent a message, desperate for help."

"Sança was already at the door, dressed to go out," Qasim said. "She insisted pirates had taken you, and she refused to stay home."

Chrétien still groused. "You should have done as I asked you."

"But, my captain," Sança said, "we are called by the Good God to protect those who own our hearts. Nothing is more important."

"How did you know that something would happen to me?" Chrétien didn't chide her. She'd already endured unbelievable hardships. And she was right about what's most important.

"Because my heart is tied to yours, my captain. Because you saved my life."

"Speaking of ties," Qasim said, "if Chrétien and I work together, we might be able to free our bonds."

"I'll help," Sança said. "But they tied pirate knots, which are very hard to untangle."

When the sext bell rang (when Chrétien, his honor smashed, should have been in the city to redeem Nuño), their guards tossed the captives some bread. Though Qasim's and Chrétien's bonds had been undone, they still stood as if helpless, with only Sança's hands free to keep the bread from falling into the mud. She fed them, whispering, "Eat every bite. Sometimes pirates forget to feed you." Then she called for water, sounding meek, begging. Which Chrétien had never heard from this fierce girl before.

"Pirates like it when you beg," she whispered, instructing them with great authority on how to survive.

"Our only hope is to act before we're taken onto that ship. We have to seize the first possible moment to defeat the closest guards and grab their weapons."

"And run for the trees?" Yusuf asked.

"No, for the church," Chrétien said, "shouting for sanctuary. It's our only hope."

"Not the church!" Yusuf, Qasim, and Sança cried at the same time.

•

"Sanctuary—begging the Church for mercy—is our only hope," Chrétien said. "I don't like it, but it's the only way through the mire."

"It's Antoni who stole the books." Yusuf sounded petulant, which wasn't usually his way. "Why do I have to beg sanctuary for his sins?"

"Beyond the magister's rotten scheme," Chrétien said, "I am in extreme jeopardy with the prelate. Our adventure only adds to it, since I didn't return with the Templars they sent to bring me to answer at the bishops' court. Worse, Durán and Foix come today to join Nuño. For the prelate's council." Chrétien needed to tell all the details. "I missed a meeting that the prelate commanded, which puts them all in danger, along with Valerós and all of the Pays d'Òc."

"Isn't that a bit grand, uncle?"

"The night before we left the city, I was sleeping in the prelate's villa." It seemed like a month ago, not just part of a day. "A man attacked me and I killed him. An assassin who sought to murder the prelate," Chrétien said. "And the assassin was one of Nuño's sergeants. That looks extremely bad for Nuño."

"What do you think has happened in Montpelhièr since we left?" Yusuf seemed pensive—and unaware that he'd struck at the perpetual worry that Chrétien carried in his belly.

"I can't guess. I'm sure it's not good for Nuño or anyone who supports him. Like Durán and the Comte de Foix."

Both young men mused on this. Even in the dark, Chrétien could tell they stared as if they read each other's mind like ancient texts. At last Yusuf said, "Not one of the expletives my father taught me is suitable for the mire in which we are caught, uncle. I'm sorry if rescuing my astrology texts made it worse for you. However, we are all still alive," Yusuf said. "We now begin the next logical action. That's what my father would say. So, uncle…"

"What next?" Qasim and Yusuf said at the same time.

"Next," Chrétien said, "we throw ourselves on the Church's mercy and beg sanctuary. Otherwise, we freeze and starve in a ditch while trying to make our way to Valerós."

Concern creased Qasim's face. "My…companion serves the Fire Lord and is…sensitive. I can't go into a church."

"Me too," Sança said. "My skin burns when I go into a church, because of the Seeking Quills in my arms. It's not so bad when people are praying in the open air. But in a church," she shuddered, "it's torture."

"*Xiqueta,* is that magic in your arm from the Fire Lord?" Qasim asked Sança.

"Magic? No, they came from my great-great..." She paused, calculating, then slipped into her Catalan dialect. "*La meva gran-gran-àvia.* She says there is no magic."

Qasim pointed with his chin to the welts on Sança's arm. "She gave you these so you could find the lord of Morella?"

"Yes. She's Don Miquel's baby sister, but she's now old as the trees. She was eight when the lord of Morella went on crusade."

Chrétien could see it in her face now, her faint resemblance to his brother as a child. Perhaps that's why he thought her a boy. Her ancient relative, who must be an aunt to Tomás. Although Miquel often told stories of his fighting life, he never spoke of life in his home village. An entire family that Chrétien had never before had any curiosity to know. Quelling a desire to ask much more, Chrétien instead listened closely to Sança's story.

"My ancient grandmother put these Seeking Quills in my arm and said prayers to lead me to the lord of Morella." Sança glanced up at Chrétien. "But it's not magic. That would be heresy. And I'm not a heretic."

Their plan to sprint for sanctuary was interrupted when Feris was also thrust into their flimsy shelter. The shelter wasn't restored properly, so it flapped whenever the wind blew, dumping rain on them. Miquel joined them, too, as if he could help keep Sança warm.

"We are four against—what?" Qasim said. "Eighteen men?"

"Three," Chrétien said. "Feris won't help us, but he won't be in the way. Correct?" He nudged Feris with his elbow, clumsily bumping the monk's ear.

"Yes," Feris whispered.

When their guards stepped aside for another wagon to pass down to the harbor, Chrétien whispered, "Be ready on my count."

"Six men for me," Qasim pretended to count, "eight for you, and four for Yusuf."

"*Vivètz Valerós!* Valerós defeats all enemies. Even pirates." Yusuf responded to the whispered tease.

"Pirates can only be defeated by weather." Sança asserted her wisdom. "If you fight, they'll cut us open to feed the fishes."

Antoni joined them, lifting a corner of their crude shelter. He'd overhead Sança's last claim. "Bonaventura is not a pirate. He's a privateer, licensed by the consul of Genoa."

"I was on that pirate's ship last summer." Sança pointed to Bonaventura, who directed the loading of boxes onto the ship. "They cut up a boy who was captured with me."

"Last summer?" Hands on his hips, Antoni inspected Sança. "I was on his ship last summer. We tried to save one of the oarsmen, but the young man had already been called to God."

"You barbarians fed him to the fishes."

"No one can preserve the dead on a ship." Antoni sounded lofty, but Chrétien didn't trust that Antoni meant well about anything, having discovered the depth of the man's betrayal.

While this argument between the orphan and the magister continued, Chrétien sought a way to capture Antoni, to use him as a hostage to negotiate their freedom. With no weapon, he could only grab the man and threaten injury, but he'd have to depend on Qasim's bare hands to protect them when the guards came. Not good enough. Yet with the others there, he refused any private notion of despair.

"Are you the butcher who cut my friend open?" Sança had perfected that pointy-nose air of disdain. Chrétien couldn't determine whether she sensed Miquel beside her, as if a ghost could protect a mortal being. "I should have known when I smelled pirates."

"Your friend was destined to die. No other physician could save him. And I was bold to challenge God for a soul He already intended to take." Antoni's nostrils flared, visibly losing patience with the urchin. "But I promise you, child, that I stopped your friend's pain before he passed beyond the help of medicine."

"Magister, you are a good and kind man. You can let us go now." Chrétien tried reason, guessing that Bonaventura didn't want them to return to Montpelhièr, so they couldn't report the privateer's movements. "It will take us more than a day to walk back to the city. You'll be far away before then. Neither the count nor the Church can pursue you."

"My cousin insists that you come with us to Genoa," Antoni said. Chrétien couldn't read his face or hear in his voice how the magister felt about betraying men who called him a friend.

"You can't get two *sous* for us in ransom," Chrétien said. "I'm only a poor country seigneur. Yusuf is a scholar of no wealth."

Thankfully, Yusuf didn't resent that description. Qasim agreed vigorously with Chrétien.

Antoni said, "Bonaventura believes you'll call the Church down on us." Chrétien strained to hear the charming notes Antoni had employed while drawing them into his scheme.

"I have never once," Chrétien said, "called on the Church to help me. Let us go."

"Rome can pursue us farther and longer than anyone in Montpelhièr," Antoni said. "My new school in Genoa must come before your temporary discomforts."

While Chrétien badgered Antoni, Yusuf had been quiet, like the others, but then he implored, "Why, magister? Why bind our fate to yours? There must be another way to—"

Antoni cut him off, his voice rising with passion. "You know, dear Yusuf, that if we do not continue the work of the great philosophers, then we surrender to pain and misery, the kind born of devils, of evil, not the deliverances that God promised."

"And your school in Genoa will solve all that?" Yusuf fumed. Chrétien also had doubts, because every impassioned believer he'd met in this life caused peril for others. While Yusuf and Antoni argued, Chrétien shuffled, seeking a position from which to capture Antoni, because having such a hostage remained their sole hope.

"We must try." Antoni switched to another register, still addressing Yusuf. And he stepped back, perhaps a natural reaction to Yusuf's ire. "When you see Genoa, you'll want to join me."

"You betrayed your friends. And your own honor." Yusuf's voice was as brittle as yesterday's ice while his dark eyes burned in fury. Antoni looked away, not meeting his gaze. Chrétien stepped to Yusuf's side, prepared to snatch Antoni.

Antoni still wanted to recruit Yusuf. "You can lecture at our new university in Genoa. You'll enjoy more prestige than you do in Montpelhièr."

"I'll lecture in the dark halls of the Fire Lord before I ever speak or break bread with you again. You dream-eating *baquelar*." Yusuf spit the last word, calling Antoni a rogue. Their flimsy canvas tent was ripped away.

"Get them onto the ship," Bonaventura commanded. "The tide won't wait any longer."

Guards surrounded them as rain splashed from the canvas down Chrétien's neck. He'd lost the final chance to free them while still in the harbor.

"*Aiieee*, damnable mongrel rogues!" Miquel added a string of curses while the captives were herded onto ship. "I get seasick. That's why I never left Cyprus."

"Ghosts don't get seasick," Chrétien muttered.

"What do you know about it?" Miquel growled.

"Only what you taught me."

25
Oars

"Put them with the oarsmen." Bonaventura shouted instructions. "We don't have space for seigneurs of leisure."

As shipmaster, Bonaventura got busy with his sailors, who were hauling up anchor and setting sail. No horses had been brought on board, only the heavy boxes of books along with four captives, eight sailors, and Antoni. One of the sailors was Zorzi, Chrétien's nemesis, though it now seemed that Bonaventura had masterminded all the chaos that had plagued Montpelhièr. The outlines of the village of Maguelone could barely be seen in the drizzle as they left the harbor. Too misty to see the bishop's church, but the nones bell rang while they were still in sight of the village.

The four grown captives were shoved into the oar-pit under the cover of a folded sail lashed to the ship's rails. Their legs were fettered to the bars for rowers to brace themselves. Four sailors settled into the ship's oar-pit in pairs of two on the bench in front of the captives. Each pair shared a large oar.

"Why are we rowing into a storm?" One of the oarsmen called up to another sailor, the question followed by an extensive series of what must be expletives. Chrétien guessed at that, but those men all spoke a Genoa dialect, so he couldn't catch every word.

"Bonaventura wants us far from port right now," a sailor said. "Storm or no storm. Untie our guests' hands and show them how to row."

However, the other sailor-oarsmen couldn't be bothered to do more than untie the captives. They didn't either speak to or teach the captive oarsmen, leaving them to figure out for themselves how to row. Their captors had parted the Gemini twins, so Qasim was paired to row with Feris, and Chrétien rowed with Yusuf. Feris had little natural strength to contribute, and Chrétien saw in a heartbeat that Qasim decided to take on all the oar work on his side of the bench. For his part, Chrétien had never rowed so much as a raft on a cow pond.

"I'll follow your lead, uncle." Yusuf put his thin shoulders and strength into the effort, his eyes on Qasim's broad back.

Chrétien kept pestering the free oarsmen, occasionally getting an answer. This small ship was to sail close to the shore, then join one of Bonaventura's regular merchant ships at Marseille for the journey to Genoa.

"Why don't we have oarlocks?" Chrétien asked. That's what he'd seen in galley transports. This small ship had only wooden pegs stuck in the top edge of its sides. The sailor-oarsmen used theirs as a fulcrum. The captive oarsmen suffered, because the pins didn't hold the oars down like oarlocks would. So, Chrétien and Qasim often raised their oars too high, and then too often dipped their oars too deep in the rough brine when trying to stroke with power. Every mistake earned them curses from the sailor-oarsmen.

Soon, Sança was sick. Qasim was also sick and then was kicked in the ribs by the sailor-oarsman at his left side because Qasim had let go of his oar and Feris couldn't manage it. Chrétien and Yusuf fared better than the others, but the gusting winds made the day's bumpy wagon ride seem like a feather bed. Besides the rain, they were splashed with salt water that ran bitter in their mouths. The lashed sail that served as overhead shelter was quickly saturated by rain and spray from random waves. They'd all been cold and wet before these new miseries. Yusuf shivered beside him.

"*Fadrin,* relax. If you resist, you shake. Your blood can't warm your muscles." Chrétien was last this cold when he and Durán rode over the Pyrenees in winter, returning from Andalusia, and learning how to stay warm together. Spray from the waves splashed over him, but it felt as if he were sprayed with regret rather than chilly salt water. Regret, for all the mistaken turns he'd taken over the past two days.

And loss. By now, Durán had found Chrétien gone from the city. Durán must be hearing how Chrétien had failed Nuño and the other counts. Perhaps Nuño was explaining how Chrétien failed to protect him and the city from the plots and chaos. But only if, however,

Nuño hadn't already been found by the bishop to be complicit in the assassination attempt.

Chrétien had failed Nuño and his own true love.

And yet here he was, with a specific duty. He had four people to protect, even if the shivering, miserable Feris preferred to suffer for his misplaced, unrequited love. Those sensations flooded his veins like ice. Chrétien again bashed back any sensation that took his mind away from calculating possible action.

The small ship had two platforms raised above the deck, one at the rear and another at the fore where the anchor dangled. It had two masts, but when they left the harbor, only a smaller triangle sail had been unfurled at the fore of the ship. That must be because of the storm. None of the sailors climbed to the nests above the sails, which must also be because of the storm. Instead, a sailor on the fore platform called to others to steer the small ship. Apparently, the man could peer through the veil of rain to watch for the shore, which lay too far away to swim to, even without the storm.

The boxes—containing the books that lured Yusuf into this adventure and spurred Antoni to act on his passion—had been stored under the platforms at the rear and fore of the ship. Sança huddled under the platform's overhang at the rear of the ship.

A voice called out a command, and Sança uncurled from her shelter and ran to the oarsmen. Miquel shadowed her. "Here's water, my captain. You must drink when it's offered."

After losing her insides into the Great Sea, Sança had been given the job of bearing water to the oarsmen, a leash around her neck, water dripping from her nose. At least the coat and boots from Mme Marguerite seemed to keep her warm.

"I'm not happy to see you treated like a dog, *xiqueta,*" Chrétien said. "I promise to save you."

"This?" Sança touched the cord around her neck. "I am used to the cruelty of pirates, my captain."

When she passed him again after offering water to the other oarsmen, she whispered, "They stashed swords and knives under that cover, where they let me huddle. I'll get you free. But until then, you must do what they tell us."

"Chainmail?" Chrétien whispered.

"I haven't seen any."

One of the sailors called the orphan away. "Take shelter, stupid brat. Before the waves take you."

She huddled down once more among the heavy crates. Chrétien watched to see if the boxes moved with the tossing ship, worried that the devil's own books might crush Sança. But the boxes seemed well stowed, tied down with ropes.

"The most important action is to go to Morella." Miquel had remained beside Chrétien when Sança left for shelter. The ship tilted and shuddered, but his father remained steadily upright. Unwavering in the late light. "With an army."

"The most important action," Chrétien said, "is to get off this boat without drowning."

"That's merely the next step on the way to Morella," Miquel said. "I recommend a song."

It took only a heartbeat for Chrétien to choose the song. Two lines into it, Yusuf sang along. First, they traded lines and figured how to harmonize. Then they sang it as a round, teaching the other rowers, including the four who weren't captives.

> I never complain of my suffering.
> I'm better than a poor man
> Living in a rich house.
> But my lord committed a grievous sin.
> He knows my heart is in the battle.
> Fighting is my only work.
> So why does he commit folly,
> Giving me nothing with which to fight?
> Send me away. Don't make me suffer.
> I do what I love, but it costs silver to live.

They changed songs when a jagged line of wine-red sunset peeked out at the western horizon, a thin gap between the sea and the sky. Chrétien proposed another song, this one about Miquel's adventures in Syria. He said to Yusuf, "Did you know that song is about Miquel of Morella?"

"You told me the first time I heard you sing it," Yusuf said.

"That's not the right way to tell it." Sança appeared with a bucket of water again, and also brought strips of sailcloth to wrap their hands, to fend off blisters. "I know that story about Don Miquel. Your song doesn't tell it right."

"You know stories about Miquel?" Chrétien hadn't yet passed all astonishment for what Sança might claim. There was always more revealed. He glanced about, but Miquel wasn't there to agree or dispute the stories.

"From the cradle, like everyone in my village." Sança was wrapping Feris's hands to protect them, though the monk hadn't worked hard enough to gain blisters. "That's why the village cheered us when we went to find Miquel to beg him to save us. They cheered because we did what Miquel did, going off into the world to help our village. He always sent home the silver he earned as a crusader. For so long, that was the burden God gave him. But now we need Miquel of Morella in the flesh again."

Zorzi stood over them, Antoni at his side. "Miquel of Morella? That knight's been dead and gone for a decade."

That man must have been born cruel. May the Fire Lord burn his soul, now, even before the man shed life's coil. Zorzi turned his back on them, his arm around Antoni, dragging him away.

"*Aiieee!*" Sança shrieked. "Don Miquel dead? Who will save us?"

"Hush," Qasim said. "Stop crying. We'll all save Morella."

"But we need the don of Morella. We need our lord's army."

"My father is the don of Morella. He and Uncle Chrétien will bring an army," Yusuf said.

Qasim said, "We know how to go to battle."

"Don Miquel is dead!" She laid her head on Chrétien's shoulder, trembling with tears, her thin body shaking with sobs.

"He was my father, *xiqueta*." Chrétien felt Sança's grief as if he were losing his father yet again. "And I miss him every day. But can't you feel his spirit is with us?"

And today, Miquel's ghost was standing right there, unable to help. When the next spray of salt water doused them, it seemed to wash away all the grief and failure gnawing at his insides, over losing Miquel and failing to save his brother Tomás from torture. All that was over and gone. Instead, as salt water drenched them,

Chrétien swore on his own honor that he'd drain every last drop of his own blood if he had to, to save these people. However, his roiling insides were so concerned about Sança's grief and his next possible action, it took a heartbeat before he realized Sança had a knife and was sawing at his bonds while sobbing in his lap.

Then she slipped his long throwing knife into his freed hand. Yusuf sang while Sança slinked among them with her knife.

> But my lord committed a grievous sin.
> He knows my heart is in the battle.
> Fighting is my only work.

"Shut up!" A loud whisper called in the gathering dark. "We have company."

The Wandering Bishop

From the Secret History of the Flaming Cross
—Andonis de Zêna

To the outside world, I like to appear grateful. However, as a youth, I quickly absorbed and outstripped the various sciences and natural history that Abbot Rodolfo and his monks could teach. The Order of the Flaming Cross did not then have a tradition of medicine as science, and little knowledge from Salerno and elsewhere had reached the bucolic world of the monastery.

And, although I earlier told the story of Abbot Rodolfo dying of pleurisy...well, perhaps. But he was ancient when I first met him and, like most of the resident monks, given to the good life that's available for a monastery with one hundred lay brothers, rich orchards and farmlands, happy vineyards, and fat cattle. He was called "Rossellini," which means tiny in our tongue. Although he was diminutive in stature, I never knew him as a small man. It's not as if he passed before his time, but it is most likely that he died of the good life that the monastery allowed him to live.

I never learned how Francisco, my mentor in Toulouse, became a wandering bishop of our order. The man could be evasive when you asked anything personal. One other story I never got out of him was how God revealed to him that it was possible to keep a wife and a passel of children and still be a priest serving mass and baptizing infants. But it was with Francisco that I first understood that allegiance to God and independence from the Roman Church was a Flaming Cross custom shared with others from Genoa. It was from Francisco that I learned our duty, to send translated texts back to our order's home near Genoa.

Francisco shared two secrets with me, as brothers of the same order. As he'd learned in Salerno, he took every opportunity with a patient who required surgery to explore and understand what lies beneath the skin. Therefore, his surgery patients were liberally dosed with poppy syrup, and lovingly stitched at the end, and well-cared for until they healed. Or died.

I was not in Francisco's house two months before he shared this work and knowledge with me. And so, unlike most physicians in Christendom, I am well versed in how the muscles and ligaments and organs of the body are arranged and do their work.

I should share one more element from my life studying with Francisco in Toulouse. A man of insatiable curiosity, he'd stay up all night in conversation with scholars passing through the city. One science he encountered through such exchanges is called alchemy, which is both a philosophy and a systematic study of how the elements of earth and fire can be altered to create new substances. Some unlearned fools scoff, calling alchemy merely sympathetic magic. But new ways of healing and other new sciences shall enter the world through this profound discipline.

But its precepts served me well when God upended my world and sent me where I'd never dreamed that I might be called to serve. I am the most fortunate of men.

‡

Cançons de Montpelhièr

The stingy bishop had so much gold,
He forgot learning and made wealth his God.
But this many years before the Last Judgment,
I have made him pay
For betrayal and deceit.
With my beloved cousin,
We shall make the world right.

26
Cursed by the Fire Lord

AS THE WORD *PIRATI* flew in whispers among the sailors, Bonaventura's words trickled down to the oar-pit. "They'll want what they can ransom and sell. We're small, so they don't expect us to fight."

"But we will fight, won't we?" Antoni sounded worried. "We can't let them have my books."

Zorzi said, "Your books aren't worth their weight in goat dung to a pirate."

Antoni's voice quavered. "Tell me you'll fight."

"Yes, we will, my idiot cousin." Bonaventura slapped Antoni's shoulder. "These are mere salt-marsh thieves. Local fishermen out on a raid. They won't know how to fight like we do."

Bonaventura then called commands in an exalted whisper, his back to the sea so that his words weren't carried to the oncoming visitors, but Chrétien was certain he understood the commands. *Take position on the decks. A crossbow at each end. Draw the oars and lock them.*

The sailor-oarsmen silently slipped their oars through the pins on the rail. They grabbed the captives' oars, slipped them too, and then scrambled up with the other sailors. Sança dodged in the deep shadows to bring swords to Chrétien and Qasim while Chrétien sliced Yusuf's and Feris's bonds. Chrétien ran his hand over the pommel of the sword Sança brought him, feeling the strange sword's heft.

Beside Bonaventura on the platform at the fore, one sailor clumsily bent to wind his crossbow. Zorzi climbed up onto the rear platform, a crossbow over his shoulder. The sailors stared out into the dark, choppy waters, awaiting *pirati* visitors. Chrétien and his now-freed friends gathered in the darkness under the rear platform two heartbeats before grappling hooks skittered across the deck and locked on the ship's side, shaking the vessel at the same moment that another random wave crashed on the ship's other side.

After a day bound in fetters, Chrétien tensed in the proper way, prepared for battle, the thump of his heart sending blood hot enough to fire his muscles.

"We fight?" Qasim whispered.

"No, you all surrender. I'll fight if anyone comes for you."

The *pirati* called commands. Chrétien listened closely to hear what Saracen tongue they spoke, fooling his own ears for a heart-beat until he heard merely the local dialect.

The visiting crew swarmed over the side, battling with the sailors. Crossbow bolts stopped a couple of the pirates, but then the bowmen turned to close-hand fighting, having no time to rewind their bows.

"Take their boat." Miquel's whisper tickled Chrétien's neck. "Your best option."

"*Fadrins*," Chrétien didn't need to whisper in the din of the fight. "We're taking their boat."

Shoulders tight with the burden on his soul—getting his friends off this boat—he made a single motion, waving them forward. His captive friends slipped over the rail, onto the pirates' ship. Muscles twitchy with the rush to escape, Chrétien reached up without thinking to grab Zorzi's boot and toppled him into the water. The man's surprised shout didn't rise over the noise of the melee and surprise, but Chrétien heard enough, while leaping to join his friends, to enjoy for one heartbeat the satisfaction of petty revenge.

Qasim wrestled with the one sailor left on the pirates' ship. Pulse still racing, Chrétien bashed the fellow with the pommel of his sword. While Yusuf and Sança scrambled to unleash the grappling ropes, Qasim and Chrétien prepared the oars. Sança untied the tiller, preparing to steer them away. Yusuf pushed away from the Genoa ship with an oar. That crack between heaven and earth at the horizon widened, and the last of the ruddy sunlight shone on Bonaventura's ship. Feris stood, a ghost face at the ship's edge. Chrétien motioned for him to jump. The monk shook his head and slipped back under the platform.

When Chrétien put all his muscle into pushing the ships apart, it rocked both ships. Bonaventura and the pirate captain stiffened for two heartbeats. Then the pirate captain called out, "Stop them!"

Before any man responded, Sança shrieked curses in the common tongue of the Pays d'Òc.

"Demons from the Fire God shall eat your souls!"

A quartet of pirates about to pursue them paused at the Genoa ship's rail. While Qasim and Chrétien put all their strength into rowing away, Sança shouted again, words tearing from her throat, this time in Catalan.

"The Fire God shall scorch your family forever if you harm us."

Bonaventura's sailors took advantage of the pirates' uncertainty and began attacking them again, drawing everyone away from the ship's rails. But the pirates responded quickly, their numbers greater than the Genoa sailors.

Still fierce, the tiller in her hand, Sança hovered over the fellow Chrétien had silenced, who lay on the tiny deck. He proved to be a half-grown boy, only a bit larger and older than Sança. Yusuf untied the last of his own bonds, still hanging from his arms after he'd been cut free. He bent to bind the boy's hands just as the boy roused from the hard knock Chrétien had dealt him.

"Chop off his head. Else, he'll come back to life like pirates do."

"No, Sança." Chrétien had restrained men still wild after a battle ended, but never a child. The hot-blooded energy that seeks battle still flowed through his own veins, yet he yearned to wipe away the murderous fury in her face. "This boy did us no harm. We will not murder him. We'll put him on shore when we get there."

"All pirates are cruel and stink of dead fish." Sança spit, but into the sea, not onto the boy, who shivered.

Their own little boat rocked.

Yusuf and Qasim leaned over to fish a thrashing man from the water, hauling a water-logged Zorzi aboard. This time, it was Chrétien who wanted to spit on that sodden excuse for a nemesis.

"Tie him up!" Qasim shouted to Yusuf. "I need to row."

But Yusuf had already proceeded to knock Zorzi on the temple, which made it easier to truss the man so he couldn't thrash or disturb the boat.

"Gag him so he can't call to his friends." Chrétien wanted that pleasure for himself, but needed to row, to put distance between their little boat and the Genoa ship.

Yusuf shoved Zorzi into the space at Chrétien's feet, then stashed the ship's boy under an oiled sailcloth at the rear of the boat.

"Can you row, *fadrin?*" Chrétien asked Yusuf. Back on the Genoa ship, in the last of the day's light, he'd seen how blistered Yusuf's hands were. It was a tribute to Yusuf's valor that he'd handled their captives so well.

"Of course." Yusuf took up oars along with Chrétien and Qasim, while Sança held the tiller. Chrétien enjoyed a moment of spiteful pleasure, bracing his boots on the bound nemesis at the bottom of the boat. If they all lived, he had at least possession of Zorzi as a portion of proof with which to protect Nuño.

"O my captain! What direction do we sail?"

Her question dashed his relief from escaping the Genoa ship. All Chrétien knew about the Great Sea was that it swallowed men whole, sucked them down to their deaths.

In the deepening night, the only sounds were the splash of the oars and the lapping of the storm waves against the side of their stolen boat. They were alone at night on a stormy sea, and not one of them was a sailor.

.

Sança's question drained the last of intrepid battle power from Chrétien's veins. On the Genoa ship, Chrétien had heard sailors call directions to each other and believed he knew where the shore lay. But he'd lost that sense of direction in the rush to get away from the other ship. He couldn't answer Sança.

His muscles pulled the oars, not guided by his mind. His mind wrestled with the sensation that the Great Sea was a force seeking to pull them down to a watery death.

His insides shivered. His belly collapsed on itself.

So, this was what fear felt like.

This is what some men felt when they seized up, unable to enter a battle. He'd always been one of those who prodded fear-frozen men with spears and swords, moving them forward to do what must be done. How to be his own prod, to drive onward? Looking out, all he saw was black. All he felt was cold water, as if it whispered, seeking to suck him under the waves.

He closed his eyes, then blinked away the salty water to clear his vision. So black. Were his eyes open or not. He squeezed them tight, resisting the whispering waves.

And saw again that unwanted but branded vision. Durán and Numa before the flames.

"Captain?" Sança's voice drifted in the night.

Yusuf said, "If I could see the stars, I could tell the direction."

"I could too." Chrétien forced far more courage into his voice than he felt.

The boat rocked when Qasim and Sança both leaned over the rail, sick. They'd been so sick on the Genoa ship, how could they have anything left in their bellies to lose?

"You need to keep rowing." Miquel whispered, as if sharing a secret in the tiny fisher boat. "You want to get to shore before the storm returns."

"You and your careening thing haven't been helpful," Chrétien muttered, reconsidering why he'd longed for his father's wisdom. He kept rowing with all his physical power, gritting his teeth to add all the force of his fear-struck soul.

"The qareen says to steer in that direction." Miquel pointed a fraction to the left of where the boat now sailed. "At least that infernal creation can see in the dark, even better than a horse."

While the boat rocked with lapping waves, Chrétien tussled with that profoundly disagreeable sense of fear along with the lack of choice. They had to keep rowing. And it seemed Chrétien had to fully believe that Miquel was actually there and could translate directions from an invisible creature that perched on Qasim's neck.

Qasim again leaned over the rail, sick. Too ill to translate for his magical creature.

Chrétien called for everyone to take a brief rest. His boots pressed against his captive to stop Zorzi from squirming, Chrétien forced his eyes to do the best they could in the dark, to assess what they had on the boat. This boat was much smaller than the Genoa ship, with a single small square sail and places for only four oarsmen.

"How do we sail this beast?" Chrétien asked.

"I don't know," Yusuf said. "I've only been on large merchant ships. And only as a passenger."

"I don't know," Qasim said. "I grew up on the wharves, not on boats."

"I know." The pirate-boy called from under the sailcloth where Yusuf had stashed him.

"You're a pirate!" Sança said.

"No, I'm not. You spared my life. Let me help."

"What's your name?" Chrétien asked the boy.

"Tibaut."

"That's a good Christian name for a pirate."

"You are pirates," Tibaut said. "We are just fishermen."

"And now," Miquel's voice drifted from where he hung close by Sança, "my son has one more child in jeopardy to save."

Chrétien bit back a rebuke about his father not helping. He said, "We aren't pirates either, Tibaut. The Genoa men kidnapped us. And this isn't the best night for fishing."

"We hate Genoa's privateers," Tibaut said. "Haughty lying *baquelars*. Think God Himself should make way for them. So, we followed them from port to teach them a lesson."

"Will your friends back there win against Genoa?" Chrétien said.

"We often fight real pirates. We always win. But we've never fought Genoa before." He spat over the rail, though not with the vehemence Sança showed earlier. "I pray that the saints will bring them safely home. Can I help row?"

They took up the oars again. Sança insisted she could handle the tiller, that none of her friends knew how, and they couldn't trust a pirate to steer them right.

So, Chrétien called directions for Sança to steer, as received from a ghost who translated for an invisible beast sent by the Fire Lord. Qasim still had his head over the rail more than he rowed, unable to speak. Thankfully, Tibaut the fisher-boy agreed with every course correction that Chrétien called.

The next time Chrétien commanded a rest, Sança tied the tiller with a rope, then hunted amid the casks on the boat.

"What do you want, *xiqueta*?" Chrétien called.

"Food. You all need to eat. I only found the water cask."

"Check the casks in the bow," Tibaut said.

Sança didn't answer, because her back was still up about pirates, but she opened casks until she found hard biscuits and cheese wrapped in waxed linen. She also produced oiled-canvas rain cloaks, each with a wool blanket lashed to its inside, the most glorious garment Chrétien had ever worn. Because his father had taught him about mercy, he threw a cloak over the bound Zorzi. And also warned that he'd throw the *baquelar* back in the sea if he didn't stay still and not rock the boat.

While they gnawed the hard biscuits, Tibaut indicated the direction that Miquel had insisted they steer. "We're coming close. Can you see the prime signal fire?"

In the misty night, Chrétien couldn't perceive a light where Tibaut pointed. Neither could Yusuf or Qasim, but Sança, even with her nose out of joint with disdain, agreed that she could see it. One hand rested on Chrétien's shoulder when she pointed to a pinpoint of light.

"Steer for it," Tibaut said. "You'll see smaller fires when we're close, to guide us into the harbor."

"If you lie to us about the fires," Sança said, "the Fire Lord will consume your soul and—"

"Stop, *xiqueta!*" Chrétien wanted obedience, but he spoke too vehemently, and Sança shrank once more into the beaten orphan. She stood so near, he felt her heart beating. He said, "The Fire Lord can mind his own damned business and keep his nose out of ours."

"Ow!" Qasim batted his ear.

Yusuf said, "Sança, how did you know the curses you shouted?"

"On one pirate ship, the captain was a bad man who always shouted at his crew." Sança bit her lip. "But I didn't mean it. I'm not a heretic or a Saracen."

"We know you aren't, *xiqueta*." Qasim stroked her head. "You are our hero. You saved us all."

When they rowed again, Yusuf asked Tibaut, "You are Christian? Why did the Fire Lord's curses frighten your friends?"

"It's what we always hear," Tibaut said, "when pirates decide to fight instead of fleeing."

"When pirates say that," Sança's voice drifted in the night, a harsh whisper, "you have to cut off their heads to stop them."

"We are not cutting off anyone's head." Chrétien had shaken off that frigid fear and once again pondered how to free this fierce girl of her nightmares...now that he knew too well what fear felt like and what she must have endured.

"Then please row harder, my captain," she said. "If Genoa won the battle, the pirates will catch us and slice us open and then—"

"Feed us to the fishes," Yusuf and Qasim said.

27

Safe Harbor

EACH GUIDING BONFIRE RESTORED more of Chrétien's good sense. The Great Sea hadn't swallowed them. He could again seize control and ensure his friends' safety, which warmed whatever ran through Chrétien's veins.

Which might be sea water, after the night's adventures.

"The first thing we do on shore—" Chrétien began.

Yusuf jumped in. "We tell the village about their sailors being on the Genoa ship."

"Yes." Chrétien, however, had not been thinking about the fishermen. "And after that, we will go to the church."

Yusuf, rowing, lifted his oar too high and befuddled their efforts for a moment.

"I'm not thrilled." Qasim offered more words than he'd coughed out in a long while.

"Nor I," Chrétien said. "But it's the only path from these blood-freezing waves back to Montpelhièr."

"And then we go to Morella," Sança said.

"Yes, Sança." Chrétien rested his hand on her shoulder as if she might run to Morella from the ship. "We will find my brother in Valerós, and he will lead an army to save Morella."

A truce had fallen between Sança and Tibaut by the time she began following his instructions to wend their way into the harbor. Tibaut leaped onto the wharf to tie up the boat in a way that must have been his daily duty.

As they walked toward the inn at the edge of the harbor, Sança was telling Qasim about escaping fishermen who'd rescued her after her pirate-captors were shipwrecked. Walking on her other side, Tibaut punched her shoulder the way boys do. "You are a brave, strong fellow. Your family must be proud of you."

That might have cracked her shell, but instead of acknowledging Tibaut's tributes to her bravery, she said only, "It was easier this time, but just as wet as when I came to Maguelone at Christmas."

A large dog—the people in this part of the country never have any dog smaller than a wolf—bounded up to Tibaut, happy to see his master. As happy as the travelers were to be back on firm ground.

"Is this truly your dog?" Sança asked. "Pirates don't have dogs."

"He's called Christophe," Tibaut said, "because he fished me out of the harbor when I was a baby."

"Oh, a hero!"

She petted his dog while Tibaut told the night's tale to the fishermen who met them by the wharf. He finished, saying, "We're only alive because of this brave little fellow. He cursed the *baquelars* of Genoa into the fiery flames, and then steered us home."

"And the others?" the tallest fisherman asked.

"They were winning when these folks sailed away. These are the captives we saw the Genoese captain force onto his ship."

"We thought your friends were pirates." Chrétien answered the querying, anxious faces of the fishermen. "And we needed to escape from the Genoese. I'm sure your friends have defeated them and taken their ship."

The fishermen began to make plans to sail out at dawn to find their friends. One said, "Young Tibaut, take your friends up to the inn. Your mother Joaneta has been kicking our tails all night for letting you go to sea."

"Come." Tibaut pointed Chrétien and his friends to the inn. "I promise you a warm fire and the best food in Maguelone."

"Senhórs," Chrétien said. "Can I beg you to watch the gentleman from Genoa? I'd like to leave him bound in the boat for a moment while I make sure my friends are safe."

If Sança hadn't been sufficiently tamed while Tibaut proclaimed her virtues, his dog finished that job. At the inn, where Tibaut's mother was mistress, Sança curled up beside the dog to eat her bowl of pottage. She made room when Tibaut also wanted to sit by the fire with his dog.

"I'm sorry I thought you were a pirate," she said.

"And I'm sorry I thought you were," Tibaut said.

She was asleep with her head on the dog's broad back before Joaneta finished commanding all the accommodations to be made for these visitors. She had a wool blanket for each of them, but no extra pallets, only the woven mat on the pounded dirt floor.

"Senhóra, you cannot imagine how much this resembles a palace." Chrétien, drenched to the skin, persuaded Joaneta not to fret that she didn't have clothes to loan or sell to him. "A wool blanket is enough. We are grateful for your kindness."

"*Aiieee*, senhór, no more grateful than I am. You saved my son from infernal Genoese privateers. Those men will sell your soul for you and keep all the silver to themselves."

Chrétien had to go to the church but insisted that his friends stay at the inn. "As far as anyone is concerned, you are my servants, and far too filthy to appear before the bishop. I'll go alone to beg protection."

"Are you confessing the stolen books?" Yusuf quietly voiced what he most worried about.

"I'll say we tried to stop them. That's why we were kidnapped." Chrétien wiggled his nose, because that part of the plot still stunk of treachery. "After the way we were betrayed, and after Antoni's confession about his real business, there's no other story to tell the bishop besides that truth." Chrétien stretched. "I'm off to find the bishop's house."

"But the bishop is in Montpelhièr," Yusuf said.

"They must have left someone at home." Chrétien walked back along the wharf to retrieve his captive.

When Chrétien glanced back from the inn door, Miquel sat with Sança by the fire, cupping her head with one hand, rubbed her shoulders with the other.

Chrétien returned to the wharf where a pair of fishermen debated whether they should wait any longer before doing something with the man writhing at the bottom of the boat.

"Help me reel him up," Chrétien said.

They dragged Zorzi onto the wharf. Chrétien slung the bound man over his shoulder. He'd made his way twenty paces toward the church when a pair of Knights Templar approached, their swords drawn. Fortunately, it was two Templars he knew by name.

"*Hola*, Fabien. Olivier. I should say *bonsoir, non?*" Chrétien spoke to them in French, in spite of his wretched accent. They still had their swords at ready. "*Je suis arrive!* I have found the malefactor that I warned you about."

"You missed the prelate's meeting," Fabien said. "When we found your special license from Comte Nuño on our way here, we didn't know what to believe."

For one heartbeat, all the fear that swamped him on the Great Sea flooded his veins again. But Chrétien was back on dry ground, and no gambler was better at bluffing, even his brother Tomás.

"*Ça n'est pas grave.* You can help me with this fellow, though it's too awkward to get him down now that he's over my shoulder." Chrétien shifted his load roughly. "My new friend Zorzi needs to go to church with me for a good shriving. For he has sinned and fallen short of the glory of heaven."

•

"Please, senhór, you must share in this divine cheese tort. And try the salt cod. You'll agree with me that the wives in this village are angels of genius in the kitchen."

The priest who invited Chrétien into the bishop's personal refectory was the ancient red-headed cleric who'd blown him a kiss at Twelfth Night. His name was Paulus, and his voice seemed too deep for his small frame. Calling him "red headed" was generous, since Paulus had retained only a few long strands of rusty grey in a fringe that circled his head.

The room was austere, in contrast to the bountiful post-matins breakfast Paulus offered him. Not even a cushion offered comfort on the hard bench where Chrétien sat, getting ready to beg the Church for mercy because it had all been a colossal misunderstanding laced with trickery. Chrétien glanced around, feeling cautious, repressing a welling tide of apprehension. His clothes, still damp, clung to him when he moved. He still clutched the borrowed blanket like a cloak.

The little cleric behaved with friendly warmth, but the door to the next room had been left ajar, so Chrétien could hear the knights eliciting details from Zorzi. While the door might be ajar to allow Chrétien the joy of hearing Zorzi's confession, instead he felt it to be a threat. Zorzi might reveal Chrétien's and Yusuf's involvement with the books, and Chrétien did not enjoy the methods used to evoke Zorzi's confession.

Chrétien said, "Thank you for your kindness, Frere Paulus. Especially since I'm an utter stranger here, seeking mercy and help. There's a great deal to my tale. More than pirates and fishermen."

"You must try this tisane. It is quite invigorating." Not waiting for an answer, Paulus poured a steaming mug full from a clay pitcher. He sipped at his own tisane. "Did you know that people from here built Montpelhièr to escape pirates? And our fishermen still battle pirates and privateers plaguing the salt marshes and the Great Sea. So, my friend, your tale won't seem unusual in this town."

From the next room, a muffled wail rose, then words in that Genoa dialect. *"Mercy. For the love of God!"*

Chrétien coughed, prepared to deliver his own confession—not the kind where the Church absolves sin, but the kind where you confess your failures to a man who's feeding you a cheese tart while another man is being tortured in the next room.

Paulus savored another bite of his tart. "A dozen Templars rode with me yesterday when I returned from Montpelhièr. We enjoyed grand feast days this year, didn't we?"

"Twelfth Night seems like a long time ago." Chrétien speared a chunk of salt cod. What would Miquel do? How to proceed?

"We were still singing songs from the holiday on our way here yesterday when we reached the peak on the trail. Because of the gathering crows, we discovered a tangle of murdered Knights Templar. The men who attacked them had carefully removed all the arms and armor," Paulus sipped his herbal draft, "but they left your license from Comte Nuño to carry a sword in Montpelhièr."

Chrétien also sipped the bitter, foul tisane. If he was about to be seized by Templars, he had no way to send a message to Yusuf and the others, warning them to flee. And how could they run?

"Òc, Frere Paulus. I came here to tell you that tale."

But Paulus wanted to finish his own story first. "Then village folk told us that the only people who'd come down the trail were disagreeable Genoese merchants, some of whom boarded a ship with a privateer captain while the rest of the merchants continued on the road east."

A thud echoed from the next room. *"Bonaventura is my cousin. I only did what he ordered. I had no choice."*

Another thud, and a cry. Chrétien masked that the sound made him flinch. What if Nuño had been found responsible in the attempted assassination of the prelate? Would the prelate turn on Nuño's friends? What if those Churchmen in Montpelhièr discovered how Durán prayed? Would Durán be forced to suffer the same treatment as Zorzi? Something worse?

Paulus continued, as if he didn't hear Zorzi weeping. "Since the Templars couldn't sail after the privateer captain, they pursued the merchants' train. And found their dead friends' chainmail and weapons in the wagons."

"I'm happy your Templar guard managed to learn what happened." After that grim night, an unexpected giddiness seized Chrétien, making him want to laugh at this blessing of a priest and a company of Templars who could confirm his story.

"The Genoa traders confessed to using a Celt seigneur to guard their departure from the city, a knight that the privateer captain took as captive. So, we've been eager to hear the rest of the story." Paulus spoke cheerily. "I've argued that a knight like you carries a burden of filial duty and personal honor that forbids betrayal and murder."

Chrétien pretended to swallow a bite of tart, mouth dry as he also swallowed humiliation. "That's true, which makes it humbling to be safe now only because those fishermen pursued the privateers who kidnapped us."

"And we shall pray that our fishermen return safely." Paulus still sounded jaunty, out of character with the conversation. "But here you are now, with no need to worry." Paulus nipped crumbs from his tart, savoring them for a moment. "Now, tell me your tale."

Chrétien told the story, skipping the adventures with his orphan and leaving out Yusuf's role with the library. Paulus listened closely, encouraging more at each pause. At last he spoke again.

"Let me understand. You were persuaded to assist a wandering bishop of the Order of the Flaming Cross?" Paulus poured more of the ghastly tisane into Chrétien's cup. "An order that never held an authentic charter from the pope?"

"I didn't know that. Antoni claimed to have been ordained in the Flaming Cross monastery outside Genoa."

"Which proclaimed itself autonomous before the first of the crusades." Paulus set aside his breakfast, stroking his chin. "However, they say the Flaming Cross has been subsumed into a secret order called the Wheel and Serpent."

"We've heard rumors about Wheel and Serpent, too. In fact, I hunted an assassin and riot monger who was a member." Chrétien shivered, remembering the mark on Vincent's arm, the would-be assassin. "Zorzi is the man I found. Though I believe his cousin Bonaventura was the ringleader from a distance"

Zorzi wept in the room next door, calling on the names of saints Chrétien had never heard of.

"Ask any sailor on this side of the Great Sea," Frere Paulus said. "Your friend Zorzi—"

"Not a friend."

"We heard him confess to being a cousin of the privateer Bonaventura de Zêna, who traveled with a man known as *Il Priore Moresco* who, they say, has magical powers," Paulus said. "Could your magister be this Black Prior?"

"The man we knew as Magister Antoni is also Bonaventura's cousin," Chrétien said. "The magister did heal me in a way that some might call magic. My hand was torn open. First, he stitched it. You can still see traces of the silk thread." He offered his hand as testament. "Later, he rubbed it and sang prayers over it. That was only two days ago, so you should still see a raw, half-healed wound. But it's already pink and closed, as if it's been a week. But I do not know if he is your Black Prior."

"Sailors say the Black Prior uses sorcery, which superstitious sailors consider very bad practice."

"But Antoni has been in Montpelhièr, lecturing in medicine. Before that, he studied in Toulouse."

"Still, the Black Prior was seen last year in privateer attacks on Venetian and Saracen ships. Don't look surprised. This village hears every rumor floating around the Great Sea. And rumors say that the Black Prior knows how to heal with magic songs."

"It isn't magic," Chrétien blurted. "It happened to me. And there's no such thing as magic."

"That's not what the merchantmen from Genoa claim." Paulus steepled his hands, the way he had at Twelfth Night, and smiled over his fingertips at Chrétien. Zorzi's sobs once more drifted into the breakfast room. "The drovers and guards claim they were beguiled, tricked by the Black Prior's magic."

"Do the Templars believe that?" Chrétien strove to focus on what Paulus reported, not letting his mind wander over everything he'd been persuaded to believe in the past few days.

"The Templars found their brother-knights' kits and swords in the wagon train. Along with what must be your chainmail and weapons, judging from the size. The knights do not believe that such steel manifested in the wagons by magic."

Chrétien's heart swelled. He might get back his own sword and his father's knives. "Did the Templars also recover my horse?" How did that idea bubble up? Chrétien should instead be relieved that one priest and a clutch of Knights Templar might believe his tale. Perhaps he could return to Montpelhièr—where Durán waited—without fearing for his life. "I can't afford to lose a horse."

"Indeed. I can't imagine that Don Miquel of Morella left his sons with vast wealth. At least, not a wealth of gold and silver. I'd wager he left you only with a penchant for finding trouble."

Chrétien didn't answer, too surprised.

Paulus's deep voice rumbled. "And I should know better than to lay a bet with any son of Miquel's. You see, I knew your father many years ago in Edessa. The best years of my life."

"Everywhere I go," Chrétien surrendered his astonishment that Miquel entered every episode of this affair, "men claim Miquel of Morella was a remarkable man."

"No one I've met since can manage to find riotous joy in the most difficult of circumstances." Paulus offered the plate of salt cod, shaking his finger to admonish Chrétien to accept a generous serving. "I wasn't with the Church then, so I enjoyed my share of disorderly adventures living in the same camp as Miquel."

The young and wild Miquel wasn't the man who'd raised Chrétien and Tomás. Chrétien knew that bold knight only from stories shared by his old friends and from troubadours' songs.

The priest offered more of his wretched tisane, and Chrétien watched with trepidation as the little man refrained from touching Chrétien's hand. Did he want to offer comfort or restraint?

After that fumbled moment, Paulus said, "What the Templars have been unable to learn from the men of Genoa is why the Black Prior was traveling from Montpelhièr to the Great Sea, and why Bonaventura ordered the murder of those knights. Perhaps you can answer that, along with why you and your young friends were dragged into this adventure."

"Magister Antoni stole the entire library from the school of Science and Medicine."

Paulus drew back, obviously astonished.

"Antoni claimed he was removing only a few texts, to prevent a zealous priest from proclaiming heresy and destroying them." Although he felt free with Frere Paulus to discuss that—an old friend of his father's—but Chrétien chose not to explain how Yusuf had first drawn him into the plot. "I now know it isn't true, but Antoni asserted at first that he was removing only a few texts temporarily. That the texts would be restored after the prelate's council leaves Montpelhièr. And I believed him because of what's happened with other lecturers and magisters in the city."

"Ah. You mean Bernardo, the zealous disciple of that teacher Dominic Guzman. All those big ideas about how the Church must purify itself." Paulus pinched his lips, which seemed to be a habit when he pondered a problem. "But you said 'a few texts.' Not the entire Science and Medicine library."

Chrétien locked into the priest's kindly eyes. "It wasn't until the peak on the trail to Maguelone that I learned that Magister Antoni had stolen the entire library." In the long, excruciating night, Chrétien hadn't yet grappled with Antoni's treachery.

A man he believed to be a friend caused chaos in Montpelhièr for his own personal desires.

Vincent died by Chrétien's hand, a serpent in their midst, a tool of the Wheel and Serpent, likely led to evil by Zorzi.

Nuño may yet be in danger, because of Antoni and his prideful insistence that he was owed the knowledge in those books.

Chrétien rolled his shoulders, ready to fight. His energy surged back, wanting to make Antoni pay for the trouble he caused.

Paulus tapped his hand, drawing Chrétien's attention back. "May I pour the last of this in your cup?"

Chrétien refused any more of the bitter tisane. He'd swallowed as much medicinal healing as he could stomach. "Will the Templars be returning to Montpelhièr soon? I missed an appointment with the prelate yesterday and need to present my apologies."

"The Templars plan to leave at the terce bell. I'm sure they'll be happy to escort you. And your *servants*." Paulus smiled at that, clearly not believing the minor falsehood meant only to protect them. Frere Paulus then promised he'd write a note to the bishop. When he had ink, a quill, and parchment, and got busy with that task, he asked in the mild-mannered way of happy old men, "What did you learn from your adventure?"

Chrétien's first notion, which he'd never share with a soul, was that he was no longer angry with his father for dying and leaving him alone in the world. Instead, Chrétien answered the opposite of what he'd said to Yusuf not so very long ago.

"Not every problem can be solved with steel."

"A sage thought," Paulus said. "That must have been an astonishing lesson for a son of Don Miquel."

"I also learned—"

"Yes, my son?"

"There is no magic. It only looks like magic when we don't have enough information to use the gift of reason that God gave us." Sweet words, intended to make sure Frere Paulus was on his side. And perhaps it was true, for what could the help from Miquel and the careening thing to steer them to shore be except a gift—from who knows what source? "You can only solve problems by undertaking the next possible action."

The note the little priest wrote was brief, and he soon set aside his quill. "But you're a gambler. Do you believe in luck?"

"No," Chrétien said. "As my father taught, I believe only in happenstance and skill."

"Then the other lesson I hope you'll see in this adventure is that you are the same kind of hero as your father."

"You are too kind." Chretien looked at his hands, feeling unworthy of such praise. He resented that it felt like the same honeyed talk with which Antoni had beguiled him.

As if reading Chrétien's mind, Paulus said, "I'm serious, senhór. If you hadn't used all the skills your father taught, the thieves from Genoa would have escaped with no one knowing who and what they'd stolen."

"They still might escape. And I was forced to leave those fishermen in jeopardy."

"At the time, you thought they were pirates. Therefore, at that moment, you were the hero who saved your young friends."

Chrétien caught a whisper of the lesson that Paulus wanted to teach. He'd previously considered one piece of good fortune amid the catastrophe. "Even if I'd never left Montpelhièr, Antoni would have kidnapped my friends. He wanted…one of the young men as a lecturer in his new university. If I weren't taken, too, I wouldn't know what had become of my friends."

"Ah, yes. Now you see. As the only man in the adventure who possessed great talent, with skills only a son of Miquel might learn, you have served as a better savior than the knightly heroes in many songs."

Chrétien swallowed his last portion of salt cod, pondering Paulus's lesson. "I'm still struggling to forget the humiliation. But I suppose if there were a second chance, I'd do it all again. Except I'd follow my father's greatest teaching."

"What was that, *fadrin?*"

"Don't get caught." Chrétien nudged his clay mug, longing for a long drink of pure water.

"Ah! What I learned from Miquel, I try to practice every day." Paulus pitched his voice, imitating Miquel's unique Catalan accent. "Be the first on the field, and never surrender."

Chrétien laughed, perhaps the first time in days.

Paulus turned away from discussing the perils of Chrétien's current world, and instead asked gently about the end of Miquel's life. He then demanded a song, a particular song.

"One moment first, Frere Paulus."

Chrétien went to the door where the Templars were discussing the nature of sin and judgment with Zorzi. "Please ask Senhór Zorzi about the riots. And about the Wheel and Serpent attempt to murder the prelate."

Then he sang the song Paulus requested.

> If the greatest scholar testifies
> By reading the stars
> That truth and honesty will come,
> Or that noble action will return,
> I would not give odds on that proof.
> Evil grows robust and tall.
> Justice does not bring peace of mind,
> Whether ordained by God or men.
> So truth wanders away,
> Unable to separate dreams from life.
> If God does not wake and take care,
> Truth will quickly vanish.

28
The Bishop's Portico

CHRÉTIEN RETURNED TO THE harbor, finding it empty, since the fishermen had left in search of their friends. The day proved to be clear and fine. At the inn, he accepted a second breakfast of lentil porridge from Tibaut's mother. Sança was still asleep in front of the hearth, slumped across that dog, which was so huge it filled half the space before the hearth. Cloaks had been spread to dry, and the odor of drying wool and leather made the inn smell like a dockside midden heap. He roused his friends, explaining they were due to join the Knights Templar, who would take them back to Montpelhièr.

"We are free?" Yusuf asked.

"I think so," Chrétien said. "The priest gave me this scrap of parchment, to be delivered to the bishop for our safe passage."

The note was in Latin, so he asked Yusuf to read it to him.

Yusuf studied it, then swiped at his eyes. The corners of his mouth quirked with a smile. "What ghost stories did you tell this priest to win safe passage?"

Chrétien folded his arms and gave Yusuf a stern glare. "Please read it aloud."

Yusuf read a simplified version of the story Chrétien had told Paulus over breakfast. Yusuf stopped reading for a moment and rubbed his eyes, as if the story raised strong emotion. Then Yusuf read the ending, "'This man speaks truth and is an honor to his father, a great crusader.'"

Seeing how this affected Yusuf, while resisting all the emotion Paulus had stirred in his own heart, Chrétien glanced about, seeking Miquel, to see his response at hearing this, but the irritating man could not be counted on for anything.

"And so," Yusuf said, "we're saved by ghosts."

"He means, *gai sauvatge*, that your own brave heritage won our freedom." Qasim had relaxed back into pet names.

"Do you not perceive, *ma belette muet*," Yusuf again called Qasim a mute weasel, "that I seek to restore casual comradery with my fierce warrior uncle? It's been lost since—"

"Since those Genoa fiends scared the linen off our nether parts?" Qasim said. "Did you not see how those moments pleased me?"

"What? To be trussed like sausages and tossed in a wagon?"

"No, to see you transform into a warrior the moment you knew the scholar Yusuf had been betrayed."

"You doubted me? I am the son of Tomás of Cyprus, and Miquel of Morella. They placed a sword in my hand at birth."

"At birth, your nurse placed a toy quill in your hand and used a toy inkpot to suckle you," Qasim said. "From my cradle, I had to fight thieves who'd steal my swaddling clothes. But you? You lived where they stab each other in the back with penknives in order to curry favor with other scholars."

Relieved at the return of their usual squabbles, Chrétien fought against the wave of emotions that threatened to sweep him away, since all his relief came with regret. However, there was no time. The Templars were already at the door, ready to return to Montpelhièr.

Fabien had Chrétien's sword and chainmail, which the Templars had recovered (with Chrétien's horse) from the Genoa wagon train. Even though the plan was to ride with well-armed Templars, Chrétien eagerly shrugged on the chainmail, then flushed with unexpected elation when he buckled on that sword he'd taken from his father's armory. He spoke to his horse, soothing it, and also himself, apologizing for leaving it with strangers.

As Qasim and Yusuf prepared to ride the mounts that the Templars were lending them, Sança hesitated. She wanted to like the horses, but she trembled and had to be coaxed forward. Qasim showed her how to talk to the horse and pet it while he got ready to ride. Then he mounted and lifted Sança to ride in front of him, wrapping his cloak to enfold her.

"See? He likes you, *xiqueta*," Qasim said. "A horse knows his friends, even if they've only just met."

"Like a dog knows a friend?" Sança settled into the ride, while Yusuf rode close by Qasim.

Chrétien followed them. Fabien and Olivier rode beside him. The Templars split into two sets, with eight knights riding slowly, escorting the captured Genoa drovers and guards. A quartet would ride rapidly to the city with Chrétien and his friends. And Zorzi, bound to a horse, with two of the Templars guarding him closely.

By the time Chrétien and the others reached the pinnacle that had been the site of the previous day's catastrophe, Fabien and Olivier had begged the story of Chrétien's journey into Andalusia with Pedro *le Roi*. As they traveled onward into the suburbs to Montpelhièr, he told them about the battle at Las Navas de Tolosa, emphasizing the heroic actions of Durán, the seigneur of Montcava. That the hero was a Goodman heretic did not enter into Chrétien's story.

Olivier kept asking questions, verifying rumors he'd heard about the Aragón army's journey into Iberia to defeat the caliph. "Then are you the knight who saved Pedro *le roi* from an assassin?"

"No," Chrétien pointed behind him. "That was Yusuf of Valerós. He and Qasim are the unsung heroes of Las Navas de Tolosa."

Fabien and Olivier both turned, saluting Qasim, who looked like a warrior, even without chainmail and arms. Qasim pointed at the other half of the Gemini twins.

"That's Yusuf of Valerós," Qasim said. "Most people only know him from his lectures at the Mathematics school."

Although they'd all dried out after the night's adventure, Yusuf looked like a half-drowned greyhound, his long hair cascading in lank locks, dressed in clothes that might have been rescued from a midden heap. But he waved and smiled at the Templars' salute.

"People know hardly any of the stories from that crusade." Fabien frowned. "Why haven't your poets written songs? How will anyone know what happened?"

"I have no song about Pedro in Andalusia. But I can sing another song." Yusuf must have heard all of Chrétien's tale. He proceeded to sing, minor notes the way he'd learned to sing in Cairo, as mournful a song as any hymn about the loss of Jerusalem. An odd choice, since Pedro had been victorious in Iberia. But it set the right mood as far as

Chrétien cared. He was riding back to the city, not knowing what had happened since he left, ready to do whatever was needed for Nuño.

After a while, Yusuf insisted it was Chrétien's turn to sing. Yet, all he cared about was riding rapidly down the road that led to where the love of his life waited.

> When I am parted from him
> My heart broods sadly.
> When I come near that beauty,
> My heart fills my veins with sweet joy.
> I'm like a man with a blackwater fever.
> First I am hot and then shivering cold.
> Because he is vibrant and joyful
> And free of evil, I love him more
> Than Jonathan did David.

•

The Templars led the way through Montpelhièr's western gate when the nones bell was ringing. They rode straight to the stables in the mews behind the bishop's villa, since the horses had been ridden harder that any of them liked.

"Qasim." Chrétien motioned the man to his side. "Please take my horse and rub it down with the others. I'll meet you later at Nuño's villa."

"Of course." Qasim took Chrétien's reins to lead the horse into the stable, Sança clinging close to his side amid the commotion and crowd of the dismounting Templars and welcoming stablemen. "*Xiqueta,* do you want to learn how to care for horses after they've worked hard?" Qasim's voice was always gentle with the orphan.

Qasim, Sança, and Yusuf were quickly too far away for Chrétien to hear more. Stable workers appeared to take the Templars' horses. Fabien and Olivier removed Zorzi from the horse he rode while claiming, in a false friendly way, that the bishop would love the man's company.

"You shall be treated to sweet cakes and wine, *mon ami.*" Fabien led Zorzi as if on a leash, the Genoa man's hands still bound, leaving him no chance to escape.

Olivier said, "The bishop and the Templars' master shall love to hear you sing." He picked up the binding that had tied Zorzi to the saddle, forcing Zorzi to hobble between them.

"We agree?" Chrétien said. "We take him to the prelate and Comte Nuño, and explain that these *baquelars* from Genoa are the source of unrest in the city."

"Yes," Fabien said. "I have the scribe's record of Zorzi's confession. Our comrades will gather others to search their villa here."

Chrétien turned down the narrow winding alley that led from the Templars' mews to the square near the bishop's villa. Behind him, there was a scuffle and a series of oaths in French and Genoese dialect.

"Go ahead!" Olivier called. "We'll catch up in a moment."

Enjoying the familiar sense of chainmail under his cloak and the swing of his own sword at his side, Chrétien stomped through the alley, eager to find Durán as soon as possible. He stepped from the deep shadows of the alley into the glaring sun that lit the square.

A ramshackle crowd meandered about the square, coalescing into knots of men. Chrétien quickly identified huddles of men he'd confronted two nights before. The *gardes du corps* in the square were outnumbered and seemingly dispirited. They hovered at the edges, making no motion to control the crowd. Absent from the square were any Templars or knights from the counts' armies. The knots of men began shouting their calls from the riots.

"*Stranger, go home.*"

"*No heretic saviors.*"

"*Jew and Saracens, God will deny you heaven.*"

"Go home, fools!" Chrétien shouted, annoyed rather than threatened. The crowd was only a barrier to what he wanted, which was to find Durán. And deliver Zorzi to Nuño.

The chants again. He shouted over them.

"The *baquelars* who hired you left town. You will never be paid."

At least two groups of men had determined that the *gardes du corps* posed no threat and advanced into the square.

"Stop. Those men betrayed you." Chrétien had a sword and a desire to stop chaos for Nuño's sake, but he was only one man in the crowd. "Make peace in your city."

The chants again.

"*Stranger, go home.*"

"*No heretic saviors.*"

"*Jew and Saracens, God will deny you heaven.*"

A shriek in Catalan from the far side of the square. "Demons from the Fire God shall eat your souls!"

Chrétien sprinted across the square to where Sança stood shouting. He couldn't see Yusuf or Qasim, but he threw his cloak over her and headed for the bishop's villa. They hadn't taken four steps when the villa's heavy doors were thrown open with a bang. Four Templars stood at the edge of the portico, calling for silence.

The people in the square became more subdued, but silence didn't take hold.

The prelate appeared alongside Nuño. Ramón-roger, the Comte de Foix, was behind Nuño. Yet no sign of Durán's beautiful auburn hair in that crew of old men. When Nuño stepped forward, half the crowd roared a greeting, the other half moaned.

Chrétien kept his arm around Sança, murmuring words his mother might use to calm her down; he had his eye on the parts of the crowd that he believed to be most dangerous. He finally spied Yusuf and Qasim in the crowd. He nodded their way, unhappy that they'd let this fierce girl loose again.

Nuño, a cloud over his face, his shoulders slumped, called for silence, but his words didn't further quiet the crowd until he shouted, "Let the punishment begin."

Across the way, where the narrow alley emptied into the square, the *gardes du corps* were binding a man's hands and then lifting him into the pillory barrel. Two of them stepped aside.

A man with the body of a god. Broad shouldered. Auburn hair. Durán.

"Stop!" Chrétien shouted. He shoved Sança toward Yusuf and Qasim and sprinted back across the square, knocking men out of his way. "That is not the man you want!"

He couldn't wrestle four guards and couldn't use his sword. But he tugged hard at one guard's arm, who jerked his prisoner when he stumbled. The man being pushed into the barrel wasn't Durán. It was Guillaume, the corporal from the *gardes du corps* quartered by the east gate. Sergeant Vincent's friend. Shining auburn hair around a long-ago burned and ruined face.

Pietro, the prelate, called from the portico. "Perhaps not. But he is your assassin's comrade. Though he refuses to confess what he knows."

"Because he doesn't know anything." Chrétien recovered from his mistake, his heart still beating wildly over perceived danger to Durán. "He has nothing to do with the chaos in this city."

Fabien and Olivier emerged from the narrow alley with Zorzi hobbling between them. They'd gagged Zorzi, and one side of the man's face was bright red from a blow.

The strain of the last few days settled on Chrétien. He just wanted this all over. He ran to the mouth of the alley and grabbed Zorzi from the two Templars. He thrust the man over his shoulder, and bounded for the portico, lengths of Zorzi's bindings whipping out behind him. His chainmail made it awkward, and the steel links pressed painfully into his shoulders. He stopped at the steps, so that he had to look up to the prelate and Comte Nuño as if he were a supplicant.

"This is the man who provoked the riots," Chrétien hoisted Zorzi off his shoulder and held him so that his toes didn't touch the pavement. "Zorzi de Zêna used lies and treachery to convince Sergeant Vincent to undertake murder."

"Senhór Chrétien—" Nuño began.

"Monsenyor, this wretch," Chrétien let the man's feet touch the pavement while he pulled up Zorzi's sleeve, revealing the serpentine tattoo, "is the Wheel and Serpent traitor who wants everyone to think he's a magical swordsman."

"Do you have proof?" Pietro said.

"Monsenyor," Fabien had caught up with Chrétien, "we have a far more fantastic tale than you could ever dream. And a scribe captured his confession."

Two hands on Zorzi's shoulders, Chrétien climbed halfway up the portico and then whirled to face the muttering crowd in the square, dangling Zorzi. "If this man promised you anything—money or glory—he lied. He came here only to create chaos while privateers robbed the city."

Chrétien, being tall, could make Zorzi dance like a puppet.

"What did he promise you for chanting in the streets? *'Stranger, go home?' 'No heretic saviors?'* Is he your champion now? He sought only to make you serve as his fools. Go home."

A dozen Templars appeared, armed. The folly of the pillory barrel had been abandoned, though Chrétien hadn't seen Nuño pass a message to the guards. At the edges of the square, people slipped up side streets. The disparate elements of the crowd appeared to forget their various purposes.

Olivier, the Templar, mounted the steps, speaking to the prelate and the bishop. "This man and a pack of Genoa merchants stole a trove of books from the science school and then murdered four Templars."

Fabien came closer but didn't seem to want to step into the whirlwind of Chrétien's anger. "Seigneur Chrétien," he said quietly, "please let us have our prisoner back."

While Comte Nuño shouted for peace, sending everyone home, Chrétien dropped Zorzi at the Templars' feet.

He slowly mounted the steps of the portico, slower than it took Fabien and Olivier to bring Zorzi before the bishop. The two Templars were explaining what they believed must be done next. Chrétien reached in his jerkin for the letter from Frere Paulus, and handed it to the bishop.

"Your good man at Maguelone wrote this for your attention."

Nuño, tears brimming, embraced Chrétien while whispering *se vos plai* over and over, calling him the hero of Montpelhièr who'd come just in time. Yet Chrétien searched the small crowd on the portico. Comte Ramón-roger, standing behind Nuño, raised a hand in greeting. But Chrétien was looking for Durán.

"Do you agree, Senhór Chrétien?" Nuño asked.

"I'm sorry?"

"Should I do what these Templars suggest? Banish every man from Genoa and seize the merchants' villa?"

"Of course. If the Templars haven't already begun a search." Chrétien remained distracted, looking for Durán, when this was the moment to proclaim he had performed his duty for Nuño. "I've done what I could. All I want now is—"

"To tell your story? No, you need…" Nuño released Chrétien from the initial embrace but still held the sleeve of his chainmail, as if not wanting Chrétien to get away again.

That close, Chrétien could murmur in the count's ear. "You weren't wrong about the plot. The one I found came from Genoa, not the Church." Chrétien was relieved not to be entwined in a deep plot between the Church and the lords of the south.

Nuño stepped back to examine him, still holding the sleeve of his chainmail. "That was one plot solved. You didn't actually prove the first assassin—or future ones—aren't part of a different plot. You didn't prove that the lords of the south are safe."

The count released his sleeve, and the linked chains rang up Chrétien's arm as he accepted the truth of what the count said. The man wasn't mad…and the council likely presented as much danger as if Chrétien had never gotten involved.

Nuño bashed Chrétien arm like a true comrade. "We have no hope but to feel our way forward. You need to get out of your chainmail, senhór. Then join us at supper. It will take all night to hear your story, won't it?"

Ramón-roger, the Comte de Foix, hovered. He undoubtedly shared Nuño's view of the remaining dangers for the lords and cities of the south. "If you don't mind me saying so, Senhór Chrétien, you look as if you were drowned in a horse pond and hung up as a scarecrow to dry."

"That's close to the truth," Chrétien said, still shaking off the chill from Nuño's words. He asked Ramón-roger for all he wanted at that moment. "Where's Durán?"

"He's inside, holding my place in the prelate's council. They're debating at length who should be regent for the king of Aragón."

"Can you—"

"Fetch him for you? It's the least I can do after what you've done for us, *bonfraire*." Ramón-roger disappeared.

"Monsenyor the count." A small voice beside him spoke in Catalan dialect. "Can we please have our captain back? He's going to lead us on a crusade and we have to get ready."

Chrétien picked her up. "*Xiqueta,* we will go when our duty is done here. You have been so brave this far. Just be a bit patient. At least, now you can forget pirates and Saracens and slavers."

Nuño said, "Perhaps it will take longer than just supper to hear your story."

29
A Crusader's Song

THE CROWD HAD DISPERSED. Chrétien stood, arms folded, towering over Yusuf and Qasim. He wanted to glare at them, but he kept watching the villa door, hoping to see Durán, and he had to drop an arm to keep Sança at his side. He didn't have to ask questions about why they weren't at Nuño's villa, as he'd instructed, because Qasim was eager to explain.

"We're on our way to pack," Qasim said. "We can leave in the morning if you're ready."

"You're giving up on school?" Chrétien hadn't been sure that Yusuf would leave Montpelhièr rather than return to school.

"No, not giving up," Yusuf said. Qasim glared at him, shaking his head. "Nothing is more important to me than university."

"Even if they can't get along well enough in this city to form a university," Qasim said.

Yusuf ignored that. "Qasim has to go to Morella because of his companions, Sança and…the qareen. It's my turn to follow Qasim for a year."

"And I decided that if Yusuf's qareen has free will," Qasim said, "then I must also be able to choose. We need to go to Morella, to take Sança's village back from bandits."

"Lord love all the whirling angels! You have not done your duty!" Miquel stood over Qasim, shouting in the way he did when his young sons broke inviolate household rules.

Qasim glanced around as if confused.

Miquel shouted again. "If you have free will, then use it. Make things right." He paused as if listening.

Qasim rubbed his ear.

Miquel ranted again. "You plagued me for seventy years. Now you're bothering this perfectly nice boy. Use your damn free will, demon. Do what your blasted Fire Lord created you to do. Take care of my family."

Qasim tried to stand, but Miquel pressed both hands down on Qasim's shoulders, so he couldn't move. Miquel lowered his voice, which if you were his son, meant you were now in dire straits.

Movement across the now-empty square distracted Chrétien from Miquel's inexplicable tirade. The door to the prelate's villa opened again. Durán stood in the opening, hesitated, as if getting his bearings. Elated, Chrétien waved at Durán to get his attention, but then Qasim twitched, like a man with the falling sickness. Yusuf caught him, arms wrapping his friend to keep him from tumbling to the pavement. He leaned on Chrétien for support, while Chrétien was still trying to shelter and steady Sança. A blast of air forced Chrétien to step back. The air rushing past him smelled of smoke and autumn decay.

An enormous bird hung in the air above him, its claws out, as if to attack his face. Its wings blocked the sun, casting a black shadow. Chrétien reached up to protect himself. His hand burned where he brushed it, as if he'd reached into a raging flame.

The huge bird-thing pulled back, hovered higher, its beating black wings revealing its face, which seemed human. Except it had a beak like an imperial eagle. It called to Chrétien, in that weak way eagles call their mates, with a high-pitched whistle.

"Don't strike it," Miquel said. "That would not end well."

Its shadow blocked the sun over Chrétien, its wings so wide that he remained in the shade as it rose higher. For the second time in recent memory, fear burned along Chrétien's nerves. Then the beast plunged, flying straight down, as if to pluck Chrétien from the ground like a raptor seizing a mouse.

But before he could duck or offer protection, it settled gently on Sança's shoulder, while she was murmuring comforts to the no-longer-twitching Qasim. She stepped back, startled. And the bird-beast disappeared.

The full winter sun shone on Chrétien again. He stared around the square but no one appeared to have noticed the gigantic creature that hovered there seconds before.

Sança tipped her head, listening, in that way she often did. Whatever she heard, a smile crept over her face. She giggled for a moment, one hand over her mouth. The smile spread over her face. She finally appeared her age, without cares, the usual bitter unhappiness vanished. Her bone-sharp shoulders relaxed, as if she no longer needed to keep her back up against the world. As if she'd been soothed, not by magic, but by something that reason did not yet understand.

Durán descended the villa's stairs, walking toward Chrétien, which distracted him from supporting Sança, Yusuf, and Qasim. When Chrétien tried to move to join Durán, Sança wrapped her arms around his waist, which he had never once before allowed.

"O my captain! The lord of Morella has sent us a guide. A companion. You and I shall never be lost again."

Miquel had his hand on her head, stroking her the way he did his own children when they were wee tykes. He looked up at Chrétien. "Never could get that damned bird-thing to do what I asked. But I suppose this solves the problem. Your little cousin seems as stuck on you as a qareen might be." He caught Chrétien staring across the square at Durán. "*Aiieee!* That man is handsome as an angel. No, he's like one of the old gods who used to walk this earth."

Chrétien couldn't resist asking. "How would you know?"

"You'd be surprised," Miquel said. "Since I left this world, I've been places. Seen things."

Chrétien opened his arms at Durán's approach. But Sança still clung to him, and Yusuf still steadied himself against Chrétien's back, while Qasim struggled out of Yusuf's embrace.

"Leave off, *gai sauvatge*. I'm fine."

"What will you do, *ma belette muet?*" Yusuf remained stiff with worry for Qasim.

"I'm going to the jakes. Alone. And giving you the chance to do the same for the first time in a year." Qasim gave Yusuf a relieved smile then stroked Sança's shoulder. "*Xiqueta*, are you well?"

She hugged him. "Never better, my brother. Our friend says thank you for carrying it." She smiled again, so brilliantly Chrétien was painfully aware that he hadn't seen her smile since Twelfth

Night. Sança looked between Chrétien and Qasim. "But you promised we'd find our supper soon. I'm hungry. Aren't you?"

"Look over there." Qasim pointed to a corner of the square, where an innkeeper was unrolling the canvas shade over his street stand, ready to sell his wares now that the angry crowd had drifted away. "One of our Templar friends lent me some silver for our dinner. Let's see if he has my favorite sausages."

Freed from his orphan's embrace, sure that all three of his companions were indeed well as they crossed the square, Chrétien walked to meet Durán, repressing the impulse to run.

They grasped each other's forearms, like soldiers greeting their brothers-in-arms, which was not what either of them longed for. Durán's touch set his blood on fire, and the blaze coursed through Chrétien's veins. Warm at last.

"Chrétien de St-Joachim?" A man rushed toward Chrétien and Durán, one of the Templars who'd guarded the Genoa drovers on the road out of the city. Agitated, having obviously ridden hard, he addressed Durán. "This is the seigneur who captured Zorzi, the Genoa pirate. The hero of Maguelone!"

Chrétien wanted to kiss Durán's amused smile, but instead he answered the messenger. "Have you already brought the other men of Genoa to Montpelhièr? May I help deliver them to Comte Nuño for justice?" Chrétien did want that, but he felt Durán's fingers on his wrist. He needed to see Nuño again—but only much later.

"I rode ahead with a message from a relay rider." The Templar was in too much of a hurry to even introduce himself. "The fishermen have captured the Genoa ship. They are sailing that ship to Marseille, because the privateer Bonaventura has promised a large ransom if they return him to his fleet."

"What good luck!" Chrétien spoke the words, though he was a gambler who didn't believe in luck, only skill and happenstance.

The exhausted Templar looked dubious. "The fishermen give thanks to St-Peter and St-Andrew."

"Of course," Chrétien said. "All the dancing angels in heaven know how earnestly I am praying at this moment."

The Templar glanced between Chrétien and Durán, as if becoming aware that he had intruded on a private moment. "Excuse me, I must find my master. We need to take a force to Marseille to demand justice from Bonaventura de Zêna."

After failing at introductions, the Templar failed to even say farewell. He bolted for the alley that led back to the mews and then to the Templars quarters.

"The hero of Montpelhièr *and* Maguelone?" Durán's fingers sneaked up Chrétien's sleeve to stroke bare skin. Like sunlight on a spring day, the heat of that touch chased the last of ice and sea water from his veins. "I missed you. It was beyond what a man should have to endure, coming here and finding you gone."

"Every dancing angel knows how badly I've missed you." Even with the scant touch they could manage in this public square, Chrétien's fingers confirmed that this was the real Durán, not another dream. "This winter was the loneliest I've known in years."

"Then why, my dear one," Durán thumped Chrétien's chest with a knuckle, "did you never answer my letters?"

"Me not answer? I thought it was the other way around." Bad happenstance? A cruel trick of unreliable messengers? He felt too happy at the moment to curse the waywardness of the universe. "When you didn't answer my messages, I plotted to punish you."

"I didn't want to scold you," Durán laid his warm hand on Chrétien's, tilting his head. "I only wanted to run and find you. Then when I get here, I find that you are once more busily serving as other men's hero."

Whatever Durán said, whatever scolding Chrétien had earned or not earned, he just wanted to hear Durán's voice, watch the knob at his throat bob.

"I was ready to run to you, but I waited when I learned you were coming here. One kind of honor, which I learned from my father, led me away to protect Yusuf. And Nuño."

"Of course it did." Durán laughed. His breath, white in the Montpelhièr winter air, brushed Chrétien's lips like a breeze in May. "I'd expect nothing less."

"And that's why I'm standing here in chainmail, when I wish we were—"

"I'm happy to help you shrug off that chainmail, as soon as you're free from…" He seemed puzzled, staring over Chrétien's shoulder (oh joy! A man tall enough to do that!) "What's happening with our friends?"

Durán pointed to Yusuf and Qasim, who were instructing Sança, though their words didn't carry across the square.

"*Ai, cor dolç.* It's a long story. Let's go where we can—"

"*Hola,* Yusuf! Qasim!" Durán called.

Chrétien made a gesture to hush him, which always annoyed Durán, and which always proved counter-productive.

"Does that girl have a pet eagle from Africa? Am I supposed to be quiet so the bird isn't frightened?" He'd released Chrétien's forearms, but wound his finger through a loop on the belt that held Chrétien's sword sheath. "You can't bring a wild animal into the city and expect—"

"No, it's called a...a...qareen." He took care to remember the correct word, while surprised that Durán could see the creature. Since there was no magic, then Durán possessed a skill Chrétien hadn't yet discovered.

"Who's the fellow by Qasim and Yusuf? From across the square, I thought at first it was your brother. But Tomás is at Valerós."

"Can you see ghosts?"

"I saw my mother's ghost for a few years after she died." Durán spoke as if this were a normal conversation. "Then she drifted away. I've never talked about it. The priest I told said that it wasn't possible. That my grief made me imagine things."

Though disconcerted that his heretic lover could see ghosts and also the qareen, Chrétien broached his drastic news. "That's my father's ghost. And the girl is a distant cousin from his home village on the Aragón frontier. She claims I'm the lord who's supposed to save her village. So, I need to fetch Tomás from Valerós and then go to Morella, instead of returning to Toulouse."

"Even though you've never been to Morella?" Durán wrinkled his nose, as if amused.

"The girl asked my help—her name is Sança. And the ghost said I should go. Yusuf and Qasim are going. It's...it's going to take a bit to explain."

"It's fine. If it's what you have to do." Durán once more stared into Chrétien's eyes. He licked his lips in a way that always distracted Chrétien whenever they had serious business. "But I'm not surrendering you to ghosts and crusades. I'm coming along. Do we get a moment to enjoy being safe and together before we pack?"

"I want nothing more than—"

"O my captain!" Sança cried out, though Chrétien longed to be free to lose himself in Durán's eyes forever. "Come share our supper. Bring your friend." She paused, then shouted for everyone in the square to hear. "He's so handsome!"

■

When I see meadows grow green in April,
When the orchards flower,
And I see the streams run pure
And hear the songbirds trill,
When the odor of flowers and grass fills the air,
My heart sings with the birds,
My joy renewed, like the buds on boughs.

When I see the fruit orchards in leaf
And summer is coming in again,
My heart draws me toward wild pleasures
In the company of my true comrades.
Heart's joy and birdsongs beg me to sing merrily.
As my father did in days long gone.

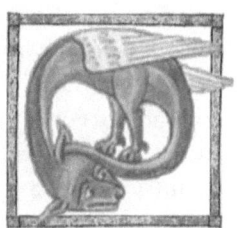

A Farewell

From the Secret History of the Flaming Cross
— Antun al-Abbas

At one point in my nearly forgotten past, I became enamored of the writings of the great physician Rhazes, who wrote the most precious of the medical manuscripts that I took from my old mentor Ezra Ibn Isaac in Toulouse.

Those books, like the other treasures I harvested in Toulouse and Narbonne and Montpelhièr, were taken from me when our ship was captured off Maguelone on our way to Genoa. To regain command of his ship, my cousin Bonaventura, always a business-man, sold most of my books in Marseille to pay ransom to a band of ragged fishermen in return for his crew's freedom. I was still then loath to part with what I consider the treasure of a lifetime.

Bonaventura and I could not align our desires, and he was im-mensely unhappy that I could not repay his expenses for our adventures in Montpelhièr and Maguelone. We boarded a ship in Marseille that was part of his fleet and prepared to sail for Genoa. But as a consequence of his disappointment, Bonaven-tura betrayed our blood alliance and sold me and my friend Feris to Saracen pirates.

However, when you enter into a foreign place, you learn that other men's world is not the horror you'd heard. Things aren't always what they seem. Those men weren't pirates but merely Arab merchants. In the same way my own family did business, these merchantmen sailed the Great Sea seeking resources in one sphere that might be more highly valued in another.

When a leader among the sailors became deathly ill, I set to prove that I was more valuable than a mere surgeon or village physician. So, I promised to heal the man. But his affliction was past the point of mortal help. An unquenchable fire burned in his blood, and God was already calling the man home. For my failure, his brother blinded me. I could heal the injury and prevent the tiny evil that turns wounds putrid. But I never saw anything except blackness again.

However, my value diminished in the marketplaces of the Great Sea. Those Arab merchants sold my few remaining medical books to another trader, who intended to sell them again in Cairo. My treasure has likely become as great a world traveler as I have been. So, what did I preserve from that adventure in Montpelhièr? Only the songs that told tales of Miquel of Morella. They seem to have no market value in the Arab side of the Great Sea. I kept them safe until I could carry them no more and now they too are on a ship with a messenger, bound for the current lord of Morella, whom I am told resides in Valerós.

I have written elsewhere to describe the adventures that took me from those Arab merchants to here, the native city in Persia of the great physician Rhazes. Here, however, I learned to say his name properly: Abu Bakr Muhammad ibn Zakariyya al-Razi. And I've learned to speak his native tongue fluently, without the accent from my childhood on Sardinia. I am more confident in my translations, though I must trust my caretaker Feris to correctly record the words I can no longer see.

Here, I am called Antun al-Abbas. With Feris's assistance I teach in the hospital Rhazes founded, where our days and nights are each divided into equal segments, tracked by a mechanical device that an earlier caliph gave to the hospital. With the advance of the Khan into Persia and surrounding lands, I have enormous opportunity to learn a great deal about battlefield medicine without suffering the discomforts and deprivations of traveling with an army. I am bound forever with Feris, who reads books to me and describes the world I can no longer see.

It is possible, as my old friends in Dalmatia taught, to find heaven on earth. But God does not answer all prayers. My comrades among the lecturers and physicians here share my understanding of the world. After I work to heal the sick each day, each night many of my comrades sing with me in the *souks*. What more could a man want who believes he's called by God to do as much good as possible in this world?

In Christendom, in the days of what I consider to be my past life, the Church's raids into medical libraries decreased our ability as healers to share revealed knowledge of God's goodness. Here, in my new land, we are free as physicians to provide healing, or at least comfort, to the afflicted.

Together with my comrades, I seek to uncover the scientific principles that govern the mind and body. Few men of science here believe in demons. Instead, we understand tales of possession and devilry as old-fashioned ways to describe how men come together with other creatures in this particular world.

Here, in this ancient land, it remains possible to learn from wisdom gathered in older times, from before the Apostles and Prophets brought our modern teachings. Like my friends in Dalmatia, the Children of God, the ancients here preserved the methods by which you can speak to—and command—creatures made by God who are otherwise invisible to men. Using peculiar knowledge gained here, I have attempted to call to my service a companion creature of greater worth than any dog or enslaved spirit. But I have not yet attained this wisdom. These secrets must be read to me by Feris, who stumbles on ideas that offend him. My apprentices read the Persian and Arabic texts to me, and I translate for Feris to write a vernacular text. But then I hear Feris sniff if he disagrees with ideas in a text, so that I'm uncertain how faithfully he records my words. I have no one else who can read the vernacular text back to me. So, Feris and I move in a merry circle together. He is always at my side, ready to protect me and guide me along the safest paths—and perhaps to protect me from secrets in books that offend his Christian faith.

Here in our new home, Feris records these words for me. Whenever Genoa traders appear, I entrust them with these rags and notes, to carry them back to my family and my monastery in my old country. I hear nothing in return, so perhaps I am forgotten in my homeland.

However, here I am. Each day, at every hour as shown on the gilded mechanical clock and reported by Feris, I continue to live in service to God, to heal and to record revealed truths.

‡

Cançons de Montpelhièr

No scholarship or sorcery
Allows a king or count or seigneur
To live longer than heaven allows.
Any reputation for evil will outlive him.
Hence, all men must take great care,
While they breathe and walk the earth,
Not to leave a bad name
When they have gone.

From Chrétien's Earlier Adventures

An excerpt: *Bone-mend and Salt,*
Book 1 in the Accidental Heretics Series

Fishers of Men

AT MIDDAY, CROSSING THE last hill but one, Isabella urged her horse ahead. She wanted to celebrate the success of the morning's hunt.

"Let's race. I'll be at Valerós before any of you."

Benito, the Valerós master at arms, called out, "Senhóra Isabella, Pèire wouldn't approve." Isabella considered Benito the best example of Catalan knights; dark, handsome, tidy, thoughtful. However, he did not rule her. She urged Al-Malik ahead.

"What can happen here in the lower hills?" Marshal Guillem said. "We killed the wolves. Let her go."

Launching the race, she rode off the soft Turkish saddle, curled along Al-Malik's side like a Seljuk horse-archer, or so Pèire said when he taught her to ride that way.

"Go fast, Al-Malik."

When she rounded a turn, she urged Al-Malik onto a lower path she often rode with her son Sebastián, a path that Guillem claimed was merely a sheep's trail. Midway along the narrow path, her horse kicked loose a hail of rocks, which knocked several boulders free and raised a cloud of dust. As Al-Malik skittered away from the landslide, she urged him forward to a flattened space under a large oak. He reared and threw her off.

Stunned and bruised, she called to the nervous horse. Dust filled her throat from the fall, her voice a jagged gasp. She reached for Al-Malik, but the earth abruptly dropped away. Her stomach lurched, and she struggled as a hempen net jerked her into the air.

"*Bon Dèu!*"

Dizzy and angry, she saw only rocky ground, far below.

"The Scripture is without error!" a man's voice called. "Jesus said, 'I will make you fishers of men,' and lo! The nets were let down and caught a man."

She thrashed in the net, turning to see a tall, slender stranger who gazed up, a fishpole over his shoulder. His long blond hair hung free as if he'd just risen from sleep. He didn't look like a hunter who'd set a trap. She called out, her voice husky and yet breathless.

"Blessed Savior and the golden angels! Let me down!"

"I don't see how I can, my friend. You are too high."

"*Punxor!* Why the devil did you set this trap?" she shouted, cursing like one of Pèire's bordoniers. "I could have been killed!"

"It's not my trap. I only came up here because the rockslide ruined my fishing. Though your curses would also scare the fish."

"*Ai Dèu*, damn the fish!"

"The rockslide already did."

"Get me out of here, senhór." She intended the same voice Pèire used to command his men, while trying to calm the panic she felt from dangling so high.

"You shouldn't have got up there if you can't get down," the fisherman said.

"I didn't choose to be here, *baquelar*." The man drove her to curse in a fury, which at least relieved her panic.

"We none of us choose, do we?" he asked. "Aren't we all just sent wherever God flings us?"

"Am I being punished by God? For what?" she cried.

Enraged, she reached for her dagger to tear the cage open, but lost hold of the blade. She tumbled over in the next, ending up staring up at the oak canopy, forcing her mind to rational thought. Who had laid this trap? Men use metal traps to catch a wolf, not hemp. The only purpose for such a trap was to catch or kill a human.

She quelled panic. No one rode this decrepit trail except Isabella and her son Sebastián.

Who wanted her captured? Or killed?

She tussled with the net, like a fly caught by a giant spider. On the ground below, despite his laconic talk, the stranger studied the tree and the nearby rock face, seeking a way to help her.

He carefully folded his faded, crimson silk surcoat and set it beside his fishpole. The embroidered linen sleeves of his quilted undershirt had been patched, as if he'd assembled his wardrobe from the back-alley rag-pickers of Narbonne, where crusaders sold their Outremer silks for coin to travel home. But he couldn't be that destitute, because his silver-handled dagger and embossed leather belt could buy passage all the way to the Pays de France, or wherever this man called home.

His hair flying behind him like a banner, he ran and leaped to grab the lowest branch of the tree. But, tall as he was, he couldn't reach the lowest branch.

"It appears God is not yet done with you today, my friend."

"Catch my horse and stand on him."

"I don't see any sign of your horse," he said.

"Then we'll have to wait until my men circle around the upper trail." She let loose of the death-grip she had on the net, preparing to wait for Guillem.

"Your men?" he asked. "People say Pèire Leteric leads all the men in these parts."

She sank into the net, disappointed that even a stranger knew her privilege to lead a band of men came from her grandfather.

"I'm the steward at Castell-de-Valerós," she said. "Until my son comes of age."

"*Ai*, you're married. That's a pity." He attempted another leap. And once again failed to seize a branch.

"Not married." Isabella was glad to be distracted from fear by his casual chatter. "I was freed by the blessed angels of mercy. And shall stay free ever more."

Her horse reappeared, stamping and snorting through foam-flecked nostrils.

"Here's your savior," the man said. "A beautiful animal."

"His name is Al-Malik."

"A king, eh?" He spoke softly, soothing the horse, which let him move closer. Soon, Al-Malik was nuzzling the man's hand, while Isabella remained unnerved, pondering who laid this trap for her.

Or for Sebastián, who also rode this trail.

The fire of her old terrors kindled once more, the nagging fear that her dead-husband's family still pursued her, determined to snatch Sebastián from her.

While Isabella's fear about the meaning of the trap increased with every heartbeat, Al-Malik let the stranger mount him and circle under her. In a swift, graceful movement, the fisherman stood in the saddle and then scrambled out along the branch from which she hung. His weight tipped the net closer to the ground.

"Put your hands over your head to protect it," he said. "Ready?"

When he cut her down, she rolled in a ball so her shoulder took the force of the fall. She lost her breath, but her leather hunter's clothes offered good protection. As she wrestled with the net to tear it away, the ground still seemed to sway. She sat down to keep from falling.

"That can't have been pleasant." The man dropped from the tree and sat beside her. "I walked right past here this morning. I might have been hanging there waiting for you to ride by. I'd have been less brave than you."

He leaned back on his elbows. One of his long legs brushed her knee. She rather liked being called brave, especially since inside, her heart hammered still. *A trap for me? Or Sebastián?*

"Who are you?" she asked. Even without considering the crimson surcoat, the way he commanded Al-Malik indicated that he was a soldier. "You aren't a squire from around here."

"A squire? I'm a bit old for that." He had a handsome face for a northerner, only slightly marred by a cynical smile. "*Ai*, the south has strange ways. Young donzels become knights while your squires grow old in the same station. Your seigneurs collect rents on the ovens, pastures, and vineyards that surround their castles, but refuse to bow to any king."

"*Òc*. It's called our domus, our entire household, for which the seigneur has special duties to uphold paratge, the honor of our grand-fathers, going back generations." She let the conversation go on, while he revealed that he didn't know the south and its ways; therefore, he wasn't an unlikely Montcava mercenary sent to hunt her down. And yet…

He prattled on. "People here say *òc* as if they're coughing, instead of saying *si* or *oui* like most Christians do. And your mothers are all goodwomen who ignore popes and priests."

"My family calls Pedro d'Aragón king," she said. "Our villages say their Creed and baptize their babies. And they're mountain people who speak Catalan more often than the common tongue of the south."

"Ah, you bow to the pope's will. How unusual here."

She didn't care to discuss her family's alliances or beliefs with a stranger. She had no reason to trust him, though his chatter distracted her from the fear that still throbbed inside. "Tell me your name."

"I'm Chrétien, a jongleur. I make my way in the world by sing-ing troubadours' songs. The minstrels I travel with are camped in a swale around the bend."

"Then perhaps you'll come to Castell-de-Valerós tonight? We haven't had entertainment since All Saints."

If she was wrong about him being a soldier, then as a jongleur he'd be accustomed to court life, which explained why he felt free to sit beside her and chat so easily. The troubadours and singers she'd known in Toulouse were impoverished cousins of the lords and ladies who supported them.

"You're worried." He examined her more closely. "Even though you're safe on the ground."

"I'm wondering who set that trap. Who seeks to harm…me."

"You could run away with us. Cast off such worries." Stretched out beside her, Chrétien returned to the laconic, teasing manner as when he first came upon her. "If you can't sing, you can do horse tricks. Or swing from a net."

"Why would I run away from the most beautiful place on God's earth? All I want in life is to make Valerós prosperous and safe."

"All you want? You don't want another marriage, with more children to succor your old age? I'm not partial to such connections myself," he said. "If you know what I mean."

"Yes," she said, though unsure. As friendly as he was, she still felt wary of him, even if he hadn't set that trap. "But truly, the safety of Valerós is all I care about. Its villages, its people. Fruitful crops and market days that bring joy to everyone."

"Then you won't run away with me?" he teased. "You're breaking my heart, you know."

"I'm not known to be a heartbreaker."

Following a whistle, Chrétien stood. "Here are my friends."

Half a dozen men spilled into the clearing. That motley band of minstrels passed through Valerós every year, the last time at Midsummer's Eve. They'd play music and offer foolish tricks at dinner that night, while she discussed with Pèire Leteric whether Sebastián needed stronger protection. And whether the House of Montcava was reviving its desire to destroy her.

The crowd of friendly, jostling minstrels helped calm her turbulent fears. When she stood to greet them, her cap fell away. Her hair tumbled down, free of its braid.

"It's the senhóra of Valerós!" one of the minstrels exclaimed.

"You're not a man." Her rescuer Chrétien frowned. Then he smirked. "The disappointment is crushing. If you were a fish, I'd throw you back."

END PREVIEW • ACCIDENTAL HERETICS

Read all the tales of Chretien's adventures with his brother Tomás.

ACCIDENTAL HERETICS SERIES: LOST IN THE LANGUEDOC
CRUSADE
Book 1: *Bone-mend and Salt*
Book 2: *Trebuchets in the Garden*
Book 3: *Crux Lunata*
Book 4: *Song of Valerós*
The Mad Woman of La Catalane: A Novella
The Blue Door… and More Accidental Heretics Tales

LEGENDS OF VALERÓS SERIES
Wheel and Serpent: 1
Traitor: 2
Hero: 3

www.eastewartauthor.com

Glossary

A – C

a mal punt: A bad state.

Adéu, el meu amic!

adieussiatz

Ai Dèu: O God.

Aviá: Grandmother.

aventail: A chainmail curtain to cover the neck and shoulders.

belette muet: Mute weasel.

baquelar: Villainous rogue.

bon amic: Good friend, or boyfriend.

bonfraires: A brotherhood.

bonhommes: The term the so-called Cathars called themselves (rendered as "goodmen" in this story).

bon nuoit; bona nuèch: Good night.

bon vèspre: Good evening.

bonjorn: Good morning.

brioix: Bread.

cabeza: Head.

cançosd'amore; canços de guerra: Troubadours' love songs and war songs.

Catalan: In the Middle Ages, a language, not a political entity.

cavaller: Cavalier, knight.

Clemencia: Mercy.

common tongue: The Romance language of the Languedoc in the Middle Ages, often now called Old Occitan.

comte: A count. A high-ranking title, below a king.

cor dolç: Sweetheart.

cruzado: A crusader hymn.

cuirass: A rigid armor covering the torso. At this period, it was still made of leather.

D – G

domus: Household, meaning the larger economic household of a
   titled landholder in the Pays d'Òc.

don: A courtesy title for a gentleman from the landed classes.

donzel: A young gentleman, in training for knighthood.

En tot mal guany: A bad outcome.

fada: Fairy.

fadrin: A lad, a term of endearment.

feliç nit dotze; I feliç any nou: Happy Twelfth Night; happy new year.

francimand: Frenchman.

furetto: ferret.

fustian: A heavy cotton fabric.

gai sauvatge: Wild jay.

gambeson: A padded jacket worn under armor or worn alone as a
   defensive covering.

gardes du corps: In this story, the city's guards (not knights).

goodmen, goodwomen: A reference to the people whom the Church
   called heretics; now commonly called Cathars.

gràcies: Thank you.

Greek fire: An incendiary of naphtha, pitch, and sulfur.

H – L

hauberk: A chainmail shirt.

hola: Hello.

homme célibataire: A celibate man.

hourra: Hooray!

Je suis désolé: I'm sorry.

jeune homme: Young man.

Jhezu del tron: Jesus in heaven.

jongleurs: Medieval minstrels who sang the troubadours' songs.

jove mèstre: Young master.

Knights Templar: A monastic crusader military order, the most elite
   of the crusader armies.

L'Espital de l'Esperi: The hospital of the Holy Spirit.

L'infern i el diable! Hell and damnation.

lo mieu aimat capitani: My dear captain.

M – R

ma dòmna: My lady.

marquis, marquesa: A lord (and his wife) whose land is on a frontier border, and so must be a capable defender.

mercé, mercés, merci: Thank you.

mestitz: A person of mixed heritage.

mio fratello: My brother.

misericòrdia: Mercy.

mon amics: My friends.

Monsenyor: An honorific, such as for a king or a bishop.

Moors: People from northern Africa who settled on the Iberian peninsula under Muslim leadership. Colloquially at this time, a person of mixed heritage with a dark complexion.

Nizari: At the time of the Crusader states, a legendary assassin cult.

Normans: Descendants of the Viking Northmen who settled Normandy and later invaded Britain and also conquered the Muslims in Sicily in the eleventh century.

òc: Yes.

oud: A lute-like stringed instrument.

Outremer: The lands across the Great Sea, where the Crusader States were founded and other territory seized by Christian invaders.

paratge: A world view from the time of the troubadours, with multiple connotations about honor, civility, nobility, grace, and tolerance, defining a culture's view of "right living."

peccador: Sinner.

per l'amor de Dèu: For the love of God.

punxor: Prick.

qareen: A kind of djinn. The word means "constant companion."

qui s'ho creu: Who'd believe it?

rebec: A medieval stringed instrument, imported into Christian Europe via Andalusia. At the time of the crusades, it was likely referred to as a lyra.

renrén: Fool.

S – Z

Saracen: Colloquial term used in Europe for Muslims.

schismatic: For members of the Holy Roman Church, a common way to refer to members of the Eastern Orthodox Church.

se vos plai; si us plau; s'il vous plaît: If you please.

seigneur: A man of rank who rules lands and a household.

senhór, senhóra: Titles of respect, equivalent to señor, señora.

Sèt Estelas: Seven Stars.

Sodalitas, fidelitas, virtus: Latin motto of the *bonfraires:* fraternity, fidelity, virtue.

sou: A French coin.

squire: In the Pays d'Òc, a fighter of rank between knights and foot soldiers, for his lifetime. In the French system, squires rose to become knights.

surcoat: A long coat worn over other clothes or armor.

taifa: An independent principality in Andalusia.

Venetians: The instigators and financiers of the so-called Fourth Crusade which changed course to conquer Constantinople.

viscount: A European noble rank, above a baron, below a marquis.

viens, mon chien! Come, dog.

Visigoths: Germanic nomads who maintained a kingdom in Iberia from the fifth to the eighth centuries.

Vivètz Valerós! Battle-cry of the Valerós knights.

woad: A plant used to create a blue dye similar to New World indigo; grown as a cash crop around Toulouse.

xin-xin: A Catalan toast.

xiqueta: Child, an endearment.

Place Names

Valerós and Montcava exist within the world of the Accidental Heretics and in these Legends, but nowhere else.

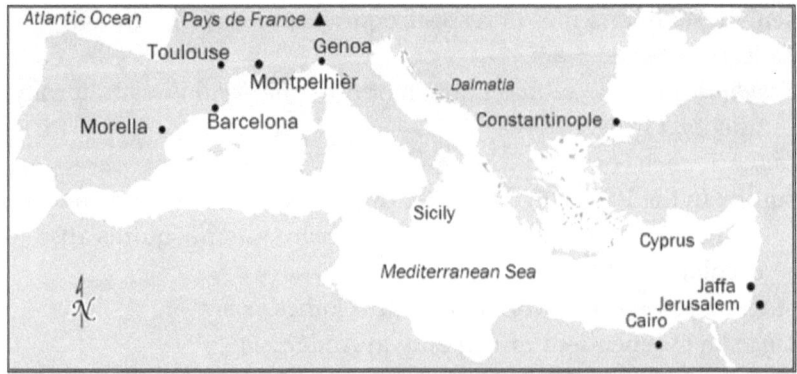

Aragón: A union of the Kingdom of Aragón and the County of Barcelona, which established the dynastic Crown of Aragón under Jaume I, *El Conqueridor*, with tributaries across the Languedoc.

Barcelona: A territory on the Mediterranean, now approximately the political entity of Catalonia, for which Pedro II held the title Count of Barcelona.

Carcassona: A fortified city in the Languedoc, which surrendered to the French crusaders in 1209.

Constantinople: Capital of the Eastern Roman Empire, sacked in the Fourth Crusade, becoming the seat of Norman rulers for the next fifty years.

Cyprus: An island in the Mediterranean, south of Turkey and north of Cairo. During the Third Crusade, its Muslim rulers were conquered by Richard Lionheart who sold it to the Knights Templar, who in turn sold it to Guy de Lusignan.

Genoa: An independent city-state on the Mediterranean, with significant trade and shipbuilding capabilities, with one of the strongest navies at the time of this story.

Jerusalem: Captured by the crusaders in 1099, recaptured by Saladin in 1187, traded back and forth for several decades until finally captured by the Mamluks and lost forever by the crusaders.

Minerve: A town in the Languedoc that sheltered refugees from the massacre of Béziers and was subsequently defeated by Simon de Montfort, and its own heretics were burned by the conquerors.

Montpelhièr: A walled city in the Languedoc, near the Mediterranean, with the second oldest university in Europe.

Morella: A town near Valencia, taken from the Moors by El Cid, lost later, then finally becoming part of Aragón in the Reconquista.

Narbonne: A rich Mediterranean port in the Languedoc that was the archbishop's seat and home to a significant Jewish community.

Outremer: The Frankish Crusader States in the eastern Mediterranean; the land overseas.

Pays de France: The original royal demesne of the Capetian kings, adjacent to Paris. A larger area was designated the Île-de-France in the Renaissance.

Pays d'Òc: The Languedoc.

Provence: A county on the Mediterranean, ruled by the counts of Barcelona; governed by Pedro's brother Alfonso at this time.

Maguelone: A seaside town south of Montpelhièr, which was the bishop's seat at the time of this story.

Roussillon: A region in the southeastern Pyrenees and foothills.

Toulouse: A county in the Languedoc, whose count owed allegiance to the king of France at the time of this story. The city, on a major trade route between the Mediterranean and central France, was a bishop's seat.

Urgell: A county in Catalan-speaking lands between the Pyrenees and Lleida.

About the Author

E.A. STEWART is an American writer whose *Legends of Valeros* and *Accidental Heretics* series explore intrigues in France and Spain in the early thirteenth century.

Ms. Stewart lives and writes in Seattle.

To learn more about
the Accidental Heretics series, visit:
www.eastewartauthor.com

Author's Notes

This story is fiction, and I'm not offering any more accurate history than the equivalent of hand-sewn costumes with no zippers, no New World foods, and weapons that match the time period. These notes might help satisfy your curiosity about some of the ideas I've drawn from history.

The History. As one result of the European crusades in the Outre-mer—the land across the Great Sea—the area we now call the Languedoc in southern France became quite wealthy. It first served as one of the departure points for crusaders setting out to capture Jerusalem, and then benefitted from the trade and science that crusaders brought home, which spawned an early renaissance.

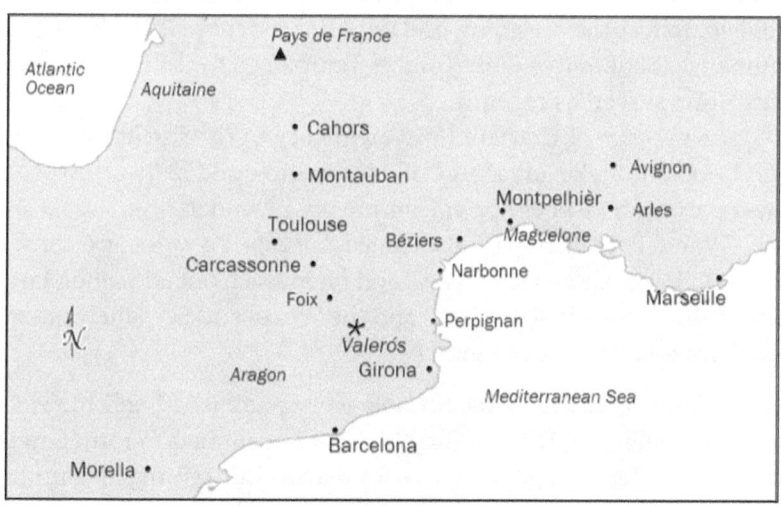

The Languedoc and Mediterranean Neighbors

In the Languedoc, a popular dualist heresy arose that is now often called Catharism, though the people who practiced these beliefs called themselves bonhommes, the goodmen. In 1209, French armies invaded the territory, an action requested by Pope Innocent III to defeat the heresy.

While the invasion continued, Pedro II, the king of Aragón, sought to establish peace through a diplomacy. Frustrated with travesties perpetuated by the invaders, Pedro brought his own army in 1213 to support the southern lords in their resistance to French aggressions. But Pedro died in the first battle.

By 1215, the south had endured five years of intermittent turmoil, waiting for their lords to solve the problem, waiting for the French armies to go home, hoping that planting could proceed, that animals wouldn't be seized by provender-seeking French infantry, that there would be grain and crops to harvest at the end of summer.

The regency for the child-king of Aragón was still in dispute. The pope sent a prelate to settle this issue — and to compel better coop-eration among Languedoc lords in suppressing the heretics. The Council of Montpelhièr in 1215 was convened to select a regent and to compel greater obedience from the lords of the south. Nuño, Count of Roussillon, and Ramón-roger, Count of Foix, attended. Pietro di Benevento was the presiding prelate. After the council, the boy-king Jaume was sent to live with Knights Templar in the hills of Aragón, and Nuño served as regent.

The practice of chartered privateers began to arise at this time, and Genoa did take advantage of its forest to build ships. However, these particular Genoese privateers are my invention.

"Wandering bishops," also called *Episcopi Vagantes*, are conse-crated in irregular or secret ways, and often teach outside canon law. The Order of the Flaming Cross and the Wheel and Serpent brother-hood are both my invention.

The Schools and the Texts. Schools were established and thriving at Montpelhièr in 1215, but they had not yet aligned to form a uni-versity. The lords of Montpelhièr in the twelfth century began the tradition of scholarly autonomy, under which (for example) any physician might lecture.

A broad tradition began in the tenth century of translating Greek and Arabic texts into Hebrew, Latin, and the vernacular, flour-ishing especially among scholars in Toledo, Toulouse, Paris, and

Montpelhièr. These translators and visiting scholar spread the advances in science and medicine that developed in Syria, Persia, Islamic Iberia, and elsewhere along the Mediterranean, like the science found in the writings and teachings of Avicenna (Ibn Sina), Averroes, and Rhazes.

The dualist Bogomil sect rose in what is now Macedonia in the tenth century. They apparently believed the adage, "your body is a temple," and were known to practice fasting, dancing, and purging. Both Orthodox and Roman Christians persecuted them as heretics, and related sects were mostly eradicated under the Ottoman Empire. "The Children of God" who taught Antoni mystical healing somewhere in Dalmatia are my invention.

The co-called Children's Crusade was a populist crusade the came out of northern France in 1212. The traditional (and unverified) accounts of the French expedition claim that those who didn't return home were given places on ships by merchants at Marseille and subsequently sold into slavery or lost in storms at sea. Sança's account might be as true or fictional as anything else that's known.

The Bells. The bells that mark the liturgical daily offices had their origin in watch changes in the Roman Empire. In thirteenth century Montpelhièr, the same bells were rung as in modern times, but the times were set in relation to sunrise and sunset, which differ based on latitude and season. So, since Montpelhièr is much farther south than England, the times were different from what some people are familiar with. The approximate canonical hours for January in Montpelhièr, 1215:

> Matins, approximately midnight
> Lauds, approximately 3–4 am
> Prime, sunrise, approximately 8 am
> Terce, approximately 9–10 am
> Sext, midday
> Nones, approximately 2–3 pm
> Vespers, sunset, approximately 5 pm
> Compline, approximately 9 pm

Places and People. Morella is a real place, not far from Valencia. It was under a Moorish general at the time of this story. *The Blue Door* offers a fictional history of Morella, Miquel's family, and our favorite qareen.

Valerós is a fictional place, a compilation of what are now called the Cathar castles on the French side of the Pyrenees. If you want to know more about Valerós, begin with *Bone-mend and Salt*, Book 1 in the Accidental Heretics series. That series also explores the relationship between Chrétien, his brother Tomás, Yusuf, Durán, and others in the world of Valerós.

Acknowledgments

Thank you to Elizabeth Bjorkman, Ajax Bell (developmental editor extraordinaire), Jacyn Stewart, Susan Urban, and Laurie Cropp for critical and editorial reading. And thanks to Waverly Fitzgerald for Mondays through Thursdays at Liberty on Fifteenth Avenue East.

Original sources that served as the basis for the author's translitics of troubadour lyrics:

"A man who finds no pleasure in song":
rialto.unina.it/GrBorn/242.30%28Sharman%29.htm

"Darius, Alexander, David":
rialto.unina.it/GlAdem/202.9%28Almqvist%29.htm

"He frightens false knights":
rialto.unina.it/PVid/364.11%28Avalle%29.htm

"He is dearer to me than my own heart":
rialto.unina.it/PVid/364.43%28Avalle%29.htm

"I never complain of my suffering":
rialto.unina.it/PVid/364.36%28Avalle%29.htm

"If a man does not follow God":
rialto.unina.it/JfrRud/262.6%28Chiarini%29.htm

"If the greatest scholar":
rialto.unina.it/GrBorn/242.30%28Sharman%29.htm

"Lord, I lived in your cloister":
rialto.unina.it/MoMont/305.12%28Mantovani%29.htm

"My dearest troubadour":
rialto.unina.it/MoMont/305.12%28Mantovani%29.htm

"My enemies sought to harm me":
rialto.unina.it/GlAdem/202.9%28Almqvist%29.htm

"My love holds me in her power":
rialto.unina.it/PVid/364.36%28Avalle%29.htm

"My ship has come to a good port:
rialto.unina.it/GlAdem/202.9%28Almqvist%29.htm

"My son shows valor":
rialto.unina.it/PVid/364.11%28Avalle%29.htm

"No scholarship or sorcery":
rialto.unina.it/GrBorn/242.24%28Sharman%29.htm

"Now that it is summer":
rialto.unina.it/GlAdem/202.9%28Almqvist%29.htm

"The other day I woke in Paradise":
rialto.unina.it/MoMont/305.12%28Mantovani%29.htm

"The plain brown rossynols":
rialto.unina.it/JfrRud/262.6%28Chiarini%29.htm

"The shepherdess set her dog": original by the author

"The stingy bishop had so much gold":
rialto.unina.it/PVid/364.43%28Avalle%29.htm

"The world is only wind and dreams":
rialto.unina.it/PVid/364.43%28Avalle%29.htm

"We choose to serve an honorable lord":
rialto.unina.it/GrBorn/242.15%28Sharman%29.htm

"When I am parted from him":
rialto.unina.it/PVid/364.11%28Avalle%29.htm

"When I rose from my first night":
rialto.unina.it/PVid/364.43%28Avalle%29.htm

"When I see the green meadows":
rialto.unina.it/PBremTort/331.1%28Harvey%29.htm

"When I see the orchards":
rialto.unina.it/GrBorn/242.15%28Sharman%29.htm

"With all my heart":
rialto.unina.it/PVid/364.4%28Avalle%29.htm

"You made a thousand promises":
rialto.unina.it/GrBorn/242.33%28Sharman%29.htm

From Jugum Press

HISTORICAL AND CONTEMPORARY FICTION

Nzinga, African Warrior Queen by Moses L. Howard

Nzinga is a brilliant leader during a time of violent upheaval. This fictional biography brings to life the 17th century flourishing African kingdom, now lost, where early explorers' maps of West Africa call out: "Here reigned the celebrated Queen Nzinga!"

Nine Volt Heart by Annie Pearson

He said, "I love you." She said, "You don't even know the real me." He said, "Great song lyrics. Key of G? Can we try close harmony?" Jason and Susi meet by accident in Seattle. Secrets, songs, and stalkers quickly entwine their lives in unpredictable ways.

This Charming Man by Ajax Bell

A chance encounter with an intriguing older man inspires Steven Frazier with visions of a more rewarding life. A vibrant snapshot of Seattle in the early 1990s, this story captures the drama of coming into one's own as an adult.

A Summer in Peach Creek by Michele Malo

Teenaged Faith travels to Peach Creek, West Virginia for a visit with relatives in 1932. When a scandalous murder occurs, Faith discovers the corrupt underbelly of Logan County. As summer progresses and peaches grow, Faith finds her own moral center.

PERSONAL VOICES IN HISTORY SERIES

Journey into Gold Country: Memories of a Forty-Niner

by Ralph Buckingham; foreword by Charles Barker

The California Gold Rush, remembered sixty years later by a New England younger son who went to seek his fortune.

We Were Walimu Once and Young, edited by Brooks E. Goddard

True stories from the Teachers for East Africa and Teacher Education for East Africa experience in the 1960s.

www.jugumpress.net